MOSCOW
EXILE

MOSCOW EXILE

A JOE WILDERNESS NOVEL

JOHN LAWTON

Grove Press
New York

Published simultaneously in Canada
Printed in Canada

First Grove Atlantic hardcover edition: April 2023
First Grove Atlantic paperback edition: April 2024

Library of Congress Cataloging-in-Publication data is available for this title.

ISBN 978-0-8021-5803-1
eISBN 978-0-8021-5804-8

Grove Press
an imprint of Grove Atlantic
154 West 14th Street
New York, NY 10011

Distributed by Publishers Group West

groveatlantic.com

24 25 26   10 9 8 7 6 5 4 3 2 1

for

Ann Alexander

First comes the imagining, then the search for reality.
Then back to the imagining,
and to the desk where I'm sitting now.

—John le Carré

Everything in life, I believe, is luck and timing.

—Pamela Harriman

Thou art poor and thou art abounding;
thou art mighty, and thou art helpless, Mother Russia.

—N. A. Nekrasov
(often quoted by V. I. Lenin and J. V. Stalin)

§

A Bit of a Prologue

West Berlin: The American Sector
Glienicke Bridge, September 28, 1969

Frank was wondering if he should buy shares in the Glienicke Bridge. Or maybe buy a small lot just inside the American sector. Put up his own shack. Find out what fishing was for. Become the CIA's answer to Elmer Fudd. He seemed to end up here far too often, three times in as many years, freezing his balls off at midnight and some. Why did the fuckin' Russians have to do everything at midnight? What was wrong with two in the afternoon? Back in time for tea. What was wrong with four in the afternoon? Back in time for dinner. Midnight, fuckin' midnight and his stomach was talking to him. It was saying, "Jack Daniel's and a hot dog! Jack Daniel's and a hot dog!" over and over again.

He had only himself to blame. It had been his idea. Perhaps taking it to the British had been a mistake. They'd been responsive, couldn't deny that, but they no more trusted him than he trusted them.

And the British were late.

He looked at his watch. The hands weren't moving. Fuckin' Rolex. He had only himself to blame, choosing a Madison Avenue status symbol over something that actually worked. Next time a Longines. Maybe the British weren't late?

He was expecting Eddie Clark. MI6 had insisted on one of their own being present so had prised Eddie out from behind his desk, as the one man they trusted for a positive identification. That Eddie regarded Frank Spoleto as the spawn of Satan didn't seem to figure.

He was also expecting some diplomat or other. They trusted Eddie so far and no farther—what was clear was that they didn't trust him with the money. So there'd be a diplomatic bagman. So there'd be a talking suit, a talking suit chained to a briefcase full of the folding stuff, just like a Pinkerton agent.

He wasn't.

When the Merc pulled up, Eddie got out of the driver's seat and opened the rear door for the bagman, who wasn't chained to anything. He was a little guy, no taller than Eddie—a snazzier dresser: silk scarf, pigskin gloves, black cashmere overcoat, collar turned up against the night air.

The bagman picked up a nifty-looking attaché case and the two of them approached Frank.

"What kept you?"

Eddie looked at his watch. He appeared to have one that worked.

"We're bang on time."

"You're late!"

"No we're . . . oh fuck you. I might have known you'd start summat. Frank, this is—"

"Forget it, Ed, let's just get out there and get this done."

Frank walked off and hearing no footsteps turned and glared at Eddie. The bagman spoke: "It's fine, Eddie. Stay here. I can handle this."

"I'm supposed to ID him."

"Damn right you are," Frank yelled.

"I can do that," the bagman said.

Frank wasn't sure just who he was talking to, but the bagman joined him with a witheringly polite English fuck-you: "Lead on, Mr. Spoleto. I'm at your service."

"In about fifty yards we're gonna meet the US border guards. Do not call me by name."

"Then what do I call you?"

"Colonel. Just call me Colonel."

"Colonel who?"

"I forget. Murphy, Moriarty. Something Irish. Just stick to 'Colonel.'"

Fifty yards on, a uniformed US Army captain saluted and raised the barrier. Frank returned the salute.

Another fifty yards and they'd be at the centre of the bridge. There was a three-quarter moon peeping in and out of clouds and the river mist danced around them playing now-you-see-it-now-you-don't.

"Are they there?" the bagman asked.

"No idea. Maybe they keep time as well as you. But let's take it slow for now. Nice 'n' easy."

"Whatever you say."

"You say you can make the ID?"

"Of course."

"So you knew him?"

"I did."

"Hmm. So, what's your name?"

"Freddie."

"I don't ever recall him mentioning any Freds."

"Then call me Troy. He always did."

"So—Mr. Troy."

"Actually it's 'Lord Troy.' Not that it matters."

"Damn right it doesn't. Why'd they send a lord? I thought you guys just wore ermine and sat around on wool sacks."

"Simple. I put up the money."

"What? All twenty-five grand?"

"Yes."

"You think he's worth twenty-five grand?"

Troy did not answer. They'd reached the middle, the line over the Havel that marked the border between West Berlin and East Germany—and there were no Russians and, worse, no Joe Wilderness.

§

A Bit Less of a Prologue

Poland, West of Oswiecim
January 1945

Auschwitz was remote now, no smell of burning flesh, no film of grease at the back of the throat. Vienna remoter still. No music. She could not recall a day without music. Silence was . . . unheard. They were alone, painted onto a fairy-tale landscape, at one with a mute, near-translucent nature—two children, Kay and Gerda, waiting/not waiting for the appearance of the Snow Queen on her silver sleigh. Silent upon a plain in Poland.

Méret recognised this for what it was—the onset of madness, a madness she had held at arm's length, at bow's length, for the best/worst part of a year.

Magda broke the spell.

"Why . . . why aren't we dead?"

Méret put an arm under Magda, lifted her to her feet.

She looked back at the German soldier. Motionless, expressionless, his rifle held carelessly, pointing at nothing.

"He's Wehrmacht. He's not SS. Maybe he just doesn't care anymore."

And they followed the soldier's footsteps in the snow.

Inside the shepherd's hut, half the roof had collapsed, and he was gathering wood and straw from the debris to light a fire. Méret scooped a clear space on the ground, and the soldier turned out his pockets for scraps of paper and a box of matches. Between them they fuelled the fire well into the night. Their eyes never meeting.

When he was ready to sleep, the soldier slipped his arms from the sleeves of his greatcoat and sat inside it like a wigwam, head down, below the collar, snoring. Méret copied him, buttoned her greatcoat around both of them—Méret a human blanket for Magda, Magda a human blanket for her—and slept.

She awoke alone. No soldier. No Magda.

It was light.

She heard feet on snow.

Magda put her head in the door.

"He's gone," she said. "He was gone before I woke up."

And as she spoke, Méret heard a diesel engine and watched Magda turn in the doorway and vanish.

"Magda? Magda?"

Then feet, running feet crunching across the snow, and Magda's scream.

Méret stood in the doorway. Half a dozen men in quilted, white winter overalls, giant babies in romper suits with tiny red stars on their foreheads, were standing around watching as a comrade ripped Magda's rags from her body and fumbled at the zips on his white suit.

Magda screamed. Méret stood rooted to the spot, facing Russian troops, wrapped in a German greatcoat.

Behind the troops, two officers approached without urgency. One short, one tall, major and lieutenant. The short major put a revolver to the rapist's right ear, and what she said needed no translation.

The man spat, cursed and ignored her.

She shot him in the head, turned her gun on the spectators and waited until they slowly turned away and walked back to the road.

The tall lieutenant came right up to Méret.

"At last. I was beginning to think we'd never find you," he said in flawless German.

It was as though he was talking to a wayward child lost now found in a street market.

"Don't worry. You're safe now. Both of you."

Her own helplessness appalled her. She let the man take her by the arm, hustle her past Magda. The woman major was helping her dress. The rapist lay sprawled on his back, blood melting the snow around his head.

She wanted to see Magda's eyes, to look her in the face, but they moved too quickly.

The lieutenant opened the rear door of an armoured half-track and gently pushed her in.

"Trust me," he said. "Your friend will be fine."

A minute later the woman major joined them, and the half-track started up—a fug of smothering heat and diesel.

"Where is Madga? I want to see Magda."

The man answered.

"She's fine. No harm will come to her."

§

Even Less of a Prologue

**Hampstead, London
June 1941**

Charlotte had had a problem—with God and Marx and Stalin. On the night of June 21, 1941, Hitler had solved it for her. Her conscience was no longer conflicted. She poured herself a very large gin and lime, sat back, kicked off her shoes, stretched her legs, flexed her toes and smiled as two and a half million German troops invaded Russia—Barbarossa.

Charlotte

§1

Chartwell, Kent

August 1939
In the Shadow of War

Hubert Mawer-Churchill was a gent. Quiet, vaguely handsome in a bespectacled, boyish sort of way. Since a bye-election in 1933, at the age of thirty-three, he had been Conservative MP for Ashbourne and Hartington, where family connections were somehow deemed to have helped in what was by any definition a safe Tory seat. He was loosely related to the Marquess of Hartington. He was less loosely related, although he could not give chapter and verse on this, to Winston Churchill, MP for Epping, a backbencher, but nonetheless quite possibly the most recognisable politician in the country.

"I can offer you a job, Hubert. Parliamentary Private Secretary. No money. I no longer qualify for a PPS in the strict sense of those words. Even if I did, there'd still be no money."

Hubert accepted.

His wife, the former Charlotte Young, was delighted. She was fond of Cousin Winston and he of her. She suggested that perhaps "advisor" might be a more appropriate title for her husband's new position.

"That," Hubert replied, "assumes I have advice to give."

Charlotte was never so modest. She had advice aplenty and then some to spare.

When Churchill consulted Hubert, more often than not he was consulting Charlotte. Hubert hunkered down over his papers, pen in hand, and seemed either not to notice or not to care.

They were out in the garden. Churchill had paused while building another of his wavy walls—bricklaying being the odder of his two hobbies—for tea and natter.

"There will have to be changes," Churchill said, not looking at Cousin Hubert but at Charlotte.

Even when she replied, Hubert did not look up from his smudgy typed pages, and she let one turn before speaking.

"Of course. Starting at the top."

"So you'd sack the Prime Minister?"

"In the blink of an eye."

Churchill laughed gently.

"And Halifax?"

"Slimy bugger. He'd sup with the devil."

"And if the devil was called Adolf Hitler?"

"Quite."

"And poor old Clem?"

"Oh, you're going to need Mr. Attlee. The workers haven't forgiven you for Tonypandy. They'll get behind him, and if he's behind you . . ."

"Morrison?"

"Our little cockney terrier? The Jack Russell of Hackney? Find him a job where he can do the least damage. Do we have a Ministry of Toad Protection?"

"You know, we could go on like this all afternoon, but—"

"But playing fantasy cabinet from the backbenches presumes too much."

"It do, indeed it do."

"Just when your country needs you? Just when it might be asking for you?"

"Enough, Charlotte. No one is asking. But—one last roll of the dice. General Young? Back on the Imperial General Staff?"

"Dad? He's seventy-three. You'd want to bring him out of retirement at his age?"

"He's still a soldier. A man can only take so much riding to hounds and bridge evenings. He was a good man in his day."

"His day was sometime during the Boer War with a second bite of the cherry in the Great War. Even he admits he was past his prime by then. And he's never chased after a fox or played a hand of bridge in his life. Leave the old man be. He's perfectly happy with his model train set and the Brunel bridges he makes out of matchsticks. If Ma lights up a cigarette he lands on the ashtray like a swooping owl. The next thing you know, the spent match is propping up the Saltash Bridge."

§2

On the train home, Westerham to London Victoria on the old South Eastern and Chatham line, Charlotte amused herself, as she often did, in observing her husband. Hubert liked to work on railway journeys. Occasionally Charlotte would point out something through the window, and for the merest flicker of a moment she would have his attention before his eyes returned to his papers. She did not mind. She liked to read on trains—in fact she had in her handbag, as she mused on Hubert—"spied," as she thought of it—*The Gift* by Vladimir Nabokov, in the original Russian. Trains relaxed her so much she wished the journeys longer. It had something to do with the precise rhythm of steel wheels on steel rails, a near-soporific clicketty-clack, and the regular heartbeat of smoke and steam from the engine. Her favourite poem in the English language was *Adlestrop* by Edward Thomas. Every station stopped at was a potential Adlestrop. And when not reading she observed her husband.

His appearance never varied.

A three-piece suit. Plain black, more often than not. He did not seem to care for stripes. No watch chain. She had persuaded him to give up his father's old timepiece and chain for that modern contraption, the wristwatch, and had bought him a Girard-Perregaux. All the same, several times a day his right hand fumbled across his chest looking for the old watch before he would turn to his left and find the new one.

His grooming was immaculate. Nails trimmed and filed. All trace of nicotine removed with pumice and lemon. Not a hint of dandruff. One gold tooth. A smile that said "harmless."

Beneath the suit . . . she imagined the hair on his chest, dark and thick and at odds with his boyish features. At thirty-nine he was greying a little on top, but not . . . down below. She imagined his cock uncircumcised. She was not sure she had a preference. If she did, it might be that Hubert were not quite so shy after nine years of marriage, that he would not get so swiftly into pyjamas, that he might not put on a dressing gown just to nip to the loo. That once in a while they might leave the light on.

It would have pleased Charlotte to be able to pretend that she did not love Hubert. But—she did. An unfortunate complication that did not stop her falling head over heels for Avery Shumacher.

§3

Hubert hated the Undergound simply because he'd never adapted to it. Anywhere he couldn't spread out papers and sit with a fountain pen in hand was a foreign country to him. Charlotte, on occasion, liked the descent into a netherworld, she liked the unified design of London Transport . . . so very modern, so very "now," and, rush hour apart, she relished the noise, the assault on her senses, the vascular roar of a train emerging from the tiny tunnels so painstakingly bored into the London clay.

The only thing to be said for cabs was precision, to be deposited on your own doorstep, and, perhaps, if the cabby shut up, the silence—as important in a cab as the noise was underground.

Often after a trip to Chartwell, and today was no exception, she would have to nudge Hubert and say, "We're home, darling." And while he fumbled for the half crowns and florins in his pockets she would dart up the steps of their house in Flask Walk, Hampstead NW3, glad to be home.

By the time Hubert had plonked his briefcase down Charlotte would have a scotch and soda ready to put into the hand that had finally surrendered the pen.

"Cook says half an hour. Time for you to scrub the ink off your fingers."

Hubert set down his glass, looked at his spotless right hand.

"I always fall for that, don't I? Tell me, Charlotte, is every day April first in your calendar?"

"I couldn't possibly say."

Gin and tonic in hand, she stood over him, wondering how long it might be before he went bald.

An arm snaked up around her waist as though not risking her bottom.

"That's my girl. A pocketful of secrets. Now, tell me. Did I overhear you and Winston rejigging the cabinet?"

She parted a few strands of hair to reveal a thinning pate.

"Just a game. The little woman knows her place."

"You're right, of course."

"I am?"

"Half the buggers will have to go once war is declared."

"And Winston will be back?"

"Darling, I'd put five bob on it at Ladbrokes."

There was something oddly sexy about watching Hubert age.

She kissed his bald spot.

"I can't tell you how much I love you, you old man."

An unfortunate complication that did not stop her falling head over heels for Avery Shumacher.

§4

Britain declared war on Germany on September 3. Before the day was over Churchill had been recalled to the Admiralty as First Lord, the very same post he had held at the onset of the previous world war. He paused a moment for photographers on the steps of the Admiralty—gloves and cane in hand, a battered ministerial red box at his feet—something that had no doubt lain ten years gathering dust in a cupboard—chomping on the last couple of inches of his cigar, grimly refusing to look into the lens.

Shrewd commentators remarked that really it was one world war with a tea break or with the peace merely a long weekend of village cricket until "rain stopped play."

Charlotte and Hubert's lives changed.

For one thing, Hubert was paid.

And when Churchill became prime minister eight months later, Hubert, an appointed, elected off-cabinet MP of no particular title other than the derogatory "Winston's bum boy," found himself at the heart of the matter, of all matters. His workload doubled. Charlotte ordered more ink in three colours: black, blue and red.

For reasons of security Hubert read less on trains, but he brought home box after box of papers, most of which his wife, both unappointed and unelected, read. And her pocketful of secrets swelled to bursting.

§5

Flask Walk, Hampstead NW3

June 1942

"I say."

Charlotte hated "I say."

Why couldn't her husband just call out her name? Surely after twelve years he knew it?

Hubert was standing by the hatstand, where the maid dumped the morning mail so Hubert could snatch it on his way out. The afternoon mail went straight to his desk.

"Amazing."

"What is?" asked Charlotte.

"An invitation to dinner from Sir Alexei Troy."

"Do you know him?"

"We've met. On the rare occasions when he and Winston aren't at daggers drawn. Darling, accept, would you?"

He handed her the embossed card requesting "the pleasure."

"I haven't looked at the diary."

"Whatever is in there for Friday, scrap it. Winston would personally carry us there in a sedan chair if he thought we'd get old Troy's newspapers on our side."

"Oh, I'm included, am I?"

"Peevish, Charlotte, peevish. You'll find it a treat. A chance to polish your languages. I hear Lady Troy speaks French out of preference, and the old man lapses into Russian every few minutes. You'll be the only guest at table who understands him if he does."

§6

The Troys lived walking distance from the Churchills, in Church Row on the far side of Heath Street. Before the war this journey might well have required a cab, but since the war began, who wore evening dresses that scraped the ground? There was far more cachet in appearing in uniform than gown, and for the last few months women between twenty and thirty could be called up for the Auxiliary Territorial Service. Charlotte was thirty-seven and would volunteer, but Hubert had been adamant that her secretarial work for him was more important than anything she might do for the ATS.

They walked to Church Row.

Hubert as ever in his black suit.

Charlotte in a Coco Chanel two-piece, in bold crimson. Almost military with its double rows of brass buttons, but not quite.

One of Alex Troy's daughters was in WAAF uniform—officer stripes that Charlotte could not decode on her cuffs and pilot's wings on her left breast.

Charlotte took her cold look upon introduction as the equivalent of a white feather.

At dinner, Charlotte was seated between two men—a very young, almost boyish Frederick Troy, younger son of the host, and a tall, elegant

American in his fifties, recently arrived in London as a special envoy of the American president, Franklin Delano Roosevelt. Young Troy had very little to say for himself and seemed to Charlotte to be wishing he was anywhere but here. Perhaps he relied on his good looks to get by in silence? He was film-star handsome, dark, almost saturnine. He reminded her of the English actor James Mason—too broody by a yard and a half. If Charlotte had a type, Freddie Troy was not it.

The American on the other hand was neither dark nor handsome— "distinguished" might be the uninformative cliché—but he exceeded even her husband in good manners, and appeared, though soft-spoken, to live for the word, to revel in the English language. And his smile was so beguiling, almost dazzling—disarming, as if she could see the boy within the man.

It would have been rude to ignore young Troy, but then young Troy did not seem to be particularly present.

His brother was cut from a different cloth. A hero of the Battle of Britain, now desk-bound at the Air Ministry, Rod could and did hold forth.

It was he, she surmised, who had invited the American, a colleague in the drawn-out discussion on "how to be allies," now that the USA had entered the war. She wondered too if Rod Troy had not been the one to invite Hubert. Much of what Rod was saying could hardly be for the benefit of a colleague—they could talk about this at their office and undoubtedly did—no . . . this . . . the second front, the urgency of giving Josef Stalin what he was asking for . . . this was a message for the Churchills. Both of them.

After dinner, Lady Troy gently, then less gently, beseeched young Troy to play the piano.

"OK," he said darkly.

And launched into a rapid-fire minute of C. P. E. Bach's *Solfeggietto*. And then he stopped.

Charlotte had drawn close, starved of music after twelve years of life with a man who by his own admission had a tin ear and no inclination to wind a gramophone. Troy's sister Sasha, the one in WAAF uniform, had drawn closer.

"Freddie, stop being a cunt and give Mama what she wants."

She had said it in not much more than a whisper, but Charlotte had never heard that word, even as a whisper, on a woman's lips before.

Sasha turned sharply, well aware that she had been overheard.

She looked Charlotte up and down, handing out the white feather once more.

"So, doing our bit for King and Country, are we?"

And Charlotte replied, "They also serve who only stand and bitch."

As Sasha retreated and redefined the height of her dudgeon, Troy said, "For that, Mrs. Churchill, you may request anything within my limited repertoire."

"How about . . . ooh . . . I dunno, a Schubert Impromptu?"

"How about the A flat major? Not quite as fast as the Bach. Less chance of me tripping over my own fingers."

"Oh, I know nothing about music, really. I was a dreadful pianist as a child. To me a key is just something you use to open the door."

Laughter behind her. Pleasant laughter. Not a hint of mockery.

The American.

They listened in silence, the hubbub in the rest of the room dropped to a susurrus.

Seven or eight minutes later Charlotte wanted to clap but had no idea if she should and was grateful when someone at the back of the room led the applause. The boy was good. He deserved the acknowledgement he so visibly did not want. The lid on the Bechstein was quietly closed.

"You are fond of music, Mrs. Churchill?"

She could not place his accent, apart from knowing he probably wasn't from the Bronx or Mississippi. He stooped slightly and she realised for the first time that he was at least six foot three. She took the stoop as a courtesy—a willingness to hear and to listen to those shorter than he.

"Fond of it and deprived of it."

"Do you attend the concerts at the National Gallery?"

"No, not yet."

"There's a Bach recital on Friday."

"Oh?"

"The violinist Dea Gombrich and the harpsichordist Susi Jeans, both refugees from Vienna. Hitler's loss is our gain."

"Do you know, I don't think I've ever heard a harpsichord."

"Then come with me—be less deprived."

"I'm a married woman, Mr. Shumacher."

"And I'm not."

A married woman? An unfortunate complication that did not stop her falling head over heels for Avery Shumacher.

§7

"I must dash."

Of course he must. War to be won.

He had sat through the trio sonatas for pedal cembalo and all the violin stuff, entranced. She had been a bit baffled by the first half or so. She had listened to the Bach solo violin partitas many times, but she'd never seen or heard anything quite like a pedal cembalo before. It was rather like watching a bloke play a coffin.

"May I see you again?"

"Yes."

"There's a top-level meeting tomorrow—although I've just broken several laws telling you that."

"Then perhaps next week?"

"Oh no. I meant I won't be at the meeting. Military only. So I could get away in the afternoon."

"Oh. I see."

"Tea . . . tea somewhere . . . somewhere very English?"

"Posh or not posh? Café Royal or Joe's Caff?"

"Let's start at the Café Royal and work our way down. At least I know where that is. And I would imagine there is more than one Joe's Caff. Say three o'clock?"

And with that he was gone. Heading across Trafalgar Square towards Whitehall.

Charlotte weighed up the possibilities.

Was it innocent?

Innocent or not, would they be seen?

Undoubtedly they would be seen. She didn't think she'd ever set foot in the Café Royal, Fortnum's or the Ritz without someone, usually some friend of her mother's, waving and simpering at her.

Hubert would find out.

To head that off, she would tell Hubert this evening.

You know, darling, that chap we met at the Troys'? Thought I'd show him a bit of London.

There was a war on. Married women had a touch more freedom, and if Shumacher were in uniform, scarce a blue rinse or a silly hat would turn. She would simply be doing her bit in entertaining the troops. But Shumacher wasn't in uniform. True, he worked with the RAF in the shape of Rod Troy, and probably with the Army and the Navy too, but the music had allowed no time for chatter. Actually, she had no real idea what Avery Shumacher did.

§8

At the Café Royal, in among the golds and greens—an immersive cacophony of tinkling china.

"I'm here to see the president's views are represented. I'm not a soldier, nor am I a politician. Officially I am an 'expediter.' Such is my title. Unofficially I am a burlap sack full of prejudicial opinion and unsolicited advice. Kind of thing could get me run out of town on a rail—till a war comes along and then I get to be what I've always pretended to be."

"And what's that?"

"The village wise man."

"Like a . . . witch doctor?"

"Even better. I'm Washington's witch doctor."

"And now London's."

"Not for long, I'm afraid."

"A . . . a posting?"

"You know I can't tell you that."

"Can you tell me when?"

"Week after next. Wednesday."

"So we have . . ." Counting on her fingers. "Twelve days. Hmm . . . one for every year of my marriage. I say again . . . hmm."

Charlotte looked around. The room had thinned. No nearby table was occupied, no waitress hovered, no old trout in Edwardian garb had waved at her. All the same, it was a time to speak secrets softly.

"You seem impatient, Charlotte. Are you waiting for something?"

"Yes . . . the seduction."

"Ah. Have I created expectations?"

"You have."

"So we are having an affair?"

"I'm not sure about your use of the present tense, but I have had affairs. Affairs I have kept out of London and hence kept from Hubert."

"I have had no affairs. I married in 1918 and I remained faithful to my wife till the day she died."

"When was that?"

"1936. Plane crash. You knew I was a widower?"

"I'd guessed. And since then?"

"I had two girls to raise. Seventeen and fifteen. You can imagine the rest. The details are obvious and hardly important."

"And your daughters are . . . ?"

"Grown-ups. Both of them in New York. Margaret works for the *Wall Street Journal*, Valerie studies oboe at the Juilliard."

"So . . . we are . . . free?"

"We are."

"Then why can I see a great big 'but' hanging in the air like a cloud about to burst?"

"But—"

"But I would be your first?"

"No, Charlotte, you would be my last. I am not looking for a mistress, I am not looking for a wife. I am looking for Charlotte Churchill, and I have found her."

It seemed to her to be a very tall order.

One almost identical to her own.

She had been trying to put her finger on the man's appeal ever since they'd met at Alexei Troy's house. Can charm be defined? And if it can, does it lose its . . . charm?

He was tall, as the habitual stoop indicated, and she had thought from the first that he bore an uncanny resemblance to the Hollywood star Clark Gable—pencil moustache, the same grey-green eyes . . . she'd read somewhere about Gable, a rare venture into trashy reading, that "there is danger in his eyes"; she had no idea what that meant and did not think she was looking for danger. But . . . but it was the difference that made the difference. She'd sat through *It Happened One Night*, a film which had won an Oscar for Gable or Claudette Colbert or both, bored with yet another runaway heiress plot, and felt blasted by Gable's volume and projection. Dammit, the man was too loud. Avery wasn't. He had the same rasp in his voice, but was soft-spoken; he smiled like Gable, his eyes twinkled like Gable's, but he felt no need to fill a room. He wasn't talking to a room, he was talking to her. Hence any conversation with him delved instantly into intimacy. A bubble wrapped around them no matter how many people surrounded them. Every word a seduction. The seduction of knowing a man's attention is entirely focussed on you.

And—his ears didn't stick out like the doors on a London taxi.

§9

Charlotte would not readily throw discretion to the winds. Love was like beef or butter—rationed.

If they met every day, they would be caught.

Charlotte wanted to be caught.

She did not want to be the one to inflict the pain of discovery.

But the twelve days became eleven, became ten.

§10

Three days before Shumacher was due to leave for parts unknown, Charlotte called him at Claridge's.

"Might I come and see you this evening?"

"Why wait so long? There's another top-brass meeting at three. I am excused."

Sex in the afternoon.

She hadn't thought of that. She hadn't done that. There'd always been Bunburys to cover an overnight stay. Of course, the hotels had been nothing like Claridge's, and she wondered if hotels like Claridge's had a hanky-panky policy.

Crossing the chequered floor of the foyer she felt like a figure on a chess board. An absurd image, but not one she could readily dismiss. What was she, queen or pawn? And of course everyone was looking at her, at the scarlet letter embroidered on her jacket, burning down to her skin.

She stopped. Looked around, momentarily cocooned in an illusory silence, a hundred lips parting in fifty conversations, in soundless animation.

The illusion cracked and shattered as the room seemed to explode into chatter. No one was looking at her. She was herself again, neither queen nor pawn nor scarlet woman. She was what she was—a nobody, a nobody of no interest to anyone.

§11

In his room on the ninth floor Avery was fussing with a teapot. Shirt-sleeves, socks and braces. A quick "Glad you could make it" all but thrown over his shoulder as Charlotte entered.

She had not known what to expect and whilst anticipating a thousand things had dismissed them all—including champagne, caviar, flowers and the finer accoutrements of seduction.

Oh, but he did have flowers, two dozen deep-plum-coloured roses. At least they weren't scarlet.

"I'm grappling, if that's the right word, with the English tea ceremony. I sent down for half a dozen different teas and a kettle. Electric kettles.

What will they think of next? Do you know any of these? I already tried the Earl Grey. It's a stinker."

Charlotte perched on the edge of a chair. She'd thought he might be joking, but clearly he wasn't.

Unpinned her hat. Kicked off her shoes. She wasn't expecting anything so casual, but if that was the offer—socks and tea and roses—then the absurdity of it all delighted her.

"Yes. It's a bit pongy."

"Pongy?"

"Means the same thing. Stinky."

"Ah . . . I see my English vocabulary needs a lot of building up. What do you reckon to Assam, Mrs. Churchill?"

Sloughed off her jacket.

Surely they were Avery and Charlotte by now? Or was seduction off the menu? Should she put her shoes on again?

"It's OK at the right time of day, and this isn't the right time. It's a breakfast tea, really."

"Can you stay for breakfast?"

Ah—back on the menu.

"Probably not."

"OK, then you'd better pick. Russian Caravan, Oolong, Darjeeling or Lapsang?"

"Russian Caravan would be fine."

"Milk?"

"Only Philistines and foreigners drink tea without milk."

"Ouch!"

"Well, you did say you wanted to learn."

"Indeed I did."

He said nothing while he made tea. A look of intense concentration on his face. She assumed she'd have to say something when he took the kettle to the teapot instead of the teapot to the kettle, but he didn't.

He set a tray on the low table between the chairs, with soft "voilà."

"Milk in first?"

"Entirely optional."

"Ah."

And for at least a minute that was all he said. Both of them sipping at their cups. Milk in last.

"You want more?"

"Haven't finished this one yet. But . . ."

"Yeees?"

"What happens when I do, Mr. Shumacher?"

He put his cup to his lips, not looking at her, took a sip and as though gazing into his tea leaves said softly, "Tell me, Mrs. Churchill, has anyone ever peeled off your dress and licked your spine?"

Across the top of the cup, he looked at her now. Roguish. The same air of confidence he'd shown at the Café Royal.

Charlotte stood. One hand went to the nape of her neck to flip a button on her dress, which obediently slid to the floor.

She was wearing nothing but a pair of stockings and garters. She turned her back on him, looked over her shoulder.

"I was almost certain people knew as I walked across the lobby. I felt naked. But of course no one even looked."

Shumacher set down his cup, leaned back in his chair, smiling, utterly devoid of urgency.

"Such fools," he said at last.

Perhaps we are Charlotte and Avery now?

§12

Avery Shumacher was German American. His father had immigrated from Wuppertal in the Rhineland in the late 1870s. Wuppertal being rich in coal, it was almost natural that Albert *Schu*macher would train as a mining engineer, and equally natural that on arrival in the New World he should gravitate to Mauch Chunk, Pennsylvania—a town built on coal, which by the end of the century could boast that it was home to a dozen multimillionaires.

Albert married the daughter of one of them, Harriet Davidson McKinley, of Scots-Irish descent. The McKinleys were so lapsed in devotion to any god but mammon that they seemed not to care that their daughter was marrying an equally lapsed Jew and welcomed Albert as an asset to the family. The *c* was quietly dropped from the German name, *Schu* becoming *Shu*. A simpler life in America.

Avery was their first and only child, born in 1889.

Money bought him whatever an excess of it should. Choate school, then Harvard, and a doctorate from Columbia.

None of these institutions made much of an impact on young Avery. He declined to join any alumni organisation, never used the title "Dr." in front of his name, shaking off that German fixation, and mentioned his specialist subject (summa cum laude in philosophy) only when pressed.

Freed from the necessity to work, Avery settled in Washington. Some people merely drift into Washington, but in 1915 Avery made a beeline for it.

Washington was a hive of activity . . . so many busy bees, so many bonnets. Somehow Washington had succeeded in pulling off a great American contradiction—it was busy and it was dull. It seemed to Avery the perfect place in which to develop and maintain his Montaignian calm. He could be seen to be doing nothing, like many a rich kid, whilst doing exactly what he wanted.

With parental funding he bought a tiny five-bedroom row house on N Street in Georgetown, cute as could be in the colonial style, with brick-built yellow walls and black shutters. He gave over the largest bedroom not to sleep but to work. It became the office of *AJ's Weekly*, a magazine of commentary and opinion, on sale for fifteen cents. He would have given it away but knew that people placed very little value on anything that was free.

As proprietor of, and, for many editions, sole contributor to *AJ's Weekly*, Avery Joseph Shumacher wrote about anything that caught his fancy—a new epic silent film, a visiting orchestra, a government report on armed-forces funding, a new building rising on the Mall, the blossoming of Nellie Taft's cherry trees.

His first essay was a review of D. W. Griffith's *Birth of a Nation*:

```
It is the most beautiful film I have ever seen,
and the most wicked. It can stand with Matthew
Brady's photographs, with the war poetry
```

```
of Walt Whitman and even with the speeches
of Abraham Lincoln. It is daring, it is
innovative, it will define the motion picture
for years to come. It is tragic, it is epic,
yet it is wicked.
```

This resulted in NIGGER LOVER being painted on his doorstep and dog shit being pushed through his mail slot, along with the arrival of two letters, two of many, but the two he kept—one from the president of the Washington branch of the NAACP, praising his courage (*Courage? Had it taken any courage?*), and one from a Mr. J. P. Tumulty, secretary to the president of the United States, asking if Mr. Shumacher might be free to take tea with Woodrow Wilson on the following Friday. The magazine's initial circulation was in the hundreds. Shumacher suspected the only way the president had come across it was if his father, a healthy contributor to campaign funds, had sent it to him. No matter. He could hardly decline.

By that Friday Shumacher had published Issue 2, in which he attacked the federal government for the ongoing construction of the Lincoln Memorial:

```
Lincoln needs no memorial in stone. His legacy
is everywhere—it is visible in the continued
existence of the Union. His words alone are
enough and should be enough. The Republic needs
no throne of Zeus for Abraham Lincoln to sit
upon. We are a nation of men, not gods.
    The projected cost of $3 million might surely
be better spent on indoor privies, running
water and proper drains for the residents of
the Alley Dwellings in the slum we call, with a
painful lack of irony, Capitol Hill. There are
upwards of two thousand houses needing these
basic human necessities.
    It is an odd experience for a newcomer to the
city to be able to stand on the hill and gaze
at the dome of the Capitol, so near and yet
```

`so far, whilst smelling the stench of an open`
`sewer.`

Which statement decisively killed any discussion between Shumacher and the president on the matter of the film and diverted them, not unproductively, into forty-five minutes, with weak tea and cookies, on the monumentalisation of the city, the condition of DC and the condition of the Republic.

Over the next twenty-five years the only president with whom Shumacher did not take tea or cocktails or dinner—on several occasions breakfast—was Calvin Coolidge, a man notorious for his avoidance of the English language. The rest of them, right up to but not including Harry Truman, sought the company of the "wisest young hack in Washington."

Along the way—the young hack reopened the debate over Plessy v. Ferguson, opposed American entry into World War I, urged entry into World War II, supported the New Deal, argued for justice for Sacco and Vanzetti, and in 1932 told every congressman and senator—"An Open Letter to You ALL!"—that America's shame was now bottomless when Herbert Hoover turned troops on the Bonus Army that had gathered across the river in Anacostia to demand their veterans' payments—forty thousand unarmed men, women and children versus the US Cavalry led by MacArthur and Patton.

Had he known either of them, he would never have spoken to MacArthur or Patton again—but he hadn't.

Along the way, his parents died in the Spanish Flu epidemic of 1918, leaving him the richest man in Pennsylvania and in all probability one of the richest men in the USA—not Rockefeller rich, but sufficient. His parents' death delayed his wedding, but on November 16 he married Eileen Annunziata Kennedy, a distant cousin of the rising stock market wizard and future bootlegger Joseph P. Kennedy. The following year he rented out his row house and bought Roundehay, a redbrick mock-Georgian mansion in McLean, high above the Potomac on the Virginia side. Eleven bedrooms and forty acres rolling to the river—far better suited to being a family home.

He—they—were happy. "Blissfully" would be the truth, not a cliché. But in 1936 Eileen had been on board a TWA flight, Washington to Nashville, when it crashed into the Black Mountain in eastern Kentucky.

Shumacher made what he later termed the biggest mistake of his life—he let his sister-in-law convince him that his daughters would be better off with her, with "a woman's touch," than with him in the "loneliness" of Roundehay. He agreed, regretted it a thousand times, but never reneged on the agreement. He saw his children during school holidays when they came home to him—but it was never enough. Tennis and swimming were insufficient bonds between a man and his daughters, and a process of distancing began that could never be undone.

He had not lied to Charlotte when he had said "the details are obvious"; he had understated things. And part of the understatement, the far-from-obvious, was that he had not seen either Margaret or Valerie for almost a year when FDR had asked him to put *AJ's Weekly* "on ice" and become the president's voice in London in the spring of 1942.

His final article for his magazine was on Wilhelm Furtwängler's birthday concert for Hitler on April 19—when Furtwängler had shaken the hand of Joseph Goebbels—saying to his readers that it was not an act on which to judge or condemn the conductor. He was aware that this could possibly lead to more dog shit and more graffiti. All the same, he mailed it to his secretary from London. It was lost in the mail and he thought no more about it.

Six weeks later he met Charlotte Mawer-Churchill.

§13

On the thirteenth day Shumacher shipped out for Gibraltar. A destination he resolutely did not mention to Charlotte.

§14

January 1943

The little things matter.

Charlotte wondered how Hubert had ever managed to put his cuff-links in when he was single. Buttons would be easier but, wedding rings excepted, cufflinks were perhaps the only pieces of jewellery allowable for the modern man. After persuading Hubert to hang up his pocket watch, she would never suggest buttons replace cufflinks.

He loved the twenty or so seconds of attention as Charlotte fastened them in place. A clothed intimacy. She loved the feel of the starched Egyptian cotton through which she threaded little chains of silver. She had bought him this pair on their first wedding anniversary—her mother had advised her that gold was vulgar and suitable only for sales-men in car showrooms or for lounge lizards, as loud as co-respondents' shoes.

"Did you hear that Avery Shumacher is back?" Hubert said.

"Yes, I had heard."

"Do try to be discreet, Charlotte."

§15

Claridge's

May 1943

It had been Charlotte's experience that most men lit up a cigarette after sex. Avery made tea. He had long since settled on Lapsang as the ideal postcoital beverage.

He fussed at his "new-fangled" kettle. The novelty seemed never to wear thin. Charlotte lay on the bed, sheet up to her chin, one bare leg dangling over the side.

"Have you noticed?" she said.

"Noticed what, my angel?"

"The number of Americans in this part of town."

He turned to face her, a cup of tea proffered. She sat up, plumped a pillow, lay back and took the cup from him.

"It makes sense," Avery replied. "We are spitting distance from the embassy. There'll be more and more of us the closer we get to opening a second front."

"Oh. Isn't that what North Africa was? I thought that was why you spent six months in Gibraltar?"

"Charlotte, I never told you where I was, and I will not."

"Wasn't hard to work it out."

"But since you ask. No. The only second front that will satisfy Stalin is France. Think like Uncle Joe for a moment."

"*Revenons à nos moutons*—I was trying to think like *Uncle* Hubert."

"Meaning?"

"Claridge's is getting too public. Grosvenor Square has been nick-named Eisenhowerplatz. Too much top brass swanning around. People Hubert may well have to deal with."

"Charlotte, we agreed, did we not? Hubert knows."

"Of course he knows. But he'd hate to hear about *us* from any third party."

"What do you have in mind for *us*, Charlotte?"

"Another hotel?"

Avery said nothing.

"The Connaught, perhaps?" she prompted.

Head down, Avery mused. When he looked up she could see resolution in his face.

"Hotel hopping? A sordid affair? I cannot have a sordid affair with you, Charlotte. In fact, I cannot have an affair with you, period."

"So what was this? Another quickie?"

"Quickie? I didn't think I was all that quick."

"Just a figure of speech, Mr. Shumacher. My dad says only a cad would time his coitus."

Avery laughed.

"You are joking?"

"Of course I'm joking. I shouldn't think Dad even knows the word 'coitus.' If I told him Captain Cook had set sail to discover the clitoris, he'd look for it on a map of Australia. My parents' generation may not have hidden from sex, but they certainly hid from its vocabulary. 'Shag' is a carpet, 'prick' is always prefixed with 'pin,' and I imagine they think 'fellatio' is Italian for 'cheese.'"

When he had stopped laughing and Charlotte had stopped smirking at her own wit, Avery said, "I say again—I *cannot* have an affair."

"Ah, you don't own the right shoes?"

This time he did not laugh. He looked more serious than she had ever seen him.

"It is not in my nature nor is it right by you. You must obtain a divorce from Hubert and marry me."

"Was that a proposal?"

"Yes."

"How . . . romantic."

§16

Hubert's birthday falling as it did in June, it was July before Charlotte found the emotional energy to ask for a divorce and August before such energy found words.

A Friday.

Breakfast.

Fried eggs, streaky bacon and Hovis. Everything but the bread rationed.

Hubert set down his knife and fork.

His egg yolk would set ere he picked them up again.

"Would you care to sleep on this, Charlotte?" he replied.

"I've slept on it since January."

"Ah—so you are certain in your own mind?"

"Certain and sorry."

"Why so?"

"I did not marry with any thought of divorce. I wanted our marriage to work."

"After a fashion it does. It is . . . comfortable . . . but comfortable is not enough for you, is it? It never has been."

"Marriage cannot be a pair of old slippers or a warm dressing gown, Hubert."

"Quite."

She never knew quite how to respond to "quite." It was the upper-class gent's filler word. Confirmation without a hint of enthusiasm.

"So . . . ?"

"No. I will not divorce you."

Charlotte thought she might cry, but a deep intake of breath saw her past tears.

"I cannot do that. It would not be . . . right."

"Hubert—"

"Let me finish, Charlotte. It would not be right by you."

The same words Avery had used. What did men think was right "by" women?

"You must divorce me," he explained.

Good fucking grief, are you kidding?

But she knew in her heart he was not.

"It will not be quick," he continued. "Nor will it be easy. We will need evidence and we must provide it without a hint of collusion. A whisper of collusion and the judge will undoubtedly regard us as committing perjury, and I am often minded to think that the courts regard murder as a lesser crime."

"Oh."

"The discretion I have urged upon you must not be relaxed."

"I understand. Or I think I do. You'll take the adulterer's slow train to Brighton—"

"I prefer Bognor, but, yes, that is what will happen. Leave the details to me and do not ask. Not to know is best."

Hubert returned to his congealed egg.

Charlotte had lost her appetite, he had not.

§17

Somewhat to her surprise, Charlotte found it was up to her to arrange for Hubert to be caught in flagrante.

"Really? Must I?"

"Collusion, Charlotte. Collusion."

"I don't even know where to begin."

Hubert seemed embarrassed. Not quite looking her in the eye. She could not be surprised at this.

"I am not wholly unworldly, and if I am, there are several of my old friends and acquaintances who have been in this position before me. You may recall Tony and Rosamond Claiborne's divorce?"

"Of course, but I was hardly privy to the details."

"Well, here is the only detail you need to know. Lewis Hancock, 221B Maida Vale."

"A detective?"

"No, my dear. A gas fitter."

Good bloody grief he's making jokes. I must divorce him more often.

§18

Lewis Hancock had no distinguishing features. It occurred to Charlotte that she'd never be able to pick him out in a police line-up. A huge asset in his line of work, she thought. His plain face was his fortune—or at least his twenty-five guineas.

"I have reason to believe my husband has liaisons in Bognor Regis."

"And how do you know this, Mrs. Churchill?"

"Oh, bugger . . ."

"Try to remember. You may be asked in court."

"Er . . . er . . ."

"Perhaps you were about to send his suit to the cleaners, and in turning out the pockets you found the stub of a Southern Railway ticket—Victoria to Bognor via Horsham?"

Of course. It made sense. The man probably knew the railway time-tables and routes of the South of England by heart. She'd bet a fiver he knew the layout of Clapham Junction better than his own parlour.

"Oh, yes. That was it. Silly me."

Sotto voce now, not that anyone but Charlotte was listening.

"Try to get it right, Mrs. Churchill. Learn your story and stick to it. Now, when do think your husband might be going to Bognor next?"

They'd agreed on Tuesday week.

"Well, lately," she improvised, "he's been getting home later and later on Tuesdays."

"And was the ticket stub you found dated a Tuesday?"

"Yes. Come to think of it, it was."

"Good, good."

"And a time, perhaps?"

"I, er . . ."

Sotto voce again, "Just tell him to be on the three fifteen."

"Ah, yes. Love in the afternoon."

And all timed to Bradshaw.

"Whatever."

"Will we need to meet again, Mr. Hancock?"

"I'll be called in court, almost needless to say, but no, I'll post you the photographs. No need even to look at them. They'll do the trick or my name's Joe Soap."

She hadn't thought of photographs, but what other credible evidence could there be? But now that Hancock had put the idea in her head, she couldn't stop thinking about them.

They arrived the following Friday.

Common sense told her not to open the envelope.

Common sense could just bugger off.

Hubert was on top of a woman whose face was turned from the camera. He was trouserless, stripped to his shirt, bare-arsed. She had her knees raised, legs locked to his hips. His face was turned to the camera as though Hancock had said, "Watch the birdie" or "Say cheese"—but

Hubert wasn't saying cheese. He just looked sad, infinitely sad. Too sad even to feign outrage.

He had left his socks on.

§19

"One of us must move out."

"Collusion? Again?"

"We cannot flout the law, Charlotte. I can stay at my club."

Which one? Whites? The Carlton? The Athenæum? He belongs to so many.

"Hubert. It's your house. Before that it was your dad's and before that your grandfather's."

"All the same I sh—"

"Will you stop being so fucking decent!"

Charlotte realised that stunned silence was literal. It was as though she'd slapped his face.

"It should be me," she said softly. "Really it should."

"And where will you go?"

She had not thought.

"I don't know. I suppose I could—"

Hubert was shaking his head.

"No, you can't. You cannot move into Claridge's with Mr. Shumacher. In fact, you can't see Mr. Shumacher."

"What?"

"Charlotte. You cannot charge me with adultery whilst living with another man. It may not equate to Mr. Hancock's profession or a trip to the seaside, but the hotel abounds with witnesses. Any chamber maid who has seen you come and go is a potential witness."

Charlotte was not a weeper. But she wept. She had not wept since the death of her border terrier, Nettle, when she was twelve, and it would be years before she would weep again, but she wept now.

"How long?" she said at last, drying her eyes on Hubert's proffered hanky.

"I don't know. I wish I did. We live in the era of infidelity—such is wartime—and it follows it must become the era of divorce. The courts may bottleneck with the demand, or they may speed up the process and rubber-stamp every adulterer from here to John O'Groats. I'm afraid I really have no idea."

§20

She could not and would not go "home."

Her mother, on hearing the news, said, "Are you sure you want to do this, Charlotte?"

Her father, in a significant variation, said, "As long as you're sure, Charlotte."

And neither mentioned that she would be the first divorcée in the family, for which she was silently grateful.

She accepted an offer from Cousin Prudence. Pru was pushing fifty, ten years older than Charlotte, and they did not know each other well. She suspected her father's hidden hand behind the offer.

Things could be worse. Pru owned a huge, airy house in South Hill Park Gardens, chosen for the constancy of its light. Pru was a painter of some renown. Her heyday had been before the war, when she exhibited every year or so and sold well to critical acclaim. Since the war began things were somewhat different. A gallery in Mayfair had taken a direct hit in the Blitz of '41 and twenty-two of her canvases had been reduced to ashes. Now the top-floor studio, looking north over one of Hampstead's ponds, was piling up with unsold canvases, waiting only on peace and profit.

Pru was a lesbian. She had no truck with the Radclyffe Hall look of faux-masculinity, owned no ties, nothing in tweed, and on those occasions when she shed her habitual work clothes—a paint-bespattered boilersuit and plimsolls—favoured flowery dresses and red lipstick and was not averse to heels when occasion required.

Pru asked nothing of Charlotte but discretion. Not rent, not a little something towards household costs. Nothing.

"I will get a job, you know."

"Not on my account, darling."

"I mean to say—I can't live off Hubert, can I?"

"I don't see why not. It's what men were put on earth for."

You may very well think that, thought Charlotte.

She had not married Hubert for a meal ticket, although she knew his income to the penny simply because she double-checked all his sums for him, but she had no idea of Shumacher's means, although he obviously was not poor . . . but then again, the American government paid for the suite at Claridge's (surely?) . . . and his suits, that hung so loosely about his body, weren't from a fifty-shilling or even a fifty-dollar tailor.

Yet . . . and yet . . . every Friday evening during her stay at Cousin Pru's a bunch of plum-red roses would arrive from a Berwick Street florist, card unsigned. Now—what did that cost? Was Avery Shumacher put on earth just to send her flowers?

$21

Pru held out the telephone receiver to Charlotte.

"Looks as though they've tracked you down."

"Hello?"

"Charlotte. Jock Colville here."

Jock was the Prime Minister's private secretary. One of London's most gleeful gossips. She could hardly be surprised that he was her first caller.

"Does this mean Winston knows?"

"Yeeeeeees. Not to worry. He just wants a bit of a chat. Would you be free in about half an hour?"

A bit of a chat?

"Of course, Jock. I'll be right here."

A bit of a chat!

§22

She did not ask after Hubert nor did Churchill say. There was, she knew, German bombs notwithstanding, something indestructible about Hubert. Her dad had once described her cousin Verity, younger sister of Pru, as a "word child," and that was not so much a simple confirmation of the fact that her nose was always in a book as an affirmation that words were a protective barrier. Her own motte and bailey. Hubert was not only a word child, he was a numbers child. Content—above all, secure—with page and pencil in hand, the real world held at siege beyond wall and water.

Cousin Winston was concerned about her. He no more worried about Hubert than she did herself.

"I fear, Charlotte, that you will stand too proudly on your independence."

"If you mean I won't take money off Hubert, you're right."

"A job?"

"I wish I could say I was looking. God knows there's enough work for women nowadays, but the truth is I'm only thinking about it. I'm not sure I'm qualified for anything."

"You have, if memory serves, a degree in modern languages."

"French and German getting a bit rusty from lack of use. And of course Italian. You can always count on me to read the menu in a trattoria. And I've kept up my Russian after that trip I made to Moscow in '28."

"Russian? I may have a job for you."

"That's very kind, but I can't work with Hubert. Even if I wanted to, there'd be legal reasons."

"Quite. I understand. I didn't mean here in Downing Street. I meant at the Admiralty. Across the road. Unless you and Hubert choose to eat your lunchtime sandwiches on the same bench, you need never meet."

"Er . . ."

"Just say yes, Charlotte. I had thought to commend you to the Navy as a German speaker, but we can go one better. Naval Intelligence is crying out for Russian speakers. Report on Monday. Room 39, chap name of Fleming."

"That's so . . . so kind."

"There is a quid pro."

"Yeeeees?"

"Let's not stop our nighttime games of bezique. When I can't sleep, I can't sleep. Bezique is my only relief."

They had been playing no-sleep-bezique for the best part of ten years. Since 1940, and his tenancy of Number 10, Churchill's insomnia had been made known to her by the arrival of an ATS girl driving a Humber Snipe, both in plainest khaki, outside the Hampstead house and a request for the pleasure of her company—melds and brisques and brandy after midnight.

§23

It was February 1944 before Charlotte and Hubert were granted their decree absolute. Hubert was right. It was the era of divorce. The mutterings of scandal that would have been audible before the war were now a muted "So what?"

Liberated, Avery took the tenancy of a cottage in the grounds of Kenwood House, the house itself being shut up for the duration. It was privacy made tangible.

He and Charlotte married in March at the registry office in Marylebone. Cousin Pru and an American Intelligence officer Charlotte was introduced to simply as "Frank" were witnesses, and the deed was done.

Bliss must surely subside, much as misery must, but somehow it didn't. Avery's sexual appetite after seven months apart astounded her. A fifty-four-year-old man priapic as a teenager. On one occasion when the ATS girl arrived at Kenwood to escort her to Downing Street, she had been tempted to plead exhaustion but didn't. She dreamed and dawdled her way through bezique, and when Churchill asked if anything was wrong she replied, "If you must know, I'm shagged out. Literally."

Churchill merely smiled and took the trick.

After he took the next trick he said, "I cannot pretend I am not envious."

§24

It was late August that year, still summer, still warm enough to sit outside at dusk.

Charlotte had floated tinned peach halves from Fortnum's—she hadn't seen fresh peaches in years—in a cocktail bowl full of champagne. Little orange rowing boats to which she had fancifully added cocktail sticks for oars and a lone wooden frog as oarsman.

It was a Friday. Avery appeared, still in his city clothes, after a day of meetings, clutching the by now customary bunch of roses.

"Ah. We're expecting company? I'm bushed. I was hoping we could just—"

"Only you," Charlotte replied. "Only you."

"That's a hell of a lot of champagne for two."

"Just a magnum."

"Just?"

"Y'know," Charlotte said as Avery scooped up a large glass of champagne and ignored the frog and peach slices. "I was thinking of all the things you've given me. Roses . . . dried eggs . . ."

"I've never given you dried eggs."

"I've already moved on from the Avery things to the nation, the general. An extrapolation. Beans, bacon, evaporated milk, corned beef . . ."

"Charlotte, is this leading anywhere?"

"Of course. I do not prattle. I talk. I inform. I ask."

"Ask away. Inform me all you wish."

"Paris was liberated today. The first real sign that the war is ending."

"Agreed."

"And when it ends . . . no more dried eggs, no more—"

"Stop! I don't want to hear that goddam grocery list again."

"And . . . no more roses . . ."

"Charlotte, there will always be roses."

"The war brought you here, my sweet. Will peace take you away?"

This prompted more reflection on Avery's part than Charlotte had anticipated.

For a minute or two he stared westward into the reddening sky over Cricklewood.

"Yes. And perhaps sooner than you think."

"Meaning?"

"The president is not a well man. That's hardly a secret. Running for office in November is a gamble, but I know of no one who would even suggest he not stand for reelection. What might be more of a secret is that he could . . ."

"Die at any moment?"

"Yes."

"And if he does?"

"The vice president succeeds him. That's the constitution. I would willingly serve under the current vice president, Henry Wallace—a good friend, I've known him for years—but he was dropped from the ticket last month in favour of Senator Truman. And . . . the reality is my job was done here in June. My presence is just that, a presence. FDR's eyes and ears. I contribute next to nothing in all these damned meetings. If he dies . . . I've no role at all.

"I will not serve under Harry Truman. If . . . if . . . well, you'll soon get used to Washington and you can have all the dried eggs you want. You can even keep chickens and dry the eggs personally."

"And roses?"

"My dear, the roses will never stop."

§25

President Roosevelt died on April 12, 1945. On May 2, Mr. and Mrs. Shumacher sailed for New York on the *Queen Mary*, arriving six days later, on May 8—the day of Victory in Europe.

Coky

§26

Times Square, New York

May 8—Victory in Europe

She knew what to expect of this night in London. There'd be a party, a street conga stretching from Piccadilly Circus all the way to the gates of Buckingham Palace.

Times Square was much the same, but much the different.

It seemed to Charlotte that all America must be gathered there. It might have been natural for them to be dwarfed by the skyscrapers, but the opposite seemed true. The crowd was large as and larger than life, as though she and Avery had stumbled into Brobdingnag.

After ten minutes she said, "I'm sorry to be a wet blanket, but could we go now? It's all a bit much."

A sailor in uniform proved her point. Whisked her off her feet, whirled her around, arched her back so that her hair all but swept the sidewalk, kissed her once and plonked her back in front of Avery with "You lucky son of a gun."

Charlotte was momentarily dizzy. Avery hooked his arm through hers and led her away. They'd come down Broadway but went back up Seventh Avenue.

At the corner of Seventh and Fifty-Seventh Street he stopped.

Carnegie Hall.

She knew why he'd brought her here. Music was what had brought them together. Standing by the piano while young Fred Troy played Bach and Schubert, the invitation to the National Gallery that followed and the countless evenings at the Wigmore once they had married. Music was the glue of their relationship. More important than any piece of paper they had signed.

Carnegie Hall was closed for music, temporarily, while former president Herbert Hoover addressed anyone, possibly no one, who hadn't made it as far as Times Square on the topic of victory. Charlotte could not imagine what he might have to say or who might wish to listen. One could inhale victory all around—words seemed wholly superfluous.

"Of course," said Avery, "it'll be music again soon. And we'll be back. More nights at the Plaza, more evenings here. We'll come back."

But they never did.

"Avery?"

Walking, strolling along Central Park South.

"Charlotte?"

"I can't be Charlotte anymore. Charlotte Shumacher. Too much alliteration. It'd be like being Mrs. Bun the baker's wife."

"Well . . . why not? New world, new name. You have several to choose from, after all. Whom would you wish to be, Ophelia? Katerina?"

"Whom? Really?"

"Yes, really."

She was giggling now. Such an archaism, willfully maintained in this rather old new world.

"Call me . . . Coky."

Avery looked baffled for a moment.

"Ah! *All* your initials."

"Got through school as Coky—there were far too many Charlottes. So 'Coky' will be fine. A new woman for this new world."

Avery kissed her.

"I was rather fond of the old woman."

§27

Coky and Avery walked the Roundehay estate to the craggy edge of the garden high above the Potomac. Every so often he'd say "well, whaddya know?" as they came upon a statue or a rare ornamental shrub from Japan or China or wherever that he claimed never to have noticed before.

Avery had mentioned he'd bought some thirty or forty acres and added a few more "here and there" over the years. Yet this seemed to be the first time he had remotely grasped the size of his own property. If indeed he had.

She could not understand such indifference . . . no, not indifference, perhaps neutrality. Whatever it was, the estate clearly mattered only marginally to its owner. He had a study and twenty to thirty assorted rooms around it, and he had a house and forty to fifty assorted acres around it—beyond that all he asked was that it function with the minimum of demands on his attention. How different from all those English toffs she'd grown up with, rippling with pride and burdened with history and debt. Her husband seemed blissfully free of such attachments.

Avery was at pains to explain Washington to Coky. They had passed through it so quickly that she had no grasp of its size—for all she knew it could be as large as London or as small as Luton, but judging by Union Station, London seemed the more likely.

"Think of it less as our nation's capital and more as a village."

A village?

She pondered this one. Did he mean everyone knew everyone? That everyone was related to everyone else? That the postman would stick a letter in your hand and give you five minutes of gossip? That she'd be expected to join the American equivalent of the Women's Institute?

The latter issue soon came to the fore.

An invitation from Mrs. Henry Benét to attend a "Ladies' Evening" at the Copernicus Club on Lafayette Square, a stone's throw from the White House.

"What's the Copernicus Club, and what exactly is a Ladies' Evening?"

"Well . . . ordinarily I'd say it was perhaps the most interesting club in town. It's not just for the rich. There are men with brains. The Philosophical Society meets there. And there's a rumour, not apocryphal, I'm pretty sure, that the Manhattan Project was cooked up over a lunch at the Copernicus. Ladies' Evening? Well, the club does not admit women . . . so . . ."

"I get it. So they toss them a bone every so often. Back door only?"

"Of course."

"And who is Mrs. Henry Benét?"

"My God, is she still around? She was a Washington young thing when I first arrived. She is the former Elizabeth Boscomb, self-appointed queen of the District of Columbia. If you go, be careful not to pronounce the *t*—it's 'Ben-nay,' not 'Ben-net.' And except when she 'Henries' herself, she is Bitsy Boscomb Benét."

"Bitsy? Are you kidding? It's the kind of name you'd give a dog."

"Pot and kettle, Coky."

"Touché."

"And you'll meet a few Muffins too."

"You don't mean *eat* a few muffins?"

"I do not. I'm from industrial Pennsylvania. Muck and brass, as you would call it. I have never understood this WASP fondness for silly nicknames for middle-aged women. A prolonged infantilism, perhaps. Dolly, Bitsy, Muffin . . . all nursery names."

"Why have I been invited? Because I'm Mrs. Shumacher?"

"I doubt that. I'm not part of any inner circle. Few Jews are. But you're new, you're British and you're related to Winston Churchill. They'd be even more interested if you were a lesser royal, but I wouldn't gild the lily."

"You mean I shouldn't wear a tiara? And we don't have lesser royals, only lesser woodpeckers."

"England abounds in lesser royals. I just can't remember any of their names. But . . . enough . . . look in the Washington Green Book when you get back."

"What's that?"

"A social index . . . a who's who of who's not really who . . ."

"Are you in it?"

"Of course not, but the husband of every woman you meet at the Copernicus will be. And not one of them matters a damn."

§28

Coky returned home less than elated. Avery had warned her in a dozen different ways that Washington was dull to the point of stodgy, but she had thought, had kidded herself, that politics would lift the tone of any evening, permeate any conversation in a town with only one industry and one reason to exist—only to find that politics was off the menu even if fresh shad was on it.

It was banal beyond belief—the sole subject seemed to be charity work—funds raised, causes served, the undeserving poor—and having no charities to which she contributed, organised or founded, Coky found herself with little to say to anyone once they had exhausted Cousin Winston as a topic. She wondered if the ladies had been as bored by her as she had been by them. But a voice inside told her that in the absence of anyone who'd actually met Princess Elizabeth (Coky had but would never admit this), Cousin Winston might be the inexhaustible topic.

She kept mental notes. There had been only one Bitsy, but she had glanced off two Muffins, a Dolly, a Lolly and three Migsies.

"I think I'll scream."

Avery looked up from the book he was reading.

"Could you scream quietly?"

"Waaaaaaaaaaaaaaaaaaaaah!"

"So . . . no. But may I point out: you don't have to go again. Just politely turn down the invitations."

"You mean there'll be more?"

"Just because you were bored by them does not mean that the Muffins and the Bitsies were bored by you. Just say no."

"Won't that make us social pariahs?"

"Probably, but I would not care. I was a part of Washington society while Eileen lived. When she died . . . I dropped out for mourning and never returned. Charlotte—"

"Coky!"

"I'll try, but I'm not sure I'll ever get used to that name. Coky, you have a choice. You can belong or you can believe, and many choose to belong *and* believe. Whatever you do, I will support you."

"They're . . . inane."

"I know that."

"But."

"But?"

"Part of me wanted to go in there with a shillelagh. Part of me didn't give a damn and part of me wanted to hammer change into them."

"Washington has changed. Just not enough. The war changed Washington. The building of the Pentagon, an influx of new people. A dull, narrow-minded company town opened up a little. I fear it is now in the process of shutting down again—regluing itself into its stuck old ways. It may well become as dull as it was in 1932."

"Belong or believe?"

"A tad too aphoristic. Mea culpa."

"No, it's not. I think you're right. I was born to belong. I am a general's daughter. The granddaughter of a viscount. The great-granddaughter of a man who served with Wellington at Waterloo. I just resisted it most of my life because I wanted to believe. Belonging required no thought; believing does."

"Believing in what?"

"Dunno. Perhaps I am a rebel without a cause."

§29

In bed.

Avery's long right arm cradling most of Coky.

"Of course," she said, "there was gossip."

"You don't say."

"About you."

"I refer the honourable member to my previous answer. Do I care?"

An elbow surfaced from beneath the sheets and jabbed at his ribs.

"Gossip about you. It was being said you'd turned down a seat in the Senate."

Silence.

"Well? When were you going to tell me?"

"I wasn't. I'd've told you if I'd accepted. Or would you have me tell you about every cockamamey idea that's put to me?"

"No. I suppose not. Where was it, by the way?"

"Pennsylvania. Thad Shelby there is eighty-nine. He won't run again. The party thought to shuffle out a Shelby and shoo in a Shumacher."

It was lines like that that reminded Coky of why she had fallen for the man.

When she'd stopped laughing she lapsed into silence for several minutes, pulled herself closer to him and lay still. Thinking his wife had fallen asleep, Avery reached for the cord to turn out the light.

"I won't decline invitations, not as such," she said softly.

"Milk and cookies keeping you awake?"

"I won't decline invitations . . ."

"Not quite following you."

"I'll start issuing them. Tell me, husband mine, when was the last time Roundehay opened up its ballroom?"

"That would be 1935."

"So—it'll need a bit of dusting."

§30

They took breakfast in bed. Avery had not changed the habit of a lifetime and began his working day in bed, in pyjamas, over his first cup of coffee, much as he had done in the London years. It might be noon before he dressed and went to his desk.

Coky sifted her morning mail.

"Dad's written again."

"I'll run off a printed form. Daughter in safe hands. Tick. Well fed. Tick. Not short of money. Tick. Husband has stopped beating wife. Tick."

"Very funny. He says . . . an old school chum of his will be in town next month."

"Fine. Plenty of room here. He'll be most welcome."

"No . . . not quite what he means. The old chum is Sir Allan Little."

"Titles, titles, titles. Bitsy would love it."

"That's more on the button than you think. Allan is principal conductor with Sinfonia Écosse. He's bringing over the whole orchestra."

She handed Avery the flyer that her father had enclosed.

Avery glanced at it. Then he put down his papers and seemed to study it.

Coky slipped out of bed and into her dressing gown.

"A reception," she said. "A reception for them all. I'll get me mop and me bucket and I'll dust off t'ballroom. Vim and t'elbow grease."

Avery said nothing.

He was still studying the flyer.

HOWARD UNIVERSITY
MAIN HALL

Friday, June 22nd 1945 7:30 p.m.

Sinfonia Écosse

Conductor Sir Allan Little

Vaughan Williams: Symphony No. 5

Tippett: A Child of Our Time

With the Howard University Gospel Choir

---

§31

Transatlantic telephone calls had to be booked.

Frustrating.

It was lunchtime the next day before the switchboard connected her to the Edinburgh number.

"Ah," Little said. "You took the hint."

Allan Little had been teasing her, coaxing her, since she was a girl. One of the things she liked about Dad's best friend was that he didn't seem to take life as seriously as the old man did. Allan would play This Little Piggy with her toes when she was five, let her beat him at tennis when she was ten, and from literacy on, not a birthday passed without a box of books arriving from Hatchards.

Quite why he was Dad's best friend had always baffled her. They had school in common, and after that a parting of the ways that might logically have led the one never to think of the other again—but they had.

Widowered when both he and the century were young, Allan had never remarried. He dipped in and out of the Young household as though enjoying marriage and children by proxy—but "children" was really just "child," Charlotte. Allan had never been much interested in the boys nor they in him. Perhaps he was a touch too raffish, too bohemian for a trio as conservative as they had become by adolescence. They joked about their eccentric "uncle"; as her brother Neville had put it, "You never know what Uncle Allan will do or say next." He had, after all, performed a Satie piece at her mother's piano—adapted, in the spirit of its composer, for additional blown raspberries. This, and many other instances, had left Charlotte with little choice but to silently agree with her brothers. Allan was unpredictable.

"I have the Saturday after the concert entirely to myself," he said. "We don't leave for Chicago until the overnight Capitol Limited on Sunday. How about lunch?"

"Lunch? I was thinking of a reception for the orchestra. We have a ballroom, and it's summer—we just open the windows and spill out onto a lawn Middlesex or Surrey would be glad to call a cricket pitch."

A momentary silence.

"Charlotte, there are eighty-two musicians. Eighty-six if I go overboard with the double-bass players."

"OK. That's fine. How many in the choir?"

"The choir?"

"I was at the première of the Tippett last year in London. There was a pretty big choir. How many in yours?"

"Fifty—"

"OK, so we're catering for upwards of a hundred and thirty—"

"Charlotte—the choir is local. They're all students at Howard. Do you not know what Howard is?"

"It's a university."

"It's a Black university."

"So?"

§32

"You bugger, you might have told me."

In the study. His feet up on a pouffe. A stack of papers and folders six inches high on the floor. Pencil in hand.

"I thought it better to let you pursue this until—"

"Until I hit the buffers? My very own train wreck?"

She had Avery's attention now. The pencil stopped scribbling in the margins of his papers, the glasses slipped to the end of his nose and he regarded her somewhat sternly across the top of them.

"I could not and will not veto you. I did not want you to get the impression that I would. As I believe is said in England, pissing on the chips. But—you must never forget that Washington is a Southern town. It is scarcely three generations away from slavery and a civil war. Robert E. Lee's estate is just downriver. Harper's Ferry just upriver. In the twenties Civil War veterans still marched on Memorial Day. And the town is where it is because the man it's named after wanted it handy for his own estate—a man who believed in slavery whilst endorsing the equality of mankind. George Washington bought and sold human beings and shuffled them back and forth across state lines to avoid laws that would give them their freedom. A Black was counted as three-fifths of a person. A so-called compromise written into our constitution. I couldn't tell you what the present fraction is. How much is less than zero?"

"Are you telling me the town hasn't changed in God knows how many years?"

"Eighty years. Almost exactly. No. It's changed. As I said, the war made a difference. Just not enough of a difference."

"Are you saying I should offer no invitation? That I should . . . should what?"

"Charlotte, invite who you will, and I shall back you all the way, just be prepared for the crapstorm you may unleash. Washington is a Southern, segregated city, and it was remiss of me not to have had this conversation with you weeks ago. I waited on incident when I should have stated principle. But . . . ask yourself which is the quicker social suicide . . . to shun the Bitsies or to usher in the Blacks?"

"I've no intention of committing social suicide, but if the only society on offer is Bitsy Boscomb Benét's, then it's time for a new one."

"I say again: belong or believe. You will not change Washington by these means. You must first belong. You don't have to believe for a second, but only by belonging will you change it."

A momentary silence. He'd uttered a sentence that had lain unuttered in her own mind for twenty years.

"What are you not telling me . . . Coky?"

The hesitation over her name would never cease to irritate her.

"As it happens . . ."

"Yeees?"

"As it happens . . . Allan agrees with you."

"Softly, softly, catchee monkey."

§33

"I hope this isn't a silly question. Do you have a piano in the house?"

"Yes. A Steinway. It might even be in tune. The only silly question might be asking me to play it. I was pretty awful as a child, if you recall. Never got past a rather clunky *Für Elise*."

"Indeed. My ears still hurt. However, it is I who shall play."

"Eh?"

"Traditional. The minstrel sings for his supper."

"Allan, you don't have to—"

"Oh, but I do."

§34

No one turned down the first invitation from Roundehay in more than ten years. If sheer nosiness was a part of good manners, then the Washingtonians had good manners. They accepted. They arrived. A fleet of limousines parked in the arc of the driveway.

Coky had her *Rebecca* moments as woman after woman recalled the first Mrs. Shumacher.

Such a charmer . . . beauty . . . hostess . . . delete as appropriate.

Coky smiled them away.

The party, as intended, spilled out across the giant lawn.

No one fell in the river.

Shortly before dusk it spilled back in through the French windows and into the ballroom.

Allan stood by the piano. When the chatter ceased, he tweaked the height of the stool and launched into three lively pieces, none of them lasting even a minute.

Coky got the joke, even if no one else did. Chopin's *Écossaises*.

He stood. Paused. The guests had clearly been expecting more and it took a moment for applause to begin.

Allan waved it down.

"No . . . no . . . we're not quite done yet. Ye must suffer more. Now— to break the mould for a few minutes—something completely different. David Mackie, our master of tympani, is also a fine bass-baritone. A fact unknown to millions. Our harpist, Daniela Cesarei, is also a fine guitar player—so much easier with fewer strings. And, as you might expect, our orchestra leader, Ruth McVey, is a pretty mean fiddle player. They will play two traditional folk songs—the first from our native Scotland, the second . . . the second is truly American."

Three musicians stepped out of the throng and lined up in the curve of the Steinway—a tall, barrel-chested man and two slender women, one clutching a battered violin that looked as though it had earned the name "fiddle" in battle, the other wielding a fat-bodied twelve-string guitar.

Allan, despite his stout knees, hardly ever missed an opportunity to wear his kilt—a bold red Lowland tartan with no hint of yellow—and about half the orchestra had opted for traditional dress, the fact that it was June in Virginia notwithstanding. The tympanist in a kilt that looked to be mostly mud-coloured, the fiddle player in a simple white blouse and a tartan skirt Coky was sure she'd seen on shortbread tins . . . but the guitar player with the strangely Italian name had topped them all with the earasaid and snood she was wearing.

Allan left the "stage," stood next to Coky. She wondered what he was up to, but his face betrayed nothing. The guitar led, followed by a mournful, whispering violin and a deep, dark voice:

> *O the summer time has come,*
> *And the trees are sweetly bloomin'*
> *And the wild mountain thyme*
> *Grows around the purple heather.*
> *Will ye go, lassie go.*

The applause had scarcely died down before the twelve-string struck up again, solo for a dozen bars before the violin and voice came back in, more melancholy than ever, a melody to rip out your heart and stamp on it:

> *Sometimes I live in the country,*
> *Sometimes I live in town,*
> *Sometimes I has a great notion*
> *Of jumpin' into the river and drown.*
> *Irene goodnight, Irene goodnight*
> *Goodnight Irene, goodnight Irene,*
> *I'll get you in my dreams.*

Was it or wasn't it? Was the applause somewhat muted? Coky turned around, looked into the "audience"—she saw pleasure, surprise and bewilderment. Then a Muffin or a Migsy had buttonholed Allan.

"Truly American, you said? Was it a Stephen Foster song? From a minstrel show?"

"Au contraire," he replied. "I believe it to be a song from Louisiana or Mississippi. Recorded in a penitentiary. The original recording is now in the Library of Congress."

"Oh. Oh. I see."

And the word had not passed his lips.

Just then Avery passed by, whispered in her ear.

"Well done, my dear. A chink in their armour."

"Really?" she replied. "That was entirely Allan. I had no idea. He just asked for a piano."

§35

Breakfast in bed.

Coky felt the merest throb of a hangover. Avery didn't. When she opened her eyes, the curtains were drawn back—far too bright to her eyes—and he was slicing letters open with a paper knife—far too loudly to her ears. A bumblebee buzzing in a sunbeam.

"And how is my wife this bright summer morn?"

"Confused."

"Of course."

"Am I the social pariah of Washington or the purveyor of pearls to somewhat willing swine?"

"Only time will tell. The invitations will pour in, or they won't. Only time will tell."

§36

Three Years Later

Roundehay
February 13, 1948

The roses stopped.

Coky was waiting for Larry Bergman—Avery's lawyer. The man who'd drawn up Avery's will, which was to be read any day now. Avery's daughters had declined to attend. If Avery's body was ever found, Coky was certain they'd all skive off the funeral. In four years of marriage she'd met neither Valerie nor Margaret. Washington might have been a million miles from New York rather than a morning's train ride.

"I can't see any point in the formalities, if the girls are going to behave like assholes. I'll just give you the bad news now. Avery left Roundehay to them."

"I cannot say I knew, but I'm not surprised. And I don't mind."

"Really?"

"Really."

"And . . . the good news. You are well provided for with a trust fund, and the house on N Street is yours outright."

It was the outcome she might have wished for, had she ever thought to wish. Avery had been only fifty-eight and in good health when his plane crashed into a Kentucky mountainside. The coincidence of its being the same mountain that had killed Eileen Kennedy Shumacher in 1936 was wasted on no one.

Coky had asked him not to go. Not to criss-cross the USA. Not to campaign for Henry Wallace.

"It's a chance to break the mould. The very thing you set yourself to do when you took on the ladies of Washington."

"I don't think there's any comparison."

"Coky, the two-party system is stagnant. If it weren't, we'd not have an ass like Truman as president. Henry is more likely to be true to the ideals of FDR than Truman. In fact, the way Truman is leading the country frankly scares me."

"If I accept the comparison, for the sake of argument, then agree with me that what I do is at grassroots level. Is there not more to be achieved if you stay here, in Washington?"

She had failed to convince him.

He had taken flights to half a dozen cities in only two months, spoken for Wallace in Los Angeles, Phoenix, Chicago and cities she no longer remembered. One week ago he had set off for Pierre, South Dakota, via Little Rock, Arkansas—a flight path that would take him straight over the Black Mountain.

"Of course, it'll all seem small after Roundehay," Larry said.

"You're rambling, Larry; there's nothing more to be said. This house is theirs. N Street is mine. And it's an end to soirées and dinner for forty. Words cannot convey how glad I am that that is over."

"Coky, I wasn't expecting—"

"It's showbiz, Larry. Always leave 'em wanting more. Now, if there's nothing else, I have to pack."

"Oh, there's no hurry. The girls will be happy with sometime in March or even April."

"Larry, I'll be out of here by Monday."

Charlie

§37

London, 1951
Spring Turning to Summer

Troy watched Burgess vanish around the corner—suitcase in hand, mackintosh slung over one arm. He could not help the feeling. It was overwhelming. He'd seen the last of Burgess. In this he turned out to be wrong, the momentary triumph of emotion over inevitability, but that's another story. For now, Guy was gone. One last lie—maybe two or three—on his lips.

It was a week or so before he heard from Charlie. The press speculation on the missing Foreign Office diplomats—"Where are Burgess and Maclean?"—whilst it would linger for years to come, was beginning to lose heat and steam, giving way to "When will there be a general election?"

Troy's elder brother, Rod, a junior minister in the troubled Labour government, had never cared for Burgess, nor for Troy's friendship with him.

"He was a liability to you as a serving police officer, and now he's a liability to us. The Tory press seem to think we're responsible for this fiasco!"

Troy said nothing.

Rod had his own problem with Guy. He'd never seemed to have one with Charlie. Charlie had led as louche a life as Guy but had the advantage of being heterosexual in his endless pursuit of pleasure. On some unfathomable level, Rod Troy, the happily married father of four, might well have envied the footloose . . . although "foot" was a singularly inappropriate organ to fuel such imagery . . . the footloose and fancy-free . . . no, that too is wrong—the fancies were never free, in fancies begins responsibility . . . or was it in dreams? Begin again, Freddie—Rod was delighted by and envious of Charlie Leigh-Hunt, grazing on the vicarious pleasure Charlie dangled in front of all and probably sundry too.

Troy was not impressed. Never had been. Tales of cherchez-la and cock-artistry bounced off him like pig fat off a sizzling hob.

All the same, they went back years and years, to the horror and boredom of an English school. They were the best of friends.

"Lunch tomorrow? I've booked a table at the Ivy."

This, to Troy, illustrated the divergence in the paths they had cut through life in the last twenty years. Charlie rang the Ivy and the Ivy would no doubt turf the Aga Khan off his chair and do the magician's trick with the tablecloth to make room. Troy rang the Ivy and was put on a waiting list. In his father's lifetime he had pretended to be booking for his father, but the late Sir Alex Troy being so obviously late, the ruse no longer worked. Charlie was somebody, Charlie was a contender, Troy was not.

"See you at one? My treat."

"Of course," said Troy. "Is there . . . an occasion?"

"Sort of. I'll tell you tomorrow."

My treat? The last time they'd met, Charlie had borrowed fifty pounds off Troy. Was he now using it to buy him lunch?

§38

Troy was late. Charlie had as many virtues as vices, patience being one of them. Left alone, Troy would lose himself in a book. Left alone, Charlie would strike up a conversation with a total stranger, a low tolerance for boredom.

When Troy arrived at the Ivy, a man and a woman had pulled up chairs to Charlie's table, doubtless sandbagged by Charlie en route to their own table. The man had just said something to set everyone laughing, but as Charlie's gaze moved from them to Troy, their heads turned.

Noël Coward, in the company of one of his leading ladies, Judy Campbell.

"Freddie, you know Noël and Judy?"

Troy had met both. Coward at his father's dining table, several times. Judy Campbell, backstage after the first night of the *New Faces Revue* about ten years before. She'd given the first performance of *A Nightingale Sang in Berkeley Square* to a stunned, rapturous audience. Charlie had dragged him to that. Campbell's husband, David Birkin, was something clandestine in the Navy, much as Charlie was something clandestine in the Guards. Birkin and Charlie knew each other, and Charlie seemed determined Troy should meet Judy. Not that it mattered. Neither she nor Coward remembered him. Good manners and meaningless phrases ensued, and after a few moments they crossed the floor to their own table. Troy found Judy Campbell's looks haunting but thought better of ever mentioning this to Charlie.

He wondered what Charlie had to tell him. It was so unlike Charlie not to have said "Why don't you join us?" and made up a foursome. He'd known Charlie to make up eightsomes and sometimes tensomes.

Onion soup.

A flotilla of French bread.

"Washington."

"Eh?"

"I'm being posted to Washington tomorrow."

"Really? As what?"

"As Burgess's replacement."

"Replacement what? Guy was . . . What was he? Information something or other? Bugger-in-chief?"

"Dunno. I haven't been given a job description. Just sort of 'Go to Washington and replace Burgess until . . .'"

"Until what?"

"Dunno that either. So 'indefinitely' might well be the word."

"But he was Foreign Office . . . You're . . ."

Troy could not quite think what Charlie was. He hadn't seen him in uniform since the end of the war—Charlie, like Rod, had had "a good war"—and he'd lost track of his rank. Simply put, Charlie was a spook.

"I'll be working under Kim Philby. He's SIS's man in Washington."

"Ah. Old pals."

"Not exactly."

"You've known him for years. Since Cambridge."

"True. I also knew Guy and Donald but it's hardly something I'd broadcast right now. One was more fun than a bag of weasels and the other was the most appalling whinger I've ever known. On that scale Kim is . . . hmm . . . middling. He's known as a charmer, but I never warmed to the man. I'd say he was a cold fish but that doesn't really go with 'dry,' does it? Anyway, we've never been chummy. But—huge but—it's one hell of an opportunity."

"Opportunity for what?"

"Does an opportunity have to be for something? Couldn't it just be sort of intransitive? Opportunity is. Full stop? No object required?"

"Remind me, what did you read at Cambridge?"

"I forget. Perhaps it'll come to me over the pudding. The opportunity *is* Washington—the hottest date imaginable. Diplomatic clover."

"And some of the worst architecture in the world."

"You've never been there."

"Actually, the old man took me when I was about twelve. Charlie, it's like de Chirico's paintings. Do you know how often neoclassical architecture features in nightmares?"

"No. And neither do you. You're just sneering. It is, I say again, a great opportunity. Not a bloody nightmare. You should be congratulating me."

"Oh, but I am. I'm thinking of all the opportunities you've had in London and the trail of broken hearts and discarded knickers you'll be leaving behind."

Charlie grinned. Tried to lose the smug look on his face by tilting his wine glass to his lips, but when it touched the table again he was still the cat that got the cream.

"Well," he said. "There'll be a few, I suppose."

Troy changed tack. Politics, always safer turf than morals with Charlie.

"Replacing Burgess, you say. What exactly is an information officer? Sounds like a cover story if ever I heard one."

"Dunno. And I never got the chance to ask him. But Kim is Lord High Panjandrum between us and the Americans. On Intelligence, I mean. Sort of our ambassador for Intelligence. So I'll be an under-panjandrum. If that's what Guy really was."

Troy paused, scored ski lines in the table linen with his fork, wondering whether he should say next what he knew he was going to say next.

"You know. I think I saw Guy the day he did his bunk."

"Well, did you or didn't you? You could hardly fail to recognise him."

"Oh, it was him. We chatted for quite a while. Just wasn't sure it was that particular day."

"So you might have been the last of us, apart from waiters and cabbies, to see Guy at large?"

"I think perhaps I was."

"Then I'd keep shtum about that if I were you, Freddie. Your colleagues in the Branch are pulling in everyone from his tailor to the milkman in their efforts to piece together the picture of that last day."

"Well. I've told you."

"And I am diplomatically deaf for the moment. Besides, if I tell our lot, I won't be getting on that ship to New York. And wild horses and all the pink floozies in Windmill Street wouldn't make me miss that. If no one asks, do not volunteer. After all, we both know where he is, don't we?"

"Of course. I do hope Guy has a taste for vodka. I doubt he'll be getting a lot of Scotch in his new home."

§39

Charlie got home to his terraced house in Woodfall Street, Chelsea, just before four, slightly the worse for drink. His cleaning lady had been in. Most of the furniture was draped in white sheets—shrouds, as Charlie saw them. The sitting room reeked of lavender polish, the kitchen of Vim. He really should have arranged to let the house, but there hadn't been time. Besides, he might be back in a matter of weeks. Charlie was, he considered, not a sentimental man. Life with his mother had been too chaotic and too itinerant for the attachments of sentimentality. The most stable thing in his life had been school, and he had hated school. The house, three storeys, less than fifteen feet wide—catswinging space if the cat was not too fat—might be all that he could ever feel that way about.

He really ought to pack now.

The telephone rang.

He ignored it, but the bugger on the other end was persistent.

Inspector Cobb, of Special Branch.

"Where the hell have you been?"

"Good afternoon to you too, Norman."

"You need to talk to Cock—"

"No names!"

"—in person. Doesn't trust me. Says it has to come from the Major. Quite insistent, and always uses your wartime rank. I'm just a soddin' NCO to him."

"Norman . . . I sail tomorrow."

"This can't wait."

"I thought we had it all set up."

"So did I, but he's being a twat."

Charlie wished he could wish Cobb out of existence.

"OK. When and where?"

"Now."

"Norman, you have to be kidding. I'm packing for—"

"I'm across the river. Would you believe he's come down for the soddin' Festival of Britain? He's in this Dome thing they've got. Be there in half an hour."

$40

Charlie was in Southwark in twenty minutes.

The Dome of Discovery was part of the ailing Labour government's attempt to repeat the Great Exhibition of 1851—a sort of delayed recognition that the war was over. It wasn't so much a dome as a gigantic flying saucer lifted from the cover of a kids' comic.

It was an eyesore.

The queue to get in was massive.

Cobb was at the end of it.

Charlie said, "Go in and get him. Flash your warrant card. If we have to tell it to him all over again, this is not the place to do it. There are people everywhere."

"Right—I hadn't noticed. We'll go to the Mucky Duck."

Like any English pub at five o'clock of a summer's afternoon, the Black Swan, Waterloo, was closed in accordance with licensing laws dating back to the grounding of Noah's ark. Some pubs did not serve women. None admitted children. Some of them served dogs.

Cobb hammered on the door.

Charlie read the sign over it: "K. J. O'REILLY LICENSED TO . . ."

It might just as well have read COPPER'S NARK.

Cobb hammered again, and there was movement on the other side, behind the etched glass that read SALOON BAR.

"Will yer fekk off. We're not open! Can't you read?"

"O'Reilly. It's Norman Cobb. Open up!"

Bolts slid back, a ruddy Irish face atop a stout beer-belly frame appeared in the crack of the opening. Obsequious in the face of a black-booted, flat-footed London copper.

"Sorry, Mr. Cobb. I didn't realise. Would this be official?"

Cobb pushed past him.

"No . . . it's not. In fact, I was never here. We need your back room for a while. Lock up again and piss off upstairs. Before you do, a pint and two large scotches."

Silence prevailed until O'Reilly had set drinks in front of them.

Cobb made no move to pay.

Charlie studied Cockerell. He'd met him perhaps half a dozen times. Three or so towards the end of the war, and as many since. He had been Cobb's choice. He was slight, muscular and sharp of feature. You remembered the nose, the cut of his jaw and the pencil-line Ronald Colman moustache—but . . . but the sum of the parts was less than the whole. He looked more like Edward Everett Horton than like Ronald Colman. "Weaselly" might be the word, but Charlie was never sure what that meant. Appearance or character? Cockerell did not lack character. He spoke his mind.

"I am not a traitor, Major Leigh-Hunt. I am simply a businessman down on his luck. Call it mercenary if you will, but I am no ideologue. I'm in it for the money."

Cobb looked as though he might burst out laughing, but he didn't.

"So happens I'm not a traitor either," he said. "That leaves you, Charlie. You're the only traitor in the room."

Charlie wanted to hit Cobb. To punch the fat grin off his fat face.

"Arnold . . . look upon it as a game. We take Russian money to feed them practically useless information, garnered by a team of agents who don't actually exist. You deliver the odd file and collect wads of cash. What harm can it do?"

"Well, if you put it like that . . ."

"I do."

"But why will it be useless information?"

"Firstly because there is not enough useful information to go round and secondly because I am posted to Washington in the morning . . . and I would be the primary source of any information worth imparting."

"You just lost me."

Charlie lowered his voice to a sarcastic, slow whisper. A lecture for a five-year-old. For the umpteenth time.

"Arnold. Make up a list of agents. Assign them to government agencies . . . Harwell, Jodrell Bank, the Ministry of Shellfish . . . it doesn't matter. Cobb will make up the necessary information and mingle it with enough real stuff to pass muster. When I get back from Washington, if I get back from Washington, we might well be able to deliver good stuff . . . real secrets . . . secrets that might trouble your conscience. Meanwhile, as you said not five minutes ago . . . you're down on your luck. I'm down on my luck. And Cobb is just greedy. So let's tell a few fibs, make some money and not be troubled by the illusion of a conscience until we have to be. It's a fiddle, of course it's a fiddle, just like all the fiddles that went on during the war. We're selling nylons and fags. And no one gets hurt."

Cockerell left first.

Cobb said, seemingly apropos of nothing, a fraction shy of sneering, "Nylons and fags?"

He sank the rest of his pint.

Belched.

Charlie found he suddenly had some sympathy for Cockerell. He had none for Cobb. He had very little for himself.

He would not have said he was an ideologue either, but he was a believer. Not the same thing at all. He too was in this for the money and dearly wished he wasn't. He'd love to believe and not to feel quite so compromised, he'd love to be able to work for nothing . . . but his tailor, his club, running the bloody Aston Martin, the packets of white fivers he bunged his mother every time she called him up in tears . . . it all added up, and Mother Russia simply didn't pay well enough. He said again, silently, to himself, *A few fibs . . . who does it hurt? No one.*

A chink of light crept in. Bedtime, sleepless, pushing Cobb and Cockerell out of mind . . . from tomorrow he was on overseas allowance.

§41

There can be, Charles Leigh-Hunt thought to himself, no better way to arrive in the New World than on the *Queen Mary*, ageing beauty though she be, gliding between the Narrows into New York Harbour, past the Statue of Liberty, her gaze ever fixed on Brooklyn, to be nursed into the midtown Cunard dock on the West Side of Manhattan by tugs scattered around her like ducklings.

If to arrive is good, to travel can on occasion be better, especially if one can contrive the occasion. Charlie had. He contrived to be seated at dinner on the second day out next to a widow or a divorcée (either way, nothing about her screamed "married") in her forties. She was an ageing beauty, slim and blonde, with a dirty laugh, an English accent as posh as his own, and a sexual appetite that turned out to be pleasingly voracious. The third day passed in a blur of sex and room service. They did not leave his cabin until evening. The fourth day would bring them into New York. He woke alone. He would always respect such good manners.

It was a beautiful late-May afternoon. Sun glinting on the water, clouds scudding across the sky . . . Did anything but a cloud ever scud? All that . . . poetry sort of thing. And if there wasn't a popular song called "Springtime in New York," then there should be.

They met for the last time on an observation deck at the sharp end, watching Manhattan loom.

She shook his hand.

Bit of a blokeish gesture.

"Goodbye, Charlie. It's been fun."

He would not be the one to deny that.

He didn't know her name and didn't ask now. Begin as you mean to go on, he thought, anticipating America.

§42

The hotel was awful. Typical of SIS to book him into a rathole. Creaking plumbing, lumpy mattress and a smell he couldn't identify wafting down the light shaft. Skinflints. It was in the shadow of midtown's skyscrapers, dark and dwarfed, scarcely a block from Penn Station and the roar of Seventh Avenue never lessened.

He asked a bloke he met in a bar on the ground floor of the Empire State Building.

"Move to the Carlyle. I live in White Plains. If I want to get good and shit-faced of a Friday night, I just check into the Carlyle and tell the wife I worked late."

"Ah . . . is it . . . handy?"

"Handy?"

"Close by."

"Seventy-Sixth and Madison. All depends on what you want it to be handy for. The Garden, nah. The Village, nope. But uptown is uptown, if you catch my drift. Most hotels in this town have seen better days. Carlyle? Not so. I reckon it's at its best right now. Even the president's been seen to lunch there. But maybe I just accidentally gave you the bad news. Politicians. Politicians and their wives, politicians and their mistresses. So if you have a problem with politics—"

"Oh no," Charlie said. "I can eat politics for breakfast."

"Speakin' o' which. The breakfast at the Carlyle might just be the best in town."

§43

Madison Avenue was as noisy as Seventh—but, he told himself, it was a better class of noise. In fact, a better class of everything, from the scrambled eggs and crusty sourdough for breakfast to the soft-shell crabs at lunch (he had no idea what a soft-shell crab was, but nothing ventured . . .) to the martinis and whiskey sours in Bemelmans Bar each evening. The bloke behind the bar readily accepted Charlie's recipe for a twosome martini. No gush, no splash—all to a measure: two fingers of imported Russian vodka, two cubes of ice, a sliver of lemon and two, exactly two, teaspoons of Noilly Prat. Above all, stir it—do not even think of shaking.

He'd asked for two days' layover. SIS had grudgingly agreed. He took four. And he had every intention of giving them the bill. If they got snotty about it . . . well, he was a spook. He'd been born with nine lives and by his reckoning he had at least three of them left.

All that was lacking was . . . *une femme.*

Each evening, somehow managing to seat himself at the same booth and look like a regular, he would gaze far from idly at the doorway, silently willing a middle-aged blonde, perhaps a few years older than he was himself—experience told, after all—chassis and all moving parts in good nick, to walk through that door.

None did. Every woman, of any age, seemed to walk in on the arm of some bloke with "Lucky Bastard" stencilled on his forehead.

At last it dawned on him that he was not really looking for a type but for an individual. Good grief. Had the woman on the *Queen Mary* got under his skin? He wasn't the sort to get hooked by a one-night stand (OK . . . two-nights-and-an-afternoon stand) . . . the thought of something that almost amounted to fidelity was damn close to unbearable.

Perhaps it was just the décor—the lingering, inherent decadence of Art Deco—a visual style which, to his untutored eye, constantly hinted at sex. A night at the rathole notwithstanding, he'd gone from the Atlantic Ocean to dry land, from the *Queen Mary* to Manhattan, from British sexy decadence to American sexy decadence—dinner jackets, bow-ties, long legs and curvy bottoms. Or maybe it really was the woman who'd changed things? Perhaps he should have broken his own rule and remembered her name—but that was just one remove from "Can I see you again?"—a line so corny he'd never, in twenty-five years of unfettered promiscuity, uttered it.

On his last night, on his second twosome, the bar filling rapidly, see-ing him drinking alone, the waiter asked if he'd mind sharing his table, and with a nod of the head and a shake of the hand and a trading of names Charlie found himself immersed in the world of Representative (D) and Mrs. George Madison, of New Jersey, and their friends Bob and Thelma. Charlie utterly failed to grasp Bob's last name or what he did, but George was in politics, and having boasted he ate politics for breakfast, Charlie saw no reason not to drink it before dinner.

"How very kind of New York to name an avenue after you, Mr. Madison."

This set everyone laughing. English wit and charm was a cliché Char-lie had traded on for years—the willingness of others to find wit where there might only be scorn.

"If only," George said. "It was Di Madio when my old man got here in 1890. I'm about as Italian as linguine and meatballs."

"And I'm about as English as boiled beef and carrots."

Charlie hadn't eaten this delicacy of English cuisine since school, but to say he was as English as foie gras and a decent claret, however true, would just delay the inevitable question, and some part of him was anxious to reach it. It might break the ice, it might sink the ship.

"So, what brings you to New York, Charlie?"

"Oh, I'm merely in transit. En route to Washington."

"You don't say? You're like . . . a . . ."

"Diplomat? Yes."

Oh, how little the truth, half-truth, hurt.

"I represent West New York, the Eighth Congressional District. Despite the name, it really is in New Jersey. You heard of Weehawken?"

Charlie shook his head.

"Nah, I guess not. Hoboken?"

"Ah . . . Sinatra's hometown?"

"Yep. Gets 'em every time. Anyway, I represent those towns and a few more like them in the House. Weekends here, Mondays to Fridays in DC. Maybe we should meet up down there? Show you around. I've been in Congress for five years now. I know the town. It has what every politician, every diplomat for that matter, needs."

George duly waited for his prompt. Charlie duly played the straight man, Abbott to his Costello. Timing is (almost) everything.

"And that is?"

"Good restaurants by the dozen. I mean, Washington is 'get-the-deal-done city,' and how can you do deals without restaurants? Harry Truman wants talks with Moscow—not that I really think he does—he should persuade Harvey's to open a branch in Red Square."

"Harvey's?"

"Best restaurant in town. Connecticut Avenue. A quick cab ride from your embassy. Anyone who's anyone is there."

"Ah, you're assuming I am an anyone."

"You tell me."

"Oh, I'm a lowly cultural attaché."

The old, old lie trotted out again. Smile as you tell it.

"And a cultural attaché does what exactly?"

"Dunno. I'll find out when I get there."

This produced more laughter. George and Mrs. Madison would never guess how true it was. Charlie had left England in such a hurry, he'd had no discussions with anyone, save Troy, about what his cover might be. Was he whatever Burgess had been, or was he something altogether different? If he needed to bluff his way in "culture," how long could he sustain a conversation about the Hallé Orchestra or Edith Sitwell?

Tack away.

"And you, George? What do you do in Congress?"

George looked at the tablecloth for a moment. A hint of modesty. Mrs. Madison ablaze in reflected glory.

"Oh, I'm on a House committee."

"Oh, Georgie," she chipped in. "Stop it!"

"Barbara, please."

"He's *only* the chair of the House Interstate Transportation Oversight Committee!"

"For my sins," George added.

Just my luck, thought Charlie. For Charlie's sins George would have been on a committee for defence, foreign affairs, national security . . . guns and bombs and battleships . . . perfect spy fodder—but no, it just had to be trains and boats and planes.

"Like I said," George picked up, "let me you show you Washington." He slipped his card across the linen.

If Charlie had had such a thing as a card he would have slipped one back. More in optimism than in expectation. Interstate transportation—riveting.

§44

On the Saturday, Charlie caught the mid-morning train from Penn Station to Washington. Emerging from the tunnel under the Hudson, it occurred to him that he hadn't really been in the USA until now. New Jersey was, visibly, not New York, and he began to wonder if New York was America at all. Once out of the industrial jungle of eastern New Jersey he seemed to be in a land of endless bridges and rivers so wide they made the Thames look like a trickle, and, tipped into dreamland by the passing, soothing landscape, he began to dream and in dreams to recollect.

A few years ago, it seemed to Charlie that Troy had sounded him out. The country place of the Troys, Mimram House. A cool late-August evening on the verandah, after a hot summer afternoon and three and a half bottles of chilled Orvieto to mark Troy's birthday. Of course Charlie had brought it upon himself.

"How do you spot a wrong 'un?"

"I'm a cop—it's the basic tool of the trade. Like a hammer or a spanner."

"Yes—but how—what do the villains give away? Nothing as simple as a twitchy eyelid or a sweaty collar. There must be something."

Troy said, "It's the lie."

"The lie? Just the one?"

"Yes. But it's the total lie. The lived lie. If you live within a lie, everything you say is a lie."

"Is it? Fuck me."

"All—and I do not wish to minimise the skill . . . it's not that easy—*all* the copper has to do is spot the contradictions. The new lie that doesn't fit the old one."

"Living within a lie? Not sure I get that."

Troy drank and sighed. He could not hold his drink as well as Charlie, but Charlie thought him still to be on the sober side of pissed.

"Suppose for one moment a double agent. Like those blokes you worked with in the war. One thing to us, another thing to the Germans . . . unless you were Eddie Chapman and you were all things to all men. You inhabit a lie. I don't think there's a better way to put it—you live within the lie. There's nothing you can say, even when you know you are telling the truth, that isn't rendered a lie by what you do not say, by what you cannot say."

Charlie upended the last bottle into his glass. The merest dribble. Troy squirmed in his chair, reached down to the floorboards and hefted a bottle of Calvados.

"Were you ever going to mention that?"

"Emergency rations. Help yourself. I am . . . done."

"Where were we?"

"Living the lie. If you live inside the lie, nothing you say can be wholly true."

Charlie glugged half an inch of Calvados. It burnt beautifully.

"Charles Edward Moncrieff Leigh-Hunt."

"Eh?"

"My name in full. What it says in every record since the old man registered my birth in 1914. Possibly the last thing he ever did for me, but there you are. Could have done without the Moncrieff, but as it probably entitles me to wear a kilt on Burns Night . . . so . . . Charles Edward Moncrieff Leigh-Hunt. Not a word of a lie. I defy you to find an untrue word in those four."

"Five."

"OK. Five. Find the lie. It doesn't matter what I might be in this hypothesis. Agent, double agent, the elusive fucking Pimpernel. I am who I am."

"If . . . if you were a Pimpernel or an Eddie Chapman . . . you would have a code name—come to think of it, 'Pimpernel' is a code name, his real name was something like Piers or Percy—and in stating your real name, your Piers or your Percy, you would not mention the code name and in that error of omission is the lie. The liar lies by what he does not say far more than by what he does."

Charlie swigged another half inch. Stared into the bat-swooping, insect-crackling darkness.

His code name was Dog Fox—in Russian, *Лиса*.

§45

The train was late. Something had held it up around Wilmington. No matter. It was spring, days getting longer with every blink of an eyelid. When he arrived, he caught a cab from Union Station to Philby's house in northwest Washington. Half an hour later he paid off the cabbie in front of wrought iron gates and looked across at 4100 Nebraska Avenue.

The first thing that came to mind was *Gone with the Wind*, memories of Rhett and Scarlett. Kim had done very well for himself. A beautiful southern pastiche—or perhaps it was the real thing and not pastiche at all?—a scaled-down version of an antebellum mansion.

"Where the hell have you been? I was expecting you on Thursday!"

"Hello to you too."

"You're t-t-two days late!"

"Just thought I'd see a bit of New York."

"So you've been playing the tourist? We're facing exposure . . . our biggest crisis since God alone knows . . . 1935? And you take two days off to f-f-f-fuck around in New York?"

"I wouldn't quite put it that way."

"I would. Ever the p-p-playboy, Charlie. Let me guess . . . you met some beautiful woman on your first day . . ."

That was too near the knuckle by a yard and a half. Charlie hoped Philby would just let it drop, then let him drop his bags and offer him a cup of tea.

He did, after a fashion. Turned on his heel in the doorway, yelled "Dump your bag over there" over his shoulder, and threw in a startling "You're not stopping."

"Really? I thought Guy had a room here and that I'd—"

"You can't stay here!"

"Ah."

They'd reached a sitting room. Philby waved him into a chair and paced in front of the fireplace.

"You can't stay here, because Guy did. It's as simple as that. Except nothing about this mess is simple."

For a moment Charlie thought Philby was pulling his own hair out—fingers locked tightly on top of his head—then the steam seemed to go out of him. He flopped into an armchair, pressed a bell button next the fireplace.

"I'm sorry. You've had a long journey. I've had a week of pure bloody hell. The girl will bring us tea. We'll all calm down."

Charlie had not lost his calm for a second.

He said, as tactfully as he could, "What is it I don't know?"

The pause seemed almost infinite. Philby staring at the ceiling, Charlie all but overcome by an urge to scratch his backside, what his schoolteachers used to call "fidgeting."

Before Philby spoke again a young black woman appeared with a tea tray.

"I got them cookies you like, and Mrs. Philby is awake now."

Philby thanked her almost inaudibly and then they were alone again.

"Before Aileen appears, and she may not, she knows nothing. Understood?"

"Of course."

"You know who Walter Bedell Smith is?"

"I read my brief, Kim."

"In his capacity as chief of the CIA he has written to our lord and master Stewart Menzies, demanding—not asking—for my recall to

London. He's threatened to break off all liaison. And in his capacity as chief of SIS, Menzies has agreed. I've been ordered home, the day after tomorrow. We have a million things to do in the next forty-eight hours and you choose this moment to swan around in New York."

"Oh fuck."

"How succinctly you put it. The CIA have nothing on me, but I am damned by association. Taking Burgess in was a mistake. The Old Pals Act isn't worth the paper it's printed on.

"Bedell Smith wants a clean sweep. Beginning with me. You can't stay here for the simple reason that the minute I leave for England, Hoover will send in the FBI and strip this place back to the lath and plaster. They'll find nothing, needless to say. If you were to be here . . . suspicion might fall on you. And that would ruin the otherwise delicious irony of Six sending you to replace Guy. Of all the people they could send, they sent you. Idiots."

"Yep. Sort of frying pan to frying pan and they don't even know it."

"You're sure of that?"

"Can we any of us be sure? Do we know what MI5 have on you apart from being Guy's friend?"

"I should never have taken him in. Aileen never wanted me to. If I'd thought for a moment he'd do something as completely pointless, as utterly stupid as to bunk off to Moscow with Maclean . . ."

"I've avoided Guy since Cambridge—not always possible, he was pretty damn ubiquitous—but I certainly never went to any of his rather queer parties. And I doubt I've even set eyes on Maclean since the war. I was never quite an 'apostle,' was I? Sometimes I think Blunt singled me out because he really wanted a puppy and I at least came house-trained. If MI5 are looking for a cabal, I'm not in it."

"I do hope you're right."

A timely pause for the English tea ceremony. The biscuits—"cookies," he believed, was the correct term—were awful. Baked-in lumps of chocolate fit to break your teeth.

"We have a place on P Street."

"Sorry, Kim?"

"An embassy apartment on P Street in Georgetown. You'll like it. It's comfortable, and Georgetown is a friendly maze of restaurants and bookshops. I say maze, actually it's laid out to a grid, but you'll like it.

It's not much more than a mile to the embassy. Walking distance, really. You can't take over Guy's bed, but you can take over Guy's desk. Not that it was ever his in anything but name. The words 'Guy' and 'desk' do not fit together anywhere near as well as 'Guy' and 'bar' or 'Guy' and 'bottle.' Nonetheless he had his own desk and his own office."

"Do I also take over his title? Am I the new information officer?"

"Blowed if I know. It was a meaningless job. Guy made it up as he went along . . . and if you wish to give it meaning you first have to have information worth imparting. And you haven't got any."

"I did make a useful contact in New York. A chap in Congress."

Charlie doubted very much that George Madison would prove to be a useful contact, but you play the hand you have.

Philby raised a sceptical eyebrow at this.

"There are roughly four hundred congressmen in the House. Most of them would have difficulty distinguishing an arse from an elbow. But . . . useful, you say. Useful? You want to be f-f-f-fucking useful? Fine, f-f-f-follow me."

Philby led him through the kitchen, out the back door to what appeared to be a potting shed. Funny time to want to prick out begonias, but whatever Philby was up to, Charlie would have to roll with it.

Philby pulled a dusty blanket off a rusting tin chest and raised the lid.

A tripod, a couple of cameras and odd bits of photographic clobber Charlie could not put a name to.

"Not quite following you here, Kim."

"It's my spy kit."

"Eh?"

"My Russian contact gave me this bundle in '48. It was and is preposterous. Like a ten-year-old being given a toy gun and a ten-gallon hat for Christmas so he can dress up as Hopalong Cassidy."

"Have you ever used it?"

"Only that miniature camera. The rest is just incriminating clutter. Make yourself useful, Charlie. Get rid of this lot. Take my car, get yourself over to P Street and when it's dark, drive out into the countryside and bury this joke of a spy kit."

"You're kidding."

"Do I look as though I'm kidding? Get this done. Get settled in and be back here at eight thirty tomorrow for breakfast. There are still

things you need to know. More things than I could tell you in a month
of Sundays, and we don't even have one."

§46

Charlie was pleasantly surprised by his official accommodation. Those
two words in tandem made him think of a school dorm or a prison
cell—he'd seen quite enough of both in his time—and it was neither.
It was five rooms, well furnished, well decorated, in a leafy side street
off Wisconsin Avenue. Streetcars rattled past from time to time. There
was a bar on the corner two blocks down and a suitably cramped and
crowded little bookstore opposite—I. FARBER, USED, ANTIQUARIAN & NEW,
EST. 1946. So far, so good. It had none of the grandeur of Nebraska Avenue,
but so what? So far, so good.

He'd lay out his clothes. Hang up his suits. Fill his sock drawer. Nip
into the bookstore, have a bit of ferret around in *Mod. Fic.* and prop up
the bar at Martin's Tavern. And when the sun set he would undertake
his first official duty as Moscow's man (one of Moscow's men, surely?)
in Washington and dispose of Philby's spy kit. It occurred to him that
his own contact, whoever that might turn out to be, might just issue
him the same kit, along with invisible ink and a curare-tipped pen. It
was all so silly. During the war, behind enemy lines, he'd carried a map
of France printed on a silk handkerchief. He'd had a compass in the
heel of his shoe. That was practical, inventive. This, as Philby so rightly
said, was preposterous.

Someone had left an old gabardine mackintosh in the wardrobe. He
wrapped the spy kit in it. All but one thing—the palm-sized Minox
camera. It was a masterpiece of design. German engineering at its
best. The Bechstein of cameras. He'd always wanted one, so he kept it.
Incriminating if found, but then again, so small, so easy to hide . . . but
then again . . . he'd no intention of being caught or even compromised.
And he'd certainly no intention of spending the rest of his life in Moscow

eking out a miserable life on a KGB pension—they did have a pension scheme, surely? He did not envy Guy's next few years. He did not envy his life or his death.

Charlie did not ask much of the world, merely that it should be his oyster.

§47

In Martin's Tavern he might perhaps have had one shot too many. Confronted with a wide row of bourbon bottles behind the bar, it seemed incumbent on him as a new arrival to pick one, and then to pick two, and two led to three. Jim Beam was bit ordinary—*give me a Highland single malt any time*, he thought—Jack Daniel's a bit sticky, Wild Turkey pretty damn good, Park & Tilford too, but for his last he tried Pappy Van Winkle's 1919 Reserve, for no other reason than the literary allusion. If there'd been a bottle up there labelled "Little Women," "Huck Finn" or "What Katy Did Next," he might well have tried it too. It was nectar to the tongue and, as he soon realized, major damage to the wallet. He'd have to ration himself to one or two a week.

Was he fit to drive?

What was the law if one was caught pissed at the wheel of a car with diplomatic plates? Then he remembered—that had been Guy's problem, one of many. He shook his head. A dog in from the rain. Asked for a large glass of iced water, accepted a look of barman contempt and downed the pint in one, feeling his teeth freeze and some semblance of sobriety course through his system like electricity.

§48

Just before dusk he drove roughly north-northwest.

He got lost.

He was almost certain he'd passed this street corner before. That church on the left was familiar. Was he driving in circles? What was that patch of leafy, arboreal green over there? A park? A wood? No, fuck it. It was a cemetery. It would have to do or he'd be blundering around in the dark and end up in Alabama or Missouri.

Past cross after cross. Statue after statue. Ascending angels, miserable mourners and one or two he could have sworn were copies of the Eros at Piccadilly Circus—up to heaven with cupid's arrow through your loins—until . . . he found what he needed but had not wholly dared to hope he'd find . . . an open grave, ready for some poor sod's funeral.

He threw the bundle in. He had only to scatter a couple of inches of earth over it and no one would be the wiser.

All he had was a trowel Philby had thrust into his hand. This could take all night.

"That could take you all night," said a voice from the gloaming.

A short, stout old man with a wild shock of white hair appeared, clutching an old-fashioned kerosene lantern, as yet unlit.

"Ah," said Charlie, wondering whether his imagination or his drunkenness had not conjured this spirit of death, this landlubber version of Charon, out of the ether.

"Whatcha burying? Funeral ain't till tomorrow. I should know, I dug the grave."

Charlie attempted his best Clark Gable impression, *Frankly, my dear* circling in his mind as he tried to grasp what might be distinctive in the accent. He ruled out W. C. Fields, considered Jimmy Stewart but knew that Jimmy would sound on his lips like a total caricature rather than a convincing American accent.

"Uncle Felix," he said at last. "My favourite uncle."

"What?"

Charlie pointed to the crude wooden sign standing in lieu of a headstone:

FELIX JEFFERSON FOSTER—1869–1951

"Oh, so you're kin."

"Yes. That's it—kin. My mom's eldest brother. Uncle Felix asked to be buried with one or two items. Ya know, his walking stick, his famous blue raincoat. I thought I'd do it quietly, in private. A dying man's last wish . . ."

"Well. We respect a man's last wishes. Let me give you a hand. You'll be here all night if all you've got is that hand trowel."

Out of nowhere he produced a long-handled, pointy-ended American shovel. Threw in half a dozen loads and handed the shovel to Charlie, who topped out the soil until the spy kit was no longer visible.

"You care to say a few words?"

Oh hell. He hadn't a clue what to say.

"I'm too broke up for words."

"I understand. I've been to a hundred funerals and some more. I'm used to it. Just try, think for a moment and then say whatever comes to mind. Whatever you say will be right."

Oh bloody hell.

"Er . . . er . . . Alas poor Felix. I knew him, Horatio . . . a fellow of infinite jest, of most excellent fancy. He hath borne me on his back a thousand times . . ."

Charlie thought he might never touch bourbon again.

The gravedigger was staring at him in an uncomprehending but far from hostile way. He did not ask who Horatio was. He took up his cue.

"How about . . . a well-earned peace, Uncle Felix, after . . . how many is it?"

Charlie looked at the wooden sign, rapidly retreating into darkness.

"Er . . . he was eighty-two."

"After eighty-two years on earth, asleep in the arms of the Lord. There, who could object to that?"

He shouldered his shovel, picked up the lantern he had yet to light.

"See you in the morning."

"You will?"

"The funeral? It's tomorrow."

"Oh yeah—right."

$49

He arrived at Nebraska Avenue somewhat hungover the next morning.

He was not the only one.

"You remember Charlie?"

Philby was wasting his breath. His wife looked as though she'd been on a bender with more loops and curves than Charlie had been able to navigate with a skinful of bourbon. She didn't even look at him. Pushed the hair out of her eyes, drew her dressing gown around her as though feeling exposed, grabbed her cup of coffee and vanished.

There was a momentary silence. At least two doors slammed, one after the other, deep in the house.

"As I said. Aileen knows nothing. Doesn't stop her guessing."

"Am I damned by association?"

"Without a doubt, but not by my wife. It's the Americans you need to convince. Since news of Burgess and Maclean reached here, most of my former contacts in both the FBI and the CIA have cut me dead. You need to . . . to repair some fences."

"OK. Where do I start?"

"Tomorrow, at the embassy, you'll get a couple of minutes with our ambassador. He'll scratch his head, call it all a 'frightful mess' or some such and say bugger all that means anything. He is 'lumpen-innocenti,' and if he's typical of Labour's idea of an ambassador, God help England. Then a briefing from the head of security, Gordon McKay. A different kettle of fish. He's a complete pessimist. He'll tell you this has set our relations with the Americans back ten years."

"Hasn't it?"

"That's up to you. Hear him out. And ignore him. Then get my secretary—or yours, as she now is—to book you a table at Harvey's for lunch. A corner table, far-left corner table. Harvey's is—"

"I've read the brief, Kim," Charlie lied. "I know where and what Harvey's is."

"Fine. Plonk yourself down and see if anyone speaks to you. Formal communications are at zero. So we have little choice but to rely on the informal. If no one speaks to you, keep it up till someone breaks silence. Work your way through the menu if you have to. They do a marvellous crab gumbo. Oysters Colchester might envy. The Feds and the Company will know who, or rather what, you are by where you're sitting. I've sat there several times a week for the best part of three years. May take a day or two, but curiosity will get the better of one of them—sooner or later. Jim Angleton will be too cautious, I think. He's terribly loyal to me. The sort of misdirected loyalty one cannot but admire. But Jeff Boyle can't resist nattering—he'll want to know your shoe size and your mother's maiden name—and I'd put money on him making the first move."

Neither of these names was new to Charlie. The situation, however, was. And it was baffling.

"Kim . . . who am I?"

"What?"

"I mean . . . I'm the information officer with, as you rightly say, no information to impart . . ."

"Drop this, Charlie, and drop it now. It's utter bloody fiction. Your transfer papers landed on my desk last week. They do not specify rank or role. You were sent here in an act of desperation. The day after that, Bedell Smith had me fired, so your role became obvious. You're head of SIS, Washington Station."

Oh bloody hell.

"Kim—I'm a field agent, not a station officer!"

"Try not to make it sound as though the job equates with that of a railway porter at Paddington. I say again: Sending you here was an act of desperation. When logic kicks in, they may replace you. On the other hand, they may not."

"You mean I could be here for years? I have several mistresses and a very loyal barman waiting for me back in London, cocktail shaker in hand."

"Very funny."

"But . . ."

"But what?"

"But . . . I am a man without a mission."

"Eh?"

"OK. I'll spell it out. Moscow doesn't even know I'm here. I had no contact with my contact before I got posted."

"Don't be naïve, Charlie. Of course they know. The mission got here ahead of you."

"Eh?"

"Mockingbird."

$50

Charlie reported to the embassy a matter of hours after Philby left for England. It was exactly a mile away, a walk across Dumbarton Oaks Park to Massachusetts Avenue. Received wisdom had it that one should never be late on one's first day, and whilst Charlie habitually ignored received wisdom, he managed to be at the embassy on the dot of nine.

It was beautiful in its way, he supposed. A mock Queen Anne house that was only about twenty-five years old, all high gables, slender windows and countless chimneys, put up by a Labour government at the time when Britain had pioneered embassies on what was now known as Embassy Row. He wondered what message this sent about Britain.

He was greeted by Gordon McKay.

"Check in with the ambassador, then I'll show you around. You've arrived at the worst of times, but then, you already know that, don't you?"

Charlie thought Sir James Taylor an odd choice for ambassador by a Labour government. A woolly-minded former academic—famous in circles where it might matter for being a translator of Aristophanes; Charlie had performed in his *Lysistrata* while a student—who, as Philby had said, scratched his head, literally, at moments of indecision. And whilst a knighthood might be the standard reward for doing the job, Taylor's was hereditary, the umpteenth Sir Somebody Taylor. The Labour hierarchy was chockablock with former trade union leaders— what message did Sir James's appointment send to the USA? The same one as the embassy itself? "You have nothing to fear from Socialism."

"Frightful mess."

Taylor scratched his head. Charlie wondered how many diplomats would state the obvious in the course of the morning.

"Of course . . . Guy . . . brought it on himself. But Kim . . . surely they can't suspect . . . ?"

Time to lie.

"Of course not, Ambassador. It's all routine. Kim will be back in a week or two. Normal service will be resumed, as they say on the BBC."

Kim would never be back. Charlie doubted MI5 had enough evidence to nail him, but they had enough suspicions to cut his career dead.

"In the meantime . . . er . . . we have you."

"Quite."

"Well . . . I'm sure you have . . . um . . . er . . . best of . . . and all that."

And in three half-finished sentences the meeting was over. Taylor had nothing to say to him. Charlie wondered if he ever finished a sentence to anyone.

§51

McKay insisted that Charlie take Philby's office, not Burgess's.

"All the mail, all the encoding and decoding you need to see goes there automatically. Let's not tinker with a system that works."

And Charlie now found himself facing the assembled diminished presence of SIS Washington Station. Two officers had returned to England in March, and, after Burgess's defection in May, London had not seen fit to replace them. That left four young men, well younger than he was, all looking a bit green and looking to him for leadership he did not much feel like providing.

"It's really quite simple," said Jones—or was it Smith? "The Americans won't talk to us. Cut us off as soon as the news of Burgess and Maclean reached here. CIA, FBI . . . they just closed ranks. No paperwork, no cables, no nothing. Chaps I've known for ages don't say hello in the street, and if I go into one of the regular FBI after-hours bars, there'll be a cordon sanitaire around me as though I'd just eaten raw garlic. If it weren't for stuff from home, your in-tray would have nothing in it."

"So you expect me to what?"

One of the others spoke up, Davis or Harrison: "It's imperative. We need to reestablish contact."

"I'll say to you what I said to Kim. I'm a field agent, not a station officer. However, I follow orders. So here I am. Acting station head. But—if you want me to play the diplomat, you'll have to give me some pointers."

"Did Kim . . . not have . . . er . . . any suggestions?"

"Kim told me to sit in a restaurant until somebody spoke to me."

Charlie had failed to keep the hint of sarcasm out of his voice.

McKay spoke before any of the young men: "Then I suggest that's what you do."

That, at least, sounded authoritative and briefer by far than the lecture he had expected.

Left alone with Charlie, McKay had one last word, very much in his capacity as head of security: "MI5's man would like a word as soon as you have a moment."

"Who he?"

"Tom Forrester."

"Put him off."

"It's his job."

"He'll have a file on me. He'll have read it by now. There's nothing I can add to it. All he'll want to do is quiz me about Kim, and I've nothing to add on that matter either. I'm stuck with Kim's job. I'm not doing Forrester's as well. Now, I take it Kim had a secretary . . . so perhaps I now have a secretary?"

"Her name's Kay. I'll send her in."

§52

"Would you book me a table at Harvey's for one o'clock?"

"Mr. Philby's corner table?"

"Have to start somewhere. Speaking of which . . ."

Charlie waved at the pile in the in-tray.

"How much of this has Kim actually read?"

"None of it. He stopped work over a week ago. There was a flurry of activity after Mr. Burgess was recalled and even more after he . . . you know. I don't wish to sound disloyal. Mr. Philby came into the office most days, but I'm not sure he actually did anything. Smoked his pipe a lot. Didn't do much dictation, certainly. I took to bringing in knitting, just to have something to do with my hands. You may find stuff in your in-tray that's the best part of a month old."

§53

It was his third lunch at Harvey's before anyone spoke to him. One lunchtime he'd watched J. Edgar Hoover and Clyde Tolson enter like royalty. Hoover did not so much as glance at him, Tolson looked his way just once and thereafter ignored him. Whoever had mentioned a cordon sanitaire was right. The table next to his was always empty.

Meanwhile he'd got through Beef Roquefort, Boston Schrod and Boiled Stuffed Flounder. He was worrying about his own waistline when someone else's hove into view. His eyes moved up from the trencher-man's belly to the barrel of a chest till he found himself looking at the face of a man he knew.

Frank Spoleto. CIA. He'd bumped into Frank in half a dozen European cities over the last three or four years. He seemed to be one of the Company's more active roving agents. Charlie had found him genial, if repetitive in his telling of shaggy-dog stories, and wherever he went Frank seemed to be preceded by his reputation as a "bit-of-a-rogue." There were tales of his postwar antics in Berlin that seemed to surface whenever two or three spooks got together over whiskey.

He smuggled peanut butter into the East!

Why the fuck would anyone do that?

At which point the room usually sank into drunken laughter.

The face was smiling.

"Hello, Charlie."

Then he clapped the man next to him on the shoulder and moved on.

Charlie realised that Frank had merely been confirming his identity, as though the suspicion on which all the other spooks in this restaurant had acted were not in itself sufficient.

If this other man was CIA, he broke the dress code. His suit was better than most, his hair longer than the standard crew cut most of them had sported since the war, and he wasn't hiding behind metal-rimmed glasses.

"Jeff Boyle," he said at last, sitting down. "You might be expecting me."

"Been expecting you all through the Boston Schrod and the Beef Roquefort."

"So, no real inconvenience, then?"

"Not at all. Will you be dining?"

"Sure. I ordered at the bar. They'll be right over with my chowder. Don't let me stop you. A flounder waits for no man."

"Sounds almost like an aphorism."

"Well, enough to break the ice."

"The ice, I fear, was all on your side."

"Can't blame us for being cautious."

"You've thrown the baby out with the bathwater."

"No. We threw the outrageous queer out with the bathwater."

"So we're all Guy Burgess now? We had a special relationship . . . with you, I mean, not with Burgess. Two countries that have not fired a shot at each other in . . . how long?"

"Since the War of 1812, which you always forget about, but I agree we need to put a stop to this."

"Then stay for dessert and we'll get to know one another. Shop talk can wait, even if a flounder can't. What do you reckon to their Peach Melba."

"Nah . . . be a touch more American. Try the pecan pie."

§54

Having little choice, Charlie was working through the pile of unread London communiqués bequeathed to him by Philby.

Most could just be initialled and passed to one or another of the green young men. Among the most recent reports, having arrived in Washington the same day he himself did, was a decoded message clearly sent before Philby's recall, but which had spent a while in the hands of a cypher clerk.

```
HMG are concerned that the Redmaine Committee
might pose a risk to our relationship with
the United States. While the House Un-American
Activities Committee seems to have slowed down,
and at no point seemed to concern itself with
British citizens, we have been apprised that
Senator Redmaine has subpoenaed several British
citizens currently working in Hollywood.
    It may be that they have nothing to hide.
Nonetheless the Foreign Secretary has requested
that the Redmaine hearings be monitored at the
highest level. Need we stress that the recent
exposure of an embassy official as a Russian
agent lends urgency to the matter.
                                            C
```

Highest level? Did they mean Philby? Did they now mean Charlie himself? A list of half a dozen names followed, with dates of the hearings attached. He'd heard of Redmaine. Only the deaf had not. He'd not been active long, but he'd taken Red-baiting to a new level. The first name on the list was that of Arthur Houghton, British-born film director, and his hearing was scheduled for Tuesday of next week. Suddenly, being a station intelligence officer in a time of intelligence drought seemed a tad less boring.

§55

"Arthur Houghton? The Hollywood director?" Boyle asked over their next lunch of "Hangtown Fry," which seemed to Charlie to be mostly oysters and bacon.

"Still a British citizen," he replied.

"And as he is wont to tell us over and over again, a US taxpayer. OK—this is what I think you don't get. The Redmaine hearings are more popular than *I Love Lucy*. Lucy has two stars. Three if you count Desi. Redmaine lines up a Hollywood A-list, week after week. This week Houghton. Last week Brandon Castani—the sexiest man alive if you believe the gossip magazines and accept that Clark Gable is not as young as he used to be—and three weeks ago Thomas Lowell Byrd—two Pulitzers and an Oscar to his name, the man who put Mississippi on the literary map of America. Doesn't matter that Redmaine is trying to stitch them up as commies, or that some of them might even be commies . . . they're stars . . . so the committee room is packed. The great American public queues at first light, and somehow I cannot see you doing that. And they have a right to be there. Strictly speaking, you don't. Your diplomatic passport cuts no mustard on the Hill. You'll have to take your turn like everybody else. Get in line, Mr. Leigh-Hunt. Unless . . . unless . . . you have friends in high places."

"Not sure I follow you."

"It's an odd committee. It's not HUAC, and it's not an official Senate investigation. Even though all six members are US senators. None of them are appointed—just chosen. It's all Redmaine's invention. He calls it the Permanent Sub-Committee of the General Committee on Investigations into US Internal Security. Deep breath and spit when you say it. It's complete bullshit. He might as well just call it the Bob Redmaine Show, put it on live TV and have advertisements for washing machines every ten minutes. He gets away with it because nobody stops him . . . well no one less than eighteen months before a presidential election. But . . . it meets on federal, that is Capitol, property so they must by law reserve seats for congressmen and senators. Any one of whom is entitled to see for him- or herself exactly what is being done in the name of the Republic. Of course, if they all turned up at once . . ."

"You'd need a room the size of Yankee Stadium?"

"Yep. So . . . who do you know?"

§56

"George? It's Charlie Leigh-Hunt. We met at the Carlyle about two weeks ago."

"Jeez. I thought you'd never call. You hungry yet?"

"I'm sorry?"

"Lunch, Charlie. Let's lunch. They can hear my stomach rumble in Des Moines."

§57

They met at the Occidental.

"Is it hard to find?"

"Nah. It's at Pennsylvania Avenue and Fourteenth."

"OK. That rings a bell."

"It should. It's right next to the White House. Y'know, that big building the president lives in?"

Ignorance had one, perhaps only one, advantage. No one would ever imagine he was a spy.

George was not a man to be rushed. Nor was Charlie a man to rush a man who did not care to be rushed.

Over Crab Norfolk (coleslaw optional) Charlie learnt what George thought of General MacArthur (not much), President Truman (even less), Senator Taft ("best president we never had"), Adlai Stevenson ("limp as last night's celery, but I'd have to vote for him") and Senator Richard M. Nixon of California.

"Not sure whether he's rising or risen. This I do know: he'll trample over anyone that gets in his way. The kid is ruthless. He used the Hiss trial to leapfrog from the House to the Senate."

Alger Hiss was currently serving a five-year sentence for perjury. It might have been espionage, but that charge hadn't quite stuck to Hiss.

"You don't think Hiss was guilty?"

"I don't know, and I don't think anyone else does either. I'd call it an unsafe conviction."

"Is that the same as unwise?"

George shrugged.

"I don't know that either. But I do know that Nixon's presence on the House Un-American Activities Committee was disturbing. The only gain to him being in the Senate is he had to quit the committee. Internal security matters. I would never deny that. But they just poke around with a broom handle and call it the law, looking for reds under beds. And whose interests does that serve? The interests of the country, or of the individual with the broom handle? Bob Redmaine's no different. Only difference is I can see where Nixon is heading. I have no idea where the vicious, odious Red-baiting that Redmaine indulges in will get him. He'll ruin lives before he's through, and one of them may well be his own."

How neatly George had brought him to the point he had not yet raised.

"London would like me to observe Redmaine."

"Hmm . . . wouldn't you rather go fishing?"

"Eh?"

"It's a bore. You'll hate it."

"Nevertheless . . . it's the job."

"Cultural attaché?"

"One of the witnesses in the next few days will be the film director Arthur Houghton."

"And he's English, right?"

"Yes."

"Observe, you say?"

"Observe and report."

George set down his knife and fork with a precision Charlie could only read as emphasis.

"I went along myself, March last year. Joe Tubkis was . . . dammit, there's no other way to say it . . . the man was on trial. Now, Joe wasn't the greatest writer in Hollywood. He wasn't Robert Rossen, he wasn't Mark Hellinger. He was a journeyman scriptwriter. He wrote horror movies . . . women who turned into snakes or wild cats . . . that sort of thing . . . men who sprouted hair where no man should have hair. Kept Lon Chaney Jr. in work and in prosthetics for a decade. I knew Joe all my life. Native Hobokener. In school he was the wimpy Jewish kid, no sports, his nose always in a book 'cos he'd had rheumatic fever around the turn of the century and it weakened his heart permanently. After three days of questions, badgering and bullying, Joe went back to his hotel room and quietly died. Bob Redmaine killed Joe Tubkis as surely as if he'd put a gun to his head. Why was he up in front of Redmaine's cowboy committee? He organised a writers' strike back in '34 to get a better deal for contract scriptwriters at the big studios. He didn't give Russia nuclear secrets. He didn't steal an atom bomb. He just got Louis B. Mayer and Jack Warner to dig that bit deeper into their pockets. Charlie, you go there . . . it could get nasty. Joe's widow, Ida, got anonymous letters and phone calls for weeks after Joe died: 'You must have known . . . you're a commie too . . . fuck off back to Russia, bitch.' They broke her heart and damn near broke her sanity. Charlie, I understand that this is your job, but if you see Redmaine in action you will come away with an idea of America that is not my idea of America."

"Can you get me in? I'm told it's packed out."

"I can and it is."

§58

Charlie had seen most of Arthur Houghton's films, from his ground-breaking "social justice" films of the 1930s to the dark, brooding crime tales he had been telling since the war. They had an immediacy, a currency right now—belonged to what was being termed "noir." Houghton's skill—genius, if you like—was to find novels that in themselves were not top-notch literature and turn them into top-notch cinema. The writers who'd been fashionable when Houghton, and Charlie, were young had benefitted hugely from having their plots updated and transplanted from London, or wherever, to LA or San Francisco. And his choice of leading ladies was pure delight—Gloria Grahame, Veronica Lake, Ann Sheridan and Barbara Stanwyck. Gloria Grahame had the top lip of an angel. Veronica Lake's suggestive, seductive peekaboo fringe left Charlie wondering whether she had a right eye at all. And he knew he'd queue in pouring rain to see Gloria eat a banana or to hear Stanwyck read the London telephone directory.

By contrast, Houghton was short, stout and bald. Nobody would pay to see him do anything. All the same, Cannon Building Committee Room 7 was full.

George ushered Charlie in. Pointed silently at the reserved benches and left him to it. Reluctantly, a few bottoms inched over. The woman seated in front of him removed a lethal-looking hat pin to set her hat upon her lap, and Charlie caught his first glimpse of Houghton. Sunlight striking in from a window high on the wall as if to anoint him, reflecting off his pate like a saintly halo.

"—And yet you continue to say this was not propaganda?"

Redmaine had a deep, resonant voice as though he'd learnt his political craft on the stump in the days before radio and television were dominant. It was impressive. Charlie could see how readily it might be turned to intimidate, how it might roll in a split second from an attractive bass-baritone to a hectoring boom.

"Senator," Houghton was saying. "You seem not to understand how books and films work. We depict. We do not lecture. It is for the reader, the observer to interpret. Any book, any film—that is, any *good* film—has what I would call breathing space. The space where the observer enters. If you see Barney Hogan's speech in *Stockyard 38* as Communist Party propaganda, I would ask what you yourself are bringing to the film."

Houghton's very English accent had acquired the merest American tinge. He'd been in Hollywood since the dying days of "silents." He didn't raise his voice or speed up his answers. He was unrufflable, it would seem, and as question and answer chased each other across the floor, he remained calm and "oh-so-English" while Redmaine's cool evaporated. The senator's voice grew deeper and louder, as though he equated volume with conviction. And Houghton's briefest and most frequent reply seemed but to add to his anger.

"Senator, I have already answered that question. I will not do so again. Consult your stenographer."

Redmaine was an actor. He was . . . a latter-day Willie Stark. A faker. A ham. Broderick Crawford would play him better than he played himself. Charlie found it hard to believe in his rage. As the afternoon dragged on he came to see the man as a commedia dell'arte character— a stock figure of limited and predictable responses, a series of masks to be donned and doffed, none of them real, none of them born of any wish to persuade or convince, only to dazzle and delude. It was third-rate showmanship. And the show was everything. As Jeff Boyle had said, it was a pity the hearings were not televised. They were made for the infant medium in its black-and-white crudity. And think of the washing machines to be sold.

§59

The afternoon simmered. Houghton was unmovable. He had a knack for flipping every question Redmaine put to him back to the man himself—it wasn't difficult; Redmaine's questions were sledgehammers, not scalpels, and but for the fact that much of the room seemed to be on his side, Redmaine would have emerged from this fruitless interrogation looking stupid.

For some reason, Redmaine had a gavel. Charlie thought only judges had gavels, but then, that was surely how Redmaine saw himself? He could not help but think of the mouse's tale/tail in *Alice in Wonderland*: "'I'll be judge, I'll be jury,' said cunning old Fury. 'I'll try the whole cause, and condemn you to death.'" He hadn't used the gavel, but after one final cheeky flip by Houghton ("I think that's entirely a matter for you, Senator"), at five minutes to five he called time, told Houghton to present himself at ten the next morning and brought down the gavel with a crash that might have vented one small ounce of his frustration.

The room emptied rapidly.

Redmaine was standing at the rostrum, red-faced, arguing inaudibly with the senator who had sat on his left. People squeezed past Charlie. Charlie sat still, wanting a better look at his subject. London would expect a report. He'd no idea what to put in it.

The woman in front of him stood, carefully replacing hat and hatpin, and he lost sight of Redmaine.

She turned to face him.

"Charlie," she said, nonchalant.

She showed none of the surprise he felt must be written on his face in Esperanto.

"Shall we find a bar? Preferably off the Hill. Walls have ears and so do hills."

"You have the advantage of me."

"So I do . . . mmm . . . call me Charlotte."

As they emerged into the afternoon's golden June sunshine, she said softly, "You know, Charlie . . . a gentleman might have asked me my name before he fucked me."

"Different rules apply at sea."

"*Queen Mary* Rules? I shall have to remember that one. Slimy bugger's get-out clause number 7. Now, flag a cab. We'll go to the Mayflower."

$60

Charlotte told the driver to take the long way round, along the south side of the Mall past the Washington Monument, with a loop at the Lincoln Memorial to arrive at the Mayflower Hotel on Connecticut Avenue after twenty minutes of tourism. Troy had told him it was a nightmare city. Charlie did not agree. He found himself willing to be monumentally wooed.

Charlotte said nothing of any significance until they were settled into a booth at the Mayflower—a glass of Veuve Cliquot for her and a vodka martini twosome for him—that he felt must wait on questions. "Go ahead," she said. "I can hear you tick as surely as Captain Hook's crocodile."

"Did you know who I was on the ship?"

"No."

"Would it . . . would it have made any difference?"

"No."

"And today?"

"You're Charles Leigh-Hunt."

"And you know that because . . ."

"Not saying. Do you know who I am?"

"Er . . ."

Come to think of it, he'd had the odd twinge, ever since the *Queen Mary*, that there was, that there might just be, something familiar about her face. The best he'd come up with was Norma Shearer, a blonde Norma Shearer. Same age, same bold nose, same—

"Charlie, you're a poor excuse for a spy!"

It took all his willpower not to look over his shoulder like a villainous coyote in a Looney Tune.

"OK. Time to stop the game. Just tell me."

"Coky Shumacher."

Oh fuck. So she was.

The English belle who'd taken Washington by storm just after the war. The woman who *dared*, the woman who would not leave the men to brandy and cigars, the woman who had seated Paul Robeson next to Governor Thurmond, Truman Capote next to Gore Vidal, Jack Kennedy next to Greta Garbo—every placement a risk, her dinner parties had been the stuff of legend—painters and musicians, senators and congressmen—her soirées almost Parisian in their extravagance. She'd been all over the British gossip columns. How had he failed to recognise her?

"You're right. I'm a bloody poor excuse for a spy."

He downed his martini in one and beckoned to the waiter for another.

"Am I blown?"

"I don't see why. You're still whatever the embassy pretends you are. What was it? Cultural attaché, information secretary?"

"I forget, myself."

"No matter. My sources are impeccable. My husband—"

"I thought he was killed in '49?"

"In '48, actually. I was not . . . I am not . . . suited to widowhood . . . I remarried last year. Quietly—so pleasing to be able do something out of the limelight. Someone else can host Washington. I did it for three years. Exhausting. I loved every minute of it and I do not miss it. All I miss is Avery."

"And your new husband?"

As he asked, Charlie could not help but think of Charlotte/Coky on her back with her legs around his waist, wrapped in an infidelity he had neither thought about nor cared about. Till now.

"Oh . . . he's not like Avery at all. No one could be. You've seen him. You should know."

"Not sure I follow you."

"I'm Mrs. Robert Redmaine."

§61

"What you do is this. You find a hotel—"

"We're in a hotel."

"No, Charlie. We're in the Mayflower at six thirty in the evening. By nine this bar will be full of pols and spooks and cave dwellers and muckety-mucks."

"What?"

"I know. It's gobbledygook. Let's just say that cave dwellers *are*, and muckety-mucks *do*. A muckety-muck thinks he can fix or arrange anything—buy a congressman, sell a senator—and a cave dweller thinks none of that matters as his ancestors were here long before Congress. And George Washington is just another parvenu. Muckety-mucks *are* politics, and cave dwellers are above politics. Either way, we do not wish to encounter them. So—find us a hotel . . . let's say out in Georgetown or beyond. Forget the four and five stars but don't drop below three. Room service, of course, but a good quality of bed linen is a must. And given that it's June, air-conditioning's a must. Get a room, then let me know the name you've checked in under."

She shoved a creamy-white card across the table to him.

"Polly, the housemaid, will like as not answer the phone. Just say so-and-so—whatever nom de guerre you come up with—will be at whatever hotel at three tomorrow."

"Three in the afternoon?"

"Charlie, I can hardly believe you haven't done this before. Adultery *is* sex in the afternoon. Or did you think I was going to skip dinner?"

§62

She was not in Committee Room 7 the following morning.

Arthur Houghton had a rougher time. Redmaine got off the subject of films and focussed instead on the testimony of previous witnesses and the affiliations with left-wing groups Houghton was alleged to have. Houghton could not blind Redmaine with philosophical points on the nature of art, of the observed and the observer. It was as simple as "Were you at a meeting of the Burbank Artists and Writers Socialist Forum on October 23, 1938?"

"No."

"How can you be so sure?"

"October 23 was a Sunday. Look it up. It was also my mother's seventy-fifth birthday. I was back in England."

An easy win, but as Redmaine pulled out date after date, the meeting of this group or that, Houghton had recourse to "I do not remember"—a reasonable answer in any other circumstance, but in this room, to that man, it undercut his position time and again.

"If I was there, it was for purposes of research."

Which was utterly unconvincing.

"So you were never a member of the New Writing Group?"

"I was, but it was what it was. A writers' group."

"A writers' group affiliated with the Socialist Workers Party of America. A known communist front."

"Not known to me. It was a group of talented young men trying to get their scripts filmed and get fairly paid for it."

"Communists!"

"So you keep saying."

"No, Mr. Houghton. So a dozen witnesses are saying, witnesses who, unlike you, seem to go around with their eyes open. Mr. Houghton, are you a fool or a traitor?"

Charlie's report, he knew, ought to consist of six words: "Get this man out of here." He knew that this could not end well. Houghton would lose funding, films would be cancelled and in all probability he'd end up blacklisted and back in England. England would be smeared along with him—the ally you cannot trust. The very thing His Majesty's Government wished to avoid. After Fuchs, after Burgess, after Maclean, the USA needed all the reassurance it could get, and it was getting very little from Arthur Houghton. It was wrong, it was a stitch-up. Redmaine would win this one, and no doubt dozens more before he was through.

He did not go back after the lunch break.

He found a hotel high up on Wisconsin Avenue. The John Smith.

And while the anonymity of the name all but screamed adultery, he felt pretty certain it was named for Captain John Smith of Pocahontas fame, rather than for habitual hanky-panky.

And—the staff seemed to accept the odd quirks that accompany adultery as par for the course. No luggage, no overnight stay, and the merest hesitation when he was asked his name.

On the way there the cab had passed the cemetery where Charlie had buried Philby's spy kit, and an obvious name sprang to mind.

"Felix Foster."

Then he rang the number Coky had given him.

§63

Coky walked around the room, examining everything after a cursory fashion. Not quite running a finger along surfaces for dust, but close.

"I've never stayed in a Washington hotel before," she said, plonking herself on the edge of the bed, giving it a bit of a bum bounce.

"Nor have I."

"It seems . . . well . . . clean. Not at all sure I'd go as far as pleasant, but . . . clean."

"What were you expecting?"

"I think I might have supposed the skimpy preparations of an English knocking shop. And sad to say, I visited a few of those when I was younger."

"So did I."

"Oh," she said. An air of faintest, near-imperceptible shock about her. "I do hope that's not all we have in common, Charlie."

§64

"Tell me."

Charlie shook himself out of the pale cloud of postcoital man-sleep.

"Tell you what?"

"Was it less exciting? You know, knowing my name?"

"I don't know how to answer that."

"Try *honestly.*"

"It was different," he said honestly.

"Did you like the anonymity of shipboard sex?"

"Yes," he said honestly. "But I am baffled."

"By what?"

"By your name. Now that I know, it isn't far short of anonymity anyway."

"You mean Coky?"

"I do."

"Ah. Thereby hangs a tale. Are you listening, Charlie-boy? Then I'll begin. I was christened Charlotte Ophelia Katerina Young. Too much Shakespeare? My mum wanted the lot. If Dad hadn't intervened I'd have been christened Portia, Perdita, Juliet as well . . . but Dad insisted on one plain old English name. So I am a Charlotte. Shakespeare created no Charlottes, but at school the Charlottes were only outnumbered by the Penelopes . . . so I became Coky. My very own acronym. After I divorced Hubert—such a gent—I thought it wise to adopt a new . . . would 'persona' be the word? So I went blonde . . . and after ten years as Charlotte Mawer-Churchill, I went back to being Coky once we'd landed here. Hadn't used the name since school, but it sat well with Shumacher, and Americans think it a lot less snooty than 'Charlotte.'"

"I'm happy with it."

"Just as well. You don't get to choose. Besides, Charlie and Charlotte? We're not in a picture book for five-year-olds."

§65

It was at this point that Charlie might have been tempted to tell London, "Enough is enough." He'd learnt what they needed to know about Redmaine. No Anglo-American summoned before the Redmaine Committee was going to come out of it well, and if the government back in Westminster wanted to avoid it reflecting on them, then the only solution was to advise every English star in Hollywood to return home before the subpoena arrived. Impossible to do—try telling that to David Niven or Cary Grant—and almost impossible to utter. But . . . the next famous face to drag him, mercifully, away from his desk was Deborah MacRae—a Scottish actress who, a few years before the war, had become the darling of the West End with her Desdemona and, a year or so later, her Saint Joan. Red hair, blue eyes, the cheekbones of a goddess . . . Hollywood had beckoned, and she had followed. She'd even taken US citizenship at the end of the war. In London she'd been an outspoken radical. America had not changed her.

"Miss MacRae, are you now or have you ever been . . . ?"

Redmaine used the traditional opening.

"Senator, I have never been a member of the Communist Party of the United States. If it's of any interest—and who knows, it might be—I was a member of the Communist Party of Great Britain from 1929 till 1931. Dark days. We needed hope. The CP provided none, so I left. I belonged to no other party until I settled in California, where I am now a registered Democrat."

Redmaine ignored this. Stuck to the script. Head down, not even bothering to look at her.

"Is it your intention to subvert the government of the United States?"

"Not today, no."

"Miss MacRae. It would be greatly appreciated if you could take this hearing seriously."

"God knows, but I'll try, Senator."

She stuck a king-sized cigarette into a black-and-silver holder and lit up.

"You may not smoke in here."

MacRae ignored this. Blew a smoke ring and smiled.

"Is it your intention . . ."

Anger creeping into his voice now.

"You know, Senator, that is not such an easy question. I might ask what you mean by it. Is subverting the government of the USA the same thing as subverting the USA? This is a democracy. It is inherent in the democratic system that democracy defines and redefines itself according to the will of the people, and in so doing it redefines government. What you call subversion might be termed more simply as change. Is it my intention to change the US government? Of course. That's why I register to vote. The Constitution of the United States is an expression of the will of the people, as they were in 1788. It is upon that constitution that our government rests. Jefferson himself said the constitution might be valid for thirty or forty years. Each generation must reassess it. Instead, we tinker with it in amendment after amendment, half of which get ignored. But I would ask you, where does the true definition of our democracy abide? Is it not more likely to be found in the

Declaration of Independence? Life, liberty and the pursuit of happiness. Every schoolboy or -girl can recite that. But what follows life, liberty and the pursuit of happiness? It's this: 'That to secure these rights, governments are instituted among men, deriving their just powers from the consent of the governed. That whenever any form of government becomes destructive of these ends, it is the right of the people to alter or to abolish it.' Alter? Abolish? Subvert? Senator, if I have the right to abolish the US government, I also have the right to subvert it."

Uproar followed. The audience that had heard her out in silence exploded.

Redmaine now appeared to be more purple in the face than red. With any luck he'd have a heart attack. Instead he pounded his gavel half a dozen times. MacRae blew more smoke rings.

"I will not . . . I will NOT be lectured on the history of America by a foreigner!"

"Senator, unlike you I *chose* to be an American."

Redmaine adjourned early for lunch. MacRae walked down the aisle to the exit nearest Charlie. The crowd parted around her as though encountering a leper. She was dignified, almost serene. Charlie waited for someone to spit on her. No one did.

She stopped in front of Charlie. The smile that had won her a million fans shone on him.

"Well. Here's a howdy-do. With the embassy, are you now, Charlie? Does your expense account run to lunch?"

§66

It was on the steps of the Cannon Building that someone did spit on Deborah MacRae. It was a woman, which freed Charlie from the necessity of thumping anyone. Instead he handed MacRae a clean handkerchief and escorted her to the Occidental.

"Let's make this lunch with a couple of stiff drinks, shall we, Charlie?"

Over Carolina Shad Roe (coleslaw optional) she said, "It's OK. I'm going to give you what you want."

Charlie mulled this a moment too long.

"No, Stage-Door-Charlie. Not another quickie in the dressing room. I mean I'll give His Majesty's Government what they want. I will spare them further embarrassment. I'll go home."

"You've had enough?"

"Sort of."

"How sort of?"

"Well . . . I'm going to be blacklisted, am I not?"

"After today's performance you'll get a blacklist and an Oscar, I think."

"Thank you. Most kind. But . . . I've already got an Oscar and no one in England will give a fuck about the blacklist . . ."

"True."

"Well—Arthur Rank has offered to buy my contract from RKO. Half the pay, but Pinewood is thriving, I get to pick the scripts and there's talk of a picture with Robert Donat. So . . . do I really need Hollywood? Do I want to swell the numbers of the Hollywood Ten to eleven? Do I have to be the first English person on the list? Racing Arthur Houghton into ignominy? No, I'll go home. The United States has never cared for dual citizenship, but then it never follows up. Took me at my word that I'd given up being British. Of course, I hadn't. So back to Blighty. In a year or two I'll be struck out of *Who's Who in America* and it will be as though I'd never been here. A pity. Meant what I said in there. I really did choose to be an American. I love the place. But for this ludicrous shitstorm Redmaine has whipped up, you wouldn't be able to prise me out with a crowbar."

"The gossip columnists will say you've cut and run."

"They'll be right. I am disappointed in America and disappointed in myself. But it's a slur on me, not HMG—and that's why you're here, isn't it? You're covering the great British arse in its pathetic arse-kicking contest with Uncle Sam. A contest in which Britain is the proverbial one-legged man."

"How sweetly you put it, Deborah."

"My lawyer's with Redmaine now. I've said me piece. He drew up a list of twenty-five questions I would most likely be asked, and wanted me to learn the answers. I told him it was the worst script I've ever been offered. He's very disappointed in me, but he does what he's paid to do. I've booked me passage home. I fully expect the afternoon session to be cancelled."

"You could have sent your lawyer over this morning."

"What? And miss a stage like that? Does Hamlet leave out the big soliloquy? Does Feste not sing to us with his 'hey nonny no'? Limelight doesn't come any better."

"What's that show biz saying?"

"Dunno. There are so many."

"Always leave them wanting more."

"Quite. But our revels now are ended."

§67

At around four o'clock Coky lay in a postcoital daze, Felix Foster's right arm wrapped around her. Her fingers dancing to an unrecognisable tune on his ribs.

"Is she really that bright?"

"Oh yes. If there'd been an afternoon session, I think Bob would have had to come back with a tirade of fury. There was very little left in his arsenal. I saw the look on his face when she quoted the Declaration of Independence. I honestly don't think he'd heard the words before. Life, liberty, happiness . . . of course . . . but the stuff about abolishing government? He's an ignorant sod."

"Then . . ."

"Then what?"

"Then why the fuck did you marry him?"

"Been eating at you all week, has it?"

"Yes!"

Her head slipped further down his chest. The fingers stopped dancing. Her voice dropped to a murmur.

"Orders."

"Eh?"

She ran her lips from his right nipple to his ear, nipped the lobe sharply between her teeth, ran her tongue around the rim, exhaled warm and wet—a sensation that shot straight to his groin—and whispered, "Mockingbird."

§68

Charlie stood at the loo. Dammit, he needed to piss and he needed to sit. Seat down, pissing like a woman. Fists to his cheekbones, thinking.

He'd broken one of his own rules. He'd fallen for her. Since adolescence, since that first tumble with Troy's sisters when he was fourteen, he had had a rule, a maxim: "The world is full of totty—falling for just one is pointless." Especially, as with Sasha and Masha Troy, when you could have two at once.

Worse. There was worse. He'd fallen for a woman who'd just revealed herself to him as a Soviet agent. He'd brought the job home. Well, if not exactly home, to a cheap hotel three quarters of a mile from home—clean sheets and air-conditioning, with added espionage. They weren't Coky and Charlie anymore; they were Tweedle Dumski and Tweedle Deeski. Fuck fuck fucketty fuckski.

§69

Undoubtedly there are conversations a man should not have stark naked. In all probability this was one of them. But the options were: pick up his clothes from the far side of the bed, but that could look like rejection, or get back into bed, which might send an equally misleading message. So instead he settled on the edge of the bed.

"You're going to have to tell me."

Coky pulled the sheets up to her chin, smiled at him slyly.

"Has it occurred to you that we're not supposed to have this conversation?"

"We're going to have to or else your mockingbird will remain a feathery thing that tweets in the treetops."

"OK—you first. It's like dancing. The man leads."

"Cambridge."

"Of course."

"I went to Trinity. As did Philby, Burgess and Blunt. I'm a bit younger than them. I overlapped with Burgess and Philby by a year. I did not know either of them well, and the only reason I ever knew Blunt, who is the best part of ten years older, was that he was a fellow of Trinity. He'd read modern languages, and I was reading French and German. That's what made me so useful to SOE during the war. I could pass for a Frenchman, and I could lie convincingly to Germans. I sometimes wonder what would have happened if I'd not wasted a few months faffing around with a thesis—I'm no academic, after all—because it was then, in '37, after all the others had left, that Blunt approached me. I gave up Cambridge for the Guards, the Guards for SOE, SOE for SIS. By which time, I was exactly where Moscow would have me be. Now, is there anything I've told you that you didn't already know?"

"Wasn't sure how you got recruited. Blunt's not a name I know . . ."

"Anthony Blunt. A remote cousin of the queen, and has a title like Duster of the King's Paintings."

"Well, that sounds really useful. So Moscow knows when a Titian is being restored or a Van Dyck's fallen off the wall. However—I'd guessed the rest."

"Guessed or read?"

"Well, of course I've seen your file. But do we really trust what some pen-pushing Russki-pooter has to say?"

"Your turn. I know nothing about you."

"Except that I'm the woman of your dreams."

"I'm all ears."

"It's not your ears I'm looking at right now."

§70

Charlotte thought her father was God. This lasted longer than it might have. Dudley Victor Augustus Young had been thirty-nine when she was born in 1905—his fourth child and only daughter, born some seven years after her closest sibling. That they would dote on one another was inevitable.

A career soldier . . . Sandhurst . . . Toski . . . Omdurman . . . Magersfontein—a year or two older and he might well have been a fatality at Khartoum—he'd been about to ask for his army pension in the spring of 1914, but the clouds were gathering and by August the storm had burst. When war broke out on the fourth, he was in no way surprised.

The girl Charlotte followed the war with a wax crayon, a pair of scissors and the *Times*. Her mother put up a green baize board for her in her room and, when that was full, another board.

Her father was promoted to brigadier general—a rank he had never imagined he'd attain, but the devil was driving now—and this put paid to Charlotte's daydreams of her father as a dashing cavalry officer leading men into battle. He was, he patiently explained, pointing to the red tabs on his uniform, a staff officer. He stayed behind the lines. What he thought, and wrestled with himself to say, was that rather than being a man who charged out to kill the Hun, he was now a man who sent other men out to be killed by the Hun.

Charlotte had heard him out in silence. Her mother was quietly furious.

There would be no third green baize board. The crayon and the scissors went back in the toy box.

Her father had also never been in a cavalry regiment, but that was by the bye—the romance of the Lancers had vanished in a haze of Maxim fire.

He ended his war with a chestful of medals he did not think he had earned and no wish to celebrate. The only celebration was for his sons, all of whom had, against the odds, survived—two in the navy and one in the fledgling RAF. He picked up the pension he'd put off four years earlier and resumed his fascination with the work of Isambard King-dom Brunel.

Churchill's "a good man in his day" was too sentimental a remark for Charlotte—that had been his day too. His taste of glory. She didn't think her father, quite unlike Churchill, had any idea of glory what-soever, and as she grew, she found she admired a man who could not and did not glory in war.

This began to unravel only in 1926. She had "come out" in 1923 and, to no tut-tutting from either parent, had declined the "season."

"I'm not looking for a husband and I foxtrot like a turkey."

Instead she had read Spanish and Italian at St. Hilda's College, Oxford, and learnt to row.

She had just sat her last exams, rowed in her last eight, when the TUC called a general strike.

Her father drove a London bus.

Charlotte was appalled.

She had not known him to have any "real" politics. He voted Liberal—all the "nice men" voted Liberal. Moreover, she had not known *herself* to have any "real" politics.

"One had to pick a side, Charlotte."

So—she picked hers.

§71

"You can't do nothing, darling," her mother said. Charlotte's three broth-ers had, respectively, gone into banking, banking and banking.

Morally, Charlotte agreed. Financially . . . no one in the Young family needed ever soil their hands with work.

"You know, Mummy. Interpreting is a job more and more being done by women, and by women of my age. We don't all have to rush into mar-riage or learn shorthand. I'd like to learn another language—with a third I could be very useful to . . . I don't know . . . the League of Nations."

"Do you have a language in mind?"

"Russian, I'd like to learn Russian."

And so Charlotte enrolled in the Regent Street School of Modern Languages, and decided that Russian was far and away the most beautiful, the most sibilantly seductive language she had ever heard.

Six months into her course, feeling some proficiency, she was frustrated by its narrowness. It was all "verb and vocab." Her tutors said nothing about the country whose language they taught, and perhaps they had nothing to say. If they'd read a word of Tolstoy or even a word of Lenin, they weren't letting on. It was language taken almost as an abstraction, devoid of context.

Determined to balance this, Charlotte attended a series of talks at the Haldane Institute on the matter of "Modern Russia." The third of these talks was given by the distinguished novelist Mr. H. G. Wells, based very much on his own travels in Russia, both before and after the Bolshevik Revolution. Wells had not only read Lenin—although he seemed not to think highly of his writing, "pamphleteering writ large"—he had actually met him.

"Mr. Wells?"

Never lacking courage, she approached him after the talk.

"I read your science fiction when I was a girl, but I am somewhat new to your social commentary. Where should I begin?"

Wells displayed acute author vanity in ignoring the question to pose one of his own.

"And which was your favourite?"

"Oh, *The Time Machine*, definitely. But it was—"

"Why not begin right here?"

He held up a copy of *Russia in the Shadows*. A yellow map, centring on European Russia, adorned the dust jacket—but "adorned" was not the word. Russia had been rendered deliberately smudgy and grubby as though to convey the title in imagery. Russia looked more in the mire than in the shadows.

"Yes. I've read some of that. In particular I read your account of meeting Lenin. I suppose I was wondering . . . what's next?"

"Ah, the impatience of youth. Admirable. Without it nothing would ever change. Well, my next book will be an anthology. I'm putting together a collection of essays right now. Look, why don't you come down to Essex and see for yourself?"

When Charlotte had told her mother she would be attending a lecture by H. G. Wells, her mother had said, "He's a socialist, you know."

Which Charlotte thought was meant as a warning.

When she told her father, he had said, "He's a lothario, you know. He's fathered several illegitimate children."

Which Charlotte knew was most certainly meant as a warning.

"Yes. That would be nice, thank you," she replied to Wells. "A most kind invitation."

§72

It was a beautiful October day when Charlotte alighted at Great Dunmow station—the leaves just clinging to the trees, a hint of autumn's diamond-damp morning evaporating into a sapphire sky. It reminded her of the opening of one of Wells's novels—perhaps it was the attentive presence of both station master and porter—not that she had any luggage—and the fading reds and purples of the sweet peas which, in more pots than she could count, had glorified the station all summer long.

"Miss Young?"

Only she had alighted.

"Mr. Wells 'ave sent Old George to take you over to the Glebe."

She had expected a car but was not surprised when Old George turned out to be a taciturn mumbler clutching the reins of a donkey cart. It was a typical Wellsian paradox—the prophet of the twenty-first century clinging to the vestiges of the nineteenth. Or perhaps he just liked donkeys.

A cedar-lined drive led to a simple, square-to-boxy Georgian house, the lesser house to some mansion tucked away from plebeian sight. Handsome in its way, red roofed and ivy clad. The cart pulled up at the side, rather than the front. A pair of French windows opened straight onto the lawn. A pair of squabbling red squirrels gave up the fight and scattered at the sight of the donkey. Wells stepped out. Portly, bristly, mufti. Men wearing cardigans, particularly cardigans with crosshatched leather buttons, made Charlotte want to take them shopping—but . . . and the "buts" amounted to an overwhelming argument in favour of sticking to the life of the mind. It was, she told herself, why she was there.

"A pleasant journey, I hope?"

"A slow one."

§73

Beyond the French windows was a room Wells was using as a study. In the middle, atop a threadbare Persian carpet, was a table that might once have seated twelve for dinner but which was now strewn from end to end with books and papers.

Wells pressed the bell on the fireplace.

"Tea and toast, and then work, eh?"

"Oh . . . thank you."

"Why so hesistant?"

"Am I?"

"My dear, you're as nervous as a harvest mouse. But . . . but let me answer my own question. My reputation has preceded me, has it not?"

"My father did express an opinion, yes."

"The suicide?"

"The what?"

"A young lady who had worked for me, in much the capacity for which I have engaged you, came to my London flat a few years ago intent on killing herself. She did not succeed. My wife found her and in all probability saved her life. Of course, it did not reach the newspapers, but . . . there will always be gossip."

"Mr. Wells . . ."

"Bert, please."

"Bert? Bert . . . my father does not listen to gossip, or perhaps he might if it concerned Isambard Kingdom Brunel. And for my part, I have no intention of killing myself, at least not today."

The arrival of the maid, bearing tea and toast, tilted their strained conversation towards the less strained topic of the weather.

Seated by the unlit fire, Wells showering crumbs down his cardigan, Charlotte evaluated her expectations, from the nineteenth-century donkey cart to the unpunctuated silence of the house—unpunctuated but for Wells himself. It was said in London that Easton Glebe was a "riot"—not a word she could imagine in this context—of activity, a rural salon of endless visitors, politicians and writers—Bernard Shaw and G. K. Chesterton and Hilaire Belloc—and endless games of Wells's own invention. Any or all of which might be code for *orgy*. It took less than a moment's thought to fail to imagine Shaw, Chesterton or Belloc in an orgy.

Yet—it was quiet as a nunnery.

Were they alone? Alone but for half a dozen maids, cooks and gardeners, which, in the class to which she had been born and to which Wells aspired, effectively meant "alone."

The little man read her like an open book.

"Don't worry, Miss Young. I have a wife. A man who has a wife might be considered blessed. I also have a mistress. A man who has a wife and mistress might be considered doubly blessed. A man who has a wife and two mistresses—cursed."

"And is Mrs. Wells at 'ome?"

"Switzerland. But trust me, as indeed you have, simply by arriving, Mrs. Wells is very real. Now, shall we get down to business?"

§74

The anthology Wells proposed had the title *The Way the World Is Going*. He was unsure how long it should be. Two hundred pages? Three hundred? A dozen essays? Twenty-five?

Charlotte's first task was to read as many as possible—on subjects ranging from the state of the empire to the future of the novel to reflections on immortality—and then to be ready for the five-o-seven train back to town. Any unread essays, and there would be many, she would carry home with her in a capacious carpet bag. She would be paid two pounds per day, plus her train fare. Her father had taught her never to haggle over money—"It's too vulgar, Charlotte"—simply to accept or decline. And as it was a generous offer, she accepted.

And at 4:45 Wells went in search of Old George and his donkey.

A pleasant day, a pleasant lunch, had passed uneventfully.

Left alone for a moment, Charlotte asked herself whether she had really wanted so little and whether she had fooled herself by expecting more, and doubly fooled herself in thinking that whatever her unfounded expectations, there was nothing more she might want from a little man in a cardigan.

But height was no measure. Bert was a very "big" man.

Bert was not the wicked man of London gossip, and at the same time . . . he was.

There was a large mirror in the study set a foot above the skirting that stopped only a couple of feet short of the ceiling and bounced light around an otherwise dark room. Charlotte looked at herself, momentarily asked herself if she was unattractive. The answer was no. A "no" of remarkable self-confidence, as she realised that she, a twenty-two-year-old virgin, could probably have any man she wanted.

§75

The carpet bag made many journeys on the London and North Eastern Railway. The porter at Great Dunmow met her every Tuesday, arm outstretched, ready to take the burden from her, addressing her as "Miss Charlotte." It always was a Tuesday, except when it was a Wednesday, and never a Friday or a Saturday. Charlotte readily concluded that Wells was separating work and pleasure—and in the wake of one attempted suicide by a lady amanuensis, who would blame him? She would have relished meeting Shaw or Chesterton, but in their absence, in the quiet of the weekday nunnery, she relished the work.

Amongst the essays Charlotte gathered up for inclusion in the new volume was a review of Fritz Lang's *Metropolis*, which had been showing on and off in London cinemas of late. Charlotte had seen the film, perhaps at the same cinema as Wells. She had been bedazzled by the imagery, by the sheer scale of the film. The review was scathing. She felt she needed to see the film again, scoured the London papers to see where it might still be showing, and made the journey from Marylebone to Harrow for a matinée.

Wells was right.

It was a preposterous film.

She hated to admit it.

But it occurred to her that they were looking for different things. Wells was a sceptic, a professional critic. He might stop short of pulling the wings off butterflies, but his modus operandi, with the English language as his weapon, was "test to destruction"—whereas she was looking for belief. She felt ashamed, stupid, that for a few hours she had believed in *Metropolis* and its pseudo-Christian message of love and salvation. As if that alone might defeat the machine. Wells would, she realised, for all his avowed socialism, "pull the wings off" any belief, be it religious or political, and hold up scientific rigour as his touchstone. He did not need to believe. If he had believed when he was her age . . . well, he was sixty-one now, the same age as her father. He did not care to believe—he cared about "vision," and *Metropolis* had not measured up to his own exacting standards of vision. It also explained why the two countries that seemed to interest Wells the essayist so much more than England did were the United States and the Union of Soviet Socialist Republics—both countries founded by men who saw themselves as visionaries.

She mentioned this on her umpteenth visit to the Glebe.

"I do so envy you your trips to Russia, Bert."

"I'll be going again as soon as we finish this book. Care to join me?"

The line had been crossed.

It was still work, it was still Tuesday, but the offer carried with it more than a hint of Friday.

"I'd be delighted," she said.

§76

What sounded imminent was not. The death of Jane Wells in October of that year delayed the visit, first by two months, then three, and then five.

They were guests of the USSR, boarded in an official Moscow Guest House, on the far bank of the Moskva River at Sofiyskaya Naberezhnaya, about half a mile from the British Embassy. The embassy was closed and had been for almost a year, awaiting resolution of some diplomatic tiff. Wells said this mattered no one jot—the embassy would have ignored him and he them. They were Kremlin guests, not diplomats. He expected nothing of His Majesty's representatives in Moscow.

It was April—death and funeral notwithstanding, Wells had been content to postpone the winter visit, pleading something about "old bones"—but even so, occasional sheets of ice floated past. From her room Charlotte could see the Kremlin, as solid and charmless as Buckingham Palace, and the cluster of buildings that were the architectural remnants of empire, all those pepper pots and salt cellars—somewhere amongst them, Charlotte thought, there ought to be a building in the shape of a soup tureen.

They had had six days of meetings and of visits to theatres, museums, galleries, factories, workshops, schools. Judging by his expression, little seemed to impress Wells, but his opinion did seem to change with experience. He had said all along that Russia had descended into its own brand of chaos and that only the Bolsheviks would be capable of bringing order. It was not "belief," nor was it to credit them with "vision"—it was much the same as saying they were the best of a bad bunch. Eight years had, he conceded, brought improvements, which was as close as he got to a word of praise.

The highlight for her had been Olga Knipper as Ranevskaya in *The Cherry Orchard* at the Moscow Art Theatre. She had gone alone. Wells had next to no Russian, and while hers was weak, reading Chekhov had been one of the ways she had learnt Russian, and to see the play in the original with Chekhov's widow in the leading role was unmissable.

The highlight for Wells had been a visit to a steel-smelting works out beyond the Moscow suburbs. It reminded Charlotte of *Metropolis*—for a silent film, it had seemed so noisy—and when she remarked on this, Wells reminded her that hers had been a sheltered upbringing. Indeed it had. An official translator escorted them everywhere. An affable man perhaps ten years older than Charlotte—that is, old enough to have been part of the revolution—Nikolai Denisovich Garentsky, a citizen of Lvov. He expressed surprise and delight that Charlotte spoke Russian and complimented her on it, she thought, quite unnecessarily.

Wells took a lot of naps. She found herself alone with Nikolai on several occasions, practising her Russian, accepting his gentle corrections. He smiled—he was always smiling—and chatted—about this, that, the shape of moonlight . . . the colour of angels . . . the sound of history repeating . . . and she knew she was being probed.

Word eventually came that Stalin would see Wells.

"I'll be going alone, I'm afraid. It'll be just me, Stalin and his interpreter."

"It's all right," Charlotte replied. "I'm not disappointed."

"I am," said Nikolai.

§77

Charlotte and Nikolai sat in the lobby of the Guest House, two tall glasses of Russian tea in the filigreed silver *podstakanniki* Charlotte thought exquisite, which was more than she dared say for the tea. Samovars stewed tea. It lost all delicacy. Another week in Moscow and she might kill for a cup of her mother's Co-op Darjeeling.

Her Russian-language copy of Lenin's *"Left-Wing" Communism: An Infantile Disorder* lay on the low table between them. Nikolai glanced at it. Thumbed it open to the contents page and then let it fold shut, rather like closing a door gently.

"You are not as one with Mr. Wells, I think," he said.

Was he asking about sex?

"You and he are close."

Good grief, he was.

"But you do not think alike."

Oh. So he wasn't.

"Not on all matters, no," she said.

"On Soviet Union?"

"No again. Bert feels that Russia—I quote his exact words—that 'Russia has let me down.' He speaks of the 'dope-dream of Soviet self-sufficiency.'"

"Dope? I'm afraid I do not understand."

"Put simply, Bert expects disappointment wherever he goes. I do not. Ascribe it to age."

"Rather would I ascribe it to belief."

Wells had said before they set off, by way of warning, that they would be watched wherever they went by Russia's new Cheka, the OGPU— *Obyedinyonnoye Gosudarstvennoye Politicheskoye Upravleniye.* She'd thought Nikolai might be their man. Now she was sure. He fitted Wells's description of an OGPU man—the same blue serge suit "as though the Kremlin has an account with a branch of Burton's on some provincial English high street" . . . "serious young chaps trying their best to be invisible." Nikolai wasn't all that serious or invisible. The smiling and the chatting were much more his norm. A vainer woman than Charlotte might have thought he was flirting. All the same, that he had observed her, read her, so closely was little short of shocking.

"Nikolai, what is it you want?"

"I . . . we . . . want you to help us. We need people in the West. If we are to survive, we need people in the West. We need the help of sympathetic minds like yours."

"I will not betray my country."

"No one will ever ask you to do that."

§78

Wells returned from his audience with Stalin in the evening. It was, he said, well worth the wait.

"I added up the hours I spent waiting, asking, angling, organising to see Lenin in 1920. It was around eighty. And it touched on farce. An interpreter whose Russian was minimal and a guide who didn't know north from south. All for an hour and a half of his time. Getting to see Stalin has been a damn sight simpler."

"What, if I may ask, did you talk about?"

"Hollywood."

"Hollywood?"

"Stalin loves cowboys-and-Indians films."

"Oh. Have you ever seen one?"

"No."

"So . . . ?"

"We switched to something that interested us both. The Difference Engine of Charles Babbage and the work of Ada Lovelace."

"Difference Engine?"

"A computation machine."

"Ah, I see," said Charlotte, not seeing, and wondering if it, any of it, had really been worth the wait.

§79

When Lenin had written his *"Left-Wing" Communism blah-de-blah* he had included a chapter on Great Britain. At the time, Britain had no Communist Party. It was founded shortly afterwards.

When Charlotte asked if she should now join, Nikolai and his superior—introduced over neat vodka, while Wells took an early night, as Anton . . . no patronymic, no surname—almost fell off their chairs laughing.

"No, no," Anton said eventually. "That is the last thing you should do."

"Then, what do I do?"

"You lose yourself," Nikolai answered.

"Not sure I'm following you."

"You lose the woman you are now in the woman you were.

Resume your patrician identity. Eschew left-wing causes, left-wing people . . ."

"Wells?"

"No, no . . . Wells will be fine. No one takes him seriously. If needs be, join the Conservative Party."

"No one, but no one, would ever believe that!"

"Then at least seem no more radical than an English Liberal."

"Lose myself," she mused. "How best to lose myself?"

Both men sat waiting for her to answer her own question.

"I suppose I might 'marry well'—Mummy would like that."

"Indeed," said Nikolai. "Marry well."

Anton said, "What does that mean?"

§80

In June of 1930 Charlotte married Hubert Mawer-Churchill.

§81

Charlotte's sister-in-law Ethel, wife of her eldest brother, Clive, saw herself as a society matron and matchmaker. Charlotte saw her as an idiot—a noddlehead who had reached the peak of her fulfilment in the manifestation of husband and children, all of whom she wore like combat medals—who seemed determined to inflict the same spurious happiness on those around her.

Charlotte let her.

"Up to this point," she confides to Charlie, "I had genuinely thought of myself as a good person. Wouldn't hurt a fly. Not that I hurt Hubert, at least not yet. I married him. Hurt me more than it hurt him."

She had found herself seated next to several eligible bachelors the previous summer—the Hon. Thingy, Sir Wotsisname Wostisname, Major Forgettable . . . all such dullards, whose mental span covered bridge and racing and polo, who'd probably never read a book since school . . . but then, in her mind they were all being compared to Wells, an unprepossessing little fat bloke in his sixties who would make a joint visit from Charlie Chaplin and Douglas Fairbanks seem dull. None of them had the Wells sparkle. If brains were flint, they would live in total darkness. In contrast, Hubert was . . . average, she could think of no greater compliment. He was pleasingly average, unthreateningly average, reliably average . . . he was no intellectual and he might never read a word of Lenin, but he'd probably read the latest P. G. Wodehouse and he most certainly had read the latest Evelyn Waugh. He was, in short, an English gentleman, not a hint of the cad or the bounder. And in that respect he was very unlike Wells.

§82

Perhaps she had made it too easy for Hubert. Dinner, flowers, a ring, a bended knee, followed by an audience with General Young and the request for her hand in marriage. The general and Lady Young approved wholeheartedly. Moscow did not.

She had explained, patiently—Nikolai visiting London posing as a Parisian tourist but looking like a Basque peasant—that Hubert was a cousin of the former cabinet minister Winston Churchill. She'd have gone into the seconds and thirds of cousins and the once or twice removeds, but she wasn't at all sure what "removed" meant. One had a wart removed, not a cousin.

Moscow seemed fixated on the word "former." Churchill had been Home Secretary, Chancellor, First Lord of the Admiralty, President of the Board of Trade—in fact, the only post he seemed not to have held was Prime Minister—but now he was a backbencher. Charlotte said, as firmly as she could, that Winston would not remain on the backbench,

but the 1930s turned out to be his "Wilderness Years"—voice and influence without office. However, Churchill's early denunciations of Hitler
changed the Moscow collective mind.

"Hubert went to work for Winston in 1934," she confides to Charlie.
"And from that point everything of any import that Winston said to
Hubert or Hubert said to me went to Moscow. I spied on my own hus-
band. Was I still a good person?"

Hubert could not hold her. She had married as a virgin. If it were
left to Hubert she might have stayed a virgin. Almost. He was dutiful
without enthusiasm. She knew she was missing something, surely?

"I took my first lover within eighteen months of marriage," she confides
to Charlie. "Naval commander on shore leave. A hotel in Windsor. I
was supposed to be visiting a cousin in Berkshire—not that I have any
cousins in Berkshire—I became a habitual deployer of Bunbury. A liar
and a cheat. I knew then that I really, really was not a good person."

With Churchill's return to office in 1939, the quality of Charlotte's
espionage soared and, with his assumption of the premiership in May
1940, became little short of priceless.

"I married once for love," she confides to Charlie. "Nobody told me
to divorce Hubert and marry Avery Shumacher. And I never spied on
Avery. My self-esteem got patched up a bit. I also never cheated on him.
Neither was ever necessary. Avery adored me and I him. And once he'd
resigned his wartime job with Eisenhower to return to Washington, there
was nothing to spy on. He declined appointed office, he declined to run
for a Senate seat—he got on with his memoir, and when he'd finished
that, he started on his book about Sherman's march through the South.
He was still working on it when he was killed . . . and when he was killed
I left Roundehay without a backward glance. I moved into the N Street
house. I gave three-quarters of my wardrobe to a thrift store, mostly
the evening stuff. I had played the life of the party too long. I had come
to hate the words 'dinner party' . . . to wish the dinner party had never
been invented.

"I had begun to bore myself. I would sit at those dinner parties with a
silver-bound Asprey notebook next to my plate. I compiled an alterna-
tive Who's Who in Washington . . . I collected the great, the good and
the out-and-out scoundrels like stamps. The notebook was my stamp
album. I noted down bon mots, aphorisms, off-the-record politics . . . I

can hardly believe I was so crass. It was a beautiful notebook, a present from Hubert just after he proposed. When I left Roundehay I tore out the pages and gave the frame to the cook to keep recipes in. Those pages would have fascinated the Russians . . . but . . .

"*I had forgotten I was a spy. My Russian control in London had been appalled when he found out I was divorcing Hubert, and then overjoyed when I took a job in Naval Intelligence. You may imagine, what the Admiralty knew, the Kremlin knew twenty-four hours later. Then, when I left for Washington, it was as though I had slipped through a net. They seemed to forget about me. I heard nothing from them.* I thought, Well, they'll take Berlin any minute, job done, as it were, so what further use am I?

"*I was content to forget and to be forgotten. At best I was a sleeper, napping by the political fireside. N Street was such a contrast to life at Roundehay. I had a year to myself. I read. I listened to the gramophone. I played all twenty-three Mozart concertos. One a day, and every three weeks I'd go back and start again. Haskil, Gieseking . . . the performers Avery had introduced me to. A legacy worth more than his millions. I scarcely went out. It passed as mourning. Perhaps it was mourning.*

"*Two years ago, Moscow woke me. 'Get to know Senator Redmaine.'*

"*Far easier than it sounded. He'd never married. Forty-nine and never married. I think he might have been a prozzie's regular, but he'd never own up to that. He was a fool for love, or what he mistook for love—the reality was I led him around by the prick as if he were a piggy-wig with a ring through his dong. Not sure Moscow was ever certain I would end up marrying him, but it was what they wanted, it was doable. So I did it. My self-esteem stripped back to nothing. I was not a good person. Not for anything I ever did or will do to Bob, but for what I do to myself.*"

§83

"So that's my history. You could almost narrate my life as a marital history . . . written in a sequence of husbands . . . a bumbling English toff with wonderful manners but not a lot of brains . . . a second-generation German American of terrifying intelligence and a smothering charm that stripped me of willpower, made me putty in his hands for five years and then left me washed up, beached and all but drowned when he was killed . . . and . . . and a dumb, charmless fucking Polack whose arse gets fatter by the day and who whistles through his false teeth on a frequency that triggers my tinnitus and sets half the dogs in DC barking."

"That's quite a litany."

"He's awful, Charlie, absolutely awful. A pig of a man."

"But orders are orders."

"Aren't they just? I live a fiction. Bob is his own work of fiction. I might even say pulp fiction as it's a spectacularly bad novel. Everything about him is made up. His deep-seated American identity, all those generations of Midwestern farmers, is a linguistic feint. His parents were Polish immigrants from Łodz. The family name is Redecki."

"Nothing wrong with changing your name."

"Indeed there isn't, and in many cases Immigration and Naturalization did it for you, as they couldn't be arsed to spell Polish names or Lithuanian names or Russian names and so on. It so happened the Redeckis got through Ellis Island with their name intact. They settled in Iowa. Just outside Cedar Rapids, where the old man farmed turkeys. It was young Bob who thought the name needed to be more American. This would be about 1917, when the USA entered the war. "Redecki" sounded foreign, to particularly stupid ears it might have sounded German. And he heard of the story of John Philip So, who added "USA" to his name to become John Philip Sousa, our most patriotic composer. It's utter nonsense, completely apocryphal, but it was enough to convince Bob that he should add a state to his name. Rediowa looked and sounded awful, Rednebraska would make you want to scratch or rub on ointment, and I rather think the boy Bob looked at an atlas for the only time in his life and picked out Maine. A state to which, so far as I know, he has never been. Thus was Bob Redmaine reborn.

"Those there were who were appalled when I married Robert Redmaine. Some may very well never speak to me again."

"What did you say?"

"What excuses, you mean? The nearest to the truth was I could not bear widowhood . . . further from the truth . . . that Avery's will had been kind without being generous. Depending on the level of stupidity of the person asking, I've resorted to both 'the heart has its reasons' and 'love is a many-splendoured thing,' although to be honest that last one is hard to say with a straight face.

"Of late, the last few months, I've feigned confidences and said stuff like 'it was all a big mistake' and got out my hanky. Alas, I cannot cry at will. I just sniffle a bit.

"I used to think Bob was like a chameleon, adaptable colours, but that's too subtle, so much less than total. He's more like a snake—he sheds his skin every so often. Polack to all-American boy, Democrat to Republican, this cause to that cause . . . his prewar record is full of causes adopted for a speech or two, a stump or two . . . pensions, housing, even libraries for God's sake . . . he tried to get stories of Robin Hood, 'that goddam Brit commie,' banned from public libraries . . . the amazing thing about Red-baiting is that he's stuck with it. I think he was on a quest to find out what would win, and if it turned out to be right-wing, racist, paranoid bigotry, so be it. That is the mask he has adopted. He doesn't think of himself as being any of those things—but—"

"We might become what we pretend to be."

"We *are* what we pretend to be . . . and in that is a lesson for us both, Charlie-boy."

§84

They were lying back now, side by side, scarcely touching. They—or rather she—had talked for what seemed like hours. It was turning twilight outside the window. Charlie let the silence be. Then:

"I was thinking . . . about that picture book for five-year-olds."

"Eh? Oh, I remember."

"I think it's called *Charlie and Charlotte Go Spying*."

"Yep—isn't it just a fucking farce?"

"No. It's the most dangerous game in town."

"And still a farce."

§85

When they met again four days later, same hotel, same bed, fresh linens, Charlie said, "We seem to be missing something."

Coky opened one eye.

"Do we? I'm here. You're here. Never really felt the need of an audience, but if you insist—"

"A mission! My mission . . . Mockingbird . . . what is my mission?"

"Oh. That? I didn't realise we were talking shop. OK. Easy peasy . . . we have the same mission: Bob."

"And what is the nature of your Bob-mission?"

"Why, you think it happenstance that Bob chooses the innocent and harmless to grill? I steer him away from the real Communists. For my sins I suggested Deborah MacRae. A neat little ploy to weaken the special relationship. It seems to have worked. It might be weaker by a micron or two. Every little bit counts, as I'm sure they say back in Moscow. I do hope I haven't ruined her career."

"And what do I do that you cannot do for yourself?"

"Bob brings stuff home."

"Of course he does."

"Needless to say, I read everything. But . . . the disruption caused when Burgess and Maclean defected hasn't been repaired. The British weren't the only ones in a panic. Moscow withdrew agents too. There's a gap to be filled."

"I get it. I'm the plumber or the plasterer."

"For now, Charlie, you're the go-between."

"How politely you put it. What you mean is that Moscow wants me to be a bloody courier. I'm a field agent, dammit."

Charlie flat on his back, eyes on the ceiling.

The merest thump to convey silent rage as his head hit the pillow.

Coky up on one elbow, eyes on him.

"Don't get ratty, Charlie-boy. Right now you're a field agent stuck behind a desk, surrounded by people you despise, optimistically courting the Feds and the CIA while watching your waistline expand."

Instinctively Charlie lifted his head, put a hand to the flat of his stomach. It wasn't as flat as it used to be.

He lay back, disappointed in himself.

Coky's hand snaked across and patted his stomach. A tangible "there, there." He removed the hand before "Mummy kissed it better."

"Are you listening?" he said.

"Fully, wholly and devotedly."

"Seriously?"

"OK."

"I am a believer."

"Two of us in one bed, there's a—"

He put a finger to her lips.

She propped her elbows on his ribcage and blew him a kiss.

"Just listen. I am a believer. In what, I will try to tell you. It may not strike you as obvious. I was not and am not out to further the interests of Russia except insofar as they serve my interests. I am not fascinated by, besotted with, our masters in Moscow. I am not out to create a balance of power or head off World War III. I got very, instantly, fed up with the apologetic bleeding-heart line of people like Klaus Fuchs. Once caught, tell all and say sorry? Bollocks. You will never hear me apologise for what I believe.

"It's not . . . I'm not . . . about Russia . . . I've never read a word of Lenin or learnt any more Russian than is necessary to chat up women."

"How many Russian women have you chatted up?"

"None, but I live in hope. No—I am not a constructive Communist, I am a destructive Communist and my target is England. And if I were not supposed to be a secret agent, I'd say hire a plane and write it in the sky."

"That's quite a speech."

"You caught me on a bad day."

"Are there worse days?"

"Try talking to me during a test match. I can be vitriolic about cricket. I have a rant on the matter of quintessential Englishness that can go on for an age. And never . . . never . . . get me going on Morris Dancing. 'Stands the church clock at ten to three, and is there honey still for tea?' For God's sake. It makes me want to puke."

"So—you're not an ideologue, then?"

"Oh yes. I'm that all right, but I'm not out to create something International. I couldn't give a toss about Trotsky's permanent revolution or Stalin's socialism in one country. It's England I want to change. England is my omelette. Just give me eggs to break."

"But, Charlie-boy—you served England so well during the war. You did things that most ordinary men would shit themselves over. You won a medal."

"My God, have you read every single file there is on me? Waist size? Do I dress to the left or the right?"

"Right now, as you are bollock-naked, the question is superfluous. But you won a DSO and a bar. How many men can say that?"

"Fucked if I know or care."

"In your war? I'd guess . . . fewer than a hundred."

"Usually, formally, one collects a gong from the king in person. Dress uniform, bit of a bow, hope he sticks the pin in the right place. The bars . . . less formal. I think they post them. But I couldn't collect either of mine during the war. It all had to wait until after VJ night as no one at the War Office was going to suggest I take a day off duty to pick up medals. So, eventually I made my visit to Buckingham Palace. I was one of about two hundred or more blokes at the palace one day in November '45. Felt sorry for the king. He didn't look well shaking so many hands, and when your right arm's tired you cannot simply switch to the left. I walked home afterwards. Down the Mall. Dumped the fucking medal in the first bin I came across."

"Why?"

"I hadn't fought *for* England. I'd fought *against* something I held to be worse than England—Nazism. Once the war was over, England assumed her natural place as the enemy. I serve Russia because we have a common enemy—but I don't do that to be used as a messenger boy."

"Charlie, just roll with it. Think of it as being caught in the slipstream of the shitstorm that was Burgess. Things will change."

"When?"

"Dunno."

"In the meantime?"

"I pass on to you what I learn. You pass it on to the next in the chain."

"Who's that?"

"I don't know that either. Wouldn't be much of a chain if I did. You will be contacted."

§86

Charlie met Jeff Boyle at Harvey's for one of their regular lunches. Over Smoked Alaska Salmon and Coconut Snowball, Jeff said, "As of Monday, the embassy—that is, you—will be included in our weekly intelligence summary. It may not amount to much—in fact, you may find a lot of it trivial, and there will be, for the time being, nothing on internal US matters. Fed stuff, after all. It wasn't easy, and there'll be a price to pay, but consider MI6 reinstated."

"A price? Tell me."

"Lunch is on you for the rest of the month."

"Done. Trivial or not, all the same I must thank you. Half a loaf is better than none. But—still the cold shoulder from the FBI?"

"Patience, Charlie. Not so long ago the Feds investigated countless members of your embassy staff to try and find the leak that now turns out to have been Donald Maclean. Every typist with a Ukrainian uncle, the mail-room boy whose grandfather had once visited Białystok . . . it was all time-consuming and time-wasting. If they've now got it into their heads that Kim might have been the one they missed . . . well, they're going to be pissed. Now—I have your corner. Frank Spoleto vouching for you was good, but the man himself was under a cloud not so long ago. So wait a while. It wasn't just peanut butter Frank was smuggling back in Berlin."

"I heard coffee."

Boyle hesitated a moment, toyed with his salmon, head down, then said softly, "Morphine."

"No joke?"

"No joke. Got one of your guys shot. Name of Holderness. Joe Holderness."

"Ah. Is that what Joe was up to? Well, yes, I knew he'd been in a bit of a skirmish. All hushed up fairly quickly. But that was Berlin. And Berlin is Berlin. A world away."

"It'll get better. The Feds will . . . they'll warm up. Another defection and I think you guys would be sunk—but what's the likelihood of that? Kim is back home getting the third degree. When he's cleared . . ."

Boyle let his sentence trail away.

Charlie felt no compunction to complete it with an unpalatable truth—that the Feds were right. MI5 would not clear Kim, and it would all end in prolonged doubt to no conclusion.

§87

Charlie saw no reason to the open the envelope Coky had given him at their last tryst.

If he was just a courier then he wouldn't waste headroom on the contents. He had quite enough of Senator Redmaine, attending the hearings as the committee continued to summon scriptwriters, directors and the occasional actor—most of whom Charlie had never heard of. If they weren't British he usually did not attend, but he'd break his own rules if the poor sod in the "dock" had real Hollywood cachet and the fan inside got the better of him. It was an aspect of America that impressed him—that so many of the "poor sods" refused to be poor sods and would not be browbeaten by Redmaine.

Ryan Robertson—an engaging heavy who'd risen up in film noir since the end of the war—a war in which he had served with distinction—had freely admitted to being a lifelong socialist and in exasperation, or so Charlie thought, had actually told Redmaine to "do your worst, you sonovabitch."

"What?"

"It's just my catchphrase, Senator. I first said it to Kirk Douglas in *Chiricahua Sunset* in 1947. I use it everywhere I go. Just like Bugs Bunny says 'What's up doc?'"

Even Redmaine had enough sense to let the laughter die down before he spoke again. His hand hovered over his gavel but didn't pick it up.

It occurred to Charlie that Redmaine's next move might be to subpoena Bugs Bunny.

And there was Hedda Mendelson, playwright and screenwriter who refused to take the Fifth, simply saying, "Ask me anything you like about me. Incriminating or not, I shall answer, but I won't answer any questions about other people. There is such a thing as privacy. And I would remind you, Senator, there is such a thing as decency. Would you like me to spell that for you?"

On the other hand, the film director Everett Zanak had, as the cliché had it and would have it forever, "named names."

When Charlie got home to P Street he found a printed card on the doormat.

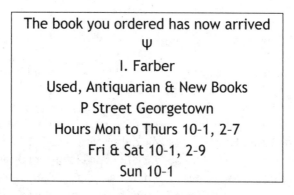

The book you ordered has now arrived

Ψ

I. Farber

Used, Antiquarian & New Books

P Street Georgetown

Hours Mon to Thurs 10-1, 2-7

Fri & Sat 10-1, 2-9

Sun 10-1

What book? He'd bought three or four from the shop across the street, but he hadn't ordered any.

He looked at his watch: 8:15 p.m. But it was a Friday, according to the card the shop's late night. Its windows were lit up. He pulled the door to and crossed the tram lines.

The last couple of times he'd been in the shop he'd been served by a near-silent woman in her twenties. Now, a man Charlie took to be at least seventy stood behind the counter.

"Mr. Farber?"

"Ja. Who else should I be?"

Charlie put the card on the counter.

"You're Mr. Leigh-Hunt?"

"Ja. Who else should I be?"

"So—a comedian. I should worry. Follow me, *Herr Shmendrik.*"

Farber lifted the wooden flap in the counter, parted the heavy green curtains that led to the back room.

There were two chairs and a steel desk, with books piled so high that even a smaller man would not have been able to see over them—but few men could have been smaller than Farber. Charlie toyed with "starved," with "wizened," both of which seemed wrong to describe the man, and settled on "desiccated," desiccated like a raisin or a prune.

"Please, take a seat."

Farber sat on the proprietorial side of the desk. Charlie lifted another pile of books off the one remaining chair and, finding nowhere else to put them, placed them gently on the floor.

"Look, there's been some kind of mistake—"

"Ignatz Farber," said Ignatz Farber.

"Charlie Leigh-Hunt, but—"

"No. There's no mistake. I believe you have something for me."

Charlie felt stupid. All those years of dead-drops and clandestine meetings, of silly hats and folded newspapers, on one occasion a green carnation, and he hadn't seen this coming.

"Oh."

"'Oh' is right. *Gevalt!* What kind of a spy are you, *nudnik?* An absolute beginner?"

Charlie took Coky's envelope from his inside pocket.

"You mean this?"

Farber held out his hand. Charlie slapped the package into it.

"Anytime you have something, just come to the store. If the girl is on watch, go away and come back another time. She knows nothing. If I need to talk to you—most unlikely, I might add—I will put a card in your letter box. Once in a while you might buy a book."

"I see—improving your cover."

"No, improving my profits."

On the way to the shop door Farber broke into a fit of coughing so prolonged Charlie wondered if he could or should offer to help, but Farber pulled a huge, dirty handkerchief from his trouser pocket. They stepped onto the sidewalk. Just when Charlie thought Farber was over it, he coughed with a gurgle like spiralling bathwater, doubled up and spat onto the flagstones.

To look down was both rude and distasteful, but Charlie could not help but notice the streak of blood in his sputum. And for the first time he noticed the club foot, neatly disguised by a well-made shoe.

Farber straightened up, scarcely level with Charlie's shoulder, a strand of drool in his wispy white beard.

"If I cough from here to eternity, I will never get the ash of Auschwitz out of my lungs."

They stood a moment, looked at one another.

"Don't look so shocked, *Engländer*. Next time come earlier. I make you best Viennese coffee and I tell you. If, that is, you wish to know. Plenty there are who don't. *Gay gezunt.*"

§88

Boyle had not overstated his case. The first shared file from the CIA was trivial to the point of boredom. Statistics for the Marshall Plan, now winding down—Charlie wasn't exactly sure what a billion dollars was, how many zeroes there needed to be on the end to turn a million into a billion. A strange failing in a man who could calculate the winnings on a racing bet placed at nine to two each way in a split second.

The USSR had told the USA where to stuff its aid programme. As Senator Henry Cabot Lodge, a man known to utter inconvenient truths, had put it, "This Marshall Plan is going to be the biggest damned interference in international affairs that there has ever been in history," which put Lodge and Stalin pretty much on the same page.

Of more interest were two pages detailing how much the "rebel" state of Yugoslavia was asking for and receiving outside of the Marshall Plan. That might very well be of interest—one small feather in an otherwise shabby cap.

The British Embassy was fortunate—farsighted, even—in possessing a Xerox model A patent photographic copier. It looked like something you'd use to press your trousers or perhaps warm up a steak and kidney pie. Unfortunately, Charlie had no idea how to use it, and according to Kay, his secretary, it was forever breaking down. But when it worked it worked and made his spy camera—he'd rescued the Minox, along with a dozen cassettes of film, the night he'd buried the rest of Philby's spy kit—pretty well redundant. Minox, Xerox? Were they related? They both sounded like brands of washing powder or shiny, green-skinned dictators of some faraway planet in a kids' comic strip. Minox, Xerox . . . Mekon?

Patiently—a faint air of superiority notwithstanding—Kay showed him how to press the right buttons and left him to do battle with the fridge-sized beast. Clutching a Latvian camera under a desk lamp illuminating pages marked SECRET might have made him feel marginally less like a cold war dogsbody, but fact beat feeling hands down, and Charlie foresaw a whole new world of espionage in which anyone with access to a secret might become an instant spy. Just add Xerox and shake well.

The following night, as soon as Kay had left for home, he photocopied twenty-seven pages of statistics. He did not understand the statistics, nor did he care about them.

§89

Just before the bookshop closed for the night Charlie called, intent on handing over the photocopies, but Farber's silent assistant was behind the counter. He browsed for a few minutes and went home.

Half an hour later his doorbell rang.

"I am done for the day. Muffin has gone. Let us drink."

"Muffin?"

"Americans," Farber replied. "But . . . they probably think Ignatz just as odd."

"We're field agents. Are we supposed to fraternise?"

"Fraternise, shmaternise . . . So? It's Friday. Fridays in America men prop up bars together, get drunk and complain about women. It's traditional."

"My only complaint about women is their absence."

"And I have been indifferent to them these twenty years. All the same I have whiskey, and my desk shall pass for a bar. Let us not disrespect tradition."

"A noble tradition, I'm sure, but aren't we here to undermine American tradition?"

"It's the weekend. I do my undermining ten till seven, Monday to Friday."

§90

Farber slid the envelope of photocopies into his desk drawer with scarcely a glance. Poured two large shots of Jack Daniel's. Charlie sipped at it—far too sweet for his taste—made a mental note to bring his own bottle next time, if there was next time, which seemed likely, as Farber gave out the impression of being Coleridge's Ancient Mariner hell-bent on telling his tale, albatross and all.

"I am a Communist by conviction. I cannot honestly say a lifelong Communist. I came to it late . . . in 1912."

"How old were you then?"

"I was twenty-three. I did not take up the cause in the heat of adolescence. I am not sure I can fully resurrect the reasons I had in 1912, but the Great War was coming, just over the horizon. I'd've been a fool not to see it."

"And you thought communism might stop it?"

"No. I never thought anything could stop it. But whether Austria won or lost did not matter—the empire would break up, there would be chaos, and I asked myself who was best placed to fix chaos. No nation state would be capable—it would be a system, not a nation, so the choice was simple, capitalism or communism. I was spared service in the war . . . the emperor did not much want a gimpy man weighing forty-three kilos and standing barely one and a half metres tall.

"I survived many a skirmish in the years between the wars. You may look upon a man of sixty-odd and not see the street-fighting man he used to be, but I could throw a cobblestone with the best of them.

"But—then came 1938. The Anschluss. Like the bullet with my name on it. A Communist, a Jew, I would not have stood a chance. So I moved to Italy, to Lucca. My wife, who was neither a Communist nor a Jew, chose to stay. We did not write, we did not meet. When the war ended I tried to trace her, but there was no trace. Like so many millions, she had vanished.

"I was safe in Italy. I can say this for Mussolini, he could stand up to Hitler on occasion. I felt safe, whatever the discrimination, until Italy changed sides and the Germans invaded the North. I'd made the mistake of growing fond of Lucca—I should have gone south, much further south, much sooner.

"In the January of 1944 I was rounded up and stuck on a train heading north. No destination given. And had they told me 'Auschwitz' it would have meant nothing.

"Irony popped its head up. Draw a straight line from Lucca to Auschwitz; where does it go?"

"Through Vienna."

"Ja, Vienna. Last time I ever saw my hometown—through a crack in the boarded-up windows of a death train."

"Don't get me wrong, Herr Farber, but I am amazed you survived."

"How so?"

"You must have been over fifty and, as you have said, as light as a bird." Farber shrugged.

"I too am amazed. I saw men bigger, younger, stronger than me pulled straight off the ramp. By this time we all knew the purpose of Auschwitz even if we did not know the name. You could smell it, you could taste it. God of the Jews, in whom I do not believe, help me . . . I can still taste it. But . . . when I dropped down from the train, the Germans began to laugh. You would think they must have seen every specimen—if not of all humanity, then of Jews—every kind of cripple, but for some reason the sight of a club-footed homunculus amused them. The bastards kept me alive for that reason alone. They took pleasure in kicking me up the arse at every opportunity, and if two or three of the bigger bastards got together they would throw me around like the ball in a game of catch. And they would have me curl up like a foetus and try to bowl me at ninepins. I rolled as far as I could. But I knew that as long as I amused them I would live—and I came to dread the day I did not amuse them."

"Did that day come?"

"Another time, my friend, another time. There is a Friday evening every week, I am told."

Charlie came again—the next Friday and many Fridays after—but not every Friday. Some Fridays, not every Friday, were Coky-time.

§91

"We're pushing our luck, you know."

"Surely Bob doesn't—"

"Of course he doesn't. I mean we're pushing our luck by using the same hotel. How often have we been in this bed? Ten times? A dozen?"

"This is the twenty-first."

"Good bloody grief, you're counting?"

"Every minute, every second."

Charlie nuzzled her left ear lobe, for emphasis.

"Charlie-boy, this is hugely flattering . . ."

He slipped a hand between her thighs, ready for a resurrection.

"Ah . . . I mean . . . it's still a risk. No, stop that, stop that."

"You don't mean that."

"Of course I don't, but we . . . we have to . . . oh fukkit, some other time."

And so they put off the conversation and stayed at the John Smith on Wisconsin another week, another month, and one month became two . . . and 1951 became 1952.

A different Charlie, a previous Charlie, would have been aware of the changes happening within him, but he was now in so deep there was no other life, no previous life—all the world had become Coky Redmaine and Coky Redmaine was all the world. Life before Coky did not matter and he could not conceive of life after Coky.

A different Charlie, a previous Charlie, might have termed such a state of heart as "letting your guard down."

§92

The Aaron Burr Hotel

Chevy Chase, Maryland
March 1952

Many a man would light up a cigarette afterwards. Charlie no longer smoked. Charlie pondered. So many things to ponder. Life, America, the world, the universe . . . the husband.

"What does the future hold for him?"

"Eh?"

"I mean . . . changes . . . changes at the top."

"Don't underestimate Bob. He has made as many friends as enemies, and there are even enemies who might think it wise to cultivate him. That said, if Adlai Stevenson is the next Democratic president, Bob is dead, as it were. If Bob Taft is the next Republican president, dead again."

"I thought Taft supported Redmaine."

"Up to a point and the point has been passed."

"He doesn't want the top job?"

"Of course he wants it. He just knows he'll never get it. He's not seeking supporters and won't put himself forward at the convention . . . far too late to throw his cap in . . . he'll wait. Ike and Taft are neck and neck. If Taft gets the nomination, Bob is fucked . . . if it's Ike then the choice of veep will be down to him. Lots of people want it . . . Thomas

Dewey might swallow his pride and play second fiddle, and he hates Bob, but I think he's happier being the power behind Ike . . . there's even a whisper that Richard Nixon wants it . . . and Bob thinks that if the job is within Nixon's grasp it's within his too. Pigs might fly . . . who knows? He'll put the word out . . . 'Barkis is willin'.'"

"Will he get it?"

"Dunno. If I were Ike being asked to choose between Bob and Dick Nixon, I'd be asking who the pot, who the kettle? If Ike wants a commie-baiting arse of a veep he'll be spoilt for choice."

Charlie reflected silently. Nuzzled her left thigh, head down, then head up . . .

"What did you mean 'cultivate'?"

"Hmm . . . perhaps that was a bit casual . . . but now you mention it, I can see anyone but Taft giving Bob a job just to get him off that damn committee. A shuttup job. Promoted into oblivion. Something where he can be all bluster and no force."

"Such as?"

"Oh no. You have to earn it first. Other leg, and all points in between."

§93

The Schuyler Old House B&B

Bethesda, Maryland
January 31, 1953

On January 28, 1953, one week after his inauguration, President Eisenhower proved Coky right and appointed Senator Redmaine to the National Security Council—an organisation just a few years old, whose function was vague and variable.

The following day the Permanent Sub-Committee of the General Committee on Investigations into US Internal Security and blah de blah de blah—otherwise known as the Bob Redmaine Show—was wound up. The price of promotion. Knowledge without power, position without influence. Effectively the president had sidelined Senator Redmaine.

"Is it usual to have a senator on the NSC?" Charlie asked. "I thought it was all generals and cabinet ministers."

"Nothing's usual. It's all too new to be usual or unusual. And it's entirely in the President's gift. Ike's appointed Bob. Caligula appointed his horse. What's the difference?"

Over the next month, one difference became clear.

"I'm swamped in . . . stuff," Coky said.

"Stuff?"

"Bob brings home twice as much paperwork as he did from the committee. I can't take notes fast enough. The only time I have is when he's gone to bed and before he wakes up. I scribble till my wrist aches. There's got to be a better way."

"Indeed, there is."

At their next tryst Charlie gave Coky the Minox and the dozen or so cassettes of film he'd saved from Felix Foster's grave. He'd thought he might use them but never had.

By March Coky had used them all.

Whereas the proceedings of the Redmaine Committee had amounted to little more than high-flown gossip, the NSC files were Kremlin gold.

"I'll get some more film," Charlie said.

"Where?"

"Dunno. Bound to be somewhere."

§94

P Street, Georgetown

Ignatz Farber had turned the first cassette over and over in his hand like a toy from a child's box.

"Fascinating. What will they think of next? The fate of America in the palm of my hand."

"How does that feel?"

"Precarious."

"Really?"

"Of course. You think I hate America?"

"I've never really thought about it."

"Liar. How many times we sit here in my shop and just talk?"

"I dunno, maybe thirty or forty times."

"I lost count—but enough for you to want to think about why I do what I do, and you have thought."

"I suppose I have."

"I don't hate America. America took me in. I am grateful to America. But I do not trust America."

"Eh?"

"I do not trust America to stop Germany if there is ever a next time. I wish I could. But only the Communist Party will stop a Fourth Reich."

"I don't think there's ever going to be a Fourth Reich, Herr Farber."

"Perhaps not, but you will understand why that possibility bothers me. I am a loyal Communist and a loyal American. I am a believer. And so the only course is to believe in the Soviet Union. But you, Charlie, what do you believe? And no, no need to answer, because I will tell you what you *don't* believe. You don't believe in England. And why should you? I have learnt the last couple of years that you hate England and that that is what you believe in. Perhaps all you believe in. And you know what? It's not enough."

§95

November 1953

"I have leave due."

"What?"

"I'm going to England for two weeks."

"You've only just bloody got here!"

"Coky, it's been two and a half years. Think of me as the English do. A sort of glorified civil servant. I'm entitled to annual leave and every two years to home leave."

"So you'd bugger off and leave me?"

"That's not the point and you know it."

"You'll miss Thanksgiving."

"I've missed thirty-eight Thanksgivings and not even noticed."

"Turkey, cranberries . . . sweet potatoes, pumpkin mush with crunchy stuff?"

"You make it sound so appetising."

"I won't be here when you get back."

"Yes you will."

"I'll have a romp with one of my other lovers."

"That's what I would do, not what you would do. Just because I think through my cock is no reason for you to think through your . . ."

"Can't say it, eh? Go on. I dare you."

§96

Clerkenwell, London EC1

Charlie met Cobb in the Dog and Trumpet in Clerkenwell, close to Smithfield market. One of those "working man" pubs that did a roaring lunchtime trade and was virtually dead in the evenings.

He'd clearly been there a while. Two empty pint glasses in front of him.

"Can I get you another, Norman?"

"Y'can. I've a fancy for a boilermaker."

Greedy bastard—beer and a shot at seven in the evening?

Charlie ordered a half of mild for himself. Watched Cobb sink most of his pint in one gulp and belch into his fist.

Of necessity Charlie had seen and heard nothing of Cobb for the last two years—he let him get on with the dodgy business of selling phony secrets to the Russians, "nylons and fags," as Cobb so sneeringly put it. Cobb was a copper in Special Branch, the Met's idiot squad, but he was far from stupid. If anything, he was dangerous. Meeting him always left Charlie with a sense of distinct unease.

"We've a problem, Charlie."

"We have?"

"Cockerell. Gone down with pneumonia or something like."

"Then let us wish him a speedy recovery."

"I said—we've got a problem. He was due on the Lisbon run this week. Y'know? The exchange? Meeting that Russian bird?"

"Can't you do it?"

"Me? I'm not some soddin' merchant banker who can pinch an afternoon to swan off to bloody Newmarket or Sandown Park. I'm a serving copper. I can't just tell the Yard I want three days holiday. You do it."

"What?"

"You're on home leave."

"Norman, I'm here to see my mother."

"You could be there and back in a day."

"A long day."

"For fuck's sake, do it or we lose a payment. After all—it's not as if you do anything else for your cut, is it?"

Cobb slapped a brown envelope on the table, splashing down on a puddle of bitter.

"What you asked for. Try earning it!"

§97

Charles Edward Moncrieff Leigh-Hunt was not a wastrel. Perhaps he was a spendthrift, as prone to generosity as he was to expensive self-indulgence. A wastrel ran through his own money and then started scrounging off other chaps. Charlie might let his tailor's bill languish a while, whereas he was always prompt with his garage in case they decided to hang on to the Aston Martin—a cute little DB1 in British racing green—but he had always been able support both self and habits—by spook or by crook.

He'd known many a wastrel. His mother seemed drawn to them. His father had been the first of many. On the way home from school on the train, each holiday—he would always spend the first couple of nights in Hampstead with the Troys until he found out where his mother was living and with whom—he and Troy would play the game they called Spot the Dad—would Judy Leigh-Hunt's new beau be a Bill or a Bob or an Uncle Bertie? They took it as read that she avoided Ruperts.

Despite numberless "dads," it seemed to Charlie that much of his childhood had been spent alone with his mother. Preferable by far to the strained times when one bloke or another was hanging around, resenting him and wanting her and thinking they could bribe him with a five-bob postal order. Had he been a Freudian, which he was not, Charlie might have attributed his lifelong promiscuity to this—he never wanted nor counted the notches on his bedpost, all he sought was the company of a woman. It was not that every woman was "Judy"—nothing so simple would serve as explanation. But on the other hand, it was and did.

Judy had settled—temporarily, no doubt—in a village just outside Lyme Regis, appropriately named Uplyme. There was no Downlyme. Charlie drove down to Up after his meeting with Cobb. The hint of Guerlain Après l'Ondée that always hung suggestively around Judy might be the antidote to Fuller's ale and Special Branch body odour— bottle that in a spray and England would have a major crime deterrent more effective than tear gas.

It was November. He found his mother in the garden of a tiny Dorset (or was it Devon?) thatched cottage, wrapped up like Captain Scott, woolly hat and fingerless gloves, deadheading something or other. Charlie knew nothing about gardening and was not sure she did either, but she had always taken an inordinate pleasure in just hacking away at things.

"I'll stop. Too cold to carry on. Let's put the kettle on."

Charlie ducked under the doorway, stepped into a room in which his hair all but brushed the whitewash off the ceiling.

He looked around. A man's mackintosh and a trilby on the hat pegs. He heard the pop of a gas ring, then his mother emerged from the kitchen.

"Take your coat off, Charlie. And stop looking around as though you'd just landed on Mars."

"Oh, just . . . y'know . . . wondering . . ."

"I know what you were wondering. You think I never knew about the silly games you and Freddie used to play? I'll save you speculating. There is no 'new dad,' no 'Uncle Bertie' at the moment. The hat and mac belong to the gardener. Although God alone knows how long I'll be able to go on paying him."

Ah, how quickly they got to the point.

As he hung up his coat, next to the supposed gardener's, Charlie reached into his pocket and drew out Cobb's envelope—tossed it onto the dining table.

"What's that?"

As if she didn't know.

"A grand."

"Charlie, you're not up to anything dodgy, are you?"

"Dodgy? No. Criminal? Of course."

"You know, I never know when you're teasing me."

"After thirty-nine years?"

"One day, my boy, you'll get caught."

"Perhaps, but not today."

§98

"Tell me . . . do you have a girl in America?"

"No. I have a woman."

"Were you ever going to mention her?"

"Perhaps."

"Ah . . . I take it she is married?"

Charlie was not accustomed to his mother turning the tables on him quite so sharply, but with a single question she'd done just that.

"Yes. She is. But, Mummy, she is the one. This time it's real."

"The one. *E pluribus unum*, as they say on the back of their money?"

"She's English."

"The one?"

"Yes."

"Real?"

"Yes."

"Oh Charlie . . . are they any of them real?"

He had the distinct feeling that the pot was questioning the colour of the kettle.

"Does she have a name?"

"Can we change the subject? You could tell me about life in a Wessex village. All those old rustics who drop from the pages of a Thomas Hardy novel—or the church flower committee you sit on—or all those whist drives you go to."

"Ha bloody ha!"

§99

At the garden gate—sweet sorrow, dead hollyhocks and the hesitation of parting. Charlie always wondered if this might be the last time. He had no idea if his mother thought the same thought.

"Speaking of dads and Berties . . ." she said.

"We weren't."

"Think back a moment, Charlie. Dads. I have heard from yours."

"Which one?"

"The real one."

"Mummy, they were none of them real."

"Perhaps not—but . . . do you want to know what he's up to?"

Charlie thought for a moment. He had not seen his biological father since . . . since . . . about 1920. He'd be something like sixty-eight now. What was the fate of a ne'er-do-well of pensionable age in postwar England? Having posed the question, he found he had no interest in the answer.

"No," he replied, and, turning over a neat phrase in his mind, used it. "He was a ne'er-do-well. All your men have been ne'er-do-wells. You don't need any of them. You never did. You have me. I'm not a ne'er-do-well. I'm a do-well."

Judy hugged him.

The fleeting wisp of Après l'Ondée.

And when she pulled back, tears in her eyes.

"Charlie, I say again. You're not up to anything dodgy, are you?"

And he laughed and laughed and hugged her one more time, but didn't answer.

$100

Lisbon

November in Lisbon still clung to summer.

Charlie sat outside, at the designated table, at the designated café, clutching the requisite newspaper.

She, whoever she was, Cobb's "Russian bird," was late and he found himself doing the crossword. He'd never cared for crosswords—he knew people for whom the day could not begin without one, more important than coffee or corn flakes—but the only other reading matter he had on him was the piffle Cobb had cobbled together as "secrets."

`3 across: Salvation Army sings for its supper.`
`Apparently.`

What the fuck did that mean?

`7 down: Spotty leopard pesters virgin.`
`Spontaneous.`

Who made this nonsense up?

Then, "What happened to the other guy?"

He looked up, a short, rather gorgeous blonde, looking about as Russian as Mae West. Eyes like conkers, and an accent he now knew to be New York. Shades of George Madison. Surely she wasn't Cockerell's regular contact? But that question beggared the answer.

"Shouldn't you begin with a code word?"

"Sure."

She sat down.

"Bloomingdales. OK?"

"Of course. Macy's. And I gather he's down with pneumonia."

He shoved yesterday's London *Times* across the table to her, with Cobb's package tucked inside.

She shoved the *New York Times*, three days old, back at him, as weighted as his own package.

"You don't count it at the table, capisce?"

And with that she was gone, and with her his crossword puzzle.

He might as well order coffee, catch up on the USA as it had been on Wednesday.

On page three his gaze froze:

President dismisses Senator Redmaine from NSC.

§101

Chelsea, London SW3

He'd been home in Chelsea less than an hour when there was a knock at the door.

A blue-jacketed postboy, with bag, with bike, with telegramme.

Get back. Coky.

§102

P Street, Georgetown

Charlie wondered how much speeding up a man's body could take. London to Lisbon, and less than a day later a BOAC de Havilland Comet to Washington National. It was exhausting. By the time he turned the key in the lock on P Street he felt as though he'd swum the Atlantic.

An envelope was on the doormat:

```
I'm at the Hay-Adams. Call when you can. Get
some sleep.
```

No signature—none required.

$103

The Hay-Adams Hotel

Washington, DC

"Ike fired Bob first thing Monday morning. Top of his agenda, but I imagine it's been simmering there since the day he was inaugurated. He set Bob up like Rip van Winkle's ninepins and finally he bowled him out. No more NSC, no more Senate Committee, and the distinct prospect he will lose his seat in the next midterms. Monday night Bob was a volcano of rage. I made myself scarce. Tuesday night I didn't see him. No idea where he went. Wednesday morning the White House press secretary gives out the news. Bob erupts again, so I bugger off all day and most of the evening.

"That day Richard came in to catch up on paperwork. You know who I mean? The young bloke who does all the bean counting for the trusts Avery put me in charge of—a two-day-a-week job. Wednesday was one of those days. Around seven, Richard is packing up—Bob comes in and comes . . . on."

"Eh?"

"I can't think how else to put it. A pass? Surely you can only make a pass at a woman? Anyway . . . Bob . . . 'comes on' to Richard, gets his cock out and asks Richard to suck it."

"Er . . . I have to ask . . . does Richard look like a poof?"

"He's young, tall and handsome. I have absolutely no idea which direction he leans. Bob may have drawn his own conclusion. I suspect he didn't care. But Richard wasn't having it. Pushed the fat bastard aside, banged on the door of the house next door and called the police. Didn't hesitate.

"Ten minutes later the cops arrive.

"Bob tells them to fuck off.

"The cops tell him to open up or they'll bust down the door.

"A thimbleful of common sense surfaces in Bob, and my front door is saved from the copper's boot.

"Of course Bob denied everything. Sat there with his flies still open and denied it all. My word against his blah-de-blah. And the cops were wary—why wouldn't they be?—five minutes ago Bob had been important. He was lucky. They did not charge him. A more zealous, dare I say a more honest, copper would have dragged him away in handcuffs. A British copper would have taken him round the back of the nick and given him a kicking. But a senator in the United States . . . ? I got home in time to see most of this. Richard in the dining room, looking offended, Bob in the drawing room, looking offensive.

"So—I packed a case and moved here. I've been here five days. My patience is wearing thin. It's my house, after all. But it's always easier to walk out than throw someone out. And it's the only way to make this thing work."

"What thing?"

Coky turned on her side to face him. A sharp intake of breath as she set sail on narrative.

"I always had a suspicion he might be queer."

"How so?"

"Not a hint of a mistress when I met him. Over forty and never been married and . . . you know the old Turkish saying?"

"What old Turkish saying?"

"It begins, 'A woman for duty' . . . well, not sure about dutiful, but his fucking was always a bit perfunctory . . . never thought his heart was in it even if his cock was. But . . . the adage goes on, 'a boy for pleasure' . . . not wholly sure about that . . . it would be too obvious, and if Bob went with boys he'd never let me find out . . . and it ends, 'a melon for ecstasy.' I rather think my arsehole is his melon. When he's getting nowhere on the western front, and more than a bit grumpy, I just flip over, offer him my arse and he goes to his own wet heaven in about fifteen seconds. What does that tell you?"

"Not much. Your arsehole is still a female arsehole. But . . ."

"But he did it. He did it. The fool even waved his cock at Richard like a drunken frat boy."

"Drunk?"

"Shit-faced. He's been drunk every day since Ike dropped his bombshell. Sober he certainly wouldn't have had the nerve and quite possibly not the inclination. But—he did it, and it is heaven-sent. Our comrades want Bob disgraced and hence discredited. They want to see his house of cards collapse. The propaganda value of this is enormous and they know it. I could not have written a better script. *The Red-Baiting Queer Commie Hunter*—in 3D and Technicolor."

"But it's not getting out. You said it yourself. The cops won't charge him."

"It will. Our orders are 'disgrace and destroy.' We'll just have to do it backwards. If we destroy Bob, his behaviour will come out, it will become common knowledge. He will be a disgrace. The police won't sit on it for a split second once Bob is dead—it will be a factor in his death."

"Death? Destroy?"

"Kill."

"Oh Jesus Christ."

"Don't worry, I'll do it."

$104

Coky went back to the house on N Street at a time she thought it likely to be empty—no cook, no cleaners.

It wasn't empty. Redmaine lay sprawled across their bed in vest, underpants and socks—the least sexy combination of garments known to woman—in an alcoholic stupor, a bottle of Hound Dog bourbon drooling onto the carpet much as he drooled onto the bed.

He'd pissed himself. Eleven in the morning—dead drunk—and he'd pissed himself.

She felt she could let off a bomb in his soggy underpants and not wake him, but she risked nothing. She tiptoed to the bathroom and examined the contents of the medicine cabinet.

Dilaudid—generically a "downer." He'd been taking them on prescription for about a month. Not long enough to have developed inordinate tolerance. Most people she knew in Washington took an upper or a downer. Dexedrine and Dilaudid being the drugs of choice for those virtuous legislators who would imprison anyone caught smoking reefer or shooting smack.

She took a packet of twenty-eight. Fifteen ought to be enough, particularly if mixed with alcohol. Hound Dog was ideal. As bourbons went, it was creosote—at ninety proof, it would mask the taste of almost anything.

She took two bottles from the cupboard in the dining room.

§105

At four o'clock she phoned Redmaine from a payphone in Farragut Square.

"Where are you?" he asked.

"Not saying."

"You're in the street. I can hear traffic."

"Well done, Sherlock."

"Still not saying?"

"No."

"What are you scared of?"

"Certainly not you."

"Whatever. If you've called me up to say you've come to your senses, all I can say is, What kept you?"

"No, Bob. You can say a lot more than that and indeed you should."

"Then get your skinny British ass back here."

"No, I will not come to you."

"So—where are you? The Willard? The Hay-Adams?"

That was close, but he prattled right past it.

"You got a hidey hole? You got some fancy man now?"

"God, you're so bloody crude. I should just let you sink."

"I am sunk, dammit! I had the press on my doorstep for a week after . . . Ike . . . you know . . . now nobody. I'm not worth a byline. I'm yesterday's cold potatoes!"

"For which you should be grateful. It's a simple choice: Would you prefer to be . . . nobody or queer? Because that's the next story."

A choking silence. Was he coughing or crying?

"Bob? Bob?"

"Yeah—I'm still here."

"I will not come to you."

"I heard you the first time."

"I will not come to you, but if you come to me, I can get you out of this mess."

"How?"

"Your stupidity—your queer stupidity—will be leaked. The cops have shown some caution regarding a senator, but it's diminishing by the second. Your immunity is a fart in a sandstorm. Your best chance is to put on a public display of the happily married man."

"Oh yeah right . . . and that's why you left."

"I can be the devoted wife again, but at a price. On my terms. If we stand firm, we can deny everything. We'll have Washington believing in your honesty and decency—gigantic fucking lie though that would be."

"How?"

"Stop saying that. You sound like Sitting Bull in a 1930s B movie. Come to me and I'll tell you. I'll show you—but if you don't meet me, I will not come to you. I will never come to you again."

Again, the choking silence.

"I'm listening."

"I'll book you a room at the Dreiser—"

"Where the fuck is that?"

"Columbia and Eighteenth. Check in. We won't use your own name. You'll be Elmer . . ."

"Fudd?"

"No, you idiot . . . Jones. Elmer Jones. Check in tonight around seven. I'll be there as soon as I can."

"Supposing I'm recognised?"

"You won't be. This is nowheresville, Bob. The only way they'd recognise you is if you were Roy Rogers or Audie Murphy. Or possibly Elmer Fudd, who knows? Trust me. You've earned a night's anonymity. Enjoy it while it lasts."

Coky hung up the telephone, silently banking on Bob being recognised.

She waited less than a minute, rehearsed her lines and dialled the Dreiser Hotel.

§106

"Good afternoon. I am the secretary of Mr. Elmer Jones. He would like a room for two nights, starting today. Would that be possible?"

She aimed for a soft Virginia accent.

She could not tell from the receptionist's monosyllabic "sure" how convincing she was—but what did it matter? Hotels like the Dreiser were just knocking shops—lies and anonymity par for the course.

"We'd like a street view, please."

"Why? Ain't nuthin' ter look at."

"Just followin' orders."

"OK. Room three, second floor. From there you can see all the way to the Piggly Wiggly. Cash up front."

"Of course."

Far too bloody English—she should have just echoed his "sure."

"Mr. Jones will arrive around seven."

"Got it."

And he hung up.

§107

Charlie rented an Oldsmobile and drove her to Adams Morgan.

She said, "Sit in the car. If I can handle this alone, I will. If I can't, I'll flash the torch at the window."

Coky got out.

Crossed the street and peered into the lobby of the Dreiser. Reception desk just inside the door, staircase to the left. One man on duty.

The minute he left the desk she'd go in.

He was patting his pockets now, looking for something, finding nothing. Coky realised he was out of cigarettes. An empty packet of Chesterfields tossed down. He looked at the clock, looked at the door. She ducked to the side and had her back to him as he came out and went to the Piggly Wiggly grocery across the street, where Charlie was parked.

§108

Bob was lying on the bed, hands clasped behind his head, pages of the *Washington Post* scattered across the bedspread, a cigarette smouldering down to nothing in the ashtray. The morning's drink seemed to have worn off. He'd changed his suit, even managed to shave, although he looked grey and grim. All the same—the level of alcohol in his bloodstream had to be at flood alert.

He swung his legs off the bed.

Stared at her. Bloodshot as sunset.

"Good evening, Elmer."

He said nothing.

She looked around. It was grubby. Worse than grubby, filthy. One chair, one dresser, one trouser press, one bed—with lipstick on the pillowcase and no doubt cum stains on the sheets. You might not want clean linen, but who could live without a trouser press?

"Shit."

"Yeah. It's quite a dive you booked us into."

Coky set a bottle of Hound Dog on the dresser. A flask of Booth's gin for herself.

The only glasses in the room were in metal hoops next to the basin, both smeared in old toothpaste. She turned a tap but only rust-brown water came out.

"And more shit."

She poured him a triple of bourbon, sluicing the toothpaste off the side of the glass. Half an inch of gin for herself that she had no intention of drinking.

She handed Bob his glass, took the only chair, leaving him arse-poised on the edge of the bed.

"We might as well be comfortable."

"Gonna be a long night, is it?"

"That rather depends on you, Senator."

"You don't say."

"I do. Do *you* have anything to say?"

"About what, Charlotte?"

"I'm not here to be your straight man, Bob. Feeding you lines like we were Dean Martin and Jerry Lewis."

"OK. I got one simple, one very simple thing to say. Can't a man get good and drunk once in a while?"

"A man can get good and drunk twice in a while—as long as he keeps it in his pants."

"I did."

"I saw you. You sat there with your flies undone and your meat on the counter."

"Charlotte . . . for Christ's sake, I'd just taken a piss and forgot to zip up."

"You got it out, you waved it about and you sang *Rally Round the Flag, Boys*, to which you gratuitously added the word 'pole.'"

"Is that what he's saying? Is that what that goddam queer is saying?"

"You know very well what Richard said to the cops."

But perhaps he didn't? Perhaps he remembered next to nothing?

"So . . . you want me to apologise?"

"Too late for that."

"You want . . . are you saying I should buy him off?"

"Might not be a bad idea."

She'd got his stress levels up now. He'd drunk the first one slowly. Now he knocked back a second and topped up for a third. The trick— hardly a precise term—would surely be to keep his stress levels up and thereby keep him drinking.

"A hundred grand should do it."

A stressful sum, she thought.

"What the fuck!"

The third went down in one, and the fourth filled the tooth glass to the brim.

"One hundred fucking grand in faggot hush money? You are pulling my johnson, Mrs. Redmaine."

"No, Bob. That's what you asked Richard to do. But . . . on the matter of Mrs. Redmaine . . . let us discuss our happy wedded bliss."

"What?"

"I'll recreate the illusion . . . I almost said 'for you,' but it's not for you, it's for everybody else, isn't it?"

"Riddles, Charlotte. You talk to me in fucking riddles."

She'd tipped away half the bottle before adding the crushed-up Dilaudid. She knew he could get through a full bottle, but she wanted to be sure he got all the drug into his system quickly. He'd downed more than half the half now. If he could taste the Dilaudid, it didn't show in his face.

"I will come back to N Street. We will pose as a married couple, but we will have separate rooms and when the shitstorm that is just over the horizon has blown out to Arkansas or Oklahoma or God knows where west of the Pecos . . . you will quietly move out and just as quietly I shall divorce you."

"Divorce?"

"Divorce."

"Shit, Charlotte. Iss the midterms in less'n a year. What divorced man ever won reelection? Do not fuckin' do this to me!"

"Bob. You won't be standing again. Go back to Iowa and pick potatoes."

"That's Idaho, you stupid bitch."

"Whatever. You're through with Washington."

"Wanna bet? Do not unnerestimate me. I will be back. I am a survivor. You hear me? A survivor!"

Glass five, or was it six, went down the hatch. There was about half an inch left in the bottom of the bottle. She hadn't touched her gin, but then he didn't seem to have noticed. He was visibly, audibly drunk. His eyes were like snooker reds just waiting to be potted. But was he also dying?

He stood up, legs like jelly, and shook himself like a wet dog. A feeble attempt to seem more sober than he was.

He yanked at the buttons on his flies, one pinged off into nowhere, and her first thought was *Oh my God, not again*, but he staggered to the washbasin and pissed.

For a minute or more he stood stock still, and then she heard him snore. He was asleep standing up, with his cock in his right hand.

Something snapped in his dreams. His head jerked up and he whirled around, hands flailing, cock flapping.

"Yea wurra durra wurra."

Bob was reeling now. Toppling but not falling. Raving but not shouting. Wobbled to the bed, wobbled to the basin. Wobbled back again. Swaying at the edge of the bed, not six feet from her—oblivious to her.

She doubted he could see her or hear her.

"On the shores of Gitche Gotcha . . ."

She pushed gently at his chest, thinking he might just topple backwards onto the bed.

He didn't.

She pushed harder.

Still he stayed upright. Dropped by just an inch or two. His arse back on the edge of the mattress.

Humpty Dumpty sat on the wall.

"On the shores of Gitche Gotcha . . . duuh . . . duuh . . . on the . . ."
She wondered how she would ever get him down and dead.
She flashed the torch in the window. Flashed again and saw Charlie
get out of the Oldsmobile.
And suddenly Bob had found his metre.

> On the shores of Gitche Gotcha,
> Of the shining Big-Sea-Water,
> Stood Nokomis, the old woman,
> Pointing with her finger westward,
> O'er the water . . . pointing . . .

He was conducting an invisible orchestra, playing every instrument
himself.
He stopped. Stared at Coky with not a glimmer of recognition. Fumbling for the next word and giving up. Starting again.

> On the shores of Gitche Bitche,
> On the shining Big Sea Water . . .

Then once more around the bed, slowing like a gramophone
unwinding.
And back again.
He grabbed the bottle.
"Gitche Bitche Gotcha Wotcha . . . jamb . . . jambally . . . filly
gumbo . . . duuh . . . crawfish pie."
Crawfish pie?
He slumped on his back on the bed.
Humpty Dumpty falling.
Eyes closed. Down.
Perhaps.
Eyes wide. Up.
"Oh . . . oh sinners . . . sinners let's go . . . down."
If only he'd just go down and bloody well stay down.
"Daisy, Daisy . . . give me your . . . wuuuuuuuuuuuuuuuuuuuh."
Humpty Dumpty breaking.
A giant sigh in exhalation, surely the breath of a dying man?

"And if that mockingbird don't sing . . . Daddy's gonna . . ."

How many damn nursery rhymes does the bugger know?

His voiced dropped to a croak, to a whisper, to a word barely breathed.

"Mockingbird . . ."

Then his chest stopped heaving, his eyelids stopped blinking, the fingers that held the bottle unwound, his mouth fell open in a round, soundless O—and he looked like a dead fish.

Humpty Dumpty broken.

All the king's horses, all the king's men . . .

Mockingbird.

His "rosebud."

His last word.

How apt.

Charlie came in. Quiet as a mouse.

"It's OK. It's over."

"You needed me?"

"I thought so, I thought he'd never go down, but . . ."

Charlie felt for a pulse.

"He's gone."

"For sure?"

"For sure."

"Were you seen coming in?"

"No."

"Then go now. I'll contact you in three or four days. I have to clean up in here, then I have to feign outrage and play the grieving widow. Call me Gertrude."

Charlie left.

Coky tucked Bob's cock back inside his trousers. She did not see why whoever found him should have to look at that.

§109

Another Harvey's lunch was looming. This time at Jeff Boyle's request.

The table was set for three.

"We expecting company?"

Jeff said, "You know Wendell Spivey?"

"Of," Charlie replied. "I know *of* him. A G-man."

"Yep. But don't use any other designation but Special Agent when he gets here. The Feds are touchy. See insult everywhere."

"He must have hated Burgess."

"He did. Guy was on his shit list . . . try to keep off it."

A man Charlie took to be Spivey was being steered in their direction. Charlie's first reaction was that if he didn't want to be called a G-man, he might try not looking like one. He looked nothing like Eliot Ness—in fact he was short and bald and fat in the face—but oh the three-piece suit with lapels like aircraft carriers and the ever-present top-pocket hanky.

Jeff made introductions.

Spivey looked at the place set for him.

"I really can't stay. I just . . . needed a word."

The waiter hovered. Jeff mouthed a silent "five minutes."

"I could use some information, Mr. Hunt."

Charlie did not correct him.

"It's what we're here for."

"Sure. Try telling that to your MI5 man."

"Forrester?"

"Yep."

"He's an awfully good man," Charlie lied.

"Good. Maybe. But I get the feeling I'm getting the runaround."

"Then you'd better tell me."

"We've been getting . . . I was about to say 'reports' . . . but that would be overstating it . . . rumours, rumours of a man named Felix Foster."

Charlie wondered what his own face might look like at this moment—but sipped at his twosome.

"A . . . a 'person of interest,' I believe the phrase is."

"Oh yeah, he's that all right. He's been around a while . . . we don't know what he's up to . . . but someone using the name John Smith—and for all we know both names are fake—bought ten cassettes of Minox film in a downtown photo store in March. You know what a Minox is?"

He hadn't used "Felix Foster" in months, and then, asked for a name, had said the first thing to enter his head. "John Smith." A little too much Freud trawling his subconscious, but surely they hadn't been able to link Smith to Foster? Where on earth was this leading?

"Of course."

"There's really no legitimate use for a Minox. So we have all the photo stores primed to report to us if anyone orders film for one. Smith ordered. The store told him 'maybe Monday,' he said 'Thursday,' so we got ready to stake out—he outsmarted us and collected Tuesday and left my guys with egg on their faces."

He hadn't outsmarted anyone. He just happened to pass the store that day and went in on the off chance.

"Two nights ago we got a lead. You know Bob Redmaine was found dead in a cheap hotel in Adams Morgan?"

"Yes. I heard it was suicide. Something about him being queer?"

"Maybe, maybe not. It happened at the Dreiser. Desk clerk there identified this Felix Foster as being at the hotel that night. Didn't see him enter, but he saw him leave. Fairly sure it was him."

Oh shit.

"Did you get a description?"

"Yes and no. The guy wears the thickest glasses I've ever seen. Didn't recognise Redmaine, just thought he looked 'familiar,' and all we got on Foster was around six foot, fair hair . . . and an English accent. Pretty much how the guy at the photo store described Smith. We got a sketch artist in and he sat with him and the guy from the Dreiser, but in the end it could have been Moe, Shemp or Larry for all the good it did. They couldn't even agree on the colour of his eyes. Still—we think Smith is Foster."

"Ah. I begin to see why you called Forrester. Surely this man, this Felix Foster, wasn't so stupid as to leave his card?"

"No, but the desk clerk used to work at the John Smith Hotel over on Wisconsin. You catch my drift here? All these John Smiths? The desk clerk knew Foster from there. A very distinctive voice, he reckons. Says Foster was a regular for over six months. Stopped some time last year. Now—despite what you might think, there's no British registered alien in DC by the name of Foster, so we assume some subterfuge. So—I thought MI5 might have a handle on some illegal Englishman. Nothing doing. Never heard of him, and when I pressed him he got aggressive. Like I was insulting him."

Yes. That was Tom Forrester's weakness, to find insult as readily as Spivey surely did.

"And . . . I think he knows who this Foster is."

"Six foot, fair hair, English accent. Could be half the chaps in my embassy and about a thousand scattered across the city."

"We have nothing else to go on. Anything you can do would be appreciated by the director. I say 'nothing else'. The desk clerk reckons all Foster used his room at the John Smith for was sex. It wasn't a different woman every time, but he reckons at least six different women came over for . . . y'know."

Thank God for poor eyesight and Coky's ever-evolving fashion sense. She had never once disguised herself, but perhaps a different dress, a different hairstyle meant a different woman to the short of sight. It was little short of a miracle the man hadn't seen her at the Dreiser. But he hadn't.

"So we're looking for an English lothario?"

"I think we're looking for a spy, Mr. Hunt."

"I'll do my best," Charlie lied.

Over Veal à la Françoise, he mused that it might be high time Six summoned him back to England. He couldn't ask. It would attract suspicion.

He didn't want to ask.

He wanted Coky.

§110

They met in a motel on the Clarksville turnpike that redefined cheap. Not even a name, just a number—Five or Nine or Ninety-Four. Afterwards Charlie could not remember.

"Why here?"

"Not that I flatter myself, but most of the DC papers have run a photograph of me in the last week. Thank God for widow's weeds. One needs something to hide behind."

"Are we hiding?"

"We're being discreet. Did you see the newspapers in the lobby? A three-day-old copy of the *Times-Herald* and a couple of sports magazines. I could have been naked on the front page of the *Washington Post* and still no one out here in Hicksville would know me."

"Blessed be the anonymous for they shall inherit the earth."

"Charlie, shut up and get your togs off."

Murder, it seemed, made Coky insatiable.

§111

Later, Postcoital

"Where are you living?"

"At home. I moved back in. That Tuesday. The night we killed Bob. Turned up with my vanity case, a dress over my arm and expressed wonder if not dismay that my husband was not there to greet me.

"In the morning I expressed some concern to the maid, but said not to worry. I'd booked that room at the Dreiser for two nights and hung out the DO NOT DISTURB sign as I left. I reckoned they'd find Bob's body sometime on Thursday morning. No such luck. Lazy buggers didn't check on him for another twenty-four hours, so I had no choice but to cover my arse. I called the cops on Friday morning and reported him missing. By Friday afternoon . . . well, you know. Shock, horror . . . blah de blah."

"Are we clear?"

"I think so. You wore gloves. I wiped down what I'd touched. If I were a cop I'd find the idea of a clean doorknob very suspicious, but I suppose by the time they arrived others had smeared their grubby hands everywhere . . . maid, concierge, what-have-you . . . so maybe not.

"I left a half-empty bottle of Hound Dog next to the bed. Bob's prints were all over it. I threw the bottle with the dope in it into the trash on the way home. And I scattered half a dozen Dilaudid onto the carpet. When they cut Bob open that's all they'd have found, whiskey and Dilaudid in a toxic quantity.

"It's all so bloody plausible, isn't it? Disgraced US senator kills himself after homosexual scandal. Our masters have what they wanted—disgraced, dead and denied. Poor Bob, did he really deserve that?"

"You tell me."

"Of course he fucking did."

§112

Later, Post-Second-Coital

"I was seen."

"What?"

"The chap on the desk at the Dreiser. Turns out he used to be the chap on the desk at the John Smith."

"How do you know this?"

"The Feds asked me, in my official capacity, to help them identify 'Felix Foster.'"

Charlie thought she'd never stop laughing, but when she finally did, she was smiling, rubbing her thumb gently at the corner of his mouth, wiping the ketchup off a child's face, darting into his lips with tiny kisses like the pecking of a sparrow.

"Oh, Charlie my love. It's over. You do see that, don't you?"

§113

Charlie was stumped as to how to engineer a return home. A posting he'd initially thought of in terms of weeks had turned into two and a half years.

For the next few weeks they changed hotels for every liaison. Each new alias stretched his imagination. He'd taken a risk hanging onto "Felix Foster" as long as he had, and in the last year he'd already run through Smith, Jones and Brown and Tom, Dick and Harry. If he'd had any skill at maths he might have worked out that the available permutations were rather limited permutations.

He'd been Wendell J. Spivey the night before. It was irresistible. He'd thrown in the *J* quite gratuitously. What self-respecting G-man did not have a middle initial? They'd gone as far as the suburbs of Baltimore to achieve anonymity and climax. It had been well past midnight when he had fallen into bed on P Street.

At seven in the morning, the phone rang.

"Major Leigh-Hunt?"

An English woman on a crackly line he took to be transatlantic. He'd not been addressed by his rank since God-knows-when.

"I have the general for you."

General? What general?

The second the man began to speak, the penny dropped. General Sir John Sinclair, the man who'd replaced Menzies as SIS chief last year. They'd never met, and a phone call from the chief? Unprecedented.

"Leigh-Hunt—time to pack. I need you back in the field."

"May I ask what field, sir?"

"Egypt. That bugger Nasser's throwing spanners in the works every day."

Well—he's been doing that since 1952. Only last month he'd banned political parties.

"I want you out there. Mohamed Naguib can't have much longer in office as president. Indeed, I wonder how much longer the man has on earth."

General Sinclair did not say "chop chop," but Charlie heard it anyway.

§114

The Mayflower Hotel

December 17, 1953

The last night had to be a good goodnight.

One calculated risk.

A night at the Mayflower. A hotel they had not visited since their first drink together in 1951.

They avoided the bar.

They arrived separately.

Coky let Charlie choose their name.

"We'll be Mr. and Mrs. Morgan Fillmore Smithers."

"Morgan? Really?"

"I'd love to be John Smith, the perfect co-respondent's name. But I've blown that one, so Smithers it is."

"And where might we be from?"

"I've given that a lot of thought. Mexican Hat, Utah."

"You just stuck a pin in a map, didn't you?"

§115

Afterwards.

The Veuve Clicquot bottle upended in the ice bucket.

"I'm not ready for this."

Coky lifted her head off his chest.

"Charlie-boy, we've . . . well, we've always known . . . well, I don't need to finish this sentence, do I?"

"Things are different. When we met, you were married."

"And now I'm not married because we murdered my husband, is that it?"

"Ouch. Ouch a thousand times."

"You surely aren't thinking we might marry?"

Charlie said nothing.

Coky rose up and thumped him on the chest.

"You bugger! You are, aren't you?"

"I haven't asked!"

Coky leapt off the bed, the top sheet swirled around her, leaving Charlie bollock-naked.

"You stupid, stupid, stupid, stupid—"

But Charlie was out of bed, arms wrapped around her, lips roaming up from her throat to kiss away the coursing tears.

"We can't, Charlie. You know we can't."

His face muffled by her hair.

"Why not?"

Coky gently prised him off, noses just touching now.

She spoke slowly.

"Because we've only survived by clarity and caution. If we marry . . . if we marry, we muddy everything. We attract the attention we have avoided for two years and we become . . . a liability. Either side might take us out. You do see that, don't you? And if the Americans catch us . . . do you think I want to die like Ethel Rosenberg?"

Her eyes on his.

"We could stop now," he said

"Stop what?"

"Stop being spies."

"And be Mr. and Mrs. Smithers forever? Charlie, we work for the KGB. We can't just apply for the Chiltern Hundreds. They won't give us a gold watch and membership of the bowls club."

"New identities? A new country?"

"Don't . . ."

"You have no mission here . . . no more Mockingbird."

"Please don't . . ."

§116

In the morning Coky sat fully dressed on the dressing table stool. Hat on, handbag at her feet.

Charlie stood by the bed, squeezing his suitcase closed.

The latches snapped to, he set it on the floor, looked at her across the infinity of the room, across dozens of hotels and countless naked afternoons of blissful adultery.

"What now?" he said simply, hoping he was keeping the desperation out of his voice.

"Well, we're hardly going to be pen pals, are we?" she replied, knowing full well she was also keeping it out of hers.

*1956–1965: An Interlude
The Ragged Sleeve Unravels
and
Maigret Goes to Moscow*

§117

The cricket on his shoulder had been telling Charlie for years that it couldn't last. He would have to be in a very miserable mood indeed not to ignore the irritating insect, so mostly he did.

He had survived the defection of Burgess and Maclean, there being bugger all to link him to them and, against the odds, he thought, he had received not a hint of suspicion or scrutiny as Kim Philby's star sank only to rise again. Last autumn some barrack-room lawyer had named Kim in the House of Commons as the "third man." Without evidence, the idiot had been forced to retract, the Foreign Secretary had issued a statement clearing Philby and, in between the two, Kim had had the balls to hold a press conference. This was unprecedented. Charlie would have given a month's salary to be a fly on the wall—he'd have given a week's just to be able to share the joke with Philby in some out-of-the-way pub. But there was nowhere in London that was out of the way enough. He could not imagine the circumstances in which he might encounter the man again. The *Observer* had made him their stringer in Beirut, which could only mean that strings had been pulled. If Charlie's time came, would anyone pull strings for him? Indeed they would, and did.

It was his own greed that betrayed him—less, far less, the role of double agent in the pay of both SIS and the KGB than the fiddles he was running on the side with Cobb and Cockerell. The cash-for-secrets, the "fibs that would hurt no one" had got first Cockerell and then Cobb killed. Hence it was not MI5 that brought suspicion and scrutiny to bear but Scotland Yard's Murder Squad, honest PC Plod, in the shape of his oldest friend, Frederick Troy.

"Bugger off."

"Eh?"

"That's all you can do. Bugger off. Follow Philby into the wilderness if you like, but resign from SIS now or so help me, Charlie, I will nick you."

"You wouldn't do that to me."

"I nick killers Charlie. You're a killer."

"Freddie, I never killed anyone. I even got through the last war without killing anyone. Please believe me."

"Of course. You had Norman Cobb do your killing for you."

"And who killed Cobb?"

Troy did not answer this.

Cobb was dead.

That was all that mattered.

"When you've disposed of Cobb's body, put in your papers to the head of SIS and look for a job. You are finished as a spy."

"I've already got rid of Cobb."

"Then you just have a letter to write to Dick White and you'll be free."

"Freddie . . ."

"Goodbye, Charlie."

"Freddie . . . it's been twenty-eight years . . ."

"We shall not meet again."

Of course they would.

§118

Charlie took his time. Troy put no pressure on him. Charlie never thought he would. All the same, he knew what he had to do. Before he resigned, or before he was pushed, he needed a job.

He called Troy's brother, Rod. Charlie was very fond of Rod. Thought him a guileless innocent, possibly only put on God's earth to be outwitted by his little brother, but by and large one of the good guys. He had none of Freddie's sneakiness or downright malevolence, was devoted to his wife and countless children, sat on the Opposition front bench . . . but, above all, he took an interest in the old family firm . . . books and magazines and newspapers.

"I need a job."

"Is something wrong, Charlie? I thought you were one of the shining lights of the FO."

"That's very sweet of you, Rod, but you know damn well I'm not and never was a diplomat."

"Of course, but one never utters it out loud. Mum's the word."

"Could you find me something? I don't mind what." (He minded very much.) *"East Fife Pictorial, Horse Hound and Moped, Pigs and Pigmen* . . . I dunno."

"Have you ever been a journalist, Charlie?"

"No. But how hard can it be?"

So it was that in the summer of 1957, more than nine months after Troy's "bugger off," having explained his resignation to Dick White with a simple "bored shitless," Charlie found himself Troy Newspapers' man in Brussels. A stringer for the near-defunct *American Week*. The explanation bothered him. It was an end too loose. A thread SIS could pull on in Timbuktu, Wagga Wagga or Brussels. Troy had forced his hand. He had not been under suspicion . . . he was 99 percent certain of that—Troy alone knew who and what he was, "the lived lie," as he had put it—at least not until his resignation, and that alone now guaranteed suspicion. Dick White had not believed his "bored shitless." Charlie had never thought he would. Even before he left London there were careless whispers that SIS had "discreetly asked for his resignation," and knowing this was the opposite of the truth helped not a bit. It was the twentieth-century equivalent of being branded.

"Hmm . . . Brussels. Not quite what I was expecting. Does anything ever happen there?"

And Rod had said, "That's for you to find out. That's what journalists do."

Troy had agreed to one last drink in a pub in St. Martin's Lane.

It was joyless, less the fond farewell than a silent reiteration of "bugger off."

"I mean . . . I ask you . . . Brussels?"

"Charlie," Troy replied. "Lick your wounds and count your blessings. Brussels is not Parkhurst or the Scrubs. Be grateful for a little anonymity."

Brussels was dull. Covering poultry shows in Scunthorpe might have been preferable, but he was out of sight and probably out of the minds that mattered back in London. Troy had kept his word. He had not ratted him out, although Charlie could not help feeling that Rod's choice of this dreary out-of-the-way posting was in some way motivated by his brother's sense of justice. To be anywhere but London was good. Rumour flared, rumour fizzled out like a damp banger on Bonfire Night—one single question in the Commons from a backbench Labour nonentity who didn't even have the balls to name him—just "yet another Intelligence Service agent." The denial was unequivocal, but came from a junior minister at the Foreign Office. Charlie had enough vanity to feel aggrieved that he did not merit a denial from the Foreign Secretary in person. There could be no clearer way for London to tell him he was second-rate. If this . . . whatever this was . . . ever blew up completely, it would be "Burgess, Maclean, Philby and . . . er . . . wotsisname." Troy was right: a touch of anonymity might be a blessing scarcely disguised.

Things livened up. After weeks that seemed like years in Brussels Charlie found himself transferred to Istanbul—the dope was plentiful and the women gorgeous—and he hoped this posting would last. He could settle here, but he doubted that he would be allowed to. Suez had changed everything. Istanbul was too far from what seemed to matter to the editors of *American Week*: the Levant, Israel . . . the canal, which was once again open to traffic.

Beirut could be, should be wonderful. A heady, immersive caravanserai of scent and colour. Even better dope than Istanbul, and women just as tempting. The crossroads of the world—well, one of them—but . . . but that bugger Philby was there. He'd been there the best part of a year by late 1957, doing for the *Observer* what Charlie was now being asked to do for *American Week*. Of course, Charlie, and anyone in the know, had seen this as a jumping-off point for Kim. He wouldn't stay, he'd cut and run—but he had stayed. The bugger simply hadn't moved on . . . and if MI5 still suspected Philby, they were also watching him, and if they were watching him they would watch those around him, even a nobody like Charlie, and it would be pathetic, absolutely bloody pathetic, to be caught in a net cast for someone else.

Charlie called Rod from Istanbul.

"Isn't there anywhere else I could go?"

"Charlie, less than six months ago you were telling me Brussels was dull. We give you a plum posting, a ripe slice of the exotic Orient, all figs and nutmeg, and you complain? I don't expect gratitude, but I do expect you to stop whinging. Now, while I have your attention, we already have a bloke in Beirut. Arthur Allis."

"Then why do you need me?"

"Because Allis is useless. You have fluent Arabic—"

"No, Rod, I get by in Arabic."

"Freddie told me you'd done a spell in Egypt."

"I did and I was slung out before I'd even mastered the past tense. I get by, but I am fluent in German and French and you're not suggesting Paris or Berlin, are you?"

"Allis hardly speaks a word of Arabic. But for the fact that he's only a few years off retirement and has a young family back in England by what must be at least his third wife, I would sack the lazy bugger."

"So I'm carrying Allis?"

§119

It was not as if Moscow left him alone. Everywhere he went someone would make contact. Twice in Brussels, three times in Istanbul and once more on a long weekend in Athens. An Ivan or a Yuri or a Vladimir. For all Charlie could remember, it was one bloke with half a dozen different hats following him around the hot and cold spots of Europe. He had nothing to give, and he kept saying so. But then, there was nothing they wanted, just the contact. As though he were on the reserve list for the second eleven at soccer. Forever the twelfth man at cricket. Not needed, but available. Just to let him know they still had him by the balls. He felt as though he had SMALL FRY tattooed on his forehead. He knew the British did not think enough of him to amount to a teaspoonful of concern. And Russia . . . for all their attention, their petty attention, was he killing time, treading water or just plain insignificant? Yesterday's man? Yesterday's spy?

$120

Charlie arrived in Beirut just in time for Christmas. And what was Christmas? Just another excuse to get drunk or stoned.

He'd passed through half a dozen times in his career (or was it just a job?)—mostly in summer, long days and balmy evenings, when he could sit out on the Raouche rocks with a bottle of chilled Chateau Kefraya Blanc and marvel at the blue beyond blue of the Mediterranean. The North Sea had nothing on this. The North Sea wasn't even blue, it was grey. And he would stay at the St. Georges Hotel on the Avenue des Français, a corniche . . . or was it an esplanade? He could never remember. Perhaps it was a promenade, but the word alone put him in mind of Clacton or Margate, and this was clearly neither, even though the St. Georges itself resembled an English multistorey car park with added balconies. It was an ugly brute of a building, but it stood on a promontory with the sea on three sides, and it was an unfortunate chap who got stuck with a room facing inland.

Much to his surprise Charlie discovered en route that he wasn't billeted in the St. Georges at all. He was down the street in the Basoul. His first reaction was "Tightwads," but that soon mellowed into an understanding of Rod Troy's rationale—everything, but everything, happened in the bar at the St. Georges. Secrets traded, lives and countries bought, sold and betrayed. A spy, even a retired (or was it merely disgraced?) spy needed to get away from it all. Philby, he knew, had taken an apartment rather than stay at the St. Georges, no doubt for the same reasons.

All the same, when he'd checked into the Basoul, scrubbed up, decided he needed a drink and ambled and over to the St. Georges for a swift tot or two, the first person he saw was Kim Philby. Or, to be precise, the first person who saw him was Kim Philby.

Philby immediately left the group he was with at their table and came over to the bar just as Charlie was choosing his whiskey.

"Laphroaig. A teaspoon of water. No ice. Absolutely no ice."

"What the hell are you doing here?"

"Delighted to see you too, Kim. What can I get you?"

"B-bugger that. Are you . . . ?"

"Spying on you, Kim? No. The irony of that would be fatal. I'd die laughing. I'm working. Just the same as you. Working."

"For who?"

"The Troys."

For more than a moment this seemed to baffle Philby.

"Troys? Which one, that big bugger in parliament or the lunatic copper?"

"I mean . . . to spell it out in words of one syllable . . . I work for the firm."

"You're a journalist?"

"Bingo. Now can I get you that drink?"

Philby might just be smiling. He stepped a few inches to his left and gestured back toward the table he'd been sitting at.

"You're his replacement?"

Charlie realised Philby meant the fat bloke sitting between a couple of handsome young Arabs.

"Is that Allis? If so, no. He's *Sunday Post*. I'm *American Week*. I have . . . hmm . . . more of a roving brief."

"Really? Make that another Laphroaig, would you?"

Charlie passed his untouched glass to Philby and gestured to the barman.

Philby knocked it back in one.

"We can't . . . we shouldn't . . . talk here. I work in the mornings. They let me have a desk in the lobby at the Normandy. Avoid it. Tomorrow, lunch at Lucullus. We can talk there."

§121

The real difference between a corniche and a promenade, Charlie readily concluded, was that on the prom in mid-December you ate greasy chips with mushy peas out of yesterday's *Daily Mirror* in a bus shelter and froze your bollocks off, whilst on a corniche you sat at a table in a rooftop restaurant in a pleasant sixty-seven degrees Fahrenheit while waiters in white jackets and bowties served you the best bouillabaisse on earth.

"This must be the last time," Philby said over lunch.

"Eh?"

"I mean the only time. Nothing p-personal . . ."

Charlie doubted that, and bit his tongue.

". . . b-but we really must avoid one another."

Prompted by his plate Charlie said, "Won't that look a bit fishy?"

"We can meet professionally, of course. But we should also keep our distance. Above all, we cannot look like a conspiracy."

"The British are watching you?"

"Of course they're watching me. Don't be so bloody naïve."

"Allis?"

"God no. The day comes when MI5 hire men as thick as Allis, we'll know we've won the Cold War. Doesn't matter who. It just demands c-caution."

"The other lot are watching me. Every so often some apparatchik shows up just to give me a prod. Bit like kicking the dog, really, just to see if it's still breathing."

"Then you prove my point. Let's give neither side cause for alarm."

"I am led to believe that Allis is a bit of an idle sod."

"He is. Those Arab chaps you saw last night do all the work. If it were left to Arthur, he'd never leave the bar. The younger one, Said Aburish, is Radio Free Europe's man here. Without him, Arthur wouldn't know what day it was."

"That suits me. I said it was a 'roving brief,' so I'll rove. If I can get him to surrender all the foreign assignments in exchange for covering Beirut from his seat in the bar . . . well, I'll be there more than I'm here with any luck, won't I?"

"Then to paraphrase our man in the Kremlin, I think you and I might achieve a peaceful coexistence."

"There is one thing," Charlie said after a prolonged, thoughtful pause with spoon in hand. "Can we ever go home again?"

"If I knew where home was, Charlie, I might be able to answer that."

§122

Being "there" rather than "here" was an arrangement that lasted more than five years—Syria, Kuwait, Iran, Iraq, Saudi Arabia, Jordan, once to Afghanistan and to Israel more times than he could count.

Charlie wasn't wholly certain what finally caused Philby to disappear early in 1963. He'd been in Aden and missed what drama there might have been. The unexpected return to Beirut of Nick Elliott, who'd been SIS station head a year or two back, could hardly be coincidental. Philby vanished in a blaze of publicity, his very own Indian rope trick—countless newspaper articles, questions in the Commons, a story that ran and ran. Only Christine Keeler would knock Philby off the top of the tabloid charts.

A few days later Charlie accepted the inevitable and followed. It might not have been inevitable, but a flying visit from the Foreign Office's number two (or was it three? Anyhow . . . a junior) in the shape of Tim Woodbridge MP could hardly be ignored. He liked Woodbridge, he felt sorry for him. It was almost as though he was a burden Woodbridge had to carry, as the poor sod had been stuck with defending him in the Commons—"yet another SIS officer"—for at least two sentences and ten words after his resignation in '57.

The visit lay somewhere between courtesy and accusation, but it was obvious no one wanted him back in the UK. It was "bugger off" in everything but words. A tip-off from Philby might have been nice, a personal touch, a simple warning, a note scribbled on a beer mat and left for him in the bar of the St. Georges or the Normandy—"You're next!"—but the man told him nothing.

Charlie left Beirut in a roaring silence, made his way to Athens, at which point the Russians had finally got their finger out and stuck him in a diplomatic "bag." And no one noticed. Not a headline, byline or sideline. It was little short of insulting. Philby was the "third man," speculation was rife about the fourth and fifth. Charlie didn't even make the top ten. He was what he believed popular-music journalists referred to as a "B side."

That winter, Philby had been welcomed to Moscow with something akin to hero status. A sumptuously furnished apartment—well, sumptuous by Soviet standards—£200 monthly salary, an offer to ship his furniture from London . . . even two of his favourite pipes were bought in a gentlemen's shop in the gentlemen's street (Jermyn Street) and sent over in the Russian diplomatic bag.

Charlie was in a hotel, and the KGB seemed to maintain half a dozen of them in Moscow as quasi-prisons, establishments he doubted merited a single star. The heating came and went, the plumbing rattled and groaned like a dying mammoth, the loo stank . . . there was no room service whatsoever and he had to all but beg for money. Thank God he'd never smoked a pipe.

One light shone on Charlie's low Moscow horizon. He had telegrammed Troy when he knew time was running out. He had pleaded with him to come to Beirut, strung out his last days to the fifty-ninth minute of the eleventh hour and, when he did not arrive, left him instructions and the paperwork to get into Russia. It was the least the Russians could do for him. They wanted him out, as much as the British seemed to, and the one card left to play was to refuse if they didn't grant him just one thing. So they did. He was somewhat surprised. They could have kidnapped him. They could have killed him. Perhaps he was still of some use after all?

Dazed and confused, clutching his three-day visa, Troy turned up in Moscow.

It was not reconciliation.

Charlie did not know what it was.

But at least he was here, at least he was speaking to him. Charlie had salvaged something from the colossal mess that was his relationship with England, a country he had sold down the Swannee, betrayed at every turn.

Troy.

He still had Troy.

He might never see Mummy again, but he still had Troy.

"Explain to her, won't you?"

"She told me all this was inevitable. Even before it happened."

"Well . . . yes. She told me that a few times too. Not that she knew everything."

"But she knew you were working some kind of fiddle?"

"Oh Freddie, what is life without a fiddle? Without a bit on the side? Answer: boring. Isn't it why you became a copper? It was the most interesting thing on offer?"

Troy said nothing.

"No," said Charlie. "I didn't think you'd answer that. When I say 'explain,' you don't need to go into too much detail. She thought I was just a bit dodgy. A vaguely crooked crook. To find out I am an honest spy must have been shocking."

§123

And when Troy left, Charlie wept buckets, entirely for himself, and cried aloud to heaven, "What the fuck have I done?"

And then he thought of his mother, Judy—alone in England, broke and lonely, with not a clue as to his whereabouts until Troy got back and told her. So he wept the more, entirely for himself—"What the fuck have I done?"

§124

The debrief was mandatory—and perfunctory, as though they knew in advance any answer he might give and considered that he had no secrets.

He hadn't.

It brought home his insignificance.

A bleak midwinter afternoon. Snow falling upon impacted snow. A brief slip-sliding walk from his hotel, with the prospect of a twisted ankle or a broken leg never far from mind.

He didn't have the right shoes for Moscow.

He didn't have the right anything for Moscow.

A windowless "meeting" room at the Lubyanka, in Dzerzhinsky Square. They might at least turn up the heating.

No different from the back room in any English nick, where he had sat occasionally while some thick plod from Special Branch managed to mangle all he'd been told, a powerless observer aching for the moment when the bloke from Five would find his voice and hit the suspect with "I'm MI5. You're in bigger trouble than you imagine."

Until that moment it was de rigueur to let the plod handle it and not play your hand too soon. And he never had a hand to play unless the silly sod cracked and confessed and Six's brief kicked in: "Turn them if possible." Most were not worth turning. The also-rans, the three-legged nags of espionage. Was that what he was now?

The Russians sent no plod. They sent a uniformed KGB captain. He'd put her in her early forties. Still a looker, though some pain had etched itself into her face and dimmed the warmth he thought might be natural in her eyes.

They spoke in German, Charlie having no Russian, his interrogator seemingly little English. Odd—but then, they surely knew everything about him, from his grasp of foreign languages to the size of his leaky shoes.

She introduced herself as "Magda Ewald."

"So you *are* German?"

"Austrian. May we get on? I haven't got all day."

Charlie was certain she had got all day, and he'd never known an interrogation, which this surely was, to be over in a single day.

She asked about his time in Washington, but every question he answered that led logically to a follow-up question had no follow-up. Captain Ewald pressed on, relentless yet cursory.

A dozen banal questions.

A dozen predictable answers.

Then she said, "Your Washington contact is dead."

And it was as if she'd hit him in the belly with a cricket bat.

"Er . . . er . . . I didn't know that."

"Do you have any suspicions?"

"What? That the Americans killed her?"

Magda flipped through her notebook.

Stabbed at a page with her chewed-up pencil.

His heart rose to his throat and stuck there.

"Not her. Him. Ignatz . . . Ignatz Ferber."

"Farber," said Charlie scarce above a whisper.

"Ah yes. Farber. Well?"

"Magda—may I call you Magda?"

"Of course."

"Magda, Ignatz was an old man. He was not in good health. He coughed all over his books, he spat blood on the sidewalk and cursed the God of the Jews under his breath twenty times a day. He was . . . a broken man. Broken by suffering. He survived Auschwitz."

"So did I."

Three words dropped like bombs, but she moved on even before the ripples had fanned out, and whatever he might have said next never surfaced.

"Charlotte Redmaine?"

"I can't hear a question there, Magda."

"You've heard from her since you left Washington?"

"No. I haven't. Not in ten years. Sentimental fool that I am, I wish I had. Do you know where she is, what has become of her?"

Madga would not rise to the bait. Head down over her notes. A rapid squiggle with the chewed-up pencil. He could even see her teeth marks on the blunt end as she waved it, thinking without speaking.

"We are done, Mr. Leaf-Hunt."

She closed her notebook.

Stood up.

He could not but smile at her mangling of his surname.

"If we are done, do we need surnames?"

"Should I call you Charles?"

"Charlie."

"Charrrrlie . . . We are done with questions. I shall make my report. Meanwhile, I thought you might like to buy me a drink at the Metropol bar."

He thought two things—first, that the interrogation probably wasn't over, it had merely changed gear and location; second, that she might be chatting him up.

Either way he felt his insignificance sink as his sap rose.

"Love to—but you'll have to pay. I have twenty-five kopecks. That wouldn't buy the lemon twist in a martini."

Never in forty years of cherchez-la had he asked a woman to pay. It felt so odd to have to ask. Almost a liberation.

$125

She walked with ten times the confidence he could muster. The little furry boots, plonking down with a careless certainty while he struggled to stay upright in his size-twelve leather-soled beetle-crushers. His last pair of bespoke Lobbs, now to be ruined by Russian snow and encrusted salt.

He'd passed the Metropol on his way to the nick. It was scarcely a block away. A glance, more than a glance . . . an envious if fleeting thought. Who was it who said the Metropol was the only hotel in Moscow in which the plumbing actually worked? John Reed? Was it as long ago as that?

It had been tempting to nip in and take a peek. It had been tempting to nip in and take a piss just to check out the plumbing. Just to be able to say, "I have seen the crapper and it works." He hadn't. He hadn't dared be late for the Lubyanka. Manners did not permit. A gentleman would no more be late for the Lubyanka than he'd be late for Alcatraz or Pentonville. But when Magda asked him if he wanted a drink at the bar, it was though she had read his mind.

The lobby was sumptuous—overwhelming, gaudy, tasteless. A Soviet endorsement of imperial splendour. A Bolshevik message to all those hifalutin visitors—the H. G. Wellses and the Lincoln Steffenses of this world—that the Soviet Union was not all austerity and functionality—it could do chandeliers and palm trees in pots and gold leaf and utterly hideous statues with the best of them.

Kitschier than thou.

All the same . . .

"It's a bit different."

"From?"

"The place you people have me in. Part hotel, part prison."

"No, it's all prison, but . . . you're staying where, exactly?"

"I was at the Moskva the first week—pretty tolerable—but your chaps moved me to the Pugachev—which isn't."

"Oh—it's a hole, isn't it?"

"I had to ask the floor attendant for the bath plug on my first day. It came with a chain long enough to bind Jacob Marley and a wooden number plate which floats in the bath. That alone would qualify the Pugachev as a hole. What is it about bath plugs?"

"I haven't the faintest idea, but it's the same everywhere."

"All the Western capitalists come to Moscow just to steal bath plugs?"

"That about sums it up, yes."

"I don't suppose you could get me in here."

"You suppose right, and you'd still have to ask for the plug. Look, find a table upstairs. Out of the melee. I'll order some demented cow's milk and find you."

"Demented cow's milk?"

"Slang for vodka."

"Make mine red top."

"It's all red top, you're in Moscow."

Upstairs was a low mezzanine, not exactly intimate but a sharp, quiet contrast to the cavernous dining room below, which put him in mind of Grand Central Station. The presence of a steam train would have added little to the hubbub. At seven o'clock of a Friday evening it was full. The mezzanine was not. He took a table set into one of the half-moon windows looking out across Sverdlov Square.

Snowflakes were falling. Floating down past the window as big as silver half dollars. You could think they were dancing, if you had a romantic twist of mind—if you forgot that this was Moscow, not Paris. If this were 1945, not 1963, and the woman in uniform were a Wren, not an officer of the world's most notorious police force.

Still . . . "red top." She'd made a joke.

Magda suddenly appeared in the chair opposite. He'd been daydreaming, carried away on a snowflake.

A waiter silently set two glasses of vodka and a plate of nibbly things in front of them and vanished.

"Zakuski," she said.

"Dumplings," he replied.

"No. So much more than that. Do you really know nothing of the country you have served so long? Drink, eat, learn. Выпить."

"Down the hatch?"

She knocked back her shot in one.

"Hmm," she replied after a couple of deep breaths. "More like 'into the valley.'"

Charlie took the hint: "Rode the six hundred."

And he downed his.

Magda raised an eyebrow.

"Tennyson," he said. "Does no one ever sip this stuff?"

"No. You knock it back in one or be thought a sissy. It's a charochka. A cup, literally. Of course, you really should raise the cup and make a toast first."

"To what?"

"Peace, friendship and understanding would be customary . . . if there's a foreigner at the table, that is. And we both are."

"That's . . . anodyne."

"No, it's 'safe.'"

"How about . . . King and Comintern? Absent apparatchiks? Gulags and gumboots?"

Magda shrugged this off.

"Not funny. Not funny at all. If you learn one thing today, Charlie, let it be that Russians hate to think they are being laughed at. Now . . . vodka. Vodka is a lethal custom, but not one we can ignore. It kills God-knows-how-many Russians every year, and their life expectancy is not great to begin with, but . . . rarely does a Russian drink without eating."

Charlie eyed the plateful of nibbles. A small mountain of gherkins, beets, salami, pirozhki and black bread—even a spoonful or two of red caviar in a chilled shot glass.

"I feel sorry for all the gherkins in this world," he said. "Nobody loves them. Always left on the side plate of life."

"I cannot pretend to understand that, but you eat a zakuska after every drink. One for one. Toast, drink, eat. That is the Russian way."

"In which case," Charlie said, "the chap might have left the bottle."

§126

"Are you sure you can't get me in here?"

"I'm breaking rules bringing you here as it is, probably upsetting both the tourists and our foreign exchange, but short of General Zolotukhina walking in, no one here will have the nerve to argue with me."

"Oh, she's a general now?"

"You hadn't heard?"

"No one's told me anything since 1956."

"Promoted on the retirement of Krasnaya last year."

"We should drink a toast to living legends of the KGB."

"You mean I should buy another round?"

"How quickly you catch on, Magda."

"You won't be at the Pugachev long. Honestly, you won't. They'll find you an apartment."

"They? Don't you mean *we*?"

"Confusing, isn't it? *You* will be found an apartment. But I can't promise you'll like it any more than the hotel. But—it will be affordable."

"Affordable? You mean on my pension?"

She was shaking her head now, pulling herself sharply together.

"There is no pension, Charlie."

"What? Hasn't Philby got one?"

"I can't answer that. But you haven't. You're simply not a big enough fish."

"Then what's the miserable pittance the old woman on duty on my floor at the Pugachev hands me each week?"

"You mean the *dezhurnaya*?"

"The plug woman, the old bat at the desk. Seems to be one on each floor. Face like vinegar, bundle of keys just like the housekeeper in *The Cherry Orchard.* I think she actually sleeps at her desk. At first I thought she was there to stop me bringing women back to my room, but every Thursday she gives me an envelope of cash."

"Oh, she's most certainly there to prevent any goings-on . . . any sex . . . Charlie, there haven't been any goings-on, I hope?"

"Haven't been that lucky."

"Good. However . . . the money . . . the money is your unemploy-ment benefit."

"What? You mean I'm on the fucking dole?"

"Yes."

"After all I've done for Mother Russia, I'm on the dole? All those years of service? If I'd worked in a factory, I'd get a pension, a card signed by all my mates and a gold watch or a ship in a bottle . . . or . . ."

"Ship in a bottle?"

"It's very English."

So saying, he pushed his empty glass towards her.

"Your round, you said far too long ago. Fine, be English. Get 'em in. And no more neat vodka. Ask for . . ."

Magda had a precise memory, it seemed.

She went down to the bar, placed her order, resumed her seat and after an awkward couple of moments a waiter appeared with martini twosomes that Charlie could not fault. The recipe followed to the letter.

"Please don't be angry about the pension," she said.

"I'm not. I'm simply disappointed. I think I exhausted anger sometime back in the mid-fifties."

"Hmm."

"Hmm what?"

"The mid-fifties. When you resigned from MI6?"

"More or less."

"That, more or less, is why you might have to earn that pension all over again."

"Because I resigned?"

"Because of all the rackets you were running."

Charlie felt mentally winded.

Said nothing.

Stared back at her.

Feeling naked.

"You think we didn't know?"

Charlie could think of nothing to say and so said nothing.

Magda said, "No one will ask you to repay all the money you cheated us out of. But 'we and they,' the whosoever of the USSR, won't be paying you a pension. On the other hand there has been no talk of punishment.

If 'we and they' were going to put you up against the wall and shoot you, 'we and they' would have done it by now. You get to live, Charlie."

"How . . . am I supposed to *live*?"

"Simple. You're going to have to get a job."

She was smiling now.

Smiling across the top of her twosome, to which she had taken like a duck to water.

He took the smile to mean she was back in off-duty mode. He could, he knew, have a bit of a thing about a woman in uniform—he was not immune to the clichés of sex—but the KGB uniform was about as sexy as a tattersall shirt, corduroy trousers and wellies caked in pig shit. Even those women who gave out parking tickets in London had more attractive uniforms.

"I've never been on the dole before," he said. "But on the other hand I've never really had what most people would think of as a job . . . MI6 didn't feel like a job. Reporting was a job, but I never had to clock in or out. I was . . . my own man."

"You still are. And we don't waste talent. You won't be bolting on tractor wheels in a factory in Volgograd. There won't be a pension, but you'll be back on our payroll, so you'll receive a modest wage and from time to time we may call on your services—as we might with all your kind."

"Kind?"

"You know what I mean. Don't get huffy. But—you will need a proper job. My role is to help you with that."

"What? You'll buy me the train ticket to Stalingrad?"

"Volgograd! Believe me, that is not going to happen. Stop behaving like a petulant schoolboy."

She reached into her shoulder bag.

Pushed a thick hardback book across the table to him—a flimsy paper dust jacket depicting a terrifying man in ankle irons, a terrified boy and, superimposed in ghostly transparency, the silhouette of a beautiful woman; an image that seemed to have nothing to do with either the man or the boy.

Большие Надежды
Чарльз Диккенс

"Do you know what this is?"

"*The Official Soviet Manual of Two-Stroke Engine Repair*?"

"*Great Expectations* by your English writer Charles Dickens."

Ah—Magwitch, Pip and wotsername.

"How very apt."

"Now—how would you feel about working in publishing?"

"Magda, as you will be well aware by now, I couldn't even translate the bar menu, but—"

"People's Publishers are looking for readers, not translators. You would read and recommend suitable books to be translated . . . from English, from German—"

"—but I am a very quick learner!"

She eyed him, still smiling her twosome smile, head tilted slightly as though trying to work out if he was joking.

Then she glanced at her watch and said, "It's not so late. Are you ready for round three?"

"Ah, Magda. We'll make an Englishman of you yet."

He didn't think it was the funniest thing he'd ever said, but Magda spluttered with laughter. And from spluttering to open-mouthed, tearful hoots. Charlie was put in mind of that moment in *Ninotchka* when Melvyn Douglas falls off his chair and Greta Garbo, the po-faced Communist until now, erupts in un-Soviet guffaws and lights up as never before—the film had been reviewed with the headline GARBO LAUGHS. Magda laughed. The light in her eyes came on, the shining glint of woman warmth inside the armour-plated apparatchik. He wondered how long it had been dimmed.

§127

The following Monday Charlie reported to the offices of People's Publishers at 3 Темнаяиубогая Аллея in the Khamovniki, to meet Grigory Gerasimovich Gogolin, a man proud to show off his English, which, Charlie conceded, was cracked but far from broken.

"Balls ache?"

Charlie gave it some thought. Several answers occurred to him, ranging from "none of your business" and "not right now" to "I should be so lucky."

He hoped for some clarification.

Perhaps the raised eyebrow had said more than words could. Grigory Gerasimovich shoved a small mountain of papers aside to reveal a book—just one of perhaps a couple of thousand that littered the room on shelves or simply in piles on the floor. It was a frayed copy of a nineteenth-century novel, *Le Cousin Pons* by Honoré de Balzac, or, as Grigory Gerasimovich would have it, "Balls ache."

"Are you asking me if I've read it?"

"Да."

"And whether you should have it translated?"

"Да."

"Then the answer is no."

"Already have we the *Cousine Bette.*"

"This book isn't quite in that league."

"What would you recommend by this man?"

Charlie gave it some thought. Grigory Gerasimovich had come at him from left field. It had not occurred to him that a writer of what might be considered the epitome of bourgeois fiction might have any appeal to the people or their publisher.

"*Illusions perdues* and *Splendeurs et misères des courtisanes.*"

Grigory Gerasimovich spun in his chair and threw up a cloud of dust searching on the bottom shelf behind his desk.

"Have only one," he said at last.

And he set a very old, very dirty copy of *Illusions perdues* on the desk.

"So sorry, have nothing newer. Is very . . . how say? Grubby?"

He smiled at his own success with the colloquial. "Да, grubby."

"It's OK. I've read it several times. You should add it to your catalogue."

Grigory Gerasimovich gently slid the book towards Charlie.

"Then you read again. Is what we pay you for."

This struck Charlie as wholly unnecessary but hardly a chore.

He opened the "grubby" book.

An 1843 one-volume first edition from Charles Furne et Cie, Paris, signed and dedicated by the author, "*à Monsieur Laurent-Jan.*"

He had only a vague idea what it might be worth, but he'd take a guess at £10,000.

"OK," he said, hoping Grigory Gerasimovich would never ask for it back and that somewhere in Moscow there might be a deeply dodgy book dealer who'd pay cash.

§128

A week later Charlie was moved from the Pugachev to an apartment in Krovyanayakolbasa Lane in the heart the Arbat district, halfway between the Smolenskaya metro station and the Arbatskaya—walking distance from just about anywhere in central Moscow.

Magda handed him a key and a hand-drawn map.

"Try not to get lost, Charlie."

"Well, if I do I'm sure you'll have a man on my tail who can set me straight."

"You're not being followed. I don't have the manpower for that."

"If I were in your position, Magda, I'd keep me guessing."

"Quite so. Perhaps I'm lying. You'll just have to keep looking over your shoulder, won't you?"

It was the first of many instances when the value of his nonentity would prove positive. It was hardly a get-out-of-jail-free card, but it was handy to have it.

The apartment block in Krovyanayakolbasa Lane, or, to be precise, in an alley *off* Krovyanayakolbasa Lane, had seen better days, but that was probably true of any street in Moscow. Magda said most of the Arbat had been utterly destroyed in the fire of 1812 and had risen, fallen, risen again and so on countless times, moving in and out of fashion, but now the street was firmly lodged in an era when fashion was meaningless.

A many-layered babushka was sweeping snow off the front step with a birch besom.

Charlie greeted her with "Прекрасное утро, товарищ."

A wonderful morning, comrade. A phrase he had memorised especially for an occasion like this.

The temperature was below zero or he would have doffed his hat to the old bat. Doffing one's hat might be suicidal. He had bought a fur hat on his second day in Moscow. On the first, almost everyone he passed had stared at him. Hatless in Moscow in winter—tantamount to madness.

She scowled at him, muttered what in all probability was Russian for "bugger off." But then again, Magda had warned him—manners were bourgeois, "please" and "thank you" counted for nothing and "bugger off" was the true mark of the revolutionary.

Once inside, his heart sank—he had hopped from the frying pan to another frying pan, a smelly, dirty hole of a room about twelve feet by twelve with a galley kitchen off to one side and a bathroom to the other, with a brown-stained, scum-rimed bath in which anyone under five foot three might just about manage to feel comfortable.

What the fuck have I done?

The bathroom also had a full-length mirror. After passing the evening consoling himself with a bottle of vodka, and needing to piss, he caught sight of himself in the mirror—stripped to shirtsleeves in the steam-powered heat of the room, braces dangling, flies gaping—and counted his chins. Troy had stared at him at Sheremetyeva a few weeks ago, an age ago, and Charlie had wondered what he'd seen. Now he could see for himself. Had he been blind or blind and stupid? Here he was . . . fat, red-nosed and pushing fifty. "Seedy" was the word.

What the fuck have I done?

But . . . but . . . Magda Ewald had flirted with him at the Metropol. Hadn't she? What had she seen? There might be hope for him yet.

He toyed with the idea of tipping the rest of the vodka down the sink but put it in a cupboard instead.

About three in the morning he slipped out of bed and poured it away. There might be hope for him yet.

§129

It is a given that in a totalitarian state everyone is on the fiddle. Charlie was disappointed, and at that mostly in himself, that he, a man with a City and Guilds apprenticeship in espionage behind him, could not find a deeply dodgy book dealer in a city that overflowed with bookshops and readers.

Everyone in Moscow read. On trams, in parks, in cafés, in Comrade Khrushchev's magnificent, mind-numbing metro.

Gorkovo, Moscow's Oxford Street—or perhaps a bit more upmarket, so . . . Regent Street—seemed to be lined with secondhand bookshops.

The first shop he went in was so crowded that he felt he could not attempt any kind of negotiation without attracting attention.

In the second, a uniformed militiaman stood reading a lurid-looking paperback right by the counter. It was probably his lunch break, but when was a copper ever off duty?

In England a secondhand book shop would resemble Grigory Gerasimovich's office. Dirty, dark and dusty with an ineradicable air of damp and decay. You could smell paper crumbling. You could feel the impermanence of the word, letters cascading into dust. Moscow, it seemed, had nothing like that.

Moscow also seemed to have no foreign-language bookshops, and it was more by luck than diligence that Charlie came across the sole example—a French-language bookshop. Why the French were allowed a shop and the English and the Germans were not might be baffling, but it mattered not a damn, and it was here that the muse snagged him. He'd mail the first edition to his mother.

He bought a modern Livres de Poche edition of *Illusions perdues*, and after a suitable interval in which he might plausibly have read the book, handed it to Grigory Gerasimovich with "Sorry, I left the old one on a tram."

Grigory Gerasimovich was delighted.

"So clean, so shiny."

He ran his thumb across the cover with childish glee.

"See? Shiny."

Charlie momentarily recalled a wonderfully cynical history teacher who had blithely told a class of thirteen-year-old boys, himself and Troy included, that the British Empire had been won not with gunboats and regiments but with trinkets and baubles—the shinier the better.

How disappointing to realise it was still true.

§130

Brevity was best, he decided.

A single folded note tucked inside the book:

`Mummy, I hope this is something you can share`
`with Uncle Jim.`

And a plain "Charlie" signature.

He had parroted enough Russian to cope with the customs form and the international post office on Komsomolskaya Square. He stated the value of the book as fifty kopecks.

"Откройте," said the woman behind the counter. Open it.

He was ready for that.

He'd no idea of the legality of his posting the book, any book—but he'd bet five bob the Russians had all sorts of rules about anything that might be dubbed "antique."

She looked at it.

She opened it

The date, thank God, was in Latin—MDCCCXLIII.

The title, obviously, in French.

Charlie didn't think she recognised what either language was, and that appeared to kill her interest and to work in his favour.

"OK," she said, in universal English.

Then she sealed up the package with gummed brown tape and took his money.

So far, so very good.

§131

Two months later he received a reply.

Judy had got the message.

An only child of a largely single mother, Charlie had few secrets from Judy—in fact they revelled in shared secrets even to a love of codes and ciphers and half-buried clues, a love they'd carried from the nursery, all through his time at school and Cambridge, to the present day.

Judy had got the message.

`Dear Charlie . . .`

For much of her life, and all of Charlie's childhood, Judy had been dependent on the kindness not of strangers but of bank managers, and her first rule was get to know them, make them less of a stranger, make a friend of them, get them to see your predicament—always "temporary, of course"—get away from "Mr. Brown" and "Mrs. Leigh-Hunt" and onto first-name terms.

The first bank manager after Charlie's dad had done a runner was Jim—Jim from Willams Deacon's. His surname didn't matter. Charlie was instructed to call him "Uncle Jim," and whilst there had been upwards of a dozen successive bank managers, holding Judy's purse strings much as she held their heart strings, while she ran the obstacle race of genteel poverty from the District Bank to Moffatt, Marriott and Hay's, they were all known to Charlie as "Uncle Jim."

He wondered who the present "Uncle Jim" might be. She'd wooed all of them, and he would guess she'd fucked half of them—not wholly without pleasure . . . there'd been Denis somebody-or-other from the National Provincial when he was about twenty who'd really stolen her heart as effectively as she stole his money—but she was sixty-nine now . . . how much sexual magic could she conjure up?

He read on:

`You were a rotter to leave me in the lurch`
`like that. I can think of a thousand reasons—a`

```
thousand reasons times twelve—why I should
never speak to you again. But I'm your mother
and mummies are forever.
     Sorry not to have written sooner. A mad dash
to Paris.
     But honestly, Charlie, I don't think you need
to worry about Mummy and Uncle Jim anymore.
```

So she'd got twelve grand for the book. More than he'd dared hope for. But the old bat nipping over to Paris, where the book was worth much more than in London, was a brainwave. He wondered what provenance she'd come up with for something so valuable. "Found it in the attic"? Where was it now? In the window of one of those exquisite little bookshops down by the Seine, or in the Bibliothèque Nationale being pored over by librarians in white gloves?

No matter. Twelve grand was twelve grand. What did the average bloke earn in England? Five hundred a year? A thousand? Very few would be on two grand . . . but Judy Leigh-Hunt was neither average nor a bloke. Twelve grand might keep Judy for five years or five months. Or, heaven forfend, five minutes.

§132

August 1963

Guy Burgess was dying. A long-overdue final act. Almost anyone who knew him had expected the curtain to fall years ago and end a tragicomedy of entertaining abuse and self-abuse.

Charlie had always liked the man, even though the excesses in which Guy had indulged had meant keeping a safe distance. His line to Philby on his first day in Washington all those years ago—"I've avoided Guy since Cambridge"—was in part true and in part not. He'd seen more of Guy than he'd admitted to in the years just after the war. Charlie, as a field agent, was often "in the field," but when they were both in London they'd meet. Not enough to attract attention. Once, perhaps twice a year. And if he'd seen nothing of him in Moscow . . . well, that was down to not alarming Magda and whichever apparatchiks worked for her, and down to the poor state of Guy's health.

By August Guy was in hospital.

Charlie knew the decent thing was to visit.

Charlie knew the sensible thing was not to hide this from Magda.

They met in the bar of the Metropol for martini twosomes. He hadn't set eyes on her for months. Nor had he spotted anyone who might be doing her footslogging for her. He was benignly neglected. He'd prefer to be benignly attended to, but . . .

"So—he was your friend?"

"More of an acquaintance, but . . ."

"Then you should go. You may well be the only Englishman in Moscow who can."

"Philby?"

"I doubt he would go. That English phrase you taught me is useful here—'covering his arse.'"

"You mean your lot won't let him go."

Magda said nothing to this.

§133

Burgess was in the Botkin Hospital on Botkinsky Proyezd, a couple of miles from the city centre. It being a fine summer's day, Charlie walked, glad of the opportunity for exercise. He'd lost ten pounds in the last two months and was finding the bathroom mirror to be a better friend.

Burgess looked dreadful. Fags and booze had taken their toll. A man scarcely older than he was himself, Burgess was the writing on the wall for Charlie, his portrait in the attic.

"Where have they got you?" Burgess asked.

"I'm in a miserable fourth-floor flat in the Arbat."

"Miserable? Really? Do you share a kitchen?"

"No. But it stinks of rancid lard."

"Everything in Moscow smells of something. Some of it far worse than lard. Mostly carbolic soap and stale piss. Speaking of which, do you share a bathroom or a lav?"

"No."

"Cockroaches?"

"No."

"Lino or carpet?"

"A sort of raggy Afghan thing."

"Do you have to step over drunks to get to your own front door?"

"The odd one, yes."

"Does anyone piss in your teapot?"

"What? I mean no. Of course not."

"Then stop complaining. You're living at a far higher standard than the average Muscovite in a kommunalka. Communal living is prescription chaos pretending to be home. In fact, you're living in one of the posh districts. Although it's a penny to a quid the KGB own the block you're in."

"The furniture's made of plywood."

"Oh dearie, dearie me. There must be another Soviet shortage . . . after wheat and barley, perhaps it's Chippendale furniture this time? Charlie, consider yourself lucky it's just the furniture that's made of plywood, not the walls . . . or you'd be listening to your neighbours fart, fuck and kill one another. Did you never see *Ninotchka*? The bit where Garbo gets back to Moscow? Living in a flat where the walls aren't walls, they're curtains, and the only privacy is between yer lug'oles? Amazing that Hollywood got that right."

"OK. I take your point."

"And, matter o'fact, they let me ship some of my furniture out here. I say 'they' . . . I suppose I mean the British let me, the Russians don't give a damn. You might as well ask. Nothing to lose. As I recall you had a sweet little house off the King's Road, didn't you?"

"I gave it to my mother a while back. Call it a tactical move."

"You may not always be in the Arbat, of course. They moved me out to Novodevichy, near the nobs' cemetery. I have me books, me harmonium. A proper little home from home if I had the faintest idea what and where home was."

A sudden pause. Charlie could all but hear the cogs turning in Burgess's mind.

"I don't suppose they got you a dacha?"

"They haven't got me anything worth a mention. It's as though they don't trust me."

"Of course they don't fucking trust you! But at least you're in Moscow. Maclean and I spent over three years in Kuibyshev. You know where that is? I bet you don't. East of Stalingrad. In Uzbekiwotsit. Imagine a Russian Stoke-on-Trent. That should do. However . . . summer in Moscow? Not bloody likely. There are only about two weeks in a year when Moscow is habitable. Either too cold or too damn hot. But I can help with that."

Burgess pulled open his bedside drawer and handed Charlie a large key on a wooden fob—the number 33 crudely burnt in with the tip of a poker.

"My dacha, out in Peredelkino. I'd be there now but for you-know-what. If I pop me clogs, make use of it. You must have realised by now that Moscow absolutely stinks in summer. Of course, the Russians may reassign it, but Soviet paperwork grinds slower than the mills of God so that could take about two years. I'll scribble you a note for Doris."

"Doris?"

"My housekeeper. Thoroughly reliable woman. She'll tell you where all the microphones are hidden. Not much English, but she understands 'gin,' 'scotch' and 'we're out of bog roll.' All the basics. And whatever you get up to, she won't be the one to shop you."

Burgess opened the drawer in his bedside cabinet again, rummaged and wrapped his hand around something small.

"Closer, Charlie. I've been saving this for you."

Charlie leaned in and found that Burgess had pinned a badge to his lapel with a faster gesture than he'd have thought him capable of.

"New boys start here."

Charlie turned his lapel and tugged at the cloth see what it was.

An enamelled, red, five-pointed star. In the middle was an engraved face, some kid or other.

"Who's the little Soviet angel?"

"That is—or is supposed to be—Volodya, the young Vladimir Ilych Ulyanov. You are now officially a member of the Little Octobrists."

"Little Octobrists? Like the Ovaltineys? You're taking the piss."

"Whenever possible, yes. 'Little Octobrists have lots of fun, they draw, they sing, they dance, they read—a very happy life they lead.'"

"What am I to say? 'Dib dib dib'?"

This set Burgess laughing, the laughing gave way to a fit of coughing, and when that had stopped he said, "You might as well enjoy Russia, Charlie. You've no other choice."

§134

Two weeks later, at the end of August, Burgess's liver, having been unfailingly tolerant of his abuse for years, finally despaired of him and left the stage. No curtain calls.

Three days after the cremation at Donskoi—marked by the absence of Philby and the presence of Maclean, who had shaken the hands of departing mourners after the manner of an English parson yet had failed to recognise Charlie—on a sunny September Saturday Charlie picked up the key Burgess had given him, packed an overnight bag and caught a train from the Kievsky Station—a Byzantine monstrosity that would dwarf St. Pancras—out to Peredelkino, about an hour southwest of the city.

Russian railways, in this instance, had followed an old English tradition—Peredelkino station wasn't actually in Peredelkino, no more than Bodmin Road was in Bodmin; it stopped two or three miles short of the village, but, according to the ancient Baedeker he had pinched from Grigory Gerasimovich's office, it was a perfectly pleasant walk.

His first reaction to seeing the village was unfortunate. It touched a memory and in so doing touched a nerve. When he was about thirteen, for reasons Charlie had long forgotten, for reasons his mother might have had at the time, he and Judy had spent a mercifully short weekend at Jaywick Sands on the east coast of England, somewhere near Colchester or Ipswich. It had probably involved another "uncle/ dad"—mostly Charlie had chosen to forget the individual uncles/dads and let them merge into one collectively unattractive figure, usually possessed of a good war record, a blue blazer, a cravat, a packet of Players Navy Cut and a couple of half crowns in bribe money. The better ones drove sports cars with dickey seats—dirty weekends with a boy in the boot, as Charlie saw it.

They arrived late and departed early, without uncle/dad and by train, but not before the true awfulness of a modern, made-to-order shanty town had had its impact. All the buildings were just one storey, clapboard walls and corrugated, rusting roofs. If paint could peel, it had peeled. If steel could rust, it had rusted.

He restrained judgement, against the demands Peredelkino was making on such judgement with its scattering of single-storey wooden houses and its peeling paint. The houses weren't so bad, perhaps they were at the stage where decay invoked charm before it induced disgust. And each house had a garden, and some of the gardens were well tended. And there were tree-lined lanes and birdsong, of which Jaywick had had neither except for the depressing, cacophonous racket made by flocks of gulls coming off the North Sea.

He walked on. The fickle gods of the USSR had added a second storey here and there, and standing in front of one of the two-storey models— white paint peeling to reveal another generation's green beneath, topped off by a verdigris copper roof—he looked at the key fob in his hand and realised that this was Burgess's dacha. In the common vernacular, Guy had "done well for himself."

There were no guards—Burgess had warned him there were never less than two and often four, "all watching me, which is to say watching paint dry," doubtless reassigned when Burgess died—but Doris appeared on the doorstep almost at once.

He handed her the "scribbled note."

"Вы—Чарли?"

That was simple enough.

"Yes. I'm Charlie."

"Тогда пришло время пить чай."

Indeed, in Russia when was it not time for tea—albeit stewed to glue in a samovar?

§135

On the floor in Guy's study—Charlie could not quite think the word without querying it in the present context . . . Guy? Study? Oxymoron?— were two big cardboard boxes. The date on the fading postmark was October 1956. Unopened, but clearly regularly dusted by Doris. The ring stains of myriad coffee cups on the top box. Why would Guy leave two parcels unopened for seven years? Answer: Because he knew what was in them. And because he didn't have a coffee table.

Charlie took a kitchen knife to them.

Inside, a twenty-two volume *Complete Works of Lenin* in the People's Publishers English-language edition of 1955, and a note he could not read, initialled "Г.Г.Г.," which he could—Grigory Gerasimovich Gogolin.

Having ruined the coffee table, he looked around for a bookshelf stout enough to take all the books Guy had not read and which he would not read either.

The sheer weight of Burgess's interests, his real interests, sagged the shelves. Why could not biographers write just one sodding volume? Why did they come in threes and fours? What had Guy found so captivating in Sandburg's *Lincoln* (six volumes), Morley's *Gladstone* (three), Churchill's *Marlborough* (four) or Soloveytchik's *Potemkin* (mercifully just one)? Combined, they took up over a yard of shelf space. Oh for Miss Blandish's Orchids or several back numbers of *Playboy* . . . oh for Bettie Page not Betsy Ross.

But—

There was also a large collection of Maigret novels in the original French in neat uniform pocket editions, shiny as a Balzac. Charlie counted more than fifty different titles . . . *Maigret et la grande perche*, *Le revolver de Maigret*, *Maigret s'amuse* and so on just shy of infinity. They looked unread, not a bent corner nor a crack to the spine.

Someone, some publisher or magazine editor, probably gave them to Burgess unsolicited, much as Grigory Gerasimovich had given him the Lenins—and sure enough, tucked into one volume was a slip of paper reading *Foire du livre, Francfort, 1961.*

This, to Charlie, was preferable to any biography or any tract by Vladimir Ilyich.

§136

Charlie meant to stay until about Tuesday, but one day led to another and it was mid-October before he felt a twinge of anything that might be mistaken for guilt. He'd taken a month's wages in advance from Grigory Gerasimovich to read and recommend (or not) several volumes of Zola and had read none, simply because he intended to say an utterly arbitrary yes to all of them.

Food was no problem. Doris shopped for him and gave him bills that seemed to him to be a fraction of what he had been paying in Moscow; he had no idea who paid Doris, but she cooked for him, except on weekends and Wednesdays, such Russian delicacies as duck stuffed with sauerkraut, or fried black sourdough bread topped with large fried duck eggs—not, he presumed, from the same duck. He thought he might become addicted to her baked, split red Irkutsk spuds smothered in sour cream and topped with dill and parsley. He might kill for her curd and raisin pashka. And he might get fat . . . again. The battle between the mirror and the belly wasn't over yet.

Fat or thin, clothes were a problem; Guy's shirts fit him, but nothing else did as Charlie was by far the taller. So he rinsed his underwear and socks (what kind of a cad would wear another bloke's Y-fronts?) and trusted Doris to let him know when his trousers began to stink.

Surprisingly (or not), Magda had not come looking for him. This surprised him. A little. If he'd been followed out to Peredelkino he hadn't spotted the tail, and, if he said so himself, he was a past master at that sort of thing. And he hadn't told Magda where he was going. Perhaps she really had exhausted her budget, if not her patience. Perhaps the flirtation that he thought had sparked when her eyes began to shine was just that, a flirtation and nothing more on the part of a lonely woman smitten not with him but with the delight of being able to converse in her own language once in a while.

He walked around the wooden village. Met people who ignored him. Met people who stared at him. (Good bloody grief, did he still really look *that* English?) Was drawn to the sound of someone playing the piano on the far side of the village, playing just the sort of pieces he could not name, but with which Troy had tried to entertain or educate him since they were boys, and thought better of introducing himself. For the first time in his life he had chosen to be antisocial and was pleasantly surprised to find he could stick his own company. He never could before. The deeply felt impulse that had led him to seek the company of others, that had driven him to club and pub, seemed subdued, dormant . . . possibly extinct. Would Troy know this version of Charlie? Would Coky recognise this wordless recluse ten years on? Would he even know himself?

And—and he had got stuck into both Simenon's Maigret and Guy's copy of the *Penguin Russian Course*—and, whilst way past the simplicity of "gin" and "bog roll," felt no compunction to ask Doris what she knew about anything, as—language barrier notwithstanding, Guy's confidence in her notwithstanding—she too was surely a KGB operative, albeit the kind that wore an apron, made the tea and mashed the spuds.

At the end of October, the end of his Indian-Russian summer, Doris told him they should close up the dacha and he took the hint.

"До встречи в апреле," she said.

See you in April. A phrase loaded with foreboding of his second Russian winter. And he'd bet a tanner to a kopeck Doris had never read T. S. Eliot.

§137

Moscow

Spring 1964

It was a given that June busted out all over on the coast of New England among crab fishers and lobstermen, but in Moscow it was April or May that "busted" when a small army of babushkas appeared with brooms and besoms and swept winter into the gutter. Spring, put simply, sprung—and if you blinked it was summer.

On the metro Charlie thought he kept seeing the same man. He saw nothing, heard nothing from Magda, not since the day she sanctioned his visit to Burgess in hospital last summer, but as she had said, he should be looking over his shoulder for the tail she could not afford. A bloke in a leather cap, head down in *Pravda* on three consecutive days. On the fourth day Charlie made a point of getting as close to him as possible. The bloke looked up as the train rattled into a station. Specs as thick as milk bottles and a grey beard. No one, not the nuttiest KGB spymaster would assign a sixty-year-old mole of a man to follow him. He chalked it up to a mild dose of paranoia—paranoia in Moscow was not mental, it was meteorological.

Grigory Gerasimovich had outsmarted Charlie over the winter.

"I want plot summaries. Everything Zola wrote."

"That's . . . that's . . . thirty-five volumes!"

"No, Comrade Charlie, that's eight hundred and seventy-five rubles a month!"

§138

In mid-April, not quite the first breath of spring, a postcard arrived from Doris.

"Ужин на столе."

Your dinner's on the table.

She had a dry sense of humour.

And: "Принесите еще кофе, Товарищ Чарли."

Bring more coffee, Comrade Charlie.

One quick, expensive foray into the black market, a suitcase packed with Grigory Gerasimovich's latest burden, the novels of Theodor Fontane—another twelve volumes, and sixteen more to be shipped—and he was on the train to Peredelkino. Two hours later, lugging his suitcase along the lane to the dacha, he would have sold his soul for a wheelbarrow had he not sold it long ago to the god that failed.

Lunch with Doris eased his burdens. Sardines and blini.

Dinner. Lamb palov and barberries, which he thought to be a tart variation on a cranberry, a bottle of Uzbeki Chardonnay and Morpheus embraced him. The god that did not fail.

§139

The morning came as a bit of a shock. Not the scant coating of frost—he'd expected that, winter lingering into spring—but the bloke in army fatigues with a donkey cart.

"Упаковать."

Pack.

He'd unpacked only hours ago.

"Where am I going?"

But the man just turned on his heel and went back to his donkey.

There was no point in arguing. Guy had mentioned the possibility that the dacha would be reassigned. It would have been more convenient had he been told yesterday.

He packed up his books and clothes.

Gave the bag of coffee beans to Doris, who thrust it back at him with tears in her eyes.

"Последние слова, Дорис?"

Any last words, Doris?

"Учитесь готовить, Чарли."

Learn to cook, Charlie.

The usefulness of such advice would depend on whether the donkey took him to the railway station or the firing squad.

Instead it took him a mile and a half to the far side of the village. And pulled up outside the house of the woman who always played the piano—another well-maintained two-storey cabin, marking her out, whoever she was, as номенклатура—nomenklatura.

"Who lives here?" Charlie asked.

He muttered a mouthful of Russian, something about donkeys. Before Charlie had worked out just what it might mean, the apparatchik had dumped his things in the road, pointed emphatically if wordlessly at the cabin next door and led the donkey back the way they had come.

Charlie was pretty sure he'd been fobbed off with something like "I'm not paid to answer questions, I'm paid to mind donkeys."

Fair enough.

The "see no—hear no—speak no" safety net of the working stiff everywhere. Russia was no different.

But—there was an American tin mailbox askew on its post by the pianist's gate. Its little red flag was up.

He looked quickly to either side like an amateur sleuth and pulled out the one envelope inside.

"Méret Voytek."

Holy shit!

She needed no introduction.

The Russian spy who had fled Britain hours ahead of a press exposé in . . . when was it? Forty-nine? Fifty? . . . and left MI5 with enough egg on their faces to keep the canteen in omelettes for a month. It had not been Six's problem. Charlie had watched, amused, cynical, from the blameless sidelines. She'd gone on to be one of the Soviet Union's greatest cultural assets—a very good pianist, quite possibly one of the greatest cellists in the world and now, perhaps, some compensation for the loss of the man who had most certainly been the Soviets' greatest asset in the cultural war, Rudolf Nureyev.

He turned his attention to the newly acquired symbol of status—his own dacha, if, that is, it really was his.

It was a small building with a steeply pitched rusting roof caked in bitumen—a lean-to that until explored could be kitchen, bedroom, loo or just somewhere to park the lawnmower, or more likely store the scythe—all in the same flaky white that concealed, in this instance, an older red, the red of lead oxide, rather than a copper green. It was as though someone had decided in the wake of the Twentieth Party Congress a few years ago to whitewash everything that didn't move—no metaphors intended or even considered.

It was a step down, but not a step out. He was thought worthy not of a two-storey dacha but of this, a superior kind of shed, a beach hut without a beach, and in that was all the reassurance he needed. He no longer mattered to them, and in that was his freedom, and in freedom, anonymity. Méret Voytek might be a problem. He knew who she was. Might she know who he was?

§140

From the road a narrow gate in the green picket fence opened into a small garden. Next to the gate was a painted sign from which the name had faded, leaving only the ghost of a number.

Ferreting around among the cobwebs and cupboards, he found an old pot of red paint, pierced its custard skin with a screwdriver and repainted the number—116.

But his dacha needed a name. He was still an Englishman, after all. And he'd no idea what the name had ever been—*Spook Cottage? Dunspyin?* What might be appropriate?

He decided on a private joke that no Russian would ever get, and if it sent them scrabbling for an English dictionary, so much the better.

Джейуик

Jaywick—one day, if the same fickle gods of the USSR permitted, a real jay might perch on it.

§141

He found he had a vegetable patch, one that the previous bloke—a minor poet in the depressing mode of "singing Stalin's praises" (Charlie had found one of his books in the house, *The Gardener of Human Happiness*)—had kept up until his death. Never having grown so much as a radish, Charlie found he could raise onions—well, small onions given the short Russian summer—a few spuds of a rather hardy variety that looked and tasted nothing like King Edward's, lots of cabbage (what was Russia without cabbage?) . . . and all the rhubarb a man could ever want.

The taste of his first homegrown carrot rewrote his life. He realised that every meal he had had in any restaurant in any country on earth was as naught compared to a freshly picked carrot from his own garden. Stuff the Ritz, bollocks to Wheeler's, nuts to Harvey's and bumholes to the Ivy. It was all a confidence trick perpetrated on gullible men with bulging wallets and no taste buds by chefs and waiters. Fukkemall. He'd never eat in any of those places again. But then again, he'd never get the chance, so what did it matter? Sour grapes made for sweeter carrots.

All he really lacked was bacon. With bacon, spuds and cabbage he could make that most glorious dish, the king of English breakfasts, bubble 'n' squeak. But then something wonderful happened: another Stalinist doggerelnik died ("Josef Vissarionovich, Gentle Shepherd of the Mighty Proletariat, who watches over us . . . etc. . . . etc.") and his dacha was given to a retired engineer who had never written a line of poetry in his life but had designed and built pontoon bridges for the Red Army during the Great Patriotic War, for which he had received instant medals and the rather belated gift of a country home—and he began to raise pigs.

And if Charlie opened the windows, he could hear Méret Voytek practising. Sometimes she played the cello, sometimes the piano. He'd never given a damn about classical music, but then he'd never given a damn about growing onions. He felt he could develop an ear for this Schubert bloke.

None of this made life in the USSR attractive, but it did make it tolerable. Nine bean rows and a hive for the honeybee would make it even more tolerable; after all, he already had the hut and the bee-loud glade, but he'd get round to beans sooner or later.

It would be the day he planted his first carrots—seed so fine a breeze would blow it off the palm of his hand. Voytek was at her piano. A piece he knew to be Fanny Mendelssohn, but only because she had told him so. Something about the months of the year. All April she had been play-ing "April." Gentle stuff. Music like water. He wondered how a musician ever knew when they'd got it right, but was well aware it was a stupid question all but begging disdain. Perhaps she was now onto "May"?

He stood and stretched. A dull ache above his hips.

In what passed for Voytek's garden a woman armed with a bread knife was slashing away ineffectually at the deadheads of last year's cow parsley—hardy buggers to have stood brittle through the winter.

Her legs were striking, not just because they were shapely but because they wore bottle-green tights. Where in Khrushchev's Russia, in 1964, did a woman get hold of anything so decadent as green tights? They went well with her dress, pale yellow with some leafy or flowery pattern, and the nondescript ragged cardigan unravelling at the sleeves. Years ago, it seemed, such a touch of careless femininity would have brought out the rogue in Charlie—a chat-up line on the tip of his tongue, but that was years ago . . .

"Aach!"

She seemed about ready to throw in both towel and bread knife. Suddenly she became aware of Charlie and looked up, eyes shining.

Magda Ewald.

"Hello, Charlie."

"Is this a coincidence, Magda?"

"Of course not."

§142

They awoke each morning to the machine-gun rattle of a woodpecker just outside the window, and Magda would slip from his bed and take breakfast with Voytek. Working against the habit of a lifetime, Charlie would not go back to sleep. He would lie listening to the trills of chaffinches and blue tits for half an hour. English Charlie, his former self, would not have been able to tell the song a chaffinch from the song of an Austin Seven.

By ten Voytek would be at her piano or her cello, and once in a while he'd hear Magda on trombone—her blues riffs . . . "St. James Infirmary" . . . "St. Louis Blues" . . . were pure delight—but never together.

"Why is that?"

"Not much written for piano and trombone, and I think nothing at all for cello and trombone. Of course, Rimsky-Korsakov wrote a trombone concerto, but we would be short a dozen or more musicians. Besides . . . no part for a cello . . . so we have a much better duet . . . her life and mine. We are . . . inseparable . . . our war notwithstanding."

"We don't talk about the war," said Charlie. "We've never talked about the war."

"Why not? You can ask me anything. After all, I know all about yours."

Ah, yet another lover who'd read his file.

§143

Predictably and strangely this conversation reminded Charlie of talking to Ignatz Farber, who had been in Auschwitz at the same time as Magda. A concentration camp was not like a Cambridge college—it was not like anything but itself—yet unbidden, stupid questions came to mind ("Did you know . . . ?") and what on earth was the point of that? *Just shut up and listen.*

"We met as girls, in the Vienna Youth Orchestra. After the Anschluss we were all enrolled in the *Bund Deutscher Mädel*, like it or lump it. Hitler's little girls in brown. But I had already joined the Communist Party. I spied for the Soviet Union for almost four years. I did not tell Méret. She was so young. She would not have understood. When I was arrested in the summer of '42, as far as Méret was concerned I had simply vanished. *Nacht und Nebel.*

"We met again in '44. Her arrest was a mistake. She sat next to the wrong person on a tram. But the Reich does not make mistakes. So we met again in Auschwitz.

"Music had saved my life, and now it saved hers. We played in the Ladies Orchestra. Death has all the best tunes.

"A year later the Russians were approaching the camp. We were among the stragglers not shipped out. We were made to walk westwards. In January. In Poland. In snow. I don't know why. Had the RAF bombed the railway lines? You tell me. I felt certain we would die. To fall behind meant a bullet—and we fell behind. A Wehrmacht private decided not to shoot us. The three of us spent the night in a straw hut. In the morning the soldier was gone—on some deep level I hope he survived—and the road was swarming with Russians. I stepped out, naïvely, to greet my comrades. I don't know what I was thinking, but I encountered rapists.

"A woman major in charge of the squad shot the man on top of me through the head. I felt the heat of his blood on my skin, the texture of his brains in my hair. After that, none dared move against us. The rest you surely know?"

§144

Charlie took every opportunity to improve his Russian. Guy had told him he might as well enjoy Russia and he'd enjoy it a lot better if he understood it.

After her initial ten days' leave, Magda returned to Moscow but came to Peredelkino most weekends. Charlie would have said it felt like being married, but he had no idea what being married felt like or looked like, his parents having provided him with no model whatsoever. They would plant and weed. They would cook and read. They would listen to Voytek play—and as the evenings grew longer the three of them would fall asleep in a heap in the garden. Like cats, Charlie said. No, said Magda, like bears.

At every visit she put his Russian through its paces.

Late one summer evening, after Voytek had crossed through the gap in the fence and gone to bed, Magda said, "Do you know what this place is called?"

"Peredelkino? Doesn't it mean 'made again' or 'made afresh'?"

"Yes. It does, but I meant its nickname. *Неясная Поляна.*"

Nyeyasnaya Polyana.

"I get it. Tolstoy's country home. The something glade?"

"Tolstoy lived at the Clear Glade. Peredelkino is the 'Unclear Glade.' The very opposite of fresh. And any synonym you care for. Personally, I would plump for 'murky.' There, a joke at my own expense."

"Because it's your presence here that makes it murky?"

"Be fair, Charlie. It's *our* presence that makes it murky. Not Méret. Not any of those dreadful poets, or the man with the pigs, or all those retired heroes of the war. It's us. Spies like us. Serpents in Eden."

He would not be the one to argue with that, regrettable though it was. He could grow carrots by the ton and not be able to see through the mantle murk he'd spent a lifetime creating—as surely as Jacob Marley had forged his chains.

§145

He wintered in Moscow.

This meant more discretion was called for, but he could not see how they could ever be discreet enough. And it meant seeing Magda in uniform. Something dark, something drab, enlivened by flashes of blue. No more flowery dresses and tatty cardigans until the sun shone again—Magda in work mode. It crossed his mind that she might be in work mode wherever she was and whatever she wore—but found he didn't give a flying fuck.

Before he left Moscow for the dacha the following spring, he put it to Grigory Gerasimovich Gogolin at People's Publishers that his Russian was up to par.

"Really? How long are you being here? Two years? Three?"

"I've always had a knack for languages."

"Knack?"

"A gift. Дар. Give me a shot at translating."

"Translating what?"

"Simenon. You have nothing by Georges Simenon."

"OK."

And with that "OK" Charlie became the voice of Maigret in Moscow.

Wilderness

§146

Somewhere East of Berlin

December 24, 1968

Wilderness wasn't sure where he was. In fact he was sure of bugger all. He just knew it hurt a lot.

He'd stick to name, rank and number, except that he'd long ago forgotten his number. But no one was asking.

A nurse came in and swapped the drip thing that hung just out of sight and fed he-knew-not-what into his right arm. No doubt she'd done this a few times before while he was unconscious, as she batted not an unmascaraed eyelash and spoke not a word. He wondered if anyone would speak to him again.

He nodded off.

When he awoke, the light had changed, there was no winter sun scraping vainly at the high, dirty window on the opposite wall, and the overhead light cast everything in an appropriately sickly, jaundice hue.

And there was a woman. A big woman, parking her big arse on a stacker chair and easing herself down with both hands on her walking stick.

General Zolotukhina.

Volga.

He didn't remember her using a stick.

What had happened?

"They shoot you too, General?"

"Eh, Joe. Eeeeeh, Joe. You are still such a boy."

"I'm twice as old as when we first met."

"And still you know nothing of the perils of ageing. How bits fall off all the time."

"What is it today?"

She shifted one buttock, her uniform squeaking on the plastic seat, more to let fly a fart than illustrate her point.

"Sciatica. Take my word for it. Hurts like fuck."

"So does being shot. Or don't they teach you that at KGB College?"

"Couldn't be helped. I am sorry."

"I note you don't say 'it was an accident.'"

"One of *your* team shot you. Not one of mine."

"So—maybe it was an accident. Just not your accident."

Volga put both hands firmly on the walking stick and eased the chair forward, a dissonant scrape across the bare concrete floor.

"Tell me, Joe—no one is listening, after all—why did you have the Koppenrad brothers there?"

"No one's listening? Volga, I don't have the energy to laugh. This is Russia and no one is listening?"

"Actually, this is Poland. You're in Łodz. You've been here more than a week. I had you taken off the train at Łodz. You were bleeding to death. I was told you would not live to see Moscow otherwise. These people, these Polish doctors and nurses, saved your life. They put ten units of blood into you."

Ten units of blood? Good grief, that was a red lake. Wilderness contained his gratitude.

"Ah—I am to see Moscow. Quaint. Almost Chekhovian."

"Don't thank me, Joe, just answer the question. Why did you have the Koppenrad brothers on the bridge at Glienicke?

"Call it an insurance policy."

"And you paid them?"

"They don't work for nothing, you know that."

"And you paid them to do what?"

Wilderness said nothing. He'd no idea who was listening, Poles or Russians, but someone surely was, and he wasn't about to admit that the Kopps had been hired to shoot Russians—if necessary.

"How much did you pay them? Surely that's not a secret?"

It wasn't.

"Four grand."

"Sterling? Deutschmarks?"

"Dollars."

"They don't come cheap, do they? (pause) And they don't make mistakes."

Wilderness was beginning to wonder where this was leading.

"Four thousand dollars. That's a lot of money, Joe. But it wasn't enough."

Abruptly, if slowly and painfully, Volga got to her feet. The door to the room opened by invisible hands. She paused on the threshold. Spoke over her shoulder.

"We paid them six."

They'd outbid him.

Well, he knew that.

The Russians had outbid Wilderness and Frank Spoleto, and they in turn had outbid the Russians . . . he was certain Volga could not know this . . . and if she did . . . it would scarcely make sense—who pays to be shot? Only . . . the Kopps were supposed to wing him in one leg. The merest flesh wound. Just enough to stop him walking, just enough to let the Russians drag him off the Glienicke Bridge into East Germany.

He wondered which one of the Kopps had shot him. Of course they didn't make mistakes—until they did. One of them had shot him in the back. Blew him off his feet into a coma from which he was only now emerging after hours or days he could not calculate or remember. Leg, back, no matter. The Russians wanted him alive. They had him alive. Just. So—why did the Russians want him alive? That question would dog him for days. For weeks.

He would sleep on it.

So he slept on it.

To very little conclusion.

§147

January 7, 1969

Days, perhaps only days, later he woke, and all the furniture had been moved around.

Ah—he was not in the same room.

Not in the same hospital?

Not in the same country?

A nurse came in. Took his pulse. Told him that it was "гораздо лучше," much better . . . in Russian.

"Where am I?"

"You're in the Semyon Timoshenko Veterans' Hospital."

"In Moscow?"

"Of course."

As she left, a man came in. No hospital whites. A plain grey double-breasted suit. Volga close behind him, still leaning on her walking stick.

The man produced a tape measure and began to measure him—his forearm, his upper arm, his chest . . .

For a split second Wilderness thought he was being fitted up for his coffin—but then logic asked him, *Why would they bother?*

And then Volga read his mind.

"We had to cut your clothes off you. In any case you would never have got the blood out. Don't expect to choose a swatch for your suit, but also do not expect a bill. A gift from the USSR."

The nut-brown eyes were smiling at him. Was she still reading his mind as he contemplated the prospect not of Russian suits but of Russian underwear, feeling his balls itch at just the thought of it?

And then he remembered the flak jacket—the bulletproof vest he had rashly handed to Bernard Alleyn only minutes before he'd been shot. Damn damn damn.

Volga asked, "How are you feeling today?"

"Hardly at my best, but apparently I can tell a tailor from an undertaker."

"Ver' funny. You have another visitor. But I can send him away if you're not up to it."

"All depends. Does your interrogator have kid gloves or a rubber truncheon?"

"Matter of fact he's clutching a bottle of vodka—Mamont, Siberia's best. You won't be allowed to drink it, but appreciate the gesture. Shall I send him in?"

"Why not?"

A minute passed. Wilderness heard indistinct conversation outside the door, hidden whispers between Volga and the bloke with the vodka.

Then he was standing before him at the bedside: older, elegant as ever, ruddier than he'd remembered . . . but that was what vodka did to you if it didn't send you blind. Wilderness paused his assumption. Ruddy, yes . . . but leaner and fitter looking, the complexion of someone who got plenty of fresh air and early nights. Not a boozer's red nose but a gardener's red cheeks? A touch of Percy Thrower? Was it possible he'd turned his life around?

He tucked the bottle into the crook of Wilderness's arm—the one without the drip feed.

"It's been a while," he said.

"About six or seven years, I reckon," Wilderness replied.

He pulled up a metal stacker chair and sat down, crossed his long legs and eased up the knee of his trousers with his fingertips.

Yes, he'd always been elegant. A bit of a peacock, to say the least.

"You're causing quite a flutter back home. Or so I'm told."

Wilderness said nothing to this. It was bait on the hook. He'd wait till he dropped it in the water.

"Of course, your people think you've defected."

Splash.

"That's because *your* people told them I defected. Why do you expect to be believed? There was a whole team on the other side of the bridge who know I did not defect."

Volga wanted him alive. Frank wanted him alive too, but whatever the Russians wanted, Frank had already got what he wanted. A personal visit from Charlie Leigh-Hunt. With any luck, the first of many. Hook, bait, bigger splash.

Frank

§148

Wilmersdorf, West Berlin

Thursday, December 12, 1968, 5:00 p.m.
About Three Weeks Earlier

Wilderness lay on the floor of his old room on Gruntümmlerstraße. The one he'd shared with Nell Burkhardt when they were young. Wilderness had been nineteen. Nell younger. He'd never been sure by quite how much, as one of the few lies Nell ever told was about her age, and that she passed off as a necessity. Wartime necessity, peacetime necessity. It really didn't matter.

What mattered was that twenty years on, she was in the hands of the KGB in the East.

Wilderness and Frank Spoleto had a plan.

It was simple.

But simple and easy were not the same thing.

They, that is Wilderness and Bernard Alleyn, aka Leonid Liubimov, would walk out to the middle of the Glienicke Bridge for the exchange. Nell would step across the border, Bernard wouldn't and then Wilderness would tell Kostya Zolotukhin that he wasn't getting Bernard. The Russians had wanted Bernard back for years. He'd served a few years in an English prison and been the object of an attempted swap only four years ago—after which Wilderness had turned him loose. He'd found him again in Ireland. Talked him into this bizarre meeting.

A lot now rested on Kostya—or more precisely on Wilderness's judgment of Kostya. Kostya, he knew, would wimp out, and unless there was anyone of higher rank or bigger balls behind him they'd just walk away without a shot fired. And if the guns came out . . . well . . . they'd hit the deck and the Koppenrad brothers had instructions to take out everyone left standing on the East German side.

He hoped to God it would never come to that.

Wilderness paused in thought as the girl who had the room now came up the stairs from the apartment below, where she slept on the sofa to keep an eye on Erno Schreiber. Neither of them knew if Erno was dying.

She set a mug of coffee on the table. Fresh-ground coffee always blasted Wilderness back to the airlift and his days as a *Schieber*, days when he thought he'd stink of coffee for the rest of his life.

"Why do you lie on the floor?" Trudi asked.

"Habit. I did it all the time when I lived here."

"And you lit a fire. Ja? Gut. Is freezing today."

"I'll pay you for the wood."

"You will pay me for everything, Joe Wilderness."

She left. Bigger feet were clumping up the stairs. He heard a muttered "bitch" and realised Trudi had just passed Frank.

The Koppenrads came in ahead of Frank. Bound in black. Gentlemen about their business.

"You gonna lie there all day?"

"If at all possible, yes."

"Suit yourself."

Frank pulled out a wooden dining chair, sat backwards on it, arms folded across the back—Robert Ryan or Kirk Douglas in some 1940s LAPD detective film, except at Frank's bulk he was more Broderick Crawford.

The Kopps remained standing, Marti all but vanishing into the woodwork.

"We have a dilemma, Joe."

"Is a dilemma the same thing as a problem?"

"Oh fuck. He's being a smart-ass. Rikki, tell 'im!"

"This morning I received a visit from the KGB, plain clothes. Would not give name or rank. He never does. I know him as Ilya. He works for General Zolotukhina. He said, 'She knows.'"

"Oh fuck."

"Shuttup, Joe. There's more. Rikki . . ."

"I was asked how much you were paying me to be on the bridge tomorrow night. I have done much business with this man, so I play straight with him. I told him. Four thousand dollars. I did not say what you were paying us to do, and he did not press me. We were to be there, that was enough. A presence, perhaps? I can shoot all the East Germans I like, the Russians would not care, but I would never tell a Russian you were paying me to shoot Russians. It would be putting my head in a noose. When he heard how much, he offered me six thousand."

"What?"

Wilderness sat upright.

"What?"

Got to his feet.

"Six thousand to do what?"

"To shoot you."

$149

"I am to . . . the word, I think, is 'wing.' I am to wing you. One leg or the other. Enough so you cannot walk. I kill you, I get no fee."

Wilderness said, "I think I just stepped through the looking glass. Bernard, Nell? What about them?"

"Ilya never mentioned them."

Frank said, "Boys, can you give us the room. Drop by on old Erno, he'll be glad of the company. Maybe Flosshilde will make you a coffee."

When they'd gone, Frank uncurled from the chair, walked across to the fire, warmed his hands, turned to Wilderness and said, "Do it."

"What?"

"Let them snatch you."

"Why would I do that, you mad bugger? They will pump out of me everything I know about SIS operations by foul means or fair."

"So tell 'em. Make it easy on yourself. You think they don't know everything already? You'd just be the confirmation."

"Frank, this is insane."

"And . . ."

"And?"

Frank inhaled deeply, left Wilderness on the hook for too long a moment.

"And . . . you'd be our man in Moscow."

He rummaged in his pockets, found his pack of Lucky Strikes and lit up. Waited for Wilderness to speak.

"Frank, I really don't get this."

"Joe . . . who do you reckon they'll send to debrief you? C'mon, think. Who would be top of the list? Your list, my list, their list."

Feeling faintly stupid, Wilderness heard the rattle of a dropping penny.

"And what might you want from him?"

"The name of the KGB agent who ran him in Washington. We've been trying to find the sonovabitch for the best part of twenty years. We know Charlie was 'Felix Foster.' All we've ever had for his contact is a codename: Mockingbird."

Now Wilderness knew exactly what to say.

"How much?"

"Fifty grand."

"A hundred and fifty."

"Whatever, consider it done. The Company will pay that to get a man on the inside. They already agreed to fifty. I'll have no problem getting one fifty."

"And how will you get this man back on the outside?"

"Swapsies. We trade for you. Six months, a year at the most. We snatch one of theirs. Another walk out to the bridge and everything is tickety-boo. Bob's your uncle."

Wilderness hated it when Frank tried to sound English. And nothing, not a damn thing that had ever happened on that bridge had ever been tickety-boo.

He sipped at the coffee Trudi had left. Watched Frank through the tinted haze of tobacco smoke.

"Will the Kopps do it?"

"Sure. I already topped Volga's offer by a grand apiece. They stick to Volga's plan but she never knows we know. They're working for us, pretending to work for her. Call it a loyalty bonus. Free money. They earn it by doing nothing they haven't already agreed to do."

"And Volga . . . what's in it for her? She wants me alive? Why?"

"Does it matter? All they ever want are bodies to trade. 'Scuse the phrase . . . I do mean *live* bodies. We may not even need a fresh snatch.

There's a list of their guys we got in prison, any one of whom they'd trade for. Shit, we should never have fried Ethel Rosenberg. We should have kept her in Sing Sing for just this sort of deal. You'd just be this year's Gary Powers . . . well, next year's, but for a hundred an' fifty big ones you shouldn't be counting the days."

Wilderness thought he could end up doing just that.

"All this for a name?"

"Yep . . . you just need to get Charlie Leigh-Hunt to utter it."

$150

Frank was on his second Lucky Strike. Dragged the first down to nothing, stubbed it out on a saucer and just lit up again.

"I've never known you stuck for words, Joe. It's out of character."

"You might want a drink with your ciggie, Frank."

"Oh—so you're sitting on bad news? Fine. Get us each a belt of whiskey and tell me."

Wilderness took a bottle of vodka and two shot glasses off the sideboard.

Frank looked disappointed.

"Is this all you got?"

"It's the right drink for what I have to say and you may do well to consider it medicinal. A prophylactic."

"That's just a fancy word for—"

"It means preventive, Frank."

"Prevent what?"

"You blowing your stack."

"That bad, eh? Enough. I can't bear the suspense."

"I killed five Russian soldiers before I left Czechoslovakia . . ."

Even as his esteem sank to rock bottom in his own eyes, he knew it had just risen in Frank's.

". . . If the Russians have the faintest suspicion it was me . . ."

Frank knocked back his vodka.

"Y'know. It tastes better than it used to. So . . . so . . . Joe. That was you? It crossed my mind it might have been you, but then I . . . y'know . . . dismissed the thought. Company was baffled. KGB appeared to be baffled. Accused us as a matter of fact. But when the Russians shot three Czech protestors picked up less than five miles from the scene and announced it was them and summary justice had prevailed . . . I dismissed the thought completely."

"They shot three Czechs?"

"Even released photos of the bodies as a warning. Everything short of heads on spikes at the city gates. You're off the hook, Joe. No excuses left."

Frank shrugged his overcoat off onto the back of his chair. The jacket followed and he sat there in shirtsleeves and shoulder holster. He put the gun, a Beretta 9mm, on the table pointing at Wilderness.

"I'll show you mine if you show me yours."

"Eh?"

"Just get your gun, Joe."

Wilderness took his Smith & Wesson out of the top drawer of the dresser and laid it alongside the Beretta, pointing at Frank.

"This the gun you shot the Ivans with?"

"Yes."

"Personally, I'd've ditched it, but . . . we just do a swap. You get caught with this on the other side and they do a ballistics test on it . . . you're dead. This—"

He slid the Beretta towards Wilderness.

"This has never been fired. Clean as a whistle."

Frank hefted the Smith & Wesson.

"Jesus, this thing must weigh over three pounds. Why do you carry such a fucking cannon?"

"It has its uses," Wilderness replied, and drew the Beretta slowly towards himself.

§151

"So, you'll do it?"

Wilderness said nothing.

"Fer fuck's sake, Joe."

"My . . . wife . . ."

"Sure, lovely woman. What's your point?"

"I'd be leaving her to raise two kids on her own for the best part of a year."

"You think Burne-Jones won't take care of her? He's her father, goddammit."

"That . . . is my job . . ."

"I'll go see her. Put her in the picture. Trust me."

"That's just it. I don't."

"A hundred and fifty thousand ought to buy me some trust."

"Frank, I trust you for the money. You've done rotten things in the last twenty years, but you've never swindled me. And you in turn trust me to get you a name. But if I let you see Judy, you'll just fuck it up. So don't."

"OK, OK."

"I know what Burne-Jones will do if I'm 'kidnapped.' He won't take the open line. He'll stay off diplomatic channels—none of it will ever make the British papers—he'll try to resolve it personally, and he'll badger the hell out of Volga. Let him. It's best he knows nothing about your scheme. The ambiguities will fry his brain."

"I guess they would, wouldn't they? He's never been one of us. Always the straight arrow."

Wilderness winced inwardly at the "one of us" but let him finish.

"OK. I stay shtum. Judy learns nothing and neither does her old man. So—you'll do it?"

"Oh yes."

§152

Glienicke, West Berlin

Friday, December 13, 1968
'Round Midnight

From the far end of the bridge, a stately, possibly fat figure lumbered towards them, the hips swinging slowly, the feet wide apart, plonking down with bodily weight, the head swathed in fur and scarves.

As it grew near, Wilderness could see gloved hands clutching a silver box—about big enough to hold a large chess set. Then proximity told, and he perceived the outline for what it was—female. And with proximity, uniform—a full-blown KGB general.

She clutched the box with one hand, and with the other pulled off her hat, a mass of greying ringlets cascaded down and Wilderness found himself looking once again into those brown and beautiful sad eyes. General Zolotukhina . . . Volga Vasilievna.

She dropped her hat and touched Nell lightly on the arm.

"Go now," she said.

Nell looked baffled, did not move.

Wilderness called her by name.

"Nell?"

Nell looked at him—eyes wide.

Wilderness said, "Nell, just walk past me, keep on walking and don't look back."

Nell crossed the line on the far side of Bernard Alleyn.

Wilderness was tempted to look back in her direction but did not want to find her looking back at him. He listened to the click of her heels on the asphalt, every step sound-diminishing, every step nearer her freedom.

Silence. Wind upon water.

Then Volga looked straight at Bernard.

"Comrade Liubimov. I am the bearer of sad news. Your mother, Krasnaya, is dead—Nastasya Filippovna died in April. Died like so many, in the first breath of spring. She was a loyal servant of the Union of Soviet Socialist Republics and was cremated with all military honours. And she was my dearest friend. Shoulder to shoulder we stood in October 1917. Side by side we took Berlin in 1945. I have here her ashes. I am sorry to drag you away from the life you have made, but I felt I should deliver them in person, and as I could not come to you, you needs must come to me. My deepest condolences, comrade. Krasnaya was a hero. May she rest in peace . . . in Ireland."

She held out the silver box.

Bernard took it, the perplexed look in his eyes yielding to tears.

Then Volga turned to Wilderness.

"You see, Joe. You need to know who to trust."

She smiled. Held out her hand for him to shake.

One shot rang out.

§153

One shot, but the wrong shot.

The bullet passed straight through Wilderness just above his right hip.

Frank kicked the gun out of Rikki's hands.

"It was an accident," Rikki said softly.

Troy

§154

The British Embassy
Palác Thun, Prague

February 3, 1969
A Freezing Cold Day

On winter mornings Anna, Lady Troy, wife to Her Majesty's Ambassador, liked to start the day with porridge. Having been married to a Scotsman before she had been mad enough to marry Troy, she would take it no other way but with salt, scorned such excesses as cream or yoghurt and could prove vitriolic on the case for maple syrup.

"Yoghurt."

"Yes?" said Troy, being unable to think of anything else to say.

"Isn't that a sort of hut Mongol warriors live in . . . in . . . er . . ."

"Mongolia?"

"Probably."

Troy liked eggs. Boiled. The sheer, the neat, the precise pleasure in slicing the top off a boiled egg. Marmite soldiers on the side.

The customary, fascinating morning routine was put on hold as Troy wielded the knife and waited for Anna's brain to kick in.

"They got to Vienna, you know."

"Who did?"

"The Mongols."

"That was the Ottomans."

"Oh."

"Quite."

"Yoghurts. Ottomans. Hmm . . . so it all boils down to a choice between a hut and a sofa, does it?"

By now Troy had had enough.

"I am out this morning."

"Dipping?"

Her word for diplomatic activity.

"Yes. A meeting with Bohdan Zloch."

"Who he?"

"He's the new bloke at the Ministry of the Interior. I mean to tackle him about our garden full of teenage refugees."

"Oh, will they be gone soon? I'd miss them. It's been a bit like living inside *West Side Story*, y'know, the Jets and the Thingies, except none of them dance and only one or two of them sing. And none of them look like Russ Tamblyn."

"I'll be sure to mention that to Mr. Zloch."

"Zloch. Zloch? Zloch! Sounds like what you'd hear if you punched a bag of wet porridge. Zzzzzloccchhhh!"

"I'll be sure to tell him that too."

When they were younger he had thought of Anna as the most sensible of women, habitually, gently warning him of his own follies. Now . . . just shy of fifty, she seemed to have developed a taste for the playful if not downright silly. It was a source of infinite delight to him. Most of the time.

"Zzzzzloccchhhh."

She might well go on saying that, a different inflection with every repetition, for several minutes. Alas, her principal pleasure, to find a rhyme for the word, would probably be frustrated.

> *There was an old man named Zloch,*
> *Who had a gigantic—*

Or perhaps not.

§155

Unfortunately, Bohdan Zloch looked remarkably like a bag of wet porridge, and for a moment or two Troy could not get Anna's voice out of his head—*Zzzzzloccchhhh!*

There was very little to distract him from the sound in his head. *Zzzzzloccchhhh!*

The room was undifferentiated brown. Brown panelled walls, brown desk, brown chair and a brown double-breasted suit on the winter-pale, sun-starved bloke sitting in the brown chair behind the brown desk. His face shone moonlike, little short of luminous against all the indelicate browns.

"Minister, I'd like exit visas for the refugees at my embassy."

Zzzzzloccchhhh!

Zloch having no English and Troy bugger all Czech, they spoke in Russian.

"You have refugees? How many?"

"Twenty-six."

"Twenty-six?"

"Twenty-six. I have already issued visas for their UK entry. All it requires is for you to issue exit visas."

"Ambassador, what do you think a Ministry of the Interior is? A shop? A travel agency? Where you buy what you want? You are asking me to release twenty-six criminals."

"Minister—they are twenty-six boys. Teenagers. They have been living in my garden since October. In all that time you have not issued warrants or pressed charges. In fact, you have ignored their presence entirely. I am asking you to shuffle off a problem you had forgotten you had. Issue the visas and within twenty-four hours I will have those boys on a bus heading for the West German frontier."

"Boys? They are counterrevolutionaries, dissidents—"

"Then you would be better off without them."

Zloch leaned back, the chair creaked, his body seemed to ripple, the illusion of liquidity, the brown bag of porridge.

He stared at Troy. Had they reached the moment? That moment?

Troy had a hardtop briefcase at his feet. He hefted it to the desktop, flipped the lid and spun it round to face Zloch.

Clearly Zloch would have loved to show no reaction, but it was beyond him to fail to react to the sight of so much money.

He opened his mouth to speak but no word emerged.

Troy said, "Five hundred dollars for each permit. That's a total of thirteen thousand dollars, US."

"You . . . you think I can be bribed?"

"I know damn well you can."

Troy kicked himself. Silence would have been so much better. Now he'd risked offending official pride. Janis Bell, MI6's "man" in Prague, had shown him the file on Bohdan Zloch. He was far from honest—a relic of the Novotný regime, dropped as spring had blossomed in Prague, picked up, dusted and stuck in a new suit and ministry as the Russians slowly marginalised Aleksandr Dubček. Troy had not expected Dubček to survive the new year. He was still nominally in office as First Secretary, but it could be only a matter of days or weeks before he was sent packing, back to Slovakia. Meanwhile . . . men like Zloch were running the country. As had been said of America's new president a few years ago, "Would you buy a used car from this man?"

Zloch would either have him thrown out or—

Zloch closed the lid. Dropped the briefcase on the floor beside him as though it was burning his fingers.

"Tomorrow. Same time."

"Thank you, Minister."

"One more thing. You leave too."

"Really?"

"Nothing personal. But we want your wife out."

Troy could not even begin to feign surprise.

"Minister. Unless you demand my recall to London, which I don't think is your intention, I will have to ask to be recalled, which will take a while. Perhaps a week or more. My wife, of course, can leave on the bus tomorrow. With the boys."

"I will book the bus myself. Noon tomorrow, Palác Thun. See that she is on it."

Zzzzzloccchhhh!

Anna glowed with pride when Troy told her.

"It's official? I'm expelled? Persona non grata? Yippee. Infamy at last."

"It's anything but official. It is a very dodgy, rather expensive deal."

"We can afford it."

"Of course. I'm made of money."

"Mind—I shall miss Prague. I shall miss being an ambassadress."

"Well . . . that's over. Back to the farm."

"Literally?"

"Oh yes. I've had quite enough of diplomacy."

"Pity. I adored it."

§156

Church Row, Hampstead

About Three Weeks Later

Troy expected to find a copper on the door of his brother's house. There'd been one there since 1964, when Rod had become Home Secretary. Helmet, truncheon, boots—the full copper kit. A cabinet reshuffle led to Rod now being Foreign Secretary, but quite why that should have tripled the police guard on his front door and included a senior Special Branch detective was baffling.

"Good evening, Lord Troy."

It was Chief Inspector Ernie Leadbetter.

"Ernie, the last time we met it was 'Fred' and 'Ernie.'"

"Can't do that anymore. What's the point of a title if no one uses it?"

"What's the point of you being here?"

"Ah . . . the Prime Minister's inside."

"Oh fuck."

"Your brother didn't tell you?"

"No. He wouldn't. Tell me, is it best bib and tucker?"

"No, the PM is in mufti."

"You mean that dreadful mackintosh?"

"Yes . . . and under that a plain blue suit that I understand is now prefaced with the word 'lounge.'"

"Well, at least I didn't come in blue jeans."

The door was yanked open.

"Freddie! Ernie has better things to do than natter to you. Inside, if you please."

Rod's voice dropped. Just above a whisper.

"And do behave yourself. For fuck's sake, do not swear in front of Harold. He was brought up a Methodist or some such bollocks, so keep it clean."

§157

Troy wondered how long it would be before Rod or Harold Wilson got to a point, the point, any point. He had long ago learnt that politicians did not "converse" with mortals—the rest of us were sources, representative opinions rather than people, voters rather than individuals.

They got through soup on the exchange rate with the US dollar.

Troy had no opinion.

They passed a delicious cut of beef on trades union "strife."

Troy had no opinion.

They ate apple charlotte on the Common Market.

Troy had no opinion.

And they finally hit the post-pudding moment.

Wilson spoke to Troy as if he cared—if you can fake sincerity, you've got it made.

"I wanted to thank you personally for the job you did in Prague. It was a job well done."

Troy found this hard to believe. It had been a cock-up from start to finish. Right down to bribing Zloch, about which he was certain Wilson knew nothing.

"I quite understand why your recall was necessary, but it was unfortunate."

Troy wondered if Wilson expected him to say anything.

Troy had every intention of saying nothing until he had to.

Rod, sensing this, stuck in his two pennorth, his three pennorth and his four pennorth.

"I know you're quite anxious to get back to your farm, but we'd be grateful if you would consider another posting."

Anxious? The pig was about to farrow. Did the man know nothing about the porcine reproductive cycle?

"Where?"

Why in God's name had he said that? He couldn't give a damn where next, he wasn't going to go there.

Rod looked once at Wilson. Was there a hint of a nod?

"Moscow."

Oh shiiiiiiiiiiiiiiiiit!

§158

Wilson knew Troy just well enough not to expect a straight answer. By half past nine, before the moment of cigars and brandy, he had left Rod and Troy to it—whatever *it* was.

Cid, the other Lady Troy, who had quietly withdrawn at the pudding stage of the meal, reappeared.

"Calvados, Armagnac or what, young Fred?"

"Whichever is the fastest route to the erasure of memory and mindless oblivion."

"Knock it off, Freddie. It's not as though I offered you a poisoned chalice."

"'Tis of Lethe I would drink."

"We're clean out of Lethe. Wolfsbane too," said Cid, setting a bottle of each spirit on the table, replacing "or what" with a Polish vodka of near-intolerable strength. Troy reached for it, Rod took the Calvados.

"I cannot go to Moscow. You know very well why."

The vodka seemed as likely to cause blindness as oblivion. Troy pushed it aside and plumped for Armagnac.

"I'm listening," Rod said.

"We're listening," Cid added. Troy took this as reassurance that she saw her role as not letting Rod steamroller him into anything.

"Do I have to spell it out? Charlie is in Moscow—or at least we have assumed that for the last six years. Does Wilson want an ambassador who is compromised the second he steps off the plane by the fact that his oldest friend is a traitor in exile?"

"There's no reason you would ever have to encounter Charlie. The Russians would no more want that than we would."

"What about what Charlie wants?"

"Doesn't matter. He won't get it. He is yesterday's man. We don't want him back. I doubt the Russians ever wanted him there."

"But . . . there he is."

"There he is. A nobody."

"Do you have any idea how annoying it is to hear you say that?"

Cid reached out a hand, put it over Troy's. Silently.

Rod would not appeal to his sense of duty—Troy had felt very little of that since the day he resigned from Scotland Yard. In fact, he had no idea what Rod's next move might be. Cid's presence was crucial—"I will not have sibling punch-ups in my house!" said after one too many punch-ups a few years ago—she held both of them back. All the same, once he and Rod had knocked back another smoothing-soothing shot apiece, Troy was gobsmacked at what Rod finally did say.

"Why don't you run this by your wife?"

§159

"Of course I want it, but there's no point in my wanting Moscow if you're not happy about it."

"I don't know what I am."

"You are a natural for the job, but I must confess to some amazement that Rod might want me there after I slapped those Czech coppers."

"Slapped? You knocked one of them cold."

"Then double my amazement."

No more was said until breakfast. Out at Mimram House. Watching the tide of frost retreat across the lawn like a winter's sundial. A season admitting defeat, so scrambled eggs on toast for Troy and some newfangled thing called Bircher-Benner Muesli for Anna, in lieu of porridge but looking much the same. Troy resisted meals that took longer to spell than to eat.

"How urgent is this thing?" she asked.

"They'd like to know by the weekend."

"Is that enough time for that deeply disturbed organ that passes for your mind to work to a conclusion?"

"Dunno. It's pig time."

A long, breathy pause as she cradled a café au lait between her hands and savoured without drinking.

"Why not," she said, "nip into town today? I'll mind the pig. I'm a doctor, after all. Only difference between her and the rest of my patients is she has four legs and eight tits."

"Nip? To what end? And it's ten tits."

"Why don't you run this by your wife?"

§160

It had been the previous November. The day after Bonfire Night, and by pure coincidence the day after the 1968 US presidential election.

Troy and Anna were in Prague, ambassador and ambassadress (a word Troy thought somewhat ridiculous), mired in the consequences of the Warsaw Pact invasion.

Rod phoned him.

"Your wife just called me. From New York."

"Please use the 'ex' or I get confused."

"Larissa phoned. As I said, from New York."

"I'm listening."

"Something about not wanting to live in an America run by Nixon."

"Who can blame her? She saw Stalin's Russia firsthand."

"She wants to come back to England."

"Then let her."

"She's asking if you will take her in."

Good bloody grief!

Rod went on. "And I thought that . . . as you don't much use the house in Goodwin's Court . . ."

"Give her the key."

"Oh. Wasn't quite ready for that. I'd worked up an entire discourse of justification."

"No need. Just give her the key. I'll be back . . . God knows when."

In 1963, Larissa Tosca had saved Troy's life. She had summoned an ambulance when he collapsed in her Manhattan apartment, kept his heart going until the ambulance arrived, and as he recovered— 'festered,' as he put it, in a sanatorium up the Hudson Valley . . . Athens? Rome? . . . he had blocked the name but had grasped why New York was called the Empire State—she had visited every weekend for six months.

The wish to die passed so rapidly that he found its space in his "deeply disturbed organ" filled with what might be gratitude.

As if that were not enough, on his release she had acceded to his request for a divorce.

He had returned to a different England—Tories out, his brother in the cabinet, an illusion of renewed optimism after "thirteen wasted years"— in time for Christmas 1964, to his pig, his Fat Man, his preposterous country house and the prospect of no more a-coppering. It might be bliss. It could be bliss. And the fact that it wasn't, he concealed artfully.

His mistress, Anna, the widow Pakenham, came out to Mimram regularly for dinner, bed, breakfast, dinner, bed. He came to expect that. He bought a fat book on French food written by three women which contained a recipe for beef bourguignon that ran to three pages (one each?) and for which he found he needed a long run-up, rather like mental hurdling . . . he also bought several thinner books by Elizabeth David . . . and upped his kitchen skills just for Anna. He could spell "lasagne." He could tell tortellini from tortelloni.

What he did not expect was Anna's proposal of marriage.

"OK," he said.

He wrote to Tosca.

"OK," she said.

And they reassured each other they would write regularly but never did. He had not heard from her for over three years.

Rod had installed Tosca in the tiny house in Goodwin's Court WC1 that Troy had owned since the 1930s.

A note arrived in the diplomatic bag from London.

"Thanks. Lx"

When this prolonged diplomatic farce was over, he had every intention of going back to Mimram, his pig and his Fat Man. He didn't need a London house. Tosca could keep it.

It was hers.

And with this in mind, key in pocket, he knocked and waited on his doorstep. The dark, almost sunless alley, the bow window of spun glass, tempting the house to burst, the oval cast-iron number plate nailed to the door centuries before, the bloodstain on the thrawl that thirteen years of rain seemed incapable of washing out.

He loved this house.

So what?

"Something up in Prague?"

"It's over."

"So, you want the house back?"

"Let me in. It's bollock-freezing out here and we need to talk."

§161

Tosca was using the dining table as a desk. A scattering of papers in two languages. The room was dimly lit by a reading lamp and the reassuring glow of the gas fire.

"What are you working on?"

"Dostoevsky. Двойник. *The Double*. Weidenfeld and Nicolson wanted a new translation of *Crime and Punishment*. I convinced them that what they really needed was *The Double*. All those people who read Dostoevsky without knowing about this short novel are missing something vital."

"I quite agree. Does it pay well?"

"I don't need a bail out, Troy."

"I wasn't offering. I have a far more sinister motive for being here."

"Kettle on?"

"I think so."

It felt very English and very comfortable to be sitting with a cup of PG Tips, either side of the fire—ex-wife and ex-husband. Tosca was, he knew, very adaptable, she could flip almost everything but her accent, which to him still sounded very, very New York.

He told her.

Briefly enough for her to listen without interruption.

"So . . . you want know what I think, is that it?"

"Sole purpose of visit."

"Are we talking one Russian to another?"

"Yes."

"Our Russias are very different."

"Well, you've lived there."

"And you've been there, what? Once? How long was the trip?"

"Four days."

"Compared to my half a lifetime. Yet . . . you're more the Russian than I am. You got brought up on stories of the old country. Your grandfather filling your head with tales of the old regime. Me? I just thought my old man talked funny, but so many dads on the Lower East Side did. Then . . . I get to be nine years old and he announces we are Russians and we touch down in Moscow. My mother gets a choice, stay Italian American—stay a 'Noo Yawker'—or become Russian . . . and keep your family. So she comes. And I become . . . Russian."

"What would you say you are now?"

"I'm a spectacularly disloyal American. Not that I sell out America, oh no, but I cannot have, cannot believe in, loyalty to a country anymore. Countries aren't worth it. Fukkem. My loyalties are closer to home."

"I've never been much of a patriot."

"Troy—the only thing you cared about was your job."

"At the time, yes."

"And now?"

"I'm still not much of a patriot. I represent a country abroad, without any sense that it is my country. As Her Majesty's ambassadors go, I am a fraud. My loyalties are much the same as yours . . . I have a wife . . . an ex-wife . . . and a pig . . . and a pigman. The list doesn't get any longer."

"How is the Fat Guy?"

"Getting old, I fear. But he can still tuck a hundred-pound piglet under each arm and demolish steak and kidney pie for three at dinner."

"Then why take the job? Seems to me you have everything you want out at the ranch."

"That's the question I keep asking myself."

"It's a mess in Moscow. It always has been. Back to the Kiev Rus. And for all I know, way beyond that. Was there ever a Neanderthal Rus? It's a nation of peasants who believe they have a mission to the West—спасители мира . . . saviours of the world. It's . . . it's like . . . a national delusion . . . they are as fucked up as can be and yet . . . do you know Nekrasov's poems?"

"I used to."

"Thou art poor and thou art something something; thou art mighty, and thou art helpless, Mother Russia. That one."

"I think the word is 'abundant,' or perhaps 'abounding.' I think it's from *Rodina*, Nekrasov."

"In two lines the guy nailed the great Russian paradox. A hundred and some years ago the Russians were serfs. Slaves in all but name. Less than a hundred years ago the Russians were peasants with hammers and sickles. In 1917 the hammers and sickles got stuck on a red flag, the Bolsheviks broke out the ammo and the Russians became peasants with rifles. Then . . . comes the Great Patriotic War and Russians become peasants with tanks . . . a costly victory and . . . boom . . . the Russians are peasants with atom bombs. Abundant and poor. Helpless and mighty. That's who you'll be dealing with. Peasants with atom bombs."

"Boom?"

"Yep. Boom."

"I met a peasant with an atom bomb."

"What? Oh . . . you mean Khrushchev?"

"Being a peasant didn't make him stupid, far from it."

"He's gone, Troy. Holed up in his dacha, writing a memoir that will never see the light of day. Brezhnev and Kosygin rule, and they make Khrushchev and Bulganin look like the Hardy Boys. You haven't really set foot in Russia. At best you stuck your big toe in the pond, but, Troy, it's an infinite pond. And I'm not talking geography. It's almost metaphysical. Russia and Russians and being Russian just goes on and on and on. Do you really want to immerse yourself in all that any more than you have done? I know it was inescapable for you. It's the nature, the substance of your upbringing, but it's contained. Contained by Mimram, by your mother, by this house."

It was, Troy knew, a sound, possibly irrefutable argument, the like of which he had often reasoned to himself and decided never to utter.

"And," he said. "There are personal reasons to consider."

"Your pal Charlie."

"Yes."

"Charlie tried to kill me."

"No . . . that was Cobb. I took care of Cobb."

"Could we not talk about Cobb? Ever again?"

"Of course."

"Are you saying you'd go just to see Charlie? You want to see Charlie?"

"No. Absolutely not. I do not want to see Charlie."

"Then that's fine. The Russians won't let you within a mile of him."

"That's what Rod thinks."

"He's right. The Charlie you'd find would not be the Charlie you knew. They got me when I was a kid. I believed, for as long as it was possible to believe. From what I hear, Philby still does. Never met the guy, but I think you have to be remarkably stubborn or stupid to go on believing once you've seen Mother Russia. Burgess? We both knew him. His existence in Russia was miserable. He could not go on believing. What's left when a believer no longer believes? He curled up at the bottom of a bottle and died. What has become of Charlie? I wouldn't care to know. Troy, the only reason to take this job, the only reason to go to Moscow is if you think you can do some good. I can't tell you that you can. You have to decide. Russia is the old immovable object. And we are neither of us the irresistible force."

Troy got up to leave.

One line, of many she had spoken, echoed in his mind.

"What's left when a believer no longer believes?"

And Tosca said, "You find something else to believe in, or you die at the bottom of that fucking bottle."

He agreed. He too would not care to know what had become of Charlie Leigh-Hunt.

§162

Troy told Rod later the same day that he would accept the posting.

"Jolly good."

"There are some conditions."

"Of course. Wouldn't be my little brother if there weren't."

"If I get fed up and have to quit, you do not argue."

"OK. Do try to stick it as long as you can. We need a good man in Moscow."

Troy concealed his surprise at being termed "a good man."

"If my wife clobbers anyone . . ."

"Don't let her!"

"And I want my choice of SIS station chief."

"Oh bloody hell."

"I don't know what you're dropping me into. I can't see a Russian crisis at the moment, but clearly you anticipate them in the future, so I want a man I can rely on completely for the spookery."

"You want me to fire . . . wotsisname?"

"I don't know his name, and if you don't then he's hardly made much of an impression."

"Who do you have in mind?"

"Janis Bell. Right now she runs the Prague station. Acting. When she gets to Moscow, drop the 'acting' and pay her properly. And—"

"You're only allowed one more 'and.'"

"And . . . I want the Rolls in Moscow."

When he got home that evening, he told Anna that Janis Bell would be arriving in Moscow ahead of them.

"Oh, good," she said. "Someone to swap knitting patterns with."

And stuck her tongue out at him.

§163

Then he called Prague.

"Janis, before you set off, arrange for the Rolls to be shipped to Moscow."

"Way ahead of you. But there will be a delay. No more than a couple of days. I'm sending it via our blokes in Berlin. It could do with some armour-plating, and a few debugging devices. Something like double glazing to stop the windows vibrating and a ring of signal-dampeners around the rear compartment."

"Is this really necessary?"

"I'm on top of bugging here, but God knows what it will be like in Moscow. The KGB could have microphones everywhere. If we know your car is safe then we have at least one place we can talk without Russian ears wagging."

Did ears wag? I thought they pricked.

"OK. But leave out the armour-plating. No one's going to take a shot at me."

§164

The next morning, the Fat Man stuck his head round the kitchen door.

"She's started. First one can't be more than a jiffy away."

Troy's teaspoon remained poised above his boiled egg.

"Your call," said Anna.

"Do I have time for breakfast?" said Troy.

"Nah, just grab a slice o' bread 'n' marge an' foller me."

"Well, you heard the man," said Anna. "A pig in labour will not wait upon a boiled egg."

Troy slipped the intact egg into his jacket pocket. Warm and smooth. He'd eat it cold. Moscow could wait a day or two. Or three.

Anna gave up waiting and set off without him.

On the fifth day Rod telephoned.

"Two military policemen will call on you at noon. Be packed and ready. There's an RAF Britannia waiting on the runway at Lyneham. It will fly you to Moscow, with a stop for fuel at Hamburg. If you are not ready, if you resist, if you string it out I shall have those chaps arrest you."

"Fuck off," Troy replied, but packed anyway.

Janis

§165

The British Embassy

Sofiyskaya Naberezhnaya 14
Moscow

"Good bloody grief. It's hideous," said Anna.

"Wait till you see the inside," Janis Bell replied.

"It looks as though it's been iced, like a soddin' cake!"

"And inside it feels as though you're trapped in granny's sewing box. I don't think there's such a thing as a good-taste embassy."

"You didn't like Prague?"

"Well . . . yes. I suppose I did. If I stay in this job long enough I may get to write the *Observer's Book of British Embassies*. Helsinki, Bonn, Prague and now this. Shall we go in?"

§166

Hideous, Anna decided on the spot, was an understatement.

She'd never liked chandeliers. Even less did she like gargoyles and dragons and flattering portraits of toffs and royalty—not that either were up-to-date, the latest monarch to grace the walls being George V, who'd died in 1936.

They walked from room to room in a silence that Anna could only feel was unnatural. Nothing buzzed, nothing hummed, no one chattered offstage. Everything echoed. It looked like an abandoned set from a Cecil B. DeMille epic. Or perhaps an Errol Flynn medieval romp. Everything was a drape or a gargoyle or a tapestry. Or Satis House before the rot set in. And it all looked fake, the colours artificial, as though it were lurid, painted plaster of paris that could be bulldozed aside at any minute to make way for a Fred Astaire musical.

It had . . . a red room . . . a blue room . . . a white room (with splashes of gold) . . . a ballroom . . . a smoking room . . . and a fireplace large enough to roast a mammoth.

"It's . . . it's . . . not your granny's sewing box," she said. "It's like being inside a can of Del Monte fruit salad."

"Same difference," said Janis Bell. "We've been here for about thirty years. Before that it was the Kremlin's guest house. Between the two, God knows how many toffs and world leaders and doomed rebels have passed through. I'm told we played host to Enver Pasha in nineteeen-and-whatever."

"I'm not entirely sure who he was."

"Nor am I, but he stayed here."

"If walls could talk."

"Alas, walls in Moscow simply listen. There is a marvellous piece of gossip that says H. G. Wells came to visit Stalin when the house was still Soviet property and had the cheek to bring a mistress with him."

Anna raised an eyebrow at this.

Janis paused.

"Don't stop now. Dish the dirt."

"It's just that . . . as I was dishing it occurred to me you might have known Wells."

"Nope. Troy did, but Troy isn't here, or we wouldn't be having this conversation."

"Weeeeell . . . it is said H. G. brought the notorious Charlotte Shumacher here."

"Before she was either notorious or Shumacher, one would presume?"

"One would."

"Troy knew her too, I gather. Or at least he admits to having met her. I wonder what became of her. All over the *Tatler*, the *Daily Mail*, the gossip columns . . . then zilch. A vanishing act, just like the one Troy is attempting now."

"Really?"

"Yes, really. I honestly think he'd be happier at home with his pigs and his piano."

"Well, there's a Lichtenthal Roial in the ballroom."

"What's that?"

"A grand piano. Clara Schumann played on it when she was in Moscow umpteen years ago. That ought to delight Lord Troy. Not a lot I can do about the pigs."

"Janis, don't even think about it. If we can fob him off with Clara's piano, we will. Now . . . a quantum leap . . . pigs to spies, if you're ready. Walls that listen?"

§167

"I think the Russians took advantage of the handover to get men inside. There'll always be Russians guarding the gate—nothing we can do about that—but I stamped me size fours and got rid of the chauffeur and the gardener. I brought in our own men from Prague. Tony Broadbent to drive, and old Sopey Glossop the gardener."

"We have a garden? Troy will be delighted. On the other hand we many never see him again."

"You'll understand if I say I'll deal with that problem when it arises. Now, on my first night here there were distinct thumps in the attic, so I think we've had a rewire.

"The clever thing is that nowadays so many bugs are voice or movement activated. They sit there in the walls and the ceiling sort of dormant. Pretty hard to detect.

"So . . . there are two solutions. Prevention and detection. I had a couple of dozen of these shipped out in the dippy bag."

Janis opened a small cardboard box on her desk. Inside were several phials of colourless liquid sitting in a bed of cotton wool.

"Prevention."

"Let me guess," said Anna. "Nerve gas?"

"Hardly. A present from my little brother. A staple in the English schoolboy's armoury. Stink bombs. I scattered the rest in the attic. The shell is spun sugar; anyone who steps on one won't hear it break. The first thing they'll know is an overwhelming stench of rotting cabbage and dog fart. Our attic is now impregnable, as a Bond villain might say. And . . . detection."

Janis hefted what looked like a large, flat battery pack onto her desk. Attached to it were headphones and something that resembled the plunger you unblocked the loo with or, if you were really unlucky, something a Dalek shot at you with. Anna did not think the Russians had Daleks—yet.

"It's called a non-linear junction detector. It can find a bug even when the bug is switched off. It works by zapping out radio waves that can read the energy reflected off a diode."

"What's a diode?"

"I've no idea. But this thing works. We've identified twenty-two bugs inside the embassy. Once we've done that, the next trick is to isolate them."

Janis pointed to a small silver box, the sort of thing a gentleman kept fags in, sitting on one corner of the desk.

"This gadget has a name so long I can't even pronounce it, but it's why we can talk in here and in most rooms in the embassy. It picks up on the frequency of the bug and sends out a countersignal. Our Mr. Fixit said to imagine an old bloke with an ear trumpet and some annoying schoolboy comes along and decides to yell down it. Essentially it smothers the bug in extraneous noise and makes it damn nigh impossible to make sense of speech.

"I had six installed in Troy's Rolls-Royce in Berlin. If absolute privacy is required we can just retreat to the car. After all, there will be bugs in here we haven't yet found. The Russians played a sneaky trick on the Americans just after the war. A group of Little Octobrists came to welcome the ambassador and presented him with a replica of the United States Great Seal, which they, as dutiful Little Octobrists, had made in their woodwork class. It was full of bugs. The ambassador hung it on the wall behind his desk and the KGB heard everything he said for the next five years. Not enough egg-on-face to make up for Burgess and Maclean, but every little helped.

"Now—outside. Moscow isn't Prague. Expect to be followed every time you leave the embassy and learn not to care, or each rustle of gabardine and every slushy footfall will have you jumping. These chaps are everywhere . . . except in the ladies', where you can assume that the granny with the mop is one of them. None of it means anything. The motto of the USSR is 'belt and braces . . . and if at all possible two pairs of trousers.' They guard against even the imaginary wisp of a threat. For example, you may wish to buy knitting wool. If you do, you will be letting the poor old dear from whom you buy the wool in for a fifteen-minute interrogation—but don't let that put you off. They're all used to it. It's as routine as a visit from the milkman. They won't pester you because they're equally afraid of a diplomatic incident—and, after all, we have Troy to create those all on his own. They'll pester embassy staff, but that's for me to handle. They'll follow you, watch you and keep their distance."

"Y'know," said Anna, "Moscow sounds so very lonely. Proximity without intimacy. Distance without privacy. A crowded emptiness."

"I think you might just have summed up the communal life."

§168

On his first morning in Moscow Troy lay abed and refused to be disturbed.

It was noon before he sat behind his desk with coffee and curiosity—neither stirred—to face an impatient Janis Bell. This woman, who normally struck sparks in all directions, did seem to be droning on a bit.

"And secondly . . ."

Secondly? What had been firstly?

"You need to present yourself."

"I do?"

"Of course you do. The only reason you didn't do that in Prague is . . . well . . . tanks and troops. Exceptional circumstances. I've researched what's required here, so there'll be no surprises. Tony drives you to the Foreign Ministry on Smolensky Bul'var, you wear the clobber—"

"Clobber?"

"The sash thingy."

"And that daft hat with plumes?"

"Yep. And any medals you might have."

"I don't have any. I try to avoid heroism."

"Then you wait a bit. They'll always make you wait. I say a bit, it will be five minutes precisely. Everything about this ritual is precise. Then you'll be shown in to meet with a minister. The only other person there will be a translator. You remain standing. You state your credentials, Her Britannic Majesty's et cet et cet, the minister reads a load of waffle off a printed page, hands it over as acknowledgement and then you leave. All rather plain, but it has simplicity going for it."

"Who's the minister?"

"Dmitry Ilyich Maslyanigit."

"And he is what exactly?"

"Third Deputy Assistant Under-Secretary to the Foreign Minister."

"A nobodnik?"

"Well . . . yes . . . but later on you do pretty much the same thing before the Chairman of the Presidium of the Supreme Thingy."

"And he is . . . ?"

"Podgorny. Nikolai Podgorny. You haven't read the soddin' brief, have you? Podgorny . . . remember? Helped oust Khrushchev along with Brezhnev and Kosygin?"

"Does he still matter?"

"Of course . . . just not as much as he did. It's the Brezhnev show now. The announcer says, 'Heeeeeeere's Leonid!' and everyone shuffles their bum down the couch."

"And Podgorny has shuffled?"

"Yep."

"Then, no," said Troy.

"What do you mean, 'no'?"

"Tell them I want to meet Gromyko. He's the Foreign Secretary. I'll present my cred to him."

"You're kidding? You're doing this just to annoy me?"

"Wouldn't dream of it. But I am Her Majesty's representative, not the umpteenth jobsworth in some diplomatic dole queue. I am the brother of a man who may well be the next prime minister—"

"Really?"

"Well, that's what he thinks . . . and I met Andrei Gromyko several times when he was their ambassador in London. I played the piano for him at my brother's house, in fact. So—tell 'em it's Gromyko or no one, no nobodniks, no bum-shufflers, and you know where you can stuff your sash and plumes. After all, he never wore them."

"Oh fuck. Is this how you mean to go on?"

"Yes."

"The gear is . . . well . . . traditional."

"Janis, we're in Moscow, not the Surbiton am-dram production of H.M.S. Pinafore. Now, any other business?"

"Yep. The first piece of Moscow gossip to come my way is really quite disturbing. There would appear to be a man under guard, and seriously injured, in the Timoshenko Hospital. Rumoured to be Joe Holderness."

"Rumoured?"

"Well, obviously the Russians aren't saying."

"Then what are our lot saying?"

"Only that Joe hasn't reported in since Prague."

"He left Prague weeks ago. Janis, what is it they're not telling me?"

"They?"

"SIS."

"I'm SIS. What is it you're not telling me?"

"Eh?"

"Nell Burkhardt got busted. Joe set off to rescue her, but it was you talked to the KGB. You struck the deal with Zolotukhina, but it was at that point you stopped confiding in me, so I can only conclude you cooked up a dodgy deal you didn't want SIS knowing about."

Troy felt nailed. Pinned to the board like a dead butterfly.

"That's . . . correct. In particular, I didn't want Colonel Burne-Jones or my brother knowing."

"I'm Janis. Tell me."

"We swapped Nell for Bernard Alleyn."

"Tell me you're joking."

"I'm not."

"Alleyn was supposed to be back in Moscow. We swapped him for a fool called Masefield a couple of years ago."

"That was the cover story. That was what Joe wanted people to believe."

"And Burne-Jones?"

"I'm sure he knew the trade didn't happen. After all, Joe went into East Berlin guns blazing like he was Clint Eastwood, and got Masefield out. My brother told me the Finland posting was to get Joe where some Commons committee couldn't put him on the spot."

"I know. He told me. Finland is where I first met Joe. But Alleyn?"

"Lived quietly in Dublin ever since under a new name."

"And Joe told you this?"

"No. Eddie Clark."

"So . . . the second trade went wrong too? The Russians now have Nell, Joe and Alleyn?"

This was in danger of turning into Abbott and Costello's "Who's on First?" sketch.

"No. Nell Burkhardt is back in Berlin. Alleyn just vanished. He's probably back in Dublin. Zolotukhina never wanted him. That was just part of her bluff."

"And Joe? She wanted Joe? It didn't occur to you he might be here?"

"Eddie has been clam-tight. And I haven't asked. Joe is a spy. For all I might guess he could be undercover in Timbuktu. I had no reason to think the swap had gone pear-shaped so long as Nell was back in Berlin, and Eddie assured me she was. The only grey area was Alleyn himself. That the Russians didn't want him is a bit baffling, but it didn't mean they'd got Joe. Until now."

"So the rumour could be true?"

"I think it most certainly is."

"Then I think I have another rumour for you. A London one. It's being said, 'muttered' might be a better word, that Joe has defected."

"Well . . . that sounds like bollocks, doesn't it?"

"Yep. Most, maybe all, defectors are ideologues. Joe isn't an ideologue, he's a chancer."

"Have you received any request to pursue this?"

"No. And you?"

"No. I am to avoid Charlie Leigh-Hunt. I would anyway. But no mention of Joe? If he really is here, then I find that a drastic omission from my brief."

Janis sighed.

"I'm sure your wife must have said this to you a few times, and I apologise in advance for the cheek, but were you actually listening? Anna and I agree, you're a daydreamer. You're often listening to the music in your head."

"I shall ignore that and ask: What is Burne-Jones up to?"

"If Joe really is here . . . if he is a prisoner . . . if neither you nor I are briefed . . . then Burne-Jones is going through the back door. Everything off the record."

"So he's talking to Zolotukhina?"

"Probably."

§169

Soviet Foreign Ministry
Smolensky Bul'var 32–34
Floor 7

A Room in Several Shades of Beige

With a wave of his hand Gromyko cleared the room.

Since standing was the formality, Troy pulled out a chair and sat down. Gromyko sat too, nose fractionally out of joint. He was a dignified, but hardly a humourless man. Humour might be all he had in common with the man who had given him power—Nikita Khrushchev. He had survived the fall of Khrushchev and as Foreign Minister seemed unassailable. The Talleyrand of the Soviet Union. He was known at the United Nations as Mr. Niet.

He was fluent in English. All the same, they spoke in Russian.

"You got some cheek," he said.

"It's a pleasure to see you again too, Andrei Andreyevich."

"Why did you take this job?"

"Duty?"

Gromyko laughed.

"You're such a liar."

"I did it to please my brother, and my brother wanted to please Harold Wilson."

"You got the bum's rush, you know that, don't you? Nothing is happening here. Moscow is just ballet, chess and dumplings. You will get fat and die of boredom. Buy a stamp album and collect stamps. It will help pass the time."

"Not planning any invasions of small countries, then?"

"No. That was last year. This year . . . I don't know . . . a bumper potato harvest . . . and a twenty percent rise in ball-bearing output. They could well be the headlines—as snappy as your *Daily Mail*. But . . . but . . . you have your brother's ear?"

"When he bothers to listen."

"You have Wilson's?"

"On occasion."

"Then get this through to him. 'Stay out of Vietnam.' Ignore the Americans and stay out of Vietnam. Convince him of that and your tenure here will have been worthwhile. It is perhaps the only good you can do."

It seemed to Troy to be an echo of Tosca's last words to him: *The only reason to go to Moscow is if you think you can do some good.*

"I'll do my best. You have Brezhnev's ear?"

"On occasion."

"Joe Holderness?"

Gromyko paused for thought. Troy could read nothing in his expression.

"Not a name I know, alas."

Troy had long been familiar with the Russian notion of враньё (*vranyo*)—a lie uttered with no expectation of belief. A few years ago Khrushchev had elevated it to the level of poetry, declining to meet a foreign politician with the excuse of "diplomatic neuralgia."

"I thought you'd say that," he said.

Wilderness

$170

Timoshenko Veterans' Hospital

Moscow
Later in February

Clearly, the nurses had been briefed. They would not speak to him except on medical matters.

There were two of them on the day shift. He was scarcely conscious of the night nurse as the last act of the day was to dope him into deep and downy sleep just shy of a coma.

They wore name tags.

V. S. Alekseyeva.

Wilderness wanted to know, Vera or Vasilisa?

N. F. Kuznetsova.

Natasha or Nadia?

But neither answered. V just carried on changing his dressings as though he had not spoken. N smiled and put a shushing finger to her lips.

He would not have thought walking quite so difficult. He had watched his daughters learn the delights of the vertical—Molly laughing every time she fell on her well-cushioned arse, Joan critically examining the carpet as though it might be at fault.

At the end of February a new nurse, not V or N, wheeled him into a physio theatre, and an elderly doctor began to put him through his paces—but that he was paceless.

He gripped the rails set at hip height, a corridor down which he must walk or crawl, and dragged his right leg behind him. The damn thing lacked traction—not that it had a will of its own but no will at all.

The doctor helped him to a chair.

"The bullet did some considerable damage to the nerves in your abdomen."

So much for the obvious. Wilderness remembered going to a cinema in Camden with Judy, perhaps fifteen years ago. A film she said he had to see called *Reach for the Sky*, which he had assumed to be a western . . . John Wayne or Audie Murphy . . . but the title was literal, and the film depicted the fall and rise of RAF fighter ace Douglas Bader. Wilderness had never forgotten the scenes of him learning to walk again after losing both legs in an accident before the war—on two tin legs—on rails identical to these.

"Will I walk again?"

"I have a good success rate. After Stalingrad, after Berlin, I saw countless men and women missing one leg or both. Most are walking around now. I had the odd failure. I'm not God. And whilst you are not young, you are healthy."

"Not young? I'm forty-one."

"As I said. Not young. In 1945 the average age of my patients was eighteen."

Exactly the age Wilderness had been in 1945.

"It will take time. Weeks. But I am confident."

It took months.

In that time he received no visitors. He'd half expected Charlie, although from time to time one of the nurses would bring in a bottle of vodka, which he could only assume was Charlie's gift. They would lock it away. V silently. N with a smiling, whispered "niet."

On the other hand, once a week an orderly would wheel in a trolley laden with books. Wilderness found he had two ways to pass the time. One way was to read all those Russian classics that had escaped him in the past—the lesser Turgenevs—and reread those he had read. *Anna Karenina, Oblomov* . . .

The other way was to work out his script for the interrogation that the Russians were surely delaying until he was fit. Once he could walk, he'd put money on Volga moving him to the Lubyanka or some lesser prison.

Questions.

Questions.

Questions.

§171

It was mid-morning, late in June. Wilderness was relishing two things: Wearing his own clothes, or at least the suit Volga's people had had made for him. Not bad, not bad at all. It wasn't Savile Row quality, but then he'd never had a bespoke suit from Savile Row—this despite the promptings of his father-in-law—so he had nothing to compare it with. And . . . and . . . walking unaided, no helpful nurse's arm, no crutch, no stick. Fourteen weeks of physiotherapy, at least six of them in exquisite pain, and he was whole again. All the bits put back together, and another scar to show—two inches away from the one Yuri Myshkin had left him with in Berlin in '47.

He stretched. He walked from one side of the room to the other and back again. Walking had its downside. More than ever the room felt like a cage, a cell—it had been the longest period he'd spent locked up since a spell in the RAF glasshouse . . . insubordination, assaulting an NCO . . . from which Burne-Jones had rescued him in 1945—the price of freedom paid ever after.

Spy.

Spy.

Spy.

He'd no real idea what he looked like. The shaving mirror was the size of a saucer. A full-length reflection in a window might be good, but there were no windows—just as there were no door handles on the inside.

The door opened.

"Chop chop, old man."

"Eh?"

"Time's up. You're fit. They need the bed for some other poor sod."

Wilderness did not know what he had expected next, but it wasn't Charlie. Surely some new "jailer" would come to take charge, and Charlie hardly qualified.

"Come on, Joe. I've a car waiting."

It was almost surreal. As though they were setting off on a picnic or going to the races.

"Got all your stuff?"

"What stuff? I'm wearing everything I own."

Wilderness would like to have said goodbye, and thank you, to N, but Charlie was bustling, a busyness that was almost out of character.

Outside, a fat-bodied government ZIL-111 was parked. A fat-bodied KGB-nik stood by the driver's door. An almost identical fat-bodied KGB-nik held one of the rear doors open as Charlie approached.

Charlie ushered Wilderness in and walked around to the other side to sit behind the driver.

Wilderness stood, one hand on the top of the door, staring. He'd almost forgotten what the outside world looked like. It was his first glimpse of Moscow. He'd been utterly unconscious when they'd brought him to the hospital in January. He relished the moment and, but for the iron look on the face of the KGB-nik, would have lingered, staring at a plain, unremarkable Moscow street as though it were the yellow brick road.

The man grunted.

Wilderness took the hint.

"Have you noticed?" he said to Charlie. "The resemblance between these two blokes and Arthur Mullard?"

"What, the actor with the boxer's face? The one who was in everybody's sitcom in the fifties?"

"Yep. You don't suppose he and his twin brother have defected, do you?"

"Quite the opposite. I think Russia manufactures them on a production line. I can only suggest you get used to them."

When the car stopped, it stopped in front of a building Wilderness knew from endless SIS briefings, like the slideshows of a bad package holiday—the Lubyanka, as recognisable as the Pentagon or the Tower of London.

He was tempted to reach for the door handle and preempt the obvious, but the car suddenly moved on and he realised they had only stopped at a traffic light.

"Charlie, where are we going?"

"Joe, you surely didn't think . . ."

The same slideshows had given Wilderness some haphazard grasp of the geography of the city, hardly a Moscow A–Z, more like a Russian

Monopoly board, but when the ZIL turned into Sverdlov Square, a few hundred yards on, he knew exactly where they were.

One Mullard stayed behind the wheel, the other got out and stood in front of the Metropol Hotel, an early-twentieth-century fantasy of a building, in its way as monstrous as the Lubyanka, also the most expensive hotel in the city and a major source of foreign exchange—one last crumb of Imperial Russia to delight the punter's palate.

"You're joking?"

"I'm not saying anything, let alone joking. This isn't my show or your show, it's Volga's. All I will say is I didn't get this treatment."

Charlie turned to the Mullard and told him to park the car and then wait in the lobby.

"Your Russian's improved," Wilderness said.

"From what? All I had in '63 was 'da,' 'niet' and 'vodka.' I've had a very good tutor, however, and in about three minutes you may well get to meet her."

§172

It seemed to fly in the face of fiction, if not of tradition, not to have a hard, upright wooden chair and an Anglepoise lamp for dazzling.

Instead, Wilderness sat in a rather snazzy bucket chair, straight out of a *Sunday Times* colour supplement, all Habitat and Conran. Charlie sprawled on one end of the sofa, long legs sticking out across the rug.

They waited more than three minutes. After ten, Wilderness said, "Should we ring for room service?"

"I'm sure we can, but let's not begin on a farcical note if at all possible."

"You don't think two English spies being in a three-room suite at the Metropol, complete with piano, is farcical in itself?"

"Of course it is. But Volga's sense of humour is never to be underestimated. She no doubt thinks it's hilarious to give you your own suite instead of your own cell. I was thinking more of Major Ewald, who . . . shall I say . . . doesn't quite share that streak of humour."

The door opened.

A small woman . . . "petite," as Charlie might say . . . a full-blown KGB major, all in brown with blue flashes, a bit like Rosa Klebb in that Bond film from a few years ago—except that she looked nothing like Rosa Klebb and, Wilderness thought, was really rather beautiful—wisps of ash-blonde hair escaping from under her bog-standard Russian forage cap with its wreathed red star badge.

The gentlemen, being gentlemen, rose to greet her.

She ignored them and took the only upright chair in the room away from the desk, to position it between Charlie and Wilderness.

It didn't look like a power play. It looked like piggy-in-the-middle.

Feeling awkward and very conscious of his size, Wilderness sat down again, wondering if Charlie might scrape up his habitually scattered wits sufficiently to introduce her.

No need. Once she had a notebook and pencil in her hand she turned to Wilderness.

"I am Major Ewald. What language would you wish?"

"As you've begun in Russian, let's stick with it, unless of course Charlie . . ."

"I'm pretty damn good, Joe. You told me so yourself not half an hour ago."

"Could do better," said Major Ewald, curtly.

"Used to get that on my school reports all the time," Charlie replied.

"Where would you like to begin, Major?"

She flicked over a couple of pages on her notepad and then flipped them back again.

"Spain. You were there in 1956."

"Yes."

"Why?"

"You're saying you don't know?"

Major Ewald looked at Charlie to take his cue.

"You know, Joe, the only smooth way to do this sort of thing is to simply answer the question without any presumption of prior knowledge on Magda's part."

"Magda?"

"Major Ewald."

"Ah. OK. I was in Madrid undercover. The British were working both ends—they despised Franco but at the same time didn't want to see him usurped by any kind of Communist coup. They didn't want a second Czechoslovakia. We knew you had people there, well concealed, all sorts of plausible guises and all capable of passing for Spaniards. SIS needed to know what they were up to. I could not pass as Spanish, but I made a passably good West German lecturer from the Goethe University in Frankfurt, taking a sabbatical from teaching something like civil engineering. It wasn't hard to find your people and ply them with Russian Kryptonite."

"Kryptonite? I do not understand."

"I mean they made it too easy for me. I found a bar where a couple of them used to hang out, bought them drinks, convinced them I was a good German Communist waiting only for the tip-off from the Kremlin to topple the Bonn government. A few more bars and a lot more alcohol and within a couple of months I'd met your entire Madrid cell."

"You were an . . . infiltrator?"

"Yes, and a very successful one."

"How so?"

"I was able to name everyone who worked for you lot in Madrid to SIS, Spanish covers *and* Russian names. We opened files on every one of them."

"Every one?"

"Domingo Márquez, José Peres, Hector Salamanca, Ramón Estévez, Raúl Ruiz, Gustavo Fring . . . otherwise known as Boris Trigorin, Konstantin Treplev, Pyotr Sorin, Ilya Shamraev, Yevgeny Dorn and Semyon Medvedenko . . . do you want me to go on?"

"You seem to have a very good memory for people you haven't seen for fifteen years."

"Training . . . and a very, very good memory. Would you like me to recite the periodic table for you? Hydrogen to whatever the latest synthetic element is? Complete with atomic numbers?"

Magda's hand stopped on the paper. There was a pause of utter stillness as though the woman had suddenly frozen. Then she got up, put pen and pad on her chair and left without a word.

"Was it something I said?"

"Hmm . . . I don't wish to be critical, Joe, but somehow the word 'atomic' does not strike me as awfully well chosen. Bit above her pay grade, really. She trained as trombone player, not a physicist. She's gone off to report it to the higher-ups. She'll probably return with a Geiger counter."

"Ah . . . I shouldn't joke with our Magda."

"Or at least choose your jokes with care. On the other hand. Are the Russian names a joke? Are any of those blokes real? I can just see them swanning around on some Chekhovian estate seventy years ago. Dreaming of Moscow, chopping down cherry trees."

"Wrong play, Charlie. But the men were real, all right."

"Were?"

"Not one of them made it out of Madrid alive."

"You're the sole survivor?"

"Yes. That's given me plenty of pause for thought over the years."

"Franco shot the lot?"

"Franco didn't touch them. I was the only one he collared. I was driven to the French border with 'undesirable' stamped on my passport, and my bollocks black from the kicking they gave me. No, the Russians took care of their own loose ends."

"The price of failure?"

"Is to be erased from history. I remember Trigorin. I remember Sorin. I remember them all. I doubt there's a file on any of them now. And that in a country of infinite bureaucracy where the filing cabinet is king."

"You realise Magda will not know that?"

"Need to know or don't want to know?"

"She's a believer."

"Then she won't believe me."

"Especially if you don't tell her."

"The KGB killed them all once it was clear they'd been, as Magda put it, 'infiltrated.' She made it sound like a dirty word and perhaps she's right."

"As a favour to me, don't tell her. And stop playing her. She may not have read Chekhov but she's far from stupid. In fact, she's an asset to us both. Her verdict on you matters."

"OK."

A momentary silence. One Wilderness ached to break.

"Trombone? Really?"

"Yes. Really."

"She told you that?"

"We have ... er ... an understanding."

"You mean a relationship?"

"I suppose I do."

"So, she's your Ninotchka?"

"Not exactly, no. I'll admit to a more than passing resemblance to Greta Garbo, but she's not Russian."

"I know. I can hear Vienna in every sentence."

"Really? Try not to be too clever, Joe. This may be just a formality to you, but we do have to get through it."

§173

Magda returned. Gathered up her things.

"Thursday," she said. "We meet again on Thursday."

"It's only Monday ... what do I—?"

"Really, Sergeant Holderness. You have the complete freedom of one of the finest hotels in Europe and you ask me how you might pass the time?"

It was the most casual thing she'd uttered so far, an almost relaxed sentence. All it lacked was the colloquial touch now readily supplied by Charlie.

"There is an English phrase, Magda—born with a silver spoon in my mouth. Родиться в рубашке comes close. Arguably I was born with one. Joe wasn't, but just now it's sticking right up his arse."

§174

Wilderness gently removed the silver spoon and explored the hotel.

Much to his surprise he found he had a reserved table in the restaurant. At dinner he was shown to it by a waiter, who addressed him as "Monsieur Alderney," which was probably as close as he could get to "Holderness," and Wilderness logged the name as a possible alias. You never knew when you might need one.

He'd stayed in hotels all over Europe, and in one or two in North America—every grade from no star to five star—but this was the first time he'd been imprisoned in one. The phrase "locked in a velvet box" came to mind, but this was a marble box, marble in shades of cream and brown, a bit like Wigmore Hall back home—a venue to which his wife dragged him three of four times a year for this pianist or that cellist—a style of decor he always thought of as a urinal for the gods on Olympus.

He looked up. A vast, domed glass roof. Art Nouveau or Art Deco, he always got the two confused—his wife would know. And he looked across, some ten or twelve small tables distant, to where one of the Arthur Mullards sat stiffly, with not so much as a menu or cocktail stick in front of him. Poor bugger.

"*Peut-être un apéritif, Monsieur?*" the waiter asked.

"*Ce serait beaucoup plus facile si on parlait russe.*"

"As you wish."

"No aperitif. How about a good red wine? Something Russian, perhaps?"

"We have a very nice Moldavia '53."

"Fine. Bring the bottle and send a glass to the gentleman over there."

When the wine arrived, Mullard looked at it as though it might be a time bomb, which in a way it was.

Wilderness hoisted his glass, mouthed a silent "Cheers, old boy," and, when Mullard made no move to touch his own glass, sipped gently at the Moldavia '53 and let his first taste of alcohol since the previous December ride roughshod across his palate.

It was . . . liberating. After prolonged abstinence, half a glass of wine went straight to his head and set loose the torrent of thought he had contained while exercising self-control and limited lies in front of Charlie and Magda—foremost among which was "What the fuck is Volga up to?"

§175

Magda did not pick up where she had left off. Orders from above or hints from Charlie. Neither mattered. Of course Frank was right all along. He could tell them very little they did not already know—betrayal was logically impossible, whatever it felt like at the point of utterance. He was relieved. To talk about the "Madrid Six" only emphasised that his side could behave as ruthlessly as their side.

Each Monday and Thursday—the lack of intensity in the frequency of interrogation said something about the operation Volga was running and most certainly about the use Magda made of a summer dacha—Magda would drum up notes on some country or other where Wilderness had been an agent. Charlie looked bored and only perked up when she drew him all the way back to Berlin just after the war. To the rackets, to coffee, peanut butter and morphine and to the *Schiebers* . . . to Joe and Eddie, to Frank and Yuri. None of this could possibly matter. Wilderness felt like the man who spun plates or juggled Indian clubs in a variety show—just filling in till "the turn" came on. All he needed was a glamorous assistant in a tasselled swimsuit and a couple of chords on a Hammond organ.

But . . . but . . . at long last the turn took to the stage.

"Finland?"

Oh fuck.

There were things about Finland in '66 that Madga would surely not know, and if she did not know already Wilderness would rather Volga didn't know either . . . that he and Volga's son had had a lucrative racket running illicit Finnish vodka into the USSR on the edge of the Arctic Circle. For all he knew Volga might have been taking a percentage . . . but if she wasn't? And then the cobalt processing in

Lapland . . . the making of a British dirty bomb . . . how to describe
that without recourse to the word "atomic."

"It was a punishment posting," he said.

So far, so true.

"Punishment for what."

"An incident at the Invalidenstraße checkpoint in Berlin. I rescued
a fellow agent from the East and crashed the barrier. I saw it as doing
my job. Her Majesty's Government saw it as a diplomatic incident. So
I was sent to run a mobile cinema in Finland."

"So there was no operation?"

"No, I'd have been glad of one. Anything to relieve the boredom."

Magda smacked of obedient, and hence unimaginative, efficiency.
Interrogation by numbers, or rather by country—every country Charlie
had told her to ask about. If she was tempted to improvise, now would
be the moment. It didn't take a genius to figure out that in all probability
Wilderness had relieved his boredom, had run a racket or two or three,
and that the racket might have been entwined like bindweed around a
field operation. He would have picked up the cue, Charlie would have
picked up the cue. Magda did not. It could almost seem that she was
on a mission to preserve his innocence.

§176

"Lebanon?"

"Lebanon?"

"You were there at the same time as Kim Philby."

"Briefly, yes. Charlie was there too."

She didn't even glance at Charlie.

"Were you spying on Philby?"

"What would be the point of that? This may be the most pleasing
answer I ever give you, Magda. I was spying on the Americans. They
were most certainly spying on Philby."

"Why not you?"

"Because we knew everything there was to know about him and were just waiting for him to bugger off."

"And the Americans? Why would they spy on him if you did not?"

"Institutional paranoia."

Now she looked at Charlie.

"Oh, they've never trusted us since Burgess," Charlie said. "Doesn't mean a thing."

"But why would you be asked to spy on the Americans?"

"Same reason you ask me the questions you do. Because it was in the script."

Was she blushing? Was she stung? Had he hit home?

Whatever, she came back at him out of left field.

"In 1961 you resigned from MI6. Why?"

Berlin again. Just when he thought they'd finished with Berlin.

If he answered honestly, what would she make of it? The fact that she seemed to have no reactions didn't mean she had no reactions.

OK, Magda, bite on this.

"It was the month the Wall went up. It wasn't much more than a few miles of barbed wire at that point, but one the of the cruellest divisions was at Bernauer Straße, where the sectors met. If you lived there, you could have your back door in the Russian sector and your front door in the French. And when the Russians bricked up the doors, they left the windows. People jumped, people broke bones, people died. The low point for me was watching an old woman dangle off the side of a building with half of Berlin and the world's newsreel cameras looking up her dress. It brought home to me what we were doing to each other. How low we had sunk, to be staring at an old woman's bloomers."

"We?"

"You and I. Me and Charlie. The serpents. The spooks. We who serve our dubious masters. People for whom expediency eclipses morality."

As Magda packed up her things, Charlie spoke to him in English.

"That was a bit harsh, Joe."

"On whom? You or her?"

"On yourself."

§177

After dinner, after many dinners, working his way through almost every plate of haute cuisine soviétique they could stick in front of him—and they refused him nothing—Wilderness decided to test the waters. He headed off, casually, slowly, to the front door and down the steps to Sverdlov Square. A Mullard was propped up in the lobby, a parcel awaiting collection, alert but inanimate, and the second Mullard, Wilderness's "dining companion"—a companion he'd never seen eat so much as a morsel—came up behind him.

"Lovely weather for the time of the year," Wilderness said, in English to no reaction whatsoever, and went back inside. June had slipped almost unnoticed into July. His prison was beginning to feel like a prison.

§178

He wondered about Prague. Session succeeded session with a lack of progress and a plethora of repetition, without a single mention of Prague. She had done Spain, again and again . . . where had he trained for Spain . . . where had he lived . . . what had Russia's own agents said to him on whatever occasion? Ancient history to Wilderness. She had touched on almost every country he'd ever set foot in, places where he'd completed a mission in less than forty-eight hours and got out before the ink was dry on his passport—but not Czechoslovakia.

Once or twice Charlie had nodded off, waking up only when his elbow slipped from his knee to jerk his head like a wobbly toy in the rear window of a Ford Cortina.

She probed, far too gently, about his time in Helsinki, and that too became dull and repetitious. But ne'er a mention of Prague. In Prague he had done "questionable things," but the questions never came.

And it seemed to Wilderness that a year or two of his life had been erased, that he had been whisked from Lapland to the Glienicke Bridge rather like Dorothy leaving Kansas. The reason might be one of two things. The KGB didn't know he'd been in Prague—Charlie certainly didn't know; after all, one of the two men who could name him was dead and the other was Kostya—or Magda was avoiding, on instruction, anything that might implicate Volga's son.

Konstantin Ilyich Zolotukhin was nowhere to be seen.

§179

July 16, 1969
A Warm Wednesday

"I've been in Turkey since May."

"Working?"

"Of course, trying to prise Turkey out of NATO."

He was wittier than he used to be. Kostya would always be a bundle of nerves—knowing his mother, who could blame him?—but perhaps the bundle was getting smaller.

They stood outside the Metropol—an Arthur Mullard to either side of them. In its way it was Wilderness's second first sight of Moscow . . . Moscow without intervening barriers, be they windscreens, windows or just curtains. Wilderness looked out across Sverdlov Square in the direction of the Karl Marx statue, a midday summer sun overhead, Muscovites on park benches silently facing the sky with eyes closed.

"Are we going any further or am I still stuck on the threshold?"

"Oh, you are free to roam. Moscow is your pearl."

"Oyster."

"Of course. Oyster. Here, you will need these."

He handed Wilderness a street map, a metro map, a wad of money and a folded card, cloth-bound in olive green and with the crest of the USSR and just one word, паспорт (PASSPORT), stamped on the front.

"Your salary . . ."

"My salary? I'm on the KGB payroll?"

"I've no idea. It . . . this . . . is all at the mercy of my mother's whims. But you cannot open your oyster without money and an identity card."

Wilderness opened the card before the oyster. A photograph of himself that he had never seen before, an approximate date of birth and a new name:

Никита Сергеевич Плохоймальчик

"Nikita Sergeyevich Plokhoymalchik? My God, she's having fun, isn't she? Naming me after Khrushchev too . . ."

"I chose the surname myself. You were ever the bad boy, Joe. And with that in mind . . ."

Kostya gestured at the Arthur Mullards, standing like obelisks.

". . . you will have company."

"Do they speak English?"

"I'm not sure they speak at all."

Wilderness turned to the nearest.

"Your mother is a ten-titted Soviet sow. Your father sucks cock in Kursk."

Not a flicker.

"You've proved your point, Joe. No more interrogation. It's over. Go out and see the city. Two cautions. Do not take a cab anywhere. They will see it as an attempt to lose them. Stick to walking or public transport. It will pay to keep them in sight at all times, even though I know you could shake them off in five minutes. And be careful who you talk to. I cannot say talk to no one, but if you seem to single someone out, you'll just be dropping them in it. Now, lecture over, reap the reward of espionage. You've earned it, after a twenty-five-year apprenticeship."

"I was hoping to reap a little of it at least with Charlie. Are we not allowed to meet?"

"It's summer. He's out at his dacha most of the time. And no, there are no restrictions on your meeting. But he'd have to come to you. You cannot leave Moscow. I do hope that's clear."

"Perfectly. And you? Do you have time to show me the city?"

"No, I have a job to do. I cannot make the Moscow version of your English pub crawl. You may have a job too. In fact, I'm quite sure you have . . . but my mother won't tell me what it is."

"You're being posted?"

"East Berlin. It brings back old memories. I rather like East Berlin."

"But only because you can visit West Berlin."

"No comment."

Wilderness took a step forward, then another and another, standing in the mythical city—Moscow warm beneath the soles of his shoes, like that first footstep onto a summer beach with sand running like liquid between your toes—Moscow, the sine qua non.

He turned to Kostya.

"Freedom of the city? Cash in hand? My own ID card? Volga really wants to give the British the impression I might have defected, doesn't she?"

"Обманщик," Kostya said simply: Trickster.

§180

It was, as he had told himself many times, the mythical city. The start and end point of his job. Mythical in that he'd never thought he'd get there, never expected to find himself there—MI6 had experts on the Soviet Union, men who made pronouncements from armchairs in London clubs but who'd never been east of Berlin—some of them had probably never been east of Margate. It was mythical too in that he'd read most of the memoirs, travelogues, what-have-you, of Russia's visiting chroniclers—John Reed, Bruce Lockhart, H. G. Wells, Crankshaw, Gunther . . . Mrs. Snowden. All those who had "seen the future," whether it worked or not. Mythical in that he had imagined the city so often.

By the Lubyanka station he unfolded his metro map, and found a demon perched upon his shoulder: *Stick to public transport. No cabs.* He descended into a gloriously golden inferno that could only have been imagined by Dante or Khrushchev. Moscow's metro was, no other term seemed to fit, a People's Palace. New York and London underground railways were far from utilitarian, but this was close to religion set in porcelain. The overall design reminded him of Marble Arch at the top of Park Lane, a Marble Arch in full colour, not dirty London monochrome. But . . . Marble Arch served no purpose. This did.

He boarded a westbound train on the Arbatsko-Pokrovskaya line. At Kievskaya he ran up the escalator, and sat on a bench at the top while the Mullards puffed up angrily behind him. Then he went down once more, switched to the Circular and caught a train anti-clockwise to Taganskaya. At Taganskaya he changed again, went one stop north to Kitay-gorod, raced up the escalator and waited for them to catch up. He smiled. No one returned the smile. They were sweating profusely. He took Kostya at his word and had no wish to lose them. He wondered how long they could keep this up and marvelled that his legs worked—a moving tribute to Soviet medicine. Run? Six months ago he couldn't crawl.

He went back down to track level and caught the next train to Krasnopresnenskaya/Barrikadnaya. At Krasnopresnenskaya/Barri-kadnaya he switched back to the Circular . . . and half a dozen times more . . . change after change . . . Kurskaya, Byelorusskaya, Park Kultury, Oktyabrskaya . . . all the way out to the Lenin Hills and back again to end up several hours later at Sverdlov Square, a short walk from the hotel. In all this the Mullards had muttered and cursed to each other but neither had said a word to him. Orders are orders, and he'd just tested one to the hilt. They daren't shoot him.

All in all a great day out with fun for all the family.

§181

Taking the air, still a novelty after three days, waiting outside the Metropol, looking across the square, a way to start the walking day. A fresh pair of Mullards bulking up behind him. A boy, fifteen or sixteen, a ragged reminder of himself at that age, accosted Wilderness, first in Russian: "Товарищ. Товарищ!" (Hey, comrade!) And then, when Wilderness just shook his head, in surprisingly good English:

"American?"

"No," Wilderness replied.

"Canadian?"

"Stop guessing. I'm English."

"Marks and Spencer?"

"Try again."

"Blue jeans?"

"You're a real optimist, aren't you?"

"Porn? *Penthouse*? *Playboy*?"

"You buying or selling?"

"Buying."

"Too late. If you'd asked me twenty-five years ago I might just have been able to get hold of a copy of *Health and Efficiency* for you."

"Health and what?"

"Forget it. I've nothing to sell you."

"Then what kind of a tourist are you? Tourists always have something. Biros, chewing gum, lipstick, tampons, all sorts of lady things, Ken and Barbie, Jimi Hendrix records. Or eight-track. I love eight-track. Randy Newman on eight-track. *I Think It's Going to Rain Today*. *Davy the Fat Boy*. Or stainless steel razor blades. Only last week at the National a man gave me razor blades and shaving foam in an aerosol. You just have to squirt it and—"

"You don't look as though you shave yet and I'm no kind of tourist. And if *you* know what I am you're way ahead of me. But the point is to be way ahead of them."

Wilderness nodded gently in the direction of the Arthur Mullards. Pulled gently on one earlobe, a Moscow code as clear as semaphore.

"Oh shit," said the boy.

"How succinctly you put it," Wilderness replied. "Now bugger off before they nick both of us."

The kid, Wilderness mused, would have no future as a *Schieber* if he couldn't spot a copper.

Moscow, surely, had to be a city of *Schiebers*? Where there is too much law, where there are too many rules and too many cops, there will be *Schiebers*. It was the fifth law of thermodynamics. And in a totalitarian state, the *Schieber* was ubiquitous, slip-slidin' between profit and arrest.

Kostya had mentioned a peasant market. Dobryninskaya. It looked to be about a half-hour walk from Sverdlov Square, south into one of the many big bends of the Moskva River, and if it lived up to its name there would be *Schiebers*.

He turned to his guardian angels.

"Давай. Следуйте по дороге вымощенной желтым кирпичом."

C'mon—follow the yellow brick road.

The Munchkin voice sounded even sillier in Russian.

§182

Dobryninskaya prompted Wilderness to coin a new phrase—"Soviet-proof," as in "idiot-proof." Fifty-two years of Soviet rule, most of it Stalinist, had not succeeded in abolishing the nineteenth century in this corner of Moscow. It made Petticoat Lane look bang up-to-date. An inept comparison—he didn't think he'd seen anything like this anywhere in England, but then, according to economists and sociologists (Wilderness was not at all sure what a sociologist was) England had no peasants.

Moscow did. A city of seven million people was never far from land and earth and peasant.

He was looking, at nothing and everything. At a shantytown of tarps and tents. At faces much like his own and at Asiatic faces from beyond the Urals, faces he had encountered in Berlin in the forties—the multi-ethnic conquerors of Aryan Germany.

He was looking for eggs. The Metropol had eggs, but not fresh eggs, and he had begun to crave a good omelette, the signature (for signature read "only") dish of his father-in-law, cooked at the table, tossed onto the plate before it was dead.

A grizzled bloke had ducks and chickens in cages.

"Do you have eggs?"

"Do I have eggs? Would I be selling these feathered fools if they were laying? Of course I don't have eggs! Nobody has fukkin' eggs. You wanna start a stampede just call out that you're selling eggs, you'll be killed in the rush."

Wilderness had no wish to unleash a rant, nodded and had turned away when the bloke said, "Amerikansky?"

The truth? Why not?

"No, I'm an Englishman."

"Ah. So no greenbacks?"

"Not so much as a red cent."

"Tourist?"

The truth? Why not?

"No. I'm a prisoner of the KGB."

Bloke doubled up with laughter, combined with spitting and ending in a fit of coughing sounding much like bathwater draining.

"Don't make me laugh, English. I got a hernia. Prisoner of the KGB? Ooh my right buttock, ooh my left buttock, ooh my bumhole . . . that is funny."

"Funny, but true."

"Really? Then we got something in common."

"When?" Wilderness said simply.

"From 1946 to 1951. I was one o' them as took Berlin. Nine months later I'd been denounced for fuck-knows-what and gulagged."

"You see those two blokes by the veg stall?"

"How could I miss 'em? I spotted them before I spotted you. Cheka down to their socks. But it'll be you they're interested in, not me."

"So you say what you like?"

"Yep. Fukkem. Fukkemall. Now—what they got you for?"

"Oh, the usual. I'm a spy."

"Whaddya spy on?"

"The Soviet Union."

"So what you spyin' on now?"

"Nothing. I am a man without a mission."

"Well . . . what do you usually spy on?"

"Nuclear secrets . . . military manoeuvres."

"None o' them round 'ere. You'll have to find somethin' else."

"I'd be interested in the *byt*. The daily life of Joe Average Russian. The sort of thing you don't learn in spy school."

"You know Komsomolskaya Square?"

"No."

"You got a map?"

"Yes."

"Then you'll find it. Three railways meet there in three separate stations. Get out there after dark. Pick a station. Sit in the waiting room, drink stewed tea, drink acorn-coffee. You'll meet Joe Average."

"People like you?"

"Nah. People far worse off than me. I'm a successful peasant entryprenoor—one step away from being an enemy of the people. Now—you wanna buy some spuds?"

"You grew them?"

"Nah. I have 'em flown in special from Idaho. You tosser."

§183

Wilderness took the bloke's advice, waited until darkness, and well into night. It seemed somehow more appropriate. For no reason he could pin down, railway stations were night places. Perhaps it had a little to do with the number of times he'd been stranded on RAF leave just after the war, out in the Essex no-man's-land, somewhere like Shenfield or Brentwood, tantalizingly short of London, sleeping on a hard wooden bench, surrounded by snoring kitbags, waiting for the milk train.

He caught the Sokolnicheskaya metro line from Manezh Square to Komsomolskaya, one Mullard fifteen feet behind him all the way, and emerged into a grey plain that might have been designed to define "dismal."

It was judgmental, he told himself. Was this any worse than the point at which Kings Cross met St. Pancras, and barely missed Euston? Yes it was. Whereas Kings Cross struck him as cluttered, mundane and functional—a series of garden sheds posing as a station—and St. Pancras as beautiful, the Three Stations were . . . preposterous. But then, so much of Moscow was, be it imperial leftovers or Soviet fry-ups, they had that in common—statements writ too large for the heavens above them.

He chose Yaroslavsky.

Paid a couple of kopecks for a white coffee—black did not appear to be an option—was surprised to find it was coffee, not acorn brew, and unsurprised to find it was so awful it might just as well have been acorns. Nothing he'd tasted in the deprived, rationing years of London in World War II had tasted quite as bad as this. He was delighted. It was Moscow, not Metropol.

Yaroslavsky Vokzal appeared to be one vast, overwhelming hall, but what in the architecture of Moscow's public transport did not aim to be vast or overwhelming? It wasn't Grand Central, although the ceiling was obviously in competition and looked like a design for bone china plates rejected by Royal Worcester or Crown Derby. It was a bit like being inside cake, he thought—cake with verdigris marzipan, a ton of icing, searing fluorescent lights and a lingering smell of stale urine . . . but then most of Moscow, certainly every doorway and stairwell, smelled of urine.

And it was all but full—a couple of hundred travellers who were waiting for the next train, had just missed the last or were, in keeping with any railway station's secondary function, just waiting intransitively under the thin, rising veil of pungent cigarette smoke.

And it had a dash of romance—you could get on here and get off in Vladivostok. For the price of a ticket all Siberia lay open before you. He could see himself momentarily—roaring along in steam and steel like Strelnikov in *Doctor Zhivago*. He'd seen the film two or three times but never managed to finish the book.

It seemed that the duck entrepreneur had been right about these people being worse off than him. It was into the Yaroslavsky that ragged humanity poured from rural Russia. They were not necessarily poor, that might be a supposition too far, but they had nothing of Moscow about them. They looked like they had been torn from the pages of the Russian novels he'd read in his "captivity"—they looked like narodniks, or more precisely, they were the people narodniks affected to be. A word he'd heard in boutiques in London, out shopping with his wife, sprang to mind—the "ethnic" look. The look would come and go, the ethnicity just shifting sands—but this was, for want of a better word, timeless. Revolution, civil war, world war, Stalin, and peaceful coexistence had done little to change it. Most of those waiting appeared to be asleep. One mournful, tuneless baritone sang something near-incomprehensible and folksy, all about a girl with wild eyes and long hair—the Russian *"Belle Dame sans Merci."* Several sleepless babies joined in. An old woman bobbed and muttered over an icon. A peasant couple, swathed in layers of tunics and rabbit-fur hats on a warm summer's night, sat with half a dozen piglets on rope leads.

He found what might have been the last vacant arse-width space on the benches. Mullard stood twenty feet off and stared. He waited for the next train to pull in. Would this lot return to the wilds, or would more join them?

An arrivals and departures board flickered on and off. Neon did not seem to be one of the Soviet Union's success stories.

In or out, there was nothing due for half an hour. Wilderness might torture his taste buds with a second coffee and break a tooth on one those small pretzel-like things that seemed to be shaped like the treble clef and cast in concrete. But—the militia were restless and, like any bored copper anywhere on earth, they got nosy when they got bored. A uniformed woman paused by him, but seeing he had no bags moved on. Her partner, as big as any Mullard, stopped by a bloke a dozen seats away—a man with a suitcase the size of a coffin. Wilderness had watched him arrive and squeeze in. The suitcase appeared to weigh nothing, he manhandled it with the ease of a flying kite.

The cop saw this as worthy of his suspicion.

"Что у вас там?"

What have you got in there?

"Свет и воздух."

Light and air.

"Ха, блядь. Откройте!"

Ha fucking ha. Open up!

Wilderness had dodged enough coppers in his youth to see the futility of the next move. The man hefted his case, tried to run for it and stumbled over a piglet. The female officer grabbed him by one arm and spun him like a top—the suitcase glided parallel to the floor and then flew out of his hand to burst open on the tiles. It sounded like a tommy gun opening up—a series of stuttering, rapid rattles, as a hundred-odd light bulbs exploded and sent travellers diving for cover.

The male cop drew his gun and motioned everyone back into their seats.

Bugger, thought Wilderness. *Bang goes my second cup of poor man's java.*

Clearly it took more than two to make an arrest. And if it was an arrest, Wilderness could not perceive the offence. Cocaine, heroin, light bulbs? They waited and waited for reinforcements. But Magda arrived first. In civvies, looking as though she'd been dragged out of bed, berating Mullard and confronting Wilderness. A quick flash of her ID and he was on his feet and stood in a corner lacking only the dunce's cap.

"My men sent for me as soon as you left the hotel."

"Fine. I'm not up to anything. I just fancied a cup of coffee in a railway station. Call me sentimental. I didn't know I was going to meet Dr. Crippen. Or is he Martin Bormann?"

"This is so petty. He is just an освещенный."

"What? 'Illuminated'? Some sort of mystic?"

"No. He steals light bulbs."

Of course. How literal. Освещенный. Lit up.

Magda seemed almost embarrassed by her own words.

"He collects spent light bulbs, sells them to workers, who swap them for live ones in the office or factory. Then, none the wiser, the office or factory replaces the bulb, and the stolen one can be used or sold. A profit at every turn. Adding up the kopecks. Joe, this is a waste of time for both of us."

"Yes, but it was fun."

"Then try to have less fun. I won't be getting out of bed tomorrow night to see what you have blundered into."

"So I'm grounded?"

"No. Those are not my orders. Will you be making a habit of this?"

"Perhaps. There is something about railway stations, particularly at this time of night."

"Really? What?"

"'All human life is there'—masthead of the *News of the World*. An English newspaper I'm sure you've never heard of."

"Indeed I have not. So, all human life in a railway station? OK. Moscow abounds in railway stations. There are two more on this square alone. Visit them all. Find your human life, but please, try to give my men no reason to call me. Is that too much to ask?"

§184

The British Embassy

Troy's posting in Prague had been at a time of crisis. A crisis that had rapidly resolved into two issues. Refugees—and how to deal with a government that was powerless in the face of Russian tanks but could not quite admit this and, by the time it did, had mostly been replaced by apparatchiks who would not unbutton their flies without calling Moscow first.

Moscow . . . was different. It had to be. Gromyko had warned him it was dull. He couldn't possibly be right, but Troy soon found out he was.

Nothing, bugger all, sweet FA was all that happened.

There was a mountain of correspondence—but he had three secretaries to deal with that.

There were receptions as the last of the British faithful sent delegations to the Soviet Union—the Amalgamated Union of Lamp Wick

Trimmers or the Brompton & South Kensington Committee for Anglo-Soviet Friendship and Cultural Exchange—but Anna saw it as her duty to organise those. He just stood around, shook hands and muttered platitudes.

He thought seriously about buying a stamp album.

He called Gromyko.

"What do you collect? Anything in particular?"

"I collect British Empire, penny red to death of George V. I gave up at the abdication. You can have my Edward VIIIs if you like."

And there were the regular meetings of Commonwealth ambassadors—Canada, Nigeria, Pakistan, Australia, Ghana, India, the newly independent and wordy "St. Kitts, Nevis and Anguilla" et cetera, et cetera—every two weeks, half the time at the British Embassy and the other half spread across the red bits on the map, as 'twere.

This was where the world would be put to rights as the representatives of the world's great democracies gathered together.

"You know, England versus West Indies this year is going to be an ordeal."

"How so?"

"Well . . . no Fred Titmus . . . and we've seen the last of Freddie Trueman. I mean to say, does England have a spin bowler as capable as Trueman?"

"For that matter they've no Ted Dexter at the helm."

"Oooh, I dunno, I think Ray Illingworth's a canny chap. He'll be a match for Gary Sobers. He'll put the right men at the crease. What he really needs is to get Geoff Boycott back on the team. What do you say, Freddie?"

Troy wanted to scream. He just about grasped who Trueman and Dexter were, he'd never heard of Illingworth or Sobers or Boycott and could not tell silly-mid-off from square leg.

After half a dozen such meetings he took a leaf out of Khrushchev's book and resorted to diplomatic neuralgia. Anna took over and after two sessions with her, the Commonwealth were so happy they didn't really want Troy back.

"How did you get round those old bores?" he said to her at bedtime after an evening session with the remnants of empire.

She tossed an illustrated book on the bed:

Teach Yourself Cricket—194 Easy Lessons.

"Easy peasy," she said. "They might as well subtitle it *Old Bores for Beginners*. But . . . I can do this, Troy, and I'm beginning to wonder if you can."

"I do not wonder. I know."

$185

Troy did not think of himself as lazy.

He detested sport.

The thought of a gymnasium turned his stomach. Far too close to schooldays . . . vaulting horses and hurdles and all that nonsense.

And ball games were for children.

Drawing up a list of psychologically sound excuses for idleness did little to alleviate the encroaching sense of loose ends.

By noon each day he'd handled everything the secretaries or Janis Bell had stuck in front of him and could have donned a cloth cap and muffler and wandered around Moscow for fun, not that there was fun, and not that Janis would have let him.

His brother called. Loudly.

"What's this guff about a war wound?"

"Eh?"

"Your wife told a meeting of Commonwealth ambassadors that, and I quote, 'my husband's old war wound is playing up.' What bloody war wound? You were never in the fucking forces!"

"How about the *police* force? Would you like me to spell that for you, or remind you of the occasions I got caught in air raids or the time I was almost blinded?"

Troy took a breathy silence as contrition.

It didn't last long.

"All the same, there's nothing wrong with you, is there?"

"Just the Moscow Blues."

"Eh?"

"You hum it, I can play it."

§186

Troy decided on a bit of a day out and sought out his chauffeur.

"Where to?"

"Yasnaya Polyana."

"Where's that?"

"Due south at about two hundred K, I should think."

"We're not supposed to leave the ... er ... *Podmoskovye*."

"We can't leave the region?"

"Something like that. Diplomatic cars have a forty-K limit. Wouldn't get us halfway there."

"Let's risk it, shall we? What's the worst that can happen? We get booked? Well, when did you last hear of a Russian diplomat paying a parking ticket in London?"

"Tit for tat, eh?"

"Quite."

§187

Yasnaya Polyana was fact and legend. Count Tolstoy had lived there, farmed there, written there.

Less than a mile away was the country home of Troy's ancestors. A small portion of the Tolstoy estate purchased by his ardent disciple Rodyon Rodyonovich Troitsky, Troy's grandfather, during the writing of *War and Peace*, when Tolstoy was short of a bob or two. His grandfather had lived there, farmed there, written there—not that anyone read anything he wrote. Красный Урожай (Red Harvest) had been confiscated by the Tsarist state after his grandfather's self-imposed exile of 1910, the year Tolstoy had died and any prospect of being protected by an international reputation blew away like a will-o'-the-wisp. The old man had settled in England, where the consolation was that the *Times* published his letters—whether anyone read them was entirely another matter.

No Troy had set foot in Красный Урожай since.

This was adventure, this was . . . the rolling back of time.

Forty-four kilometres from the centre of Moscow, two militia cars came up behind them. One overtook, the other brought up the rear, forcing the Rolls to the side of the road.

They were civil—greatly admiring the car, wanting to know its top speed. And they were absolute—"Обернитесь." Turn around.

A few miles back towards the city, a familiar smell wafted in through the open window.

Troy asked Tony to pull up by a limestone track, vanishing into the distance, wound the window fully down and inhaled.

"Turn right," he said.

"Boss . . ."

"We're still inside the *Podmoskovye*. The cops have no reason to bother us again."

A kilometre on they came in sight of the source. At the side of the track in a roughly made pen of split rails and rusting tin sheets—the earth sun-baked into crusts and ridges, not a blade of living grass in sight—were half a dozen poking, snuffling, snorting black-and-white pigs.

Tony, being a city boy, said, "What exactly is that?"

And Troy replied, "That is a fine example of Сибирская черно-пестрая—to you, the Siberian mottled pig. Now, let's find the farmer and see how much he wants for that rather fine-looking sow on the left."

Mario

§188

The British Embassy, Moscow

July 23, 1969
Another Warm Wednesday

Janis Bell and Anna Troy met each morning in the "first lady's" office. Janis was of the opinion that the government back home would have done far better to appoint Lady Troy, rather than Lord Troy, to the post of ambassador, but she didn't need to say that. It was understood by all concerned, perhaps even by Lord Troy himself.

She could see Troy right now, through the window at the back of Anna's office, sitting in the garden with Glossop the gardener, tossing beetroot to the pig.

"What's on the agenda?" Anna said.

"Two items. Joe Holderness appears to have been moved to the Metropol, and I still lack any instructions concerning him."

"Could we not accept that no news from London is good news?"

"Quite, as your husband would say."

"How do you . . . hmm . . . read the move?"

"Joe is either favoured or the Russians want us to think he is favoured. I gather the move happened about a month ago . . . we had a sighting just last week. Joe was seen in front of the Metropol in the company of Kostya Zolotukhin. Nothing since—my sources are not thorough nor are they up-to-date—so if he's still there . . . well, they're spoiling him, aren't they?"

"Quite. Either that or fattening him up for the kill."

"And . . . we need an occasion."

"For what?"

"The *Sunday Post* is sending its chief foreign correspondent, Mario Mariotti, out to Moscow. Charlie Leigh-Hunt appears to have consented to an interview."

"Bloody hell."

"Which means of course that the Russians have consented to an interview. I shouldn't think Charlie's opinion mattered a damn. SIS would like a reception, not for Mariotti specifically, but something he could attend, mingle with and get debriefed on the sly. So—we need to invent something."

"Couldn't they just talk to him when he gets back?"

"I was told that whatever Mariotti has to say about Charlie should be considered most urgent."

"OK. When's he due?"

"Middle of August. He has a ten-day visa commencing on the eighteenth, and a meeting with Charlie on the twenty-first. It would be very convenient if the Ministry of Shellfish or the Northern Counties Pig Fat Authority had a trade mission to Moscow in August, but they don't. In fact, nobody has. Hence . . . we need to invent something."

"What day is the twenty-first?"

"A Thursday."

"So the day after might be a good day. Friday, August twenty-second."

"OK . . . and the highly plausible excuse?"

"It's Troy's birthday."

"Will he roll with this fib?"

"No—I mean, it really is his birthday."

"Is Lord Troy in the habit of celebrating his birthday?"

Anna looked over her shoulder, just in time to see the pig catch a large green apple in its teeth.

"No, but what he thinks doesn't matter a flying fuck really, does it? I'll just give him twenty-four hours' notice to dust off his evening clobber and scrape the pig shit off his shoes."

"I don't suppose you could persuade him to wear the sash?"

"You suppose right."

§189

Barbara and Ugo Mariotti christened their first-born Fenchurch.

"It's a very English name," Barbara said. "It's a saint's name."

"*Che cosa?*"

"I found it on a map of London."

So saying, Barbara flipped open a London street atlas and pointed just to the north of the Tower of London.

"See? Fenchurch St. 'St.' stands for saint. Saint Fenchurch. They even named a railway station after him."

"So?" her husband replied.

"He'll find it easier to fit in."

"Fit into what? There are more Italians here than Poms."

A true statement. Turrawurra was the second largest Italian community in Queensland.

"We aren't always going to live in Turrawurra."

This was news to Ugo. He was happy in Turrawurra. There was plenty of work for a plumber. But move they did. First to Brisbane, and then further south to Melbourne, just in time for Fenchurch to start school and join a gang.

Fenchurch's gang had a Clyde, a Ralph, three Micks and a Tommo. Occasionally a Kev or a Donald would join in, but they were unreliable compared to Clyde and all the Micks.

"We can't have a Fenchurch," one of them said. "It's just such a stupid poncy name."

Fenchurch thought.

"OK. I'll be a Mick."

"We already got three. Tell you what. You can be Mario."

"Mario Mariotti? That's just silly."

But it stuck. And before long Fenchurch was happy to be Mario. It was distinctive. There weren't three of him or even two, and words could scarcely describe the sheer delight of seeing his first byline as "Mario Mariotti" in the *Sydney Morning Herald* fifteen years later, in 1947, or in the London *Sunday Post* in 1956.

$190

London

August 17, 1969

It had been reckless for Mario to plonk himself down as a freelance in the middle of the Suez crisis, but it had paid off. Roving correspondent—a staff job on Britain's leading Sunday paper.

The *Post* sent him to cover Castro's revolution in Cuba, Harold Macmillan's "winds of change" in South Africa, Kennedy in Paris, the building of the Berlin Wall, the escalating conflict in Vietnam . . . and Macmillan's visit to Moscow. He'd crammed Russian for that trip—got himself halfway fluent. That too would pay off.

In August 1969 the *Post* sent him back to Moscow. Charles Leigh-Hunt had agreed to an interview. The first since his defection some six years before. Landing the job was not so much a feather in Mario's cap as full plumage.

The day before his flight to Moscow. The boss called him in. The boss was Lawrence Stafford, editor-in-chief. The bloke with him was Rod Troy, Stafford's brother-in-law and Foreign Secretary. London was just a cesspit of nepotism and incest.

Mario gave him the quick once-over. Big bastard, almost as big as he was himself. But dapper. Not the sort of bloke to shuffle around in khaki pants with three days of beard bristling under a beaky nose.

"Have you met?" Stafford asked.

"Nah. London's never been my beat. Nice to meet you all the same. Met yer brother a couple o' times. He's a character."

"Quite," Rod said, with a hint of displeasure. "You know he's our man in Moscow?"

Mario looked at Stafford.

"You got me here to suck eggs, boss? I could be packing right now."

"Mario, please. We're sorry if it sounds like that, but there are just one or two things. Rod?"

"You'll be invited to an embassy reception. So will about a hundred others."

"I'll take me best bib and tucker."

Stafford winced and fiddled ominously with his paper knife.

"But," Rod went on, "the reception is really just for you. What I want to get across is that you and everyone there will be spied upon."

"I'm tasting raw egg again."

"I have almost finished. If he remembers protocol, my brother will greet you on arrival. I say 'if' because Freddie has a mission in life to break every possible rule. After the introduction and handshake, do not speak to him again. Avoid him. Whatever you have to say, say to Miss Bell. She will make a point of seeking you out."

"Come again, mate? 'Whatever I have to say'?"

"Well," Stafford picked up the thread. "You wouldn't be averse to a little spying, would you, Mario?"

§191

Moscow

August 18, 1969

One morning Wilderness awoke from a dream of Hampstead, of wife Judy, of daughters Joan and Molly, to find another dream had ended too. He emerged from the bathroom, still zipping up his flies, to discover a pair of Arthur Mullards in his sitting room, and a suitcase of his few belongings—his books and most probably his underpants and socks—in the hand of the marginally slenderer of the two. They'd done all this while he peed and shaved.

"Мы куда-то едем, да?"

Going somewhere, are we?

Neither Mullard spoke.

He never thought they would.

So much depended on which way the car turned as they left Sverdlov Square.

Wilderness and Mullard the Greater sat in the back, the Lesser drove. If he made a U-turn then they'd be heading back towards the Lubyanka. If he went straight on . . . God knows.

They headed southwest. Past Kropotkinskaya Metro. Along Prechistenskaya. Wilderness tried to remember what was out there and came up with just one thing, the Novodevichy Convent. It would be so ridiculous if they meant to house him there. He attempted to wind down a window just for air, and the giant's paw wrapped itself around his, squeezed till his knuckles ached.

"*Niet*," was all he said, but at least he'd finally spoken.

After three or four kilometres they pulled up at the convent. Right in front of them was a modern tower block, eight or nine storeys high: 53/55 *Bolshaya Pierovogskaya Ulitsa*, Big Dumpling Street; even with a name that ridiculous, it was more than a cut above the notorious Khrushchev-era slums—the Khrushchyovka.

"Здесь?"

Here?

Lesser Mullard handed him a key, on a wooden fob, rather like the bath plugs at the Metropol.

Wilderness looked at it: 7G.

Lesser pointed at the sky with a nicotined index finger.

Oh, you're not coming up?

$192

It was a bare apartment. Naked. Almost a blank. There wasn't a word to describe the colour of the walls. As a child Wilderness had thought the colour in his paint box labelled *Eau de Nil* was "water of nothing." This too was water of nothing. Blank walls in a noncolour. Bare but for a single reproduction of a classic Soviet painting hanging crookedly over the plywood dining table. He'd forgotten the artist if he'd ever known the name—but every Socialist Realist had depicted Lenin at the Finland Station at one time or another. This one had added an interesting touch of fiction. As Lenin pauses before getting off the train that has hauled him, Krupskaya and thirty-four fellow-Bolsheviks the length of Finland, Stalin has appeared in the doorway just behind him like the bad fairy at the christening.

The only other item of interest was that his new apartment came fully equipped with a Corby trouser press and, for good measure—belt, braces and truss, if you like—a second Corby trouser press.

There was no plug in the bath. What did it say about a nation that it would let a man have two trouser presses but not a bath plug?

In every respect but one this apartment was enough to put him in mourning for the Metropol—the missing thing had been a working telephone. There'd been one in his suite at the Metropol, but scarce a crackle came down the line. This one was active, it buzzed and it hummed, it told its own tale of tapping in the clicks just seconds after he picked up the handset. And, of course, it was odds on that it recorded every fart and whisper in the room.

Would anyone ever call, or would he be like some character in an as-yet-unwritten Pinter play waiting on the anonymity of a phone that never rang?

§193

August 20, 1969

Wilderness was beginning to think he'd be in Moscow well into the autumn. Charlie had retreated to his dacha—no doubt with his *Ninotchka*—and if he stayed there all summer . . . well . . . when did the Russian summer end? In Southend or Clacton it would be when the Punch and Judy man packed up and the last candy floss blew into the North Sea. He could not telephone him. Charlie had no phone, and if he had Wilderness could hardly call him without blowing the plan—Frank's cockamamey scheme—sky high.

Wilderness had thought he'd have to finagle contact somehow—to almost seduce Charlie into meeting—but chance and Charlie came to his rescue. Perhaps that was another reason Magda had let him have a telephone? The farts, the whispers and the Charlie?

And when it rang, the only time it rang . . .

"I'm in town . . ."

Far too London a phrase for Moscow, but all the same.

". . . Let's have a drink and a natter."

They met the next evening in the bar back at the Metropol.

"I don't get into the city often in August—it's a stinker of a month—but when I do, it would be pleasant to talk to someone who isn't a People's Publisher or KGB, and preferably in English. Magda doesn't have much English beyond 'yes,' 'no,' and 'more,' rather like a two-year-old—or did I tell you that? Sorry, I'm rambling."

Rambling was exactly what Wilderness wanted Charlie to do. To ramble all the way to revelation.

They'd met up two or three times since his interrogation ended, thankfully without Magda in tow, and there seemed to be almost nothing Charlie would not talk about—shoes, ships, sealing wax. All the same, he doubted very much that Charlie trusted him. And whatever Magda believed, he would surely never have fallen for Zolotukhina's nonsense about defection? How to "pop" the question was still a bit of a mystery. How many meetings would it take, how to measure the buildup of confidence? How to pick the moment? How to coax a man into what he would in all likelihood see as an act of betrayal? If Charlie were Guy Burgess, Wilderness would have no problem. Guy had the knack of spilling the beans and making it all sound like nonsense. He could tell the truth with his hand on the bible and still not be believed.

"What's the occasion?" Wilderness said.

"An interview. The *Sunday Post* have asked a few times. This time it's happening."

"You agreed to this?"

"Saw no reason not to."

"And the Kremlin agreed?"

"I think they think it's time."

"Time for what?"

"Time I said something."

"Such as?"

"Blowed if I know."

"Who are they sending?"

"Mario Mariotti. Do you know him?"

"Who doesn't? He was always sniffing around for a story. And I don't mean that to sound snide. He's good at what he does. The last I heard he was reporting from Ulster on what he calls a policy of unthinking neglect. I rather think he can kiss goodbye to an OBE."

"That's probably the club we're all in. The Nobeys."

"Didn't you get the odd gong during the war?"

"I did. Matter o'fact, I expected them to ask for it back in '63. Tough luck if they had, since I binned it the day I got it—but they didn't. I'm still Charles Leigh-Traitor DSO. There might even have been a bar with that. Alas, not one that served booze."

"Actually, I knew Mario quite well. He did the odd BBC programme. My wife was his producer."

"I'm seeing him tomorrow afternoon. That gives our mutual friends the morning to turn on the microphones in my apartment. Perhaps they'd care to do a little light dusting while they're there. I hardly ever am. If our friends wanted to get snotty they'd take the flat away from me. I spend far more time at Magda's or the dacha. But . . . enough about the *friends* . . . what'll you have?"

"I think I'll have one of those very precise martinis you invented, Charlie."

"OK—but I'm strictly rationed for twosomes. Magda has a verbal rolling pin to clobber me with."

She also had two of her goons cooling their heels out in the street. Not trailing Charlie but Wilderness—and it said something about Magda the apparatchik versus Magda the girlfriend that, knowing who Charlie was meeting, she still hadn't stood them down.

Wilderness never tried to shake them. As long as they were out of earshot they might as well be dogs or cats just following a scent. Short of him robbing a bank, they'd probably stay thirty feet away and never interfere—regard, remember, report. A largely pointless exercise.

At their first meeting outside of formal questioning, Charlie had shown some curiosity about life back in "Blighty," but it had soon evaporated. Wilderness realised that Charlie had adapted by a conscious decision not to look back. He'd never be a miserable drunk like Maclean nor a happy one like Burgess, both dreaming of the old country while publicly praising and serving the new. He had no more questions about London life, no requests for a visit to his tailor, no quick trip to Fortnum's, no "have you seen so-and-so . . . old Tommy, Johnny, Dickie?" He wondered how much of this was down to his highly improbable relationship with Magda. Charlie didn't talk much about Magda either—but that was understandable; if Moscow had closed an eye to them, why tempt it to blink?

"My God," said Charlie after the first sip of twosome. "I really miss these. I taught half the barmen in Washington how to make 'em."

How many twosomes would Wilderness have to get down him before he could ask the Washington question?

§194

Rambling led them circuitously to samizdat—underground writing and publication—a cultural phenomenon to which Charlie had better access than the average Russian, as Grigory Gerasimovich constantly monitored illegal fiction since one day it might be legal. Samizdat led them easily to the legal, if controversial, *Moskva* magazine, which had published Bulgakov's *The Master and Margarita*, in parts and censored, only a couple of years before, almost thirty years after the death of its author.

Charlie was reading the censored version.

Wilderness trumped Charlie.

"I read the whole thing."

"Eh?"

"Came out in English about the same time *Moskva* serialised it."

And Charlie trumped Wilderness.

"I had the idea of a walk around Moscow. Y'know the sort of thing. In Bulgakov's footsteps."

"Like visiting Anne Hathaway's cottage?" Wilderness asked.

"Nothing so sentimental. We could go by Alexander Herzen's old house. It's said to be the home of some character or other in the book. Just round the corner from my place, as a matter o' fact. Nothing much to see, though. It's not marked or anything. Not like in London, where the council puts up blue plaques everywhere. Or we could go to Bolshaya Sadovaya, the street Bulgakov actually lived on while he was writing it before the war. But it was just a communal apartment. Seen one you've seen 'em all. Come to think of it, it's probably not such a good idea after all. Traipsing around looking at . . . well . . . nothing. The poor old bugger's still in disgrace. No . . . I suppose I mean a sort of pub crawl. Except we'd have a job finding pubs. Not really a Russian thing. It's all restaurants . . . but restaurants don't admit women on their own . . . so quite how a comrade is expected to meet a single woman . . . God knows . . . not that I'm looking, you understand . . ."

"Of course not, you're . . . счастливый."

"Eh?"

"Happy."

"Happy. Good Lord. Been here six years and I keep forgetting that one simple word. Have to look it up every time."

"A mental block, perhaps. A refusal to admit that you might be."

"Let's drop the psychoanalysis or we'll never make it to the first *porto franco*. Now—I do have an ever-so-tiny brain wave. Let's go up Gorkovo, hotel by hotel. Claim our foreigners' privilege to jump the queue and get served ahead of the comrades. I don't suppose you've any hard cash?"

"No. The KGB took everything I had, even my socks."

"OK. Then the drinks had better be on me. I had about two hundred and fifty quid in cash when I arrived. My running-away-from-home fund. Gets whittled down, but then that's what it's for . . . to spend when no other currency will talk quite as loud. How else will Madga get her Liberty scarf or her Maybelline lipstick?"

Charlie looked at his watch.

"It's early. Be light for a few hours yet. Do you fancy making a start?"

"Yes. I'd be up for that. Where exactly?"

"We'll start at the National . . . hit a few other hotel bars . . . flash our foreign ID . . . Bob's your uncle."

Wilderness laid his Russian ID card face up on the table.

"I'm afraid that's all I have."

"Good bloody grief, is that who you are now? Someone's having fun, aren't they, Nikita Sergeyevich Badboy? Let no one say the Russians are humourless."

"Volga and I go back a long way."

Charlie fished in his jacket pocket to produce his own Russian ID. Wilderness read, "Igor Ignatyevich Smoktunovksy. You're an Igor? Like Bela Lugosi in the old Frankenstein films?"

"Yes. However, I have old faithful with me. We'll get in anywhere that craves foreign currency."

Charlie laid his British passport next to their Russian cards. The midnight blue was faded, the edges frayed like the sleeves of an old pullover, brown cardboard showing at the corners, the gold flaking off, the cramped letters crowded into the white window, far too small for a name as long as Maj. C. E. M. Leigh-Hunt. Wilderness opened it. Issued in 1957. Almost an antique. A tattered remnant of a former life.

"I surrendered my diplomatic passport the same year," Charlie said.

"Old faithful? Ah, I see."

Wilderness flipped the pages. Every single one covered in entry and exit stamps. Triangles, circles, squares. Like labels on a suitcase. The inky, smudgy biography of a very busy hack. He wondered whether its practicality as proof of his foreigner status might not be outweighed by its sentimental value.

"We digress," Charlie said.

With any luck.

"So . . . here . . . to the National . . . grab a bite to eat at the Astoria, then on to the Tsentralnaya . . . which is spitting distance from the Patriarch's Ponds—'the Patriki,' as people call them—where *The Master and Margarita* begins. That may be the only bit of the novel worth seeing in brick and stone and such. Five kopecks to the man who spots the cat. All in, it's about half an hour's walk. Or it would be but for all the watering holes in between. If at that point we feel the need of coffee, the Ukraine Hotel would be next . . . the caff there stays open all night."

This was more than Wilderness had dared hope for. A Charlie in, whatever the disclaimer, a sentimental mood and willing to knock back a few more than his Magda allowance.

"A *zapoy*," he said. "A pubski crawl."

"How aptly you put it, old man. Pubski indeed."

§195

Pubski 1: National Hotel
Manezh Square/1 Gorkovo

They sat on the mezzanine, above the first-floor bar—twosomes in hand—at a table for twosome, set in the curving, scalloped railing, thrust out as though specifically intended to enable better views of the floor below. A seat for watchers, not doers. A seat for spies, not those spied upon.

Wilderness said as much.

Charlie was baffled and said so.

"Why?" Wilderness asked.

"Well, we're allowed to meet."

"Yes. Kostya Zolotukhin was quite clear about that."

"Not what I meant. I meant . . . our people . . . I mean your people . . . fukkit . . . the British."

"I don't quite see what you're getting at. It's not as if they have a say. I am a prisoner of the KGB."

"But . . . you're constantly looking over your shoulder."

"As I said. KGB."

"For the British, Joe."

"Well, I'm sure they've an eye open for me but they can't get close, and I'm not sure I'd spot them if they did."

Charlie breathed in deeply, girding loins . . . getting to the point.

"There's two down there now."

He nodded to the pit, perhaps a hundred people seated, a good few dozen simply milling around.

"Where?"

"Those two blokes at the bar, sipping vodka while looking as though they'd prefer a pint of IPA."

"I've never seen either before. You know them?"

"By sight. The tall one is the embassy chauffeur, the short one is something like Troy's gardener."

"Troy?"

"He's the ambassador. Got here about the same time as you."

"Magda kept very quiet about that. Must make life a bit awkward for you."

"It won't. No chance of our meeting whatsoever. The British would never contemplate it."

"And the station head? Did he bring her with him?"

"The divine Miss Bell? Oh yes."

"And you think those two are following me, or following the KGB-niks who Magda has following me, on Janis Bell's orders?"

"No. I prefer to think it's just two blokes having a night on the town. As I said, a baffling coincidence. All the same, let's drink up and move on. My stomach's grumbling anyway. And the food here's pretty much of a muchness."

§196

Pubski 2: Astoria Restaurant
10 Gorkovo

Wilderness was baffled and said so.

By the menu. There was much too much of it. Page after page. A thousand and one ways to cook sturgeon. Smoked, marinaded, jellied. None of it remotely appetising.

"I can't believe you haven't been here before," Charlie was saying. "I mean, what have you been doing with yourself for the last month?"

"Drifting."

"Why?"

"Partly because I have no wish to play the tourist. I've no wish to see Lenin's tomb. I couldn't give a flying fuck about Lenin. Any more than I think you could. It's not as if seeing the glazed corpse would add anything to the million-odd posters and effigies scattered the length and breadth of Moscow. Of course, I've been to Red Square. Looked at St. Basil's. Didn't go in. Out to Novodevichy. The convent. Did go in. But mostly because I'm playing the game Volga set me."

"And what game's that?"

"The defector. If the British are tagging me—and if it isn't the two blokes back at the National it'll be somebody, somewhere, *some* of the time—then I am, in street terms, high profile. I'm where Volga wants me."

"Not sure I believe a word of that."

"It's what I'll do until I find out what she really wants. I do the rounds of markets and bookshops, and I hang around railway stations . . . I've been to all nine by the bye . . . looking for a Moscow I won't find in foreign exchange hotels . . . looking for the *byt*, which I've decided means pretty much the same as *craic* does in Dublin, though the Russian version is a lot more humdrum."

"Did you find your *byt*? Must confess I've never looked."

"Yes . . . and no . . . I found a Russia that seems untouched by any five- or ten-year plan. I found wooden shacks and tin huts within yards of postwar high-rises—some even had fenced yards with goats and pigs."

"Nobody, but nobody keeps pigs in the middle of Moscow."

"Yes they do. If you can buy a live duck at a peasant market, why not a live pig?"

"As I said, I never looked. But there is a modern Russia, an indisputably Soviet Russia—"

"Which I can see every time I ride the Metro, every time I glimpse a power station on the skyline, every time I see a statue of Lenin. I don't deny it's there. It's the Russia I learnt about at spook college. I learnt Russian translating papers on hydroelectricity in the Donbas, not from the pages of *Crime and Punishment*. If I wanted a tour of an up-to-date factory making thingamajigs and widgets, I'm sure I have only to ask Magda. But I don't. I rather think I've seen a Moscow we fail to mention in England or we don't know exists."

"So you walk the streets all day? That's what you mean by 'drifting'?"

"Mostly . . . and . . . when I get tired I find a park to sit in and when I get hungry I eat in prole caffs."

"Lots of spuds?"

"Lots of spuds indeed. Lots of beetroot. Lots of kasha. I ate at the Metropol until the Russians handed me the key to the city. Haven't eaten there since. You can get fed up with caviar, you know. A few weeks under even the most benign lock and key and caviar sort of blurs into Shippam's Fish Paste, and you realise it always was just Shippam's Fish Paste, just with a posh label. A few days ago, I got my own flat with my own samovar, frying pan and gas rings. If I can ever find a bloke selling eggs, I'll have my first home-cooked omelette in God knows how long."

"Actually, the caviar here is rather good."

"Fish paste. One and thruppence a jar in Sainsbury's."

"Suit yourself. I can also recommend the battered sudak. Sort of perchy-pikey."

"With chips and mushy peas?"

"You're just playing silly buggers, aren't you, Joe?"

"Yes. Force of habit."

"Like running Magda's men ragged on the metro?"

"OK. Yes. Do, please, apologise to Magda for that. I couldn't resist it."

"Actually she thought it was rather funny. The Arthur Mullards, as you call them, drive her to distraction. Not a brain cell between them."

Wilderness nodded his head towards the door.

Charlie said, "Yes. I see him. The hospital, the Met and fifteen minutes ago the National. A moveable fixture, a bit like furniture on casters."

"No. Not the bloke you met me with at the hospital. And not the bloke at the National either."

Charlie craned his neck, peered around him.

"Surely?"

"Nope. They changed shifts on the way here. He's at least the tenth Mullard since the hospital. Production model apparatchik rolled off the line in Omsk or Minsk like a T-34, exactly as you said."

"Hmm. Really? I was joking, honestly. I must be losing my touch."

Wilderness silently queried the tense.

Charlie paused in thought.

"Y'know," he said, "if you're here long enough I might be able to help you out."

"What? Get Magda to call off the dogs?"

"No. Not within my purview. I was referring to the omelette you crave. So happens Magda and I keep a few hens out at the dacha. Now . . . dare I say, if you've really defected, Joe, you may well be in line for your own dacha."

"I can't tell you how depressing that possibility is."

"Let's order. You can't rush a Russian. It'll be three-quarters of an hour before they serve anything."

Wilderness returned to the menu. One item stood out with spikes.

"Sputnik broth? What on not-earth is that?"

"Oh, it's very much of this earth. It's borscht. Tarted-up borscht. Beetroot, chicken broth, perhaps a splash of wine or sherry. Repackaged for the space age."

"That's like renaming fish and chips something like *patate pescate della luna*—it's still fish and chips."

"Quite. However, it's the best in town so I suggest you try it."

§197

Pubski 3: Tsentralnaya Hotel
36 Gorkovo

"You've got here at a rather odd time."

"How so?"

"The . . . what should I call it . . . what will discretion and microphone allow . . . the . . . er . . . the crackdown one might logically have expected after the fall of Khrushchev never really happened. There will no doubt be many who will disagree with me, and I'd certainly never call it a smooth transition, but it was pretty well bloodless. More noted for its survivors than not—Gromyko, to name but one. It's happening now, and the trigger was Prague. People are vanishing again. The slightest protest in support of Dubček is stepped on at once. It's being termed neo-Stalinism. Everyone expected it, most were surprised it didn't happen sooner—but it's happening now. People are vanishing. Just as they did right here thirty years ago."

"Here meaning Moscow?"

"Here meaning this hotel. It used to be known as the 'Gilded Cage.' Effectively a prison for dissidents—many of them communist refugees from Hitler. After '33 the place filled up, but it soon became obvious to most of them that they'd leapt from frying pan to fire. Communist or not, Stalin deeply distrusted foreigners. And so the midnight knock, the four-in-the-morning knock, the dawn knock became daily occurrences. 'Pack your bag, while we seal the doors.' I've even heard tales of blokes who slept fully dressed just in case. Within a few years, the place even had internal passports."

"And now?"

"Now it's all more discreet. Not quite deniable, but close. And one thing that hasn't changed is that it still doesn't pay to ask questions. If Uncle Fred doesn't come home one night, assume the worst and keep your trap shut."

"What might the worst be?"

"Prison probably. Exile more likely. Siberia's a pretty big place, after all. But I think the era of the firing squad is over. Perhaps a few discreet—there, that word again—discreet executions in the Lubyanka dungeons, but . . ."

"As discreet as a bullet in the back of the head?"

"Quite."

"Doesn't this give you pause for thought?"

"Joe, I'm sure you didn't mean to say anything as namby-pamby as that. What you mean is has it forced me to reexamine everything I've ever done, to wrack my conscience and wreck my soul? No—I'm enough of an egotist to have believed everything I did was right, and enough of one not to be kicking myself when everything turns out to be wrong. And if I pause for thought, what might I do in that pause? Ask to go home? They don't want me back and we both know it. What they don't know is that this is home now. So in one clear sense I was right. Even when I was wrong I was right."

Wilderness had been keeping a tally of drinks, making sure Charlie had more than him, slyly tipping his away, on a couple of occasions managing to swap glasses without him noticing. Surely the man was well on the way to being pissed, but right now Wilderness felt pissed himself. He couldn't make sense of what Charlie had just said and felt he wouldn't make sense of it pissed or sober. It was as though he'd heard Charlie's manifesto—or perhaps more a confession from the analyst's couch.

He got to his feet and pushed back the chair.

As in every hotel bar they'd visited, there was piped Western pop music burbling in the background to the delight of no one—usually way out-of-date and very bland, like being stuck in a perpetual lift going nowhere.

For some reason Cliff Richard's "Wonderful Life" struck him as an absurdly inappropriate song to be playing right now.

"I think I need some fresh air after that. Fresh air and a piss, not in that order. See you outside."

"We're almost there. Patriki are but a skip and a hop away."

At their last port of call, the Astoria, Wilderness had picked Charlie's pocket and helped himself to two blue five-pound notes—no longer legal tender in Britain, but who would ever know? He approached the bar, pointed at a half-litre bottle of Mamont and pushed a fiver across the bar. If the bloke got greedy he had the second fiver in reserve, but that would be daylight robbery.

The banknote vanished and the bottle appeared on the bar as if by magic—the quickness of the hand deceived the eye and the Arthur Mullards too.

§198

Patriarch's Ponds
Bol'shoy Patriarshiy Pereulok

Wilderness was content to let Charlie lead him from one hotel bar to the next. It was strategic. Let him think he is in control. Besides, he really had never been to any of them. No interest, no hard currency. But he had been to Patriki countless times in his brief, new freedom. When he got fed up walking the streets, dodging around the metro, hopping on and off trams or drinking undrinkable coffee at railway termini, he would go out to the ponds with a book, sit on a bench, read and watch this deliciously wet corner of the world go by. It was good for the Mullards. They soon learnt that if Wilderness sat down with a book, he would not stray for about two hours, and they would amble over to the wooden hut selling tea and fruit juice and appear to be almost off duty.

It was, he thought, as well not to mention any of this to Charlie. This was Charlie's trip, best to leave him with the clear sense that if there were strings to be pulled, he was the one pulling them. Moonlight flickered through the leaves of the linden trees, a summer night's gentle breeze rippled the water. Ten o'clock. All around them the lights of Moscow were going out. Early to bed. The city that slept rather a lot. Courting couples slipped away in whispers and giggles. An insomniac duck let rip with its ducky aria. And in minutes they seemed to have a park to themselves. Only the Mullards remained.

They sat on a bench. The half litre of Mamont sat in Wilderness's coat pocket waiting for its cue.

Wilderness pulled the cork, took a sip and handed the bottle to Charlie, not looking at him.

"Do you miss Washington?"

"I miss everything. You name it, I miss it . . . but . . ."

"Yeeees?"

"Why Washington? London, of course. You would ask about London, wouldn't you, but you haven't; you've asked about Washington."

"I suppose it occurred to me because it's the last place you were active."

"No, I was in England for three years after that. Still active. Joe, you're fishing."

Wilderness found no lie worth the telling.

"It was your greatest achievement as a spy."

"Thank you, but it doesn't compare to '56. I . . . my Khrushchev . . . adventure."

"Escapade?"

"Call it what you will. Nonetheless . . . a Russian battleship, a dead British frogman, the late Commander Cockerell—put 'em all together . . . it left Her Majesty's Government with egg all over their chops."

"And led to your downfall."

"Not to my knowledge, it didn't."

"Really? Norman Cobb disappears without trace, and not long afterwards you resign. Someone in SIS had you cornered."

"Joe, if you knew that for certain you'd not be saying 'someone,' you would know the name. But you don't, 'cos there wasn't anyone. I'd just had enough."

"Burne-Jones thinks you killed Cobb."

"I have never killed anyone, Joe. Not in my nature. I'm a lover, not a fighter, as some pop song of the fifties had it."

"Was that your role in Washington?"

Was that a painful twitch as a dart struck home . . . or an involuntary drunken wobble, as vodka-fuelled as slurring or drooling?

"Fishing, I say fishing. Tell me, Joe, what are you after? A name?"

"That would do nicely."

"Ah, would you rat out your mates? No—don't bother to answer. I'll give you a name. I'll put an end to this farce before it becomes an utter bore. Farber."

"Edna?"

Wilderness wasn't sure whether he had set Charlie giggling or Charlie had done it himself. He'd had the bottle of Mamont to his lips and sprayed vodka all down his trousers.

"Ah . . . ah . . . ah . . . the dear departed. No . . . not Edna Ferber, perish the thought. Ignatz Farber. With an *a*."

"And he is?"

"My Washington contact. It's what you want, is it not? The bloke next down the chain. I passed old Ignatz everything I received."

"And who gave it to you?"

"You've had your twenty questions, Joe, and you've got a name. Stop now. There's no way I'd rat anyone out."

"You just did."

"No I didn't. Ignatz died years ago. He had no wife, no kids. There's no one SIS can pursue. Igntaz is dead and a dead end."

"But you knew the contact next up the chain?"

"Be a crap chain if I didn't."

"So?"

"So nothing. You've had all you're getting."

Charlie got to his feet. Staggered. For all the clarity of his words he seemed very, very pissed. He held the bottle out to Wilderness.

"One last drinkie, Joe. Before the dance."

"Dance?"

"C'mon, old man. Shake a leg."

Charlie all but slithered across the gravel towards the edge of the railing that separated them from the pond. He all but fell over the railing, and just when Wilderness thought he was about to land headfirst in the water Charlie lifted his left leg and stood still, as still as being seriously pissed might allow.

"C'mon!" over his shoulder.

And then he began to sing:

> *You put your left leg in,*
> *Your left leg out.*
> *In, out, in, out.*
> *You shake it all about.*

And the left leg shook.

Wilderness knew it was over. He'd nothing left to lose. He dropped the bottle and stood next to Charlie. Right leg raised. What the fuck.

> *You put your right leg in,*
> *Your right leg out.*

In, out, in, out.
You shake it all about.

They pivoted to face the Arthur Mullards, who looked at them, then at one another, but didn't move.

You put your whole self in.
Your whole self out.
In, out, in, out.
Shake it all about.
You do the Hokey Cokey
And you turn yourself around.
That's what it's all about.
Woah, woah, the Hokey Cokey.
Woah, woah, the Hokey Cokey.
Woah, woah, the Hokey Cokey.

Wilderness fell first. Laughing longer and louder than he'd done in months—Soviet months.

Charlie offered a hand and an arm but fell himself. Arse-down on the gravel. The Arthur Mullards motionless before them.

"Oh God, oh God . . . where's the fucking bottle?"

"Broke when I dropped it," Wilderness said.

"Just as well. I really should sober up. Important date tomorrow."

Charlie tried to get up. Failed. Sat down with a schoolboy grin on his face.

"Mariotti?" Wilderness asked.

"Yep. Who am I going to be for Mr. Mariotti? The spy, the lover, the traitor, the old Harrovian, the habitual English piss-artist, the clean and sober nouveau apparatchik? Perm any two from three."

"Nouveau apparatchik. Sounds like Russian Beaujolais."

"I'd sooner drink my own piss. Charlie Nouveau Soixante-Neuf."

Wilderness thought Charlie would never stop laughing at his own joke.

And still he was no nearer knowing.

§199

Krovyanayakolbasa Lane

August 21, 1969

Charlie awoke in his own bed in the Arbat. A not wholly unpleasing rarity. Magda was his significant something rather than his indiscriminate everything.

His dreams had been close to nightmares—age thirteen, yet still fifty-five, wearing his Harrow School straw boater, trying to buy Shippam's Fish Paste in GUM with a five-bob postal order given to him by "Uncle Jim."

He weighed up his day.

Out for the morning while the Niks respooked the flat.

Then an afternoon with Mario Mariotti.

He weighed up his night before.

He finally knew what Joe Holderness was after.

And he wasn't going to give it to him.

He'd never have guessed what Joe wanted, and Joe would never be able to guess the answer. He was baffled why anyone would give a flying fuck after all this time.

Joe Holderness could be persistent. He wished Joe would just bugger off, and with a little help from Mr. Mariotti he might be able to nudge him on his way.

He'd had to play the drunk to flush Joe out.

As he had put it, "the habitual English piss-artist."

He'd noted every drink he'd had, aiming for the right side of sobriety, and every drink Joe hadn't had—pushed aside, left behind and on occasion slyly swapped for his own. Cheeky bugger. He'd nicked ten quid too.

He couldn't play piss-artist for Mario. In fact, he'd no idea who to be with Mario. Mario would have his expectations, his hack's agenda, and it was wholly in Charlie's nature to defy expectation. As Troy used to say when they were schoolboys, "If we can possibly fuck it up . . ."

But . . . but . . . the Niks . . . the comrades would be listening. And who was Charlie Leigh-Hunt to them? Was it the duty of a spy to be all things to all men? And what was the duty of a defector . . . bed . . . made . . . lie . . . in . . . put on a brave face and believe . . . slip in an odd request for Gillette razor blades or a couple of Duncan's Walnut Whips or the old school tie from Benson & Clegg's . . . just to show that a gentle touch of nostalgia was compatible with the iron fist of ideology. The old Harrovian tie was black and white—about the only soddin' thing is in this murky world that was.

Oh shit. I must have been mad to agree to this.

$200

Mario Mariotti looked more grizzled than usual. He'd never been a typical foreign correspondent. No safari suit or seersucker jacket. Mario was habitually in fatigues and boots, and often looked to have been recently dipped in dog shit.

"If yer boots are clean, you're not doin' it right," he had once said to Charlie.

He was also never keen on a daily shave and often sported a couple of days of beard. The last time Charlie had seen him in Beirut ten or so years ago it had been dark—now it was white fuzz, as though he were practising to play Santa at the office party.

"Been a while, Charlie-boy."

Charlie winced inwardly. Only Coky had ever called him that.

"Do sit down, Mario."

Mariotti dropped his Australian Army–surplus rucksack on the floor—something clunked; he didn't seem to care what—and set a notepad and a couple of ballpoint pens on the coffee table.

"No tape recorder?" Charlie asked. "One of those neat little cassette jobs the Russian kids would sell their souls for?"

"Nah. I'm old school. Shorthand and a Biro. That's me."

"I know the sun is well below the yardarm, but could I get you a drink?"

"Yardarm? Still playing the ponce, eh, Charlie? Yeah. Why not? Make mine a vodka, what else could it be?"

Charlie went to what passed as his kitchen, almost bumbling through, looked at the fresh scar on the ceiling where one of the many microphones lay scarcely concealed and muttered, "Get a grip, Charlie-boy. Or he'll rip you to shreds with every sentence."

Out loud, "Been anywhere lately, Mario?"

Mario yelled back, "Vietnam. Pig's arse. A clusterfuck."

Charlie knew he was out of touch, but *that* out of touch?

"Clusterfuck?"

"Neologism, Chaz. The Americans drop things called cluster bombs on the Vietnamese peasants . . . one bomb that just mushrooms into a hundred other bombs . . . like blowing on a dandelion . . . so a clusterfuck is a super fuck-up. Ulster's another one. I was there earlier this year. Labour's very own clusterfuck. Jim Callaghan's a twat. I wouldn't let him run a launderette let alone the Home Office. He hasn't got a clue."

Charlie set down two glasses and a bottle of Moskovskaya Osobaya. Mario reached out and poured for both—to the brim.

Charlie went back to get a plate of zakuski, to really play the Russian host, and heard Mario yell, "So is this the good stuff?"

§201

On his third slug Mario got serious.

"Time to get serious."

"Really?"

"Oh yeah. Not here for me health, y'know. Moscow in August isn't Noosa in November. More engine fumes than ozone."

"Really? Then fire away."

Mario topped up his glass. Charlie had not touched his.

"So, Charlie-boy . . . are you happy?"

Oh fuck, Mario. Ask me about the space race, Gagarin, U2s, tractor productivity, the next five-year plan, corn harvest in the Ukraine, hydroelectricity in the Donbas . . . anything but that.

§202

"You don't think I'm entitled to be happy?"

"Dunno. The only countries I can think of that have happiness as an entitlement are America and North Vietnam, and even then they say you've a right to *pursue* it—they don't guarantee you'll get it. Russia? You tell me."

"Russia isn't about happiness. It's . . ."

Oh fuck. What was all that bollocks that Troy used to rattle off . . . the great mission of Holy Mother Russia? The dark soul? The Russian Idea?

"Mario. It's the wrong question."

"What's the right one?"

"Surely you want to know why I defected. Isn't that why you're here?"

"Yeah. But it's corny as Kansas. You defected because you'd already betrayed your country, your mates, your family, so there was bugger all else you could do—"

"I did no such thing. I believed, Mario, I believed."

"In what?"

"In a cause."

"Marxism?"

"If you like."

"Marx-Engels-Leninism?"

"Yes. Of course."

"OK. Quote me something."

"Eh?"

"Anything. Just quote me a single line any one of them wrote. C'mon. You've got three to pick from."

"Er. The square on the hypotenuse is . . . fukkit, Mario. I was never an ideologue, I was literary. Ask me to quote you *To His Coy Mistress* or

Donne's *Sunne Rising* or anything Tigger says in *Winnie the Pooh* and I'm your man. I was a believer, not an ideologue, and there's a difference."

"OK. What did you believe in? And don't say a cause. We just been there."

"Why not cut the crap and just ask me why I left."

"OK. Why d'ya leave?"

"I left because . . ."

§203

Because the earth is flat.
Because I have size 12 feet.
Because it never rains on Sundays.
Because my dad buggered off and left us.
Because my mum fucked too many men.
Because I fucked too many women.
Because
Because
Because
Because
Because
Because.

§204

Charlie was left in no doubt about the point at which Mario stopped listening, or at least stopped writing.

Mario pointed at the ceiling, to another fresh white scar in the plaster, then put down his Biro, and after what must have been his fifth slug, and all the zakuski gone save the poor old salty gherkins, he reached for Charlie's glass.

Took this one slowly.

Closed his eyes after the first sip.

Charlie was telling him about Cambridge in the thirties . . . Red Vienna . . . Franco. Mario had the good manners not to yawn.

The truth, as black and white in this instance as the Harrow tie, that his "treason"—Mario had not used the word, good manners again—had as much to do with his mum as with anything else and that his present condition had everything to do with Magda . . . was unutterable. He'd love to be able to talk to Mario about Magda, to be able, just once to be the one to shame the devil, but what would be the point? Just to be able to slice through the murk?

§205

Mario stuffed his kit back in his rucksack.

"Been a treat, Charlie-boy."

Really?

"So in return I got a treat for you."

One of his huge hands dug down into the bag and pulled out something crumpled, wrapped in cellophane.

There it was, as though conjured up by some kind of Freudian word-magic—an old Harrovian tie.

Then Mario extended his arms and gripped Charlie in a bear hug. Far too Australian a gesture. His spikey bristles next to Charlie's ear.

"Spit it out, mate."

"Tell the English. Get Joe Holderness out now. He's asked one question too many," Charlie whispered back.

Mario slackened off and smiled.

"Any last message for Blighty," he said at a normal volume.

"Yes. Vote Conservative," Charlie replied, which set Mario laughing all the way down the staircase.

Charlie looked at Mario's present. A world in two stripes. Took it into the kitchen and binned it.

He sat back in his plywood armchair, staring at the ceiling. He'd set his own mind rambling . . . Pooh, Marvell, Donne . . .

Rambling, drifting . . . Pooh, Marvell, Donne . . . de la Mare . . .

". . . a host of phantoms, listening . . .
Tell them I have kept my word."
Well, comrades . . . did I pass?
". . . And the silence surging softly backward . . ."

§206

The British Embassy

August 22, 1969

Mario was uncomfortable in his "best bib and tucker," but not half as uncomfortable as Lord Troy looked as he greeted guests assembling to celebrate his birthday.

"Evenin', young Fred. Looks like quite a bash."

Troy shook hands and used the moment to draw Mario in a little closer, to the distance of a whisper.

"This is hell. Shoot me now!"

"Nah. I'll just stuff you in me tucker bag, 'cept I didn't bring one."

In a normal voice, Troy said, "I don't believe you've met my wife."

"My wife" was scowling at her husband, clearly finding it hard to fake a smile after what he'd just said.

"Mr. Mariotti. At last. One has heard so much about you."

"One has?"

And then he was set adrift on a polyglot sea of chatter, snatching Russian here, French there, until a sexy northern-English voice turned his head and a good-looking young woman in a scarlet gown said, "Mr.

Mariotti, I'm Janis Bell. Would you care for a tour of the building? We have some truly hideous oil paintings I could show you."

§207

"He tried tossing me the odd sausage. Had a go at feeding me the clichés of the defector. 'I'm a committed communist, a believer.' Blah blah blah. Could not do it. Fell at the first hurdle. 'I'm a lost soul in Moscow, drowning in booze.' I poured him a triple vodka. He never touched it. Either of those would fit what my editor is expecting, and I think the spooks on the other end of all those microphones would have been satisfied with them too—but it's not where Charlie Leigh-Hunt is at. He's happy. Killed him not to say it, but he is. So I go home with a story no one will want and you get a simple message. At least I assume it's for you. 'Get Joe Holderness out. He's asked one question too many.'"

§208

In the morning Janis told Troy.
"Do I need to do anything?"
"I'll handle it."
"You'll tell my brother?"
"I don't have that level of access."
"Neither do I. He much prefers to deal with Anna. Can't say I blame him."
"I'll tell Burne-Jones."
"Is Charlie taking a risk?"
"*Being* Charlie Leigh-Hunt is a risk. But he's a big boy."

"Janis, I've known Charlie all my life. Those two words in combination do not describe him. He's brave, without being reckless. An habitual womaniser, but no one's lover. Smart but still a fool. And before you open your mouth to speak . . . no, the pot doth not accuse the kettle."

"Can I take it you want to be kept out of it but well-informed?"

"Perk of the job," Troy replied.

"Reminds me of Macmillan's best line."

"You've never had it so good?"

"No . . . the other best line. The historic privilege of the whore has now been usurped by the press . . . power without responsibility."

"You will understand if I say 'fuck off,' but before you do . . . Holderness? Clear and present danger?"

"Not at the moment. The comrades moved him to a high-rise out near Novodevichy Convent. He can hear all the Gregorian chant a man could wish for. He's still getting preferential treatment. But I think that if we are to believe Charlie, we cannot simultaneously believe Joe is a defector. He has two goons traipsing after him everywhere. He's not allowed to leave the city—neither am I—but most of Moscow seems open to him. And of course he has occasional visits from his handler."

"Who is?"

"Major Ewald. Magda. Not Russian. Austrian. A protegé of General Zolotukhina. Her file reads like an Eric Ambler novel. I can drop it off later if you like. And . . . and . . . London thinks she may well be Charlie's mistress."

"Yes," said Troy. "Drop off the file."

Magda

§209

Novodevichy

September 6, 1969

Wilderness was at "home," bored shitless and wondering, since the evening was light and cool, whether he should wander into the city centre, seek out somewhere new to eat and drink at the same time and lead the Arthur Mullards on another pointless pursuit. He was quite sure they hated walking, and the only respite he gave them was the occasional bookish afternoon at Patriki or a sour-cream-and-spud evening in a dingy caff.

There was a knock at the door. The first ever.

A Mullard bulked in the doorway, a total eclipse of the light bulb.

"Вниз. Сейчас."

Downstairs. Now.

§210

There was Magda, staring up at the side of the building. A streetlight went out as though cued by her gaze.

A wave of her hand and the Arthur Mullards walked away and did not look back.

"Your apartment? 6G?"

Wilderness looked up.

"No. The only one with a light on. 7G."

"Really?"

"Yes. Why do you ask?"

"Oh, just memory stirring. I knew the man in 6G. Must be the apartment right underneath yours."

"A friend?"

"A friend of Charlie's. Perhaps even a friend of yours. Burgess. Since he died, the apartment has stood idle."

"Idle meaning empty?"

"No. Idle meaning idle. Most of Burgess's things are very probably still there. He didn't dispose of much in his will, although I believe Philby got the odd bequest. Books . . . a chair to read them in. It's waiting on the next defector. I had assumed that would be you. Apparently not."

"You're my handler and you didn't know?"

"We both know who's in charge, Joe. Now. Let us go where she cannot hear us. The cemetery."

§211

"Pick a grave," Wilderness said.

"What?"

"It's a game I play on days when I'm bored. Sometimes I nip into the convent. A little Gregorian chant is good for my soul. Mostly I walk around the cemetery. I pick a grave and start up a conversation with the occupant."

"Chatty, are they?"

"Bulgakov was. Couldn't get a word out of Prokofiev."

"So—I get to pick?"

She strolled off, seemingly knowing exactly where she was going.

"OK," she called and beckoned to him.

He found her standing by a life-sized alabaster statue of a seated woman—flowers, mostly dead, strewn at her feet.

Александра Михайловна Коллонтай
1872–1952

Alexandra Kollontai, one of a handful of original 1917 revolution-
aries to live to be eighty. So many bullets dodged. Not that he'd ever
stopped to chat before.

"Interesting choice. Can you hear her?"

"Loud and clear. She will be my rod and my staff."

"Yea, though you walk—"

"Joe! What do you want?"

Before Wilderness could say anything her hand went up, verbal traffic stopped.

"Don't answer yet! Do not speak! Whatever you say now will be a
lie. Listen! There is more I have to tell you.

"When I met Charlie he was on the road to join all the other Eng-
lishmen who've ended up in Russia. Drank far too much and sooner
or later drunkenness would flood with self-pity and drown him in a
pool of nostalgia for the country he had betrayed and abandoned. The
latter days of his life spent dreaming of an England he had never much
cared about—not knowing what he'd got till it was gone. Fish and chips
and the old school tie.

"Now, he has one martini while he listens to the BBC World Service . . . at weekends we share a bottle of wine each night. He is sober,
he is sane. I might even say he is happy. He'll never be Russian, but then
neither will I. We are not communism's fellow travellers—such a dis-
paraging phrase—we are the Soviet Union's willing passengers—we are
believers. But, we are different and we know we are different—so much
so that we have a home language, German, and a work language, Russian. We are what we are. There is, for want of a more romantic word, an
equilibrium. We have become a Soviet chimera—and if you sneer now, I
shall hit you—we are мещанство. Middle-aged and middle class. A far
from petty bourgeoisie. Charlie is happy with his flat in the Arbat, his
dacha out at Peredelkino, his books and his veg garden. You may choose
not to believe that. But you may not choose to fuck it up.

"When you plied him with vodka two weeks ago, he probably hadn't
drunk like that in five years. A weak moment. He let you—but he didn't
know what you were up to."

Thinking of Charlie's drunken Hokey Cokey . . . right leg in, left leg
out . . . Wilderness still didn't have a clue what Charlie had been up to.

"But then . . . you drew him on, you drew him out, you rooted around in his psyche hoping to find the old Charlie and then you asked your question. You upset our equilibrium. Charlie won't tell me what you're after. Only that you ask too much. He will not repeat your question. So, now you must answer mine—Joe, what do you want?"

"You debriefed me, Magda. You should know."

"I do what I am told. I debriefed you on instructions from Zolotukhina. I asked you what I was told to ask. You said yourself, there was a script. I did not depart from the script."

"Until now."

"Yes."

"Because I've upset your . . . 'equilibrium'?"

A sigh of utter exasperation in lieu of an answer.

"Do you think I'm a defector, Magda?"

"No."

"Do you think I was kidnapped?"

"I don't know. I just know you have your own motives, your own reasons. Reasons that might coincide with Zolotukhina's reasons but are not her reasons."

"She's pulling every string, you know. Me as well as you."

"To what end? You want what you want. But what does she want?"

"When I find out I'll tell you."

"Why not begin by telling me what you want?"

"Me first. Who is asking? The KGB officer or the spy's lover?"

"It's my job. And it's my nature. To be suspicious. So both of us are asking you."

"Even when orders say not?"

"I'm not a robot, Joe. I want to know what you want because you are a threat. You proved that out at Patriki."

"A threat to . . . ?"

"To Charlie. To my life with Charlie. To our life of мещанство."

"So, really . . . the lover is asking? About a petty-bourgeois life already under scrutiny."

"You mean Zolotukhina?"

"Of course."

"Then I'd say that whilst I do not have her blessing for what I have done, I also do not have her suspicion. She knows Charlie is no threat to the Soviet Union—better still, he is no threat to her. The threat is you. But if she suspects you, she will suspect Charlie. Zolotukhina would not need proof of anything. If she thought you were working both ends, which I think you are, she'd take out all concerned. A short trip to the Lubyanka and a bullet to the back of the head. You, him and me. Do not drag Charlie down with you. Zolotukhina holds the power of life and death over all of us. So—what do you want from Charlie?"

"A name."

"Please try to be less cryptic."

"The name of his fellow agent in Washington seventeen years ago."

"You're joking?"

"No."

"Who gives a damn about things that happened seventeen years ago? Good God . . . Stalin was still alive . . . the ark had not yet landed on Ararat . . ."

"The CIA gives a damn."

The look on her face was priceless. Wide-eyed amazement.

She had not anticipated this.

It seemed to Wilderness an age before she spoke. Head down. Weary.

"So—you're not working for England?"

"Not today."

"Joe, are you trying to get us all killed?"

"Only you know, Magda."

She kicked at the gravel, sending up a shower.

"Fuck! Fuck! Fuck! You stupid, stupid Englishman. We are dead. Do you know that? Dead!"

"She doesn't know!"

"You can't possibly say that. You haven't seen her since . . . since . . ."

"Since the week before you moved me to the Metropol."

"It was my job to . . . to . . . sound you out. To . . . catch you."

"No. You were never meant to catch me. You were meant to stick to the script. And you did. It wasn't an interrogation so much as a career review before I pick up a lifetime achievement award. Magda, it's all been a masquerade."

"No . . . no . . ."

"You played your part in Volga's masquerade. You played it well. That's all she asked of you."

There was another pause. She could not look at him.

"If I played it well it was because I did not realise it was a masquerade. Why? Why tell me now?"

"You asked."

"If I'd had the faintest inkling of your answer I would not have. I would have preferred ignorance. It's not a masquerade, it's . . . *un ascenseur pour l'échafaud*—an ascent to the scaffold."

"And . . . Magda . . . I think you know what I need to know."

"What?"

"I think you and Charlie tell each other everything."

Another long pause in which she would not meet his gaze.

"Have you never been in love, Joe?"

"Of course. I am a happily married man."

"And you and your wife, you tell each other everything?"

"No."

"And you think we do?"

"Yes."

Magda looked to the cerulean Moscow heaven and sighed loudly.

"And if I give you the name . . . if I give you this piece of ancient history, you'll leave Charlie alone?"

"Yes."

Magda turned to Kollontai.

Picked up a dead rose and plucked off a few petals, not looking at Wilderness. Lips moving silently.

"Любит? Не любит?" He loves me, he loves me not . . . a scattering of dried red flakes at her feet like bloodstains.

"Then . . . then . . . I will tell you."

Looking at Wilderness now.

"It was Coky Shumacher."

Coky Shumacher. Good fucking grief.

"Now you're the one joking."

"No—you were quite right. Charlie told me everything. Not at first. And not in the debrief. He might have assumed I knew. But I didn't. Her name wasn't in any file the KGB showed me before I was asked to interrogate Charlie. I had names—Farber, Ignatz Farber. And Charlotte Redmaine. That was it. Just the name and a single question. Had he seen her since Washington? No note to tell me who she was, and no hint of why I should be asking. But then, there never would be. I did what I always do. I stuck to the script. It's a manual for survival here. Charlie even asked about her. I had no answer. It wasn't in the script. She was just those two words. A fraction of an identity. I did not realise who she was. There was no mention of a Coky Shumacher. Later . . . summer in Peredelkino . . . he wanted to tell me about his lover "Coky." The flattery of a confession. The arrogant intimacy of telling one lover about another. And it dawned on me that she was the woman I had been instructed to ask about in the Lubyanka. His Washington contact had been his lover. Charlotte Redmaine was Coky Shumacher."

Thinking of Charlie's drunken dance . . . right leg in, left leg out . . . Wilderness realised Charlie had taken the piss. He'd answered the question and Wilderness hadn't even noticed—

Woah, woah, the Hokey Cokey.

He had to admire the sheer cheek.

That's what it's all about.

She threw the stripped rose stem at his feet.

Gauntlet down. A return to rage after the softness of a monologue. Almost shouting her words.

"Did you really think you could get Charlie shit-faced and that he would simply tell you? That he would . . . would . . . betray her?"

"Betrayal might be the name of the game."

"Not anymore. Not Charlie. I can't kid myself I'm the love of a lifetime for a man who's been as promiscuous as a tomcat . . . but perhaps Shumacher was. He'd never betray her."

"It was worth a try."

"No Joe, it was pathetic."

Wilderness shrugged this off.

"Are we done?" Magda said. "Do we have a deal?"

"We do."

"Then never come near me again."

Wilderness looked around. For some reason he could not fathom, he felt foolish. "Pathetic" was right. Why would Charlie ever have betrayed her? Charlie betrayed countries, not individuals.

"My turn to pick," he said at last. "You seem to know the cemetery far better than I do. I don't suppose you happen to know where Ivan Goncharov is buried."

"Yes. Leningrad."

"Then perhaps some other absurdist writer who might find room for someone as pathetic as me in his fiction."

"Follow me."

A short walk through the gravelled maze of angelic art, to another tomb, topped by a shining bronze cross.

Николай Васильевич Гоголь

1809–1852

Nikolai Gogol. Author of *Dead Souls*.

Inveterate chronicler of пошлость—*poshlost*—close to the English idea of "vulgarity" but with a better sense of humor.

"Is Gogol absurd enough for you? You must have plenty to say to one another. I'm surprised you and Nikolai haven't chatted before. I'll leave you two alone together—and please be so kind as to leave me and Charlie alone. До свидания, Joe."

With that she was gone, leaving Wilderness looking at a cross when he'd rather be looking at a statue with a face.

He'd got what he came for.

It felt like defeat.

An anticlimax that reached down into his socks.

He'd no idea what might happen next.

He asked Gogol.

Gogol didn't answer.

§212

Most of Burgess's things are very probably still there.

Magda had transported him to a rock above the Jordan valley and shown him all the kingdoms of the world.

It was irresistible, but for the best part of three days Wilderness did resist, and on the fourth he fashioned lockpicks out of a nail file and teaspoon worn down to nothing and went to the floor below. The cat burglar once more—his grandfather's willing pupil . . . Dodger to his Fagin.

He'd no idea what he might find.

Six years of dust?

A handwritten confession?

A pile of unpaid bills from Jermyn Street, Savile Row and GUM?

The apartment was identical to his own. A longish but not biggish living room, a small bedroom, smaller kitchen and even smaller bathroom. But there the resemblance ended. Wilderness's apartment was spartan—regulation issue—bog standard, as he thought of it— Soviet-shabby furniture and plain, colourless walls. To have put his own mark upon it, to have improved it in any way might be to succumb to the notion that he was staying rather than passing through. Burgess had stayed, Burgess had put his mark on his flat.

The first thing that struck him was the harmonium. He'd heard that Burgess was fond of the Anglican hymnal, as likely to play *Rock of Ages* as *Any Old Iron*. Somehow he must have persuaded the Russians to ship this symbol of English parishional life. Much as he had persuaded them to let him continue to buy suits and ties from his London tailor.

The second thing was the posters taped to the wall.

Burgess had never lost his sense of humour. Above his desk were several posters—some in the style of Socialist Realism, poster-paint colours and geometric angles.

An old lady in red:

Родина-Мать Совет
(Soviet Motherland Calls You)

Stirring stuff. Probably helped win the war.

A young lady, also in red, index finger pressed to her lips, urging the observer:

Не болтай!
(Keep shtum!)

And another red figure, a featureless silhouette looking far too much like a rough sketch of Guy Fawkes, telling US citizens:

THE RED MENACE IS REAL!

. . . and urging them to report anything . . . and everything.

Joe concluded it could only be a souvenir of Guy's time in Washington, a remnant of the Redmaine era, and had been pinned up with deliberate irony—as if Burgess were capable of responding to such injunctions—opposite traditional English hunting scenes of fat blokes riding to hounds in Constable-like landscapes. Wilderness's father-in-law had half a dozen lining his study in Holland Park. Wilderness sincerely hoped his wife would not inherit them.

None of this was really surprising, albeit unanticipated. After all, Wilderness had no idea what he was looking for.

One cupboard in the kitchen was locked. Why lock a kitchen cupboard? No matter. The lockpicks made a second's work of it.

Twelve jars of Frank Cooper's Coarse Cut Oxford Marmalade. Three jars of The Gentleman's Relish, Patum Peperium, a Mars Bar and a rancid-looking jar of Heinz Sandwich Spread . . . salad cream with Technicolor bits in it. Someone, clearly, came in and cleaned from time to time but threw nothing away—a *babushkapparatchik*? He'd nick a couple of jars of marmalade on his way out. Why waste them? He'd leave the Mars Bar. For some reason they'd tasted better in 1942 when they were rationed and you had to share them in slices. A whole Mars Bar to oneself was self-defeating postwar decadence.

He'd just gone through Burgess's books—well, a couple of dozen of them—shaking them to see if anything fell out—only a receipt from Collet's bookshop in the Charing Cross Road and a page torn from the menu for Giovanni's restaurant in Goodwin's Court—when a flickering above his head caught his eye. It was the red light on a fisheye camera set in the ceiling. He had noticed it when he came in and assumed it to be long dead. Stupid. He should have realised it would be motion activated. He just didn't think batteries lasted that long. He'd probably set it off seconds after he came in. He wondered how long he'd been bumbling around on camera, wondered how long he'd got, and did so pointlessly as the thought had scarcely taken shape in his mind before the door burst open and two KGB-niks took up positions either side of it.

They stood like statues. He hardly existed for them.

A third KGB-nik appeared in the doorway—a Makarov automatic in his hand—one star on his shoulder, a sublieutenant—no ribbons on his chest. A nobodnik.

"You will sit."

OK, you're the man with the gun.

He sat at the oval dining table. The nobodnik pulled out a chair and sat opposite, the Makarov on the table pointing at Wilderness.

"Waiting for someone, are we?" Wilderness said.

No answer.

And they sat like that for the best part of half an hour.

The nobodnik stared at Wilderness.

Wilderness did not stare back. Played a silent game of I Spy around the room . . . the porcelain reading lamp . . . the half-roundy thing you use as a blotter . . . the black-box Pye record player, successor to the wind-up gramophone . . . watched the blokes at the door begin to twitch with the discomfort of standing to attention.

At last Wilderness heard slow steps on the staircase. Not the leaping gait of young limbs . . . the measured, more careful tread of a man in late middle age. Then he was standing in the doorway like an illusion made manifest—Kim Philby.

"You're an ass, Holderness. A total ass. You might fool a dimwitted playboy like Leigh-Hunt but you're not f-f-fooling me. Defection, my arse. Kidnap, my arse. You're a fraud! A f-f-fucking con man. You always were! C-c-cuff 'im."

Wilderness shoved his sleeves up and held out his hands.

Well, if you're going to get busted, at least get busted by a living legend.

Troy

§213

Moscow

September 10, 1969
Sunshine

The battle lines were drawn invisibly across the tablecloth.

Poached eggs versus buckwheat kasha. Anna had forsaken porridge for a Russian variant, served up with a splash of buttermilk. The change did not alter her morning disposition.

"What does a beautiful late-summer day hold for an idle peer of a faraway rainy realm? Quality spotted-pig time? An afternoon pootlin' around on the piano with Schubert's greatest hits, or perhaps the vaguest possibility of work?"

"I'm going to London."

"What?"

"Rod has summoned me."

"No he hasn't, you fibbing little fucker. If he had, I'd know. Every phone call, telegramme and letter that comes into this place is recorded. I read the dailies . . . daily."

"Of course. Silly me."

"Silly you, indeed. You're up to something."

"I just need to talk to Rod."

"In person?"

"Yes."

"OK. So don't tell me. Leave me on me Jack Jones to run the British Empire, hold the red menace at bay, see off the yellow peril and look after your pig."

It was not a good report on the state of Troy's marriage that he had reached the point of not knowing whether his wife was serious or not.

§214

London

Drizzle

He got to Hampstead later the same night. The same uniformed copper was on the door who'd been there six months ago. No Special Branch, ergo . . . no prime minister or anything like a prime minister inside.

"Good evening, Tom."

"Evenin' . . . your er . . ."

"Forget rank, Tom, just tell me if he's in."

"In, yes. Up, I dunno. Your brother tends to go to bed early with a box of government papers. Earlier still if something on the news has annoyed him."

"That could be most nights."

"Student protests get right up his nose."

Troy looked at the light shining from the front bedroom window.

"He's awake. Would you mind ringing the bell. I have my own key but it seems a cheek to use it."

Cid, the other Lady Troy, answered.

"Freddie. What a pleasant surprise. Is Anna with you?"

"No. Someone has to run the empire. I need a bed for the night, and I need to see Rod."

§215

"It's over, isn't it?" Cid said over a cup of char.

"Yes. I've had enough. Living in Moscow is like trying to make your own yoghurt."

"A favour, Freddie. Don't tell him till the morning. Or he'll get no sleep. Been a particularly bad day. Looming prospect of a big anti-war demo at the weekend, and more trouble in the new universities . . . Essex or Sussex or somesuch . . . ungrateful bastards, as he calls them. Not his brief, but he takes the notion of collective cabinet responsibility far too seriously."

"Name me something he doesn't take far too seriously. I've been trying to find it for fifty years."

"So . . . you'll resign in the morning?"

"Better still, I will name a new ambassador for him."

"Who?"

"Anna."

"Does she know?"

"No."

§216

Rod wasn't fooled for a moment. He had arisen with the cares of yesterday dreamed to naught in the night. And straight into the new one.

Over the first espresso and buttered toast he said, "You've come home to quit."

It was not a question.

"Yep."

"The answer's no."

"Why?"

"You still have a mission."

"A mission?"

"Quite."

"Only . . . if you make it my last mission."

"Then we have a deal."

"We do? Tell me."

"Set up a meeting with Charlie Leigh-Hunt."

"The Russians will never agree to that."

"Compassionate grounds."

"Rod, we're talking about Soviet apparatchiks . . . hold on, what compassionate grounds?"

"Charlie's mother died last week. I found out yesterday. Had you not appeared as though summoned by some devilish incantation I would be drafting a telex to you right now."

So Judy was gone. The light and life of the party finally burnt out. Troy had been fond of Judy Leigh-Hunt. She was fun. His own mother had been austere, ramrod straight, strictly Russian even when she spoke her first, her favourite language, French . . . as though joie de vivre might be a sin. Judy had had enough joie de vivre for her own monstrous regiment.

"I'll tell him. I should be the one. I wouldn't let anyone else do it."

§217

Moscow

Still Sunny

After more than six months in Moscow, Troy still did not know the name of the Minister of Internal Affairs.

"I think you forget deliberately," Janis Bell said. "You've met him twice!"

"Just give me a name, Janis."

"Shchelkov. Nikolai Shchelkov."

"And?"

"And he's a rogue. I think that's what you really need to know."

"Would you have someone place a call to this rogue? I need to talk to him."

"As he's also the chief of police, might I ask why?"

"Leigh-Hunt," Troy said simply.

"We're not supposed to—"

"I am commissioned by Her Majesty's Foreign Secretary and blah de blah. Charlie's mother died. Rod asked me to tell him. I wouldn't have it any other way."

Fifteen minutes later Troy had Russia's top cop on the other end of the line. No "How may I assist you" et cetera, just a plain "What?"

"I have to ask you to arrange a meeting with Charles Leigh-Hunt."

"No."

"Compassionate grounds, Minister. His mother passed away."

A long silence.

"We are . . . not . . . inhuman, you know. Something will be done."

"Could it be done soon?"

"My man will call you."

And the line went dead.

Troy said, "Did you get all that, Janis?"

"I did. What a charmer."

Later that day an assistant at the MVD telexed, with precise instructions:

```
Noon. Tomorrow.
By the Andreyevsky railway bridge.
The entrance to Gorky Park on Pushkinskaya
Naberezhnaya.
Leading to the Rozariy.
Do not enter.
You and one other.
You have thirty minutes.
```

"Just like an invitation to an opening night," Troy said. "A plus-one. Slightly more polite than 'bring bird and bottle.' I'm sure Charlie will provide the bottle and I suppose you'll be the bird?"

"No. Tony will be. Take the Rolls," Janis said. "That way no one will be able to hear you."

"I'm not imparting secrets, Janis. Just telling him the worst news of his life."

"Of course, we don't know what he might have to tell you, do we?"

"Nothing," Troy replied. "Absolutely nothing."

§218

Gorky Park

Troy thought Gorky Park shabby. Shabby to the point of sadness. London after the war. A shadow of its former glory, but that he had no idea of any of its glory. He'd been there in the spring, when perhaps it was at its saddest. No smothering, blanketing, snow-bound beauty. Rowing boats bobbing empty on scarcely thawed ponds . . . a Ferris wheel that wasn't turning . . . roundabouts that did not spin with children . . . grittily optimistic ice cream stands and bars selling kvass and shashliki that no one queued for in the world capital of queues. The sense of things dripping, always dripping.

Summer made a different sound. The yelps of pleasure from the playground, the rapid pops from the shooting gallery. If this were London, people would come and go with dogs on leads, but Moscow seemed curiously lacking in both dogs and cats. In six months he didn't think he'd seen more than two or three of either.

He stood in Pushkinskaya Naberezhnaya on a half-moon of walkway next to the railway bridge, jutting out over the river, looking towards the park entrance.

At 12:01 Charlie appeared from the Rozariy, a light summer suit flapping around a far slimmer Charlie than he'd ever known, and two goons behind him looking overheated in gabardine macs, no doubt worn to conceal small personal armouries.

Charlie stopped. They stopped. A good twenty yards behind him.

"What a fucking farce, eh?"

He stood on the opposite pavement. Troy raised his left hand slightly and the Rolls glided into view.

"Get in."

"Eh?"

"Get in before your fan club works it out."

Charlie crossed the road, the goons burst from bafflement to life, but it was too late. The Rolls pulled away with Troy and Charlie in the back seat.

"First left, Tony. Take us along Leninsky Prospekt and then cross into the Khamovniki."

Charlie turned in the seat.

"They're running after us."

"Let them. The car is bulletproof and also bugproof. The best listening device in the world won't pick up what I have to say."

"And after six years, what might that be?"

"Your mother died."

Troy had learnt years ago, as a London copper, never to be coy about death. What hurt was the suspense. Just spit it out.

"Oh, Jesus Christ. When?"

"September third. Her heart just stopped. Her boyfriend found her sitting upright early in the morning, dressing gown, cup of coffee still warm, copy of the *Guardian* on her knees. I'm afraid I don't know which boyfriend."

"Doesn't matter. They were all the same to me. Excuse me, Freddie."

Charlie looked away. Fished around in his pocket for a handkerchief to wipe away the tears. Troy handed him a clean, folded one. The Rolls had turned off Leninsky and was crossing the river before he spoke again.

"I was a dreadful son, you know."

"She was a pretty dreadful mother."

"Wasn't she just? More fun than a wagonload of monkeys, but . . ."

"But everything."

"Yep. I don't suppose I'll be allowed home for the funeral."

"I've been told not."

"Bastards. If, if . . . there's a chance. I mean a wake, some sort of a do . . . would you speak for me? And tell the truth. I hate eulogies that sanctify the dear departed. She is departed, and she was very dear to me . . . but she spent money like a drunken Irish sailor on shore leave and fucked anything in pants. Of course, you don't have to say it quite like that . . ."

"I'll think of something."

"Odd, isn't it. I've been here six years and you . . . what . . . six months, and someone has to die before we can talk to one another."

The Rolls pulled up.

Tony slid back the glass partition.

"We're there, Your Excellency."

Charlie stared at Troy.

"How do you ever get used to that, and where the fuck are we?"

"Let's walk for a bit. It will be an age before they catch up with us."

They got out. Stood in front of a long row of ornate, dirty railings. "Since you ask, we're at Tolstoy's house. But that's not why I brought you here."

Troy pointed down the street to a house on the opposite side that seemed sombre and shuttered, and led Charlie to it.

"My dad's old house. Abandoned in 1905 and confiscated by the state. The ancien régime, not the Soviet one. I just wanted one last look. And in that is the answer to your first question. I'll never get used to it, even though Tony was only being formal because of you. I'll never get used to this fucking job. I'm going home. Judy's timing was immaculate. Brought us together at the last possible moment. I'm going home to pack. I have a Siberian pig and eight piglets to ship to England."

"Last possible? You're sure?"

"I'll be gone in a matter of days."

"Then I have to ask."

"Ask what?"

"Mario Mariotti. I gave him a message for you."

Troy thought he must have looked blank, as Charlie said it again.

"You got my message?"

"I did."

"Then why is Joe Holderness still in prison?"

"I don't know. I'd no idea he was in prison. I'd assumed he was being traded. I imagine Six have made offers."

"He's not. He's in the Lubyanka. And you need to get London to act. The Kremlin are humouring Volga Zolotukhina. It was she snatched Joe off the Glienicke Bridge. They're not averse to a little private enterprise, after all, but they're getting fed up. It's piss or get off the pot."

"Meaning?"

"That she pulls off whatever fiddle she's working—and believe me, they know she's up to something—or they'll take Holderness into their own care. And that word is loaded with irony. Freddie, they'll start to knock him about."

"Why? You had six months with him, surely he spilled the beans?"

"He did. I got a full carton of fucking Heinz out of him. Most of it worthless. No, they'll knock him about for the fun of it. If you want Joe back with any fingernails on his hands, get him out."

Troy stared for a moment or two at the ghost of his father's house.

"I may have to stay a little longer, it seems. I've dealt with Zolotukhina before. Another wagonload of monkeys. I'll have to play His Excellency one more time and call her. Now, to invoke an old cliché . . . may I drop you somewhere?"

"No. I really should walk. We're both playacting it seems, and I need to play the grieving son."

Troy knew he wasn't playing at all.

Just as Troy reached the Rolls, Charlie called out.

"September third?"

"That's what Rod told me."

"The day war broke out?"

"Yes."

"*The day war broke out . . . the missus said to me . . .*"

Robb Wilton's mournful monologue.

Troy knew how the line ended. Every Englishman of his generation did.

"*What good are you?*" he said.

"Still on the nail thirty years on, eh? What good am I indeed?"

§219

Before he called Zolotukhina Troy sent for Janis.

"Joe Wilderness. Tell me."

"Burne-Jones is . . . how to put it . . . operating under the radar. I think I told you that when you got here. But . . . we have no one the Russians want. The Americans have been somewhat cooperative, by which I mean that Burne-Jones thinks they could do better. They offered

Helmut Schwartzentruber . . . a minor spy not considered worth the death penalty in Washington. Gave the Russians the formula for hot dogs or pretzels or something of no significance whatsoever. But he's East German. The Russians most likely want a Russian. Then Washington offered Victor Miniver—he gave them NATO's strategy for the next five years, but he was born English. Naturalised American. About as appealing to the KGB as yesterday's rice pudding. It's going to take a bigger and more native fish to get Joe out."

"Do the Americans have bigger fish?"

"Oh yes. And sooner or later they'll deliver . . ."

"I don't think we have a later."

§220

"The Lordship Troy, I thought you'd never call." Zolotukhina's voice crackled down the line.

"You've been playing games."

"I am an old woman. What other pleasures do I have?"

"Meanwhile Joe Holderness rots in the Lubyanka, at your pleasure."

"'Rots' would not be the word."

"He's in the fucking Lubyanka. How could you let that happen?"

Silence.

Confessional.

"I took my eye off the ball. I was in hospital having surgery on my hip. Joe chose that moment to be an idiot and break into Burgess's old apartment. That set off an alarm, literally . . . and that summoned Philby off the reserve benches. We ask fukkall of Philby—in fact, he would love KGB rank and a full-time job, which he will never get—but anything to do with British defectors and he is our man. It would have given him immense delight to arrest someone like Joe."

"But you didn't call on Philby to interrogate Joe, did you? You sent Charlie."

"Philby would have seen through Joe. Mister Charlie was the lesser risk. He'd chat and ramble and learn fukkall."

"Fine. Get Joe out."

"He's safe where he is."

Troy did not believe this, but they were both shy of the point.

"You don't want Schwartzentruber. You don't want Miniver. So—?"

"So?"

"So how much do you want, General?"

"What took you so long? Twenty-five thousand."

"Dollars."

"Sterling."

"I do hope you enjoyed the game, General."

"I did. I did."

"Twenty-five thousand pounds and you'll deliver Joe unharmed."

"Can't guarantee he's unharmed, but I will deliver him."

"Where? Here?"

"Oh no, nowhere in Russia. The Glienicke Bridge, Berlin."

She rung off.

Troy rang his secretary and asked her to get him on the next flight to London.

Then he sent for Janis Bell once more.

§221

"Can't say I'm surprised. After the last time, I mean," Janis said.

"It does look as though Joe was snatched just for the money."

Janis pondered.

Then, out of left field.

"How long have you known Joe?"

"Met him . . . about fifteen years ago. We are not exactly mates."

"Professional reasons?"

"Yes."

"But you know Eddie Clark much better?"

"He worked for me for seven years before he moved to MI6. He's one of my closest friends."

"So . . . I'm treading carefully here . . . you know what Joe and Eddie got up to in Berlin after the war?"

"The rackets? I'd have to be deaf to both Eddie and gossip not to have heard. The first time I met him he tried to sell me nylons. But he spares me most of the details."

"They were *Schiebers*. There were four of them. Eddie and Joe did the actual smuggling. Yuri Myshkin was the buyer—he died a few years ago—and Frank Spoleto was the supplier."

"Not a name Ed ever mentioned."

"He's CIA. Runs a Madison Avenue ad agency as a very lucrative cover. Frank is a bigger rogue than Joe or Ed."

"And?"

"And . . . he was out at Glienicke the night the Russians snatched Joe."

Troy did not need or ask Janis to spell it out.

"I need to talk to Eddie."

"I'll get him on the phone."

§222

"Frank Spoleto?"

"Spawn of Satan. Judas, Oedipus and Beelzebub in one bumper package."

"Ed. That does not help."

"Sorry."

"Where is he?"

"Right now? Washington. He was here till yesterday. He and Burne-Jones have had their heads together. I just listen through the wall."

"And he was the one tried to get General Zolotukhina to agree to an exchange?"

"Yes. But—if you're asking if he blew it deliberately, the answer's no. Frank is a bastard, but he wouldn't leave Joe in the lurch like this. He's having another go at Langley right now."

"Not what I meant. Spoleto's wasting his time. She was never interested in a swap."

"Typical."

"Did you know Frank Spoleto was at the Glienicke Bridge when Joe was snatched?"

"Boss, I was there."

"And is there more to this than meets the eye?"

Eddie silence. The world's worst fibber contemplating his next battle with the truth.

"There might be."

"I'm coming to London."

"I think that's wise."

§223

Bateman Street, Soho

London

Discretion called.

They met in the Dog and Duck in Soho over pie and chips—far from any of their usual haunts, a pub the size of a wardrobe, more likely to be occupied by jazz musicians or actors—all morning-aftering from whatever had been "the night before"—than spooks or coppers.

"Why have I not heard of this Frank Spoleto?"

"Maybe 'cos you don't listen?"

"Eddie—please."

"I admit he's not a hot topic with me. Frank is the classic bad penny. I prefer not to talk about him, but that doesn't mean I haven't."

"OK. Point taken. Now, why was he on the bridge?"

"American territory. Joe couldn't get the bridge without Frank. The trade you set up for Nell Burkhardt couldn't be done at a British checkpoint. Far too exposed."

"What is it you're not telling me?"

"Joe and Frank did a deal."

Eddie paused. Surely, Troy thought, he could not think his last sentence adequate?

"I gather deals are what the three of you did."

"I wasn't party to this one. I know they did a deal, that's all."

Eddie's next pause was laden with melodrama.

Deep breath and spit it out, Eddie.

"Joe wasn't kidnapped."

"I don't understand."

"Joe *let himself* be kidnapped."

"Why? It's . . . it's madness."

"As I said, I wasn't privy to details. But . . . Joe hired two hit men—the Koppenrad brothers, kids we'd known for twenty years—to cover his arse on the bridge. Volga Zolotukhina got wind of this and bribed them to wing Joe. Just enough to stop him walking."

"So they knew she meant to kidnap him? Why did Joe even set foot on the bridge?"

"Because he'd do anything to get Nell back. But that's not all. Frank and Joe topped Volga's offer. The Kopps would go ahead. Joe would be snatched—Frank would pay Joe to be snatched. Don't ask me why or how much, because I don't know. Joe told me it would all add to the confusion on the bridge and allow Bernard Alleyn to escape. But Volga never wanted Bernard in the first place. She just let him go. It was all about Joe. It was always about Joe. And . . . bottom line, we'd get Joe back sooner or later in an exchange. Burne-Jones has been sending messages to Volga for months trying to set up a swap. You may well imagine—he's had his daughter on his case ever since Joe disappeared. Until about three weeks ago Volga ignored us. Suddenly she's open to the idea."

"But she's turned down everyone we've offered her."

"We? . . . *We* haven't offered her anyone. We've got no one. George Blake would have been perfect, but the bugger escaped from the Scrubs three years ago. So Frank offered those two the Americans have banged up. She doesn't want them either. I don't know what she wants."

"I do. She told me. Twenty-five thousand sterling."

"Oh bugger."

"Money changes things."

"No, boss. Money changes *every*thing. The twenty-five grand Volga wants . . . and whatever Frank's people have agreed to pay Joe."

"Does Burne-Jones know this?"

"Don't be daft."

Eddie changed gear. A rare note of authority entered the voice of a man who was a past master of light and bushel.

"Now, before we meet the nobs . . . be it your brother or my boss . . . don't tell 'em any of this."

"OK. But . . . I think I know why you didn't hear from Volga for so long."

"I'm listening."

"She had nothing to trade. Those kids, as you call them, didn't wing Joe. They blew him off his feet. According to Janis Bell, my MI6 chief in Moscow, the city was awash in rumours of a British agent the KGB brought in close to death last December. Janis is convinced it was Joe, and that he was in hospital for weeks. Volga couldn't swap a man on a stretcher."

"But . . . he's OK now?"

"I don't know. He's in the Lubyanka. That I do know, and that doesn't come within any definition of 'OK.'"

§224

They met in Burne-Jones's office.

Troy, Eddie, Colonel Burne-Jones and Alice Pettifer, who ran the office.

Troy decided he wanted to keep Rod out of it until absolutely necessary. As Foreign Secretary he was Burne-Jones's boss. All of MI6 answered to him, and what he did not know about MI6 operations would fill the Encyclopædia Britannica.

"How long has Joe been in the Lubyanka?" Burne-Jones asked.

"I don't know."

"And he is . . . well?"

"I don't know that either."

"I will use this word advisedly—can we 'trust' Zolotukhina?"

"I'd be a fool to answer that. I've spoken to her on the phone. Never met her face to face. Eddie?"

Troy turned to Eddie. He thought Eddie might be hoping to get through this meeting without saying a word, but that was never going to happen.

Eddie tried the quiet defiance of silence.

"Ed? Ed! You've met her?"

Eddie spoke as though he'd prefer having teeth pulled.

"Short answer? No. You can't trust her. She could take the money and run."

"Money?" said Burne-Jones.

Troy had not led with the matter of money. Wilderness's welfare came first in the mind of Burne-Jones, and Troy had not refused him.

"Volga wants twenty-five thousand pounds."

"So—no exchange of prisoners?"

"No. I think it was about money all along."

"My, this woman redefines capitalism, doesn't she? You realise I can't authorise a payment like that?"

Troy said nothing.

"Even . . . even for my own son-in-law . . ."

Burne-Jones was struggling.

Troy thought he might be close to tears.

Burne-Jones had had shining, spotless half-moon reading glasses perched on the end of his nose throughout the meeting. He took them off, wiped them pointlessly on the corner of his linen hanky and shoved them back on.

"For Joe . . ." he said opening a sentence he could not end.

Alice spoke up.

"Twenty-five grand is lunch with champagne and two helpings of pudding to the fucking CIA. Eddie . . . phone Frank!"

"Why me?"

"'Cos you know him better than any of us."

Eddie looked from Burne-Jones to Troy and back again.

Troy would let him stew for as long as it took.

"Edwin—just do it," Burne-Jones said softly.

And when Eddie had left the room, "Really, Alice. The f-word?"

§225

Washington, DC

Life went better with lunch.

What could be so urgent it could not wait until a good lunch?

So, the following day Frank Spoleto met Jeff Boyle at Harvey's.

They sat at the same table Charlie had occupied the day Frank had given the nod to Jeff way back in nineteen-and-whenever, but Frank had a short memory for anything else but insult and little regard for history.

Jeff was late.

No matter. He'd order a starter. He'd order two starters.

Oysters Rockefeller.

Why did they name a dish after him?

A gas station? Sure. But oysters?

And . . .

Artichoke Hearts Vinaigrette.

And if Jeff wasn't here after that, he'd move on to the main course.

Butterfly Shrimp?

Or Filet Mignon?

Frank was chomping on the last artichoke when Jeff arrived.

He wasn't smiling.

Jeff could bear a grudge.

OK. So their last few meetings he'd been the beggar asking for American prisoners in exchange for an English spy.

OK. So it had not worked out. The Russians had spat back Schwart-zentruber and Miniver.

So?

"Order food, Jeff. It'll put the smile back on your face."

Boyle glanced at the menu and shoved it aside.

"Frank. This has gone on too long. If you're here to ask for Sebastian Konitz, the answer's no. He's worth two of Joe Holderness."

Wow. Aim for the gut, why doncha?

"You want Felix Foster's contact or not?"

"Of course I do. This time it's personal."

"Whyzat?"

"Because eighteen years ago 'Felix Foster' sat where you're sitting and conned me and he went on conning me for another two fucking years, that's why!"

Frank saw no point in holding back. OK, so they might not get to the filet mignon, but there'd be other times.

"I don't want Konitz. The Russians don't want Konitz. They want money."

"What?"

"We can get Holderness and the contact name for twenty-five G."

"Since when did we pay for the G in KGB?"

"You didn't think they were capitalists all along?"

"Not funny, Frank. So, listen up—we're not paying so much as a nickel more. The Russkis want twenty-five G? We paid this guy $150,000 already. On your say-so. He has the equivalent of twenty years' pay sitting in his account. Let him take it out of that."

If Frank could ever look sheepish, he would, but he couldn't. He poker-faced. The $150,000 was sitting in *his* bank account in New York. He had rationalised this—Joe and his wife had a joint bank account. If he paid in $150,000, she was bound to ask where it had come from and why . . . and she was not only Joe Wilderness's wife, she was Alec Burne-Jones's daughter. And the next thing you know the whole damn thing comes tumbling down in a transatlantic shitslide.

But—big but—the money sitting in Frank's Chase Manhattan account was, temporarily, the worst kind of money after no money at all, that is, *theoretical* money. It wasn't *actually* in his account. He'd invested all but fifteen grand thinking that he could at least double it on Wall Street while Wilderness was in Russia, and pocket the profit. Alas, his investment had gone down, not up, and to cash in now would yield only 50 percent of the original sum. Enough to pay off the KGB but well short of the sum properly owed to Wilderness. OK, he'd got a few grand of his own he hadn't invested, but that would require wrestling with conscience, an organ he wasn't wholly certain existed. All might be well in six months or so . . . Wall Street might go bullish . . . and by May, at the latest, he'd get his Madison Avenue bonus. Meanwhile . . .

"I'll talk to the British."

"You do that, Frank. And get us the name. We've paid to know who ran 'Felix Foster.' Paid through the goddam nose. But don't come back to me with another demand. Come back to me with a name."

Frank was a bit of a bastard and he knew it, but he could take some consolation in knowing he worked for bigger bastards.

§226

"No go, Eddie."

"Oh, you are fucking kidding!"

§227

London

Troy visited his brother in his office in the Palace of Westminster.

When one of Rod's many assistants said into the intercom, "Lord Troy to see you, sir," Troy knew for certain he'd never get used to it. He hoped Rod would be his usual patronising, insulting, messianic self, then he could feel better about being "Lord Troy."

He explained.

"Why do I know none of this?" Rod said.

"Perhaps it was on a need-to-know basis?"

"Need to know? I'm the fucking Foreign Secretary. I run MI6. It's an FO department."

"Tell me you don't really believe that."

"Are you saying I'm naïve?"

"Yes. But if we could get past that and to the point, I'd be delighted."

"What?"

"Can you authorise Burne-Jones to pay the Russians the money?"

"Of course I can't. How could you even suppose that for a minute?"

"I don't . . . so let's move to plan B before your naïveté proves fatal. The Americans won't pay, you will tell me England cannot afford to pay, so we pay."

"We?"

"You and me."

Rod looked gobsmacked.

"We can afford it. We get Joe back. Frank Spoleto gets whatever he wants. And Volga Zolotukhina gets her pension fund."

Rod had been standing all along.

Now he sat behind his desk. Put his head in his hands. Locked his fingers in his hair as though he might pull out clumps of it.

He spoke without raising his head or moving his hands. Barely audible.

"Cheque or cash?"

"Now you really are being naïve."

§228

Grunewald, West Berlin

Thursday, September 25, 1969

Troy enjoyed one of the perks of rank. There were probably lots of perks to being Her Maj's ambassador to everywhere or anywhere, but he was oblivious to most of them. It would take one hell of a perk to make up for missing piglet time.

The perk he endeavoured to enjoy was not having to stay in a hotel in West Berlin—the best was held to be the Kempinski, which, according to Janis Bell, had more spies than bellhops and was better avoided. Eddie could stay there—he was a highly unlikely spy but nonetheless a spy, and he'd have his ear to the ground, the ceiling and all four walls and no doubt give Troy the "buzz" at a moment of his own choosing. Troy would stay at the residence of the High Commissioner for the British Sector of West Berlin . . . Sir Numpty Something, whose main job was being ambassador to Bonn, so he was hardly ever at home. It was a town house on Hohmannstraße, west of Wilmersdorf and close to the ribbon of lakes that bordered Berlin on the western side and snaked all the way down to Potsdam and beyond. Troy had looked it up in an atlas—the Glienicke Bridge straddled one of the lakes at the city's extremity. One step beyond and you were in Brandenburg, in the DDR, quite possibly the greyest country on earth.

The house was spotless and smelled of beeswax and mothballs. It had a resident housekeeper in the shape of Hedwig Butterschuhe, who showed him to his room, asked him if there was anything he needed and, when he said no, quietly returned to her own.

Troy found himself alone. Just what he wanted. He checked that the telephone worked. Pulled out the perforated page sticking up in the standard-issue British military teleprinter—it was dated 1961, something about a wall. It had been sitting there for eight years. How often had Frau Butterschuhe dusted the teleprinter without reading the printout? No matter. Everything worked. Just what he wanted.

He kicked off his shoes.

Lay back on the bed.

Locked his hands behind his head.

Time to reflect.

Rod had protested, softly.

"The messes you create, Freddie. The shit you get me into. I am bribing a KGB agent. I'm the Foreign fucking Secretary and you have me bribing a KGB general. Can you begin to imagine the row if this gets out?"

Eddie had protested, loudly.

"You don't need me in Berlin. Honestly. I've some very important filing I could be getting on with. I've luncheon vouchers to cash in. Me toby jugs need dusting. Me horse brasses could use a tub of Brasso. I've a jigsaw puzzle of *The Laughing Cavalier* to finish. And it's quiz night down the Three Tuns. They'll be lost without me. Honestly, boss. I hate Berlin."

Troy had ignored him.

"You know this Spoleto fellow. I don't."

"There's bugger all to know. He's a big fat Yankee rogue."

"So, no prejudices, then?"

"Boss, Frank is trouble. He created this mess in the first place."

"Then I hold it as a matter of honour that he get us out of it. It so behooves him."

"Don't go using words like 'honour' to Frank. He won't know what you mean. And I'm not sure I understood that last sentence meself."

"Kempinski. Thursday night. Be there. Call me at the residence."

Troy was sure Eddie's last words had been a whispered "oh bugger."

He had called Janis before he left London.

"Anna is asking," Janis said. "What do I tell her?"

"The truth. I'm on my way to Berlin."

"She wants to know."

"When I'm coming back?"

"*If* you're coming back."

"Dunno."

§229

In the morning Frau Butterschuhe asked what he would like for breakfast.

"Poached eggs on toast, please."

"*Ohne Wurst?*"

"*Ohne Wurst.*"

While he took his second cup of coffee the teleprinter burst into life. Frau Butterschuhe paused, startled, with coffee pot in hand at a perilous angle.

"*Mein Gott. Das hat es noch nie gegeben.*"

My God. It's never done that before.

Troy gently took the dripping pot from her hands and looked at the emerging printout.

It was in Russian. He glanced at Frau Butterschuhe, who took the hint and the coffee pot and went back to her kitchen.

Проснись, ваше Лордство. Солнце встало и я тоже. Мост.
Воскресенье в полночь. Понял? Волга.

WAKEY WAKEY, LORDSHIP. THE SUN IS UP AND SO AM I. THE BRIDGE.

SUNDAY MIDNIGHT. GOT THAT? VOLGA.

How on earth had she managed to get into a secure system and send a teleprinter message? How did she know where to send it?

Then the phone rang.

"Two things." His wife's voice. "Why do I have to find out where you are and what you're up to from Janis? And do you realise how bloody difficult it is to phone West Berlin from Moscow?"

"Blame the Russians. They cut the cables several years ago. You're probably routed through Norway and Chile to connect to Berlin."

"Fine, answer the easy one first. Troy, are you ever coming back?"

"Dunno."

"Is that all I get?"

"My brother and Harold Wilson might have had nothing much in mind in sending me to Moscow. Nor did I. But I have a . . . 'mission' sounds pompous . . . let's say, a task has emerged."

"Charlie or Joe Holderness?"

"Joe. Charlie has made his own Russian bed. He must lie in it. There's nothing I can do for him. Joe . . . yes."

"Russian bed? Sounds like hairy blankets, no sheets and itching all over. However, I somehow managed to miss meeting Joe in Prague. I ask . . . is he worth it?"

"He saved me from the dogs of MI5."

"When was this?"

"About ten years ago."

"The things you do not tell me."

"We were . . . estranged at the time."

"Estranged meaning 'other women'?"

Troy said nothing.

"And if you rescue Joe . . . you'll go back to your pig and pigman?"

"There is that possibility."

A pause, during which he could not read her mind.

"OK," she said. "In the meantime, Troy, do try to keep it in your pants."

§230

Sunday? Midnight? Two days to kill and an injunction to "keep it in his pants."

What an ambassador to West Berlin and Bonn did not seem to need was fiction. There was not a novel in the house. He'd finished *Myra Breckinridge* on the plane and wished he'd packed more. All this house had to offer were endless bound reports on this, that or t'other—all in German.

What an ambassador to West Berlin and Bonn *did* seem to need was music, in fact, a room devoted to music in the shape of a Blüthner aliquot-strung grand piano—made in Leipzig and dating, Troy estimated, from the 1880s.

Much to his amazement it was in tune.

He had a melody in his head that Volga had put there.

"The sun is up and so am I."

He couldn't place it and knew it would annoy the bejesus out of him until he recognised it.

He let the melody move from his mind's ear to his fingers and realised he was playing *Dear Prudence*, a Beatles song from the previous year. Problem solved.

On to other songs. A test of memory.

He pootled through a couple of Schubert's Impromptus.

He felt as though he were playing with ten thumbs and told himself that he might not only go back to his pig and pigman, he would also go back to his piano.

He'd spent an hour more getting past the pootle to a competence that was beginning to please him—the unfathomable satisfaction of getting the ripples of the E flat major to sound like a running stream rather than breaking bottles—when he became aware of a figure standing in the middle of the room, looking at him, as though summoned by his wife to test his resolve; a good-looking woman in her thirties, not very tall, thick dark hair, pale skin and a touch of almost po-faced earnestness about her.

"Your housekeeper let me in," she said in accented English.

"Well . . . as long as you're not an assassin . . ."

"Do you know who I am?"

"No."

"I am Nell Burkhardt."

§231

A further perk of being an ambassador was being able to ask for a pot of tea and two cups. Gold leaf bone china with the royal crest and motto upon them. Fragility redefined.

Nell Burkhardt thanked Frau Butterschuhe and forced a smile, but it was not a smiling day.

"There seem to be so many occasions when we might have met," she said. "We might have met in Prague last year, but you arrived there at the worst possible moment."

"Quite. I could hardly hold a reception with tanks on the streets."

"And Eddie tells me you were in Berlin during the airlift."

"I was. I got kidnapped by the Russians."

"You too? This is all so familiar."

"It wasn't for long, and I later married my kidnapper. I wonder what Freud would make of that."

Troy knew from the look on her face that Nell had no idea whether to take him seriously or not. He regretted saying it. To tell more of Tosca now would be a distraction. They had married, they had divorced, they had made their peace and this wasn't about him or her, this was about Nell and Joe . . . Eddie could blame Frank Spoleto but this "mess," as he had called it, centred on Nell Burkhardt and Joe Holderness.

He changed the subject.

"I suppose Eddie told you where to find me?"

"He arrived last night. He came to see me in Wilmersdorf. He is not a happy man."

"He never is. Frank Spoleto?"

"Not yet. Eddie expects him tomorrow night."

"And you . . . you . . . know everything?"

"I think so. Eddie cannot keep a secret, after all. He is hardly a perfect spy. We . . . I mean you . . . are buying Joe from the Russians?"

"Yes."

"Will it work?"

"Yes. I have a deal with General Zolotukhina."

"As you did last time? It was you, wasn't it? You arranged to trade Bernard Alleyn for me?"

"Yes."

"Yet you are confident. Knowing how badly wrong that went, you are confident?"

"Call me a cockeyed optimist."

"I'm sorry . . ."

"Fräulein Burkhardt, I am confident that I am giving Volga Zolotukhina what she has wanted all along. Money. Joe was simply a means to an end. But you have the advantage of me."

"I do?"

"You've met her. I have had dealings with her son. I've never met her, and everything I have learnt in meeting Kostya tells me not to judge the mother by the son. Kostya is also far from being a perfect spy. Far too human."

"Zolotukhina is unpredictable. A complicated woman. The sort of person who keeps one hand on the butt of her gun while she tells you a dirty joke."

"Then it would pay to laugh."

"I hope you are right that she may be trusted, but I fear the worst. She will play games with you. She is . . . eine *Betrügerin*." I cannot think of the English word. In Russian, *обманщик*."

"Trickster," said Troy.

"Yes. She will play tricks."

Troy knew damn well she would. He just hadn't a clue what they might be.

"I wish to be there."

That was understandable.

"No," he said.

"For my sins," Nell said.

Troy said nothing. He had so little sense of sin.

"For my sins . . . it was I who tried to smuggle a Czech boy into Berlin. It was I who got caught. It was I who cost Jiří Jasný his life and Joe his freedom. I should be there. For my sins . . . you know I should be there."

§232

West Berlin: The American Sector
Glienicke Bridge

Sunday, September 28
Midnight

Frank was wondering if he should buy shares in the Glienicke Bridge. Or maybe a small lot just inside the American sector. Put up his own shack. Find out what fishing was for. Become the CIA's answer to Elmer

Fudd. He seemed to end up here far too often, three times in as many years, freezing his balls off at midnight and some. Why did the fuckin' Russians have to do everything at midnight? What was wrong with two in the afternoon? Back in time for tea. What was wrong with four in the afternoon? Back in time for dinner. Midnight, fuckin' midnight and his stomach was talking to him. It was saying, "Jack Daniel's and a hot dog! Jack Daniel's and a hot dog!" over and over again.

He had only himself to blame. It had been his idea. Perhaps taking it to the British had been a mistake. They'd been responsive, couldn't deny that, but they no more trusted him than he trusted them.

And the British were late.

He looked at his watch. The hands weren't moving. Fuckin' Rolex. He had only himself to blame, choosing a Madison Avenue status symbol over something that actually worked. Next time a Longines. Maybe the British weren't late?

Eddie turned up in the Merc, got out of the driver's seat and opened the rear door for the bagman.

The bagman picked up a nifty-looking attaché case and the two of them approached Frank.

"What kept you?"

Eddie looked at his watch. He appeared to have one that worked.

"We're bang on time."

Another fifty yards and they'd be at the centre of the bridge. There was a three-quarter moon peeping in and out of clouds and the river mist danced around them playing now-you-see-it-now-you-don't.

"You say you can make the ID?" the bagman asked Troy.

"Of course."

"So you knew him?"

"I did."

"Hmm. So, what's your name?"

"Freddie."

"I don't ever recall him mentioning any Freds."

"Then call me Troy. He always did."

"So—Mr. Troy."

"Actually it's 'Lord Troy.' Not that it matters."

"Damn right it doesn't. Why'd they send a lord? I thought you guys just wore ermine and sat around on wool sacks."

"Simple. I put up the money."

"What? All twenty-five grand?"

"Yes."

"You think he's worth twenty-five grand?"

Troy did not answer. They'd reached the middle, the line over the Havel that marked the border between West Berlin and East Germany— and there were no Russians and, worse, no Joe Wilderness.

§233

Eddie had retreated from night and cold to the Merc. Frank noticed what he'd missed ten minutes ago. There was someone else in the back seat.

"You brought backup?"

"No. Did you? I didn't think it necessary."

"Then who the fuck is that?"

"Nell Burkhardt," said Troy.

Frank had been about to peer through the window.

At the sound of Nell's name, he pulled back.

"Then you got some explaining to do. Good luck with that. Sooner you than me. *A domani*, Lord Troy."

§234

Nell said, "I don't want to be alone."

"It's past one. If I were to say let's make a night of it, it would be an understatement. I'm sure the Treasury can run to another room at the Kempinski if you and Ed want to—"

"No. You. I must talk to you."

Troy leaned forward.

"Ed. Go straight to the residence. There will be supper, and there are beds aplenty."

"If it's all the same to you, boss, I'd as soon get some kip. Days are long. Longer still if Frank's around."

§235

Frau Butterschuhe had left a pile of chicken sandwiches and two bottles of *Spätburgunder* on the kitchen table.

"Go ahead," said Troy. "I'm starving."

"I'm not," Nell said.

She slumped on the table, head resting on her forearms.

There were sighs and sobs.

Before she looked up again, Troy had downed a glass of red and three sandwiches.

Nell reached for a glass.

Knocked back half in one gulp.

Then, "Tricks, tricks, tricks. Nothing but tricks."

And she sank the rest of the glass. Troy topped it up again.

"Well, we anticipated that," he said.

Nell was eating now, speaking through the crumbs.

"Tell me . . ."

She gulped, swallowed, cleared her throat.

"Tell me . . . do you know Joe's wife?"

"Know her? No. I've met her several times, she's a close friend of my sister-in-law, but I wouldn't say I know her. Ed would be the better person to talk to. Joe and Judy keep a bed permanently made up for Ed. He could never hold his drink and tends to fall asleep halfway down the bottle."

"No. Not Eddie. Eddie would hide from my question."

"Ed is bright but in a way he's simple. He chooses simplicity. I've never beaten him at chess. He can do a broadsheet crossword in minutes in at least three languages . . . but he avoids the complexity of emotions. He likes firm, clear facts . . ."

"And the heart has none?"

"Exactly. I can do three things Ed cannot. I can shoot straight."

Troy stood up, slipped off his jacket, squirmed out of the shoulder holster and hung his Browning on the back of the chair as he spoke.

Did Nell raise an eyebrow? Perhaps. Perhaps not.

"I can play the piano," Troy continued.

"I heard. Schubert. I play also. I have never attempted anything as difficult as that Impromptu."

The second glass was downed in one. She helped herself to a third.

"And I can wade into the quagmire that is the human heart, deluding myself about my own immunity. Ed would never bother. Far too smart. Now, what is the question Ed would hide from?"

Nell cradled her glass in both hands as though warming it, staring into it, but simply buying a moment in time.

"So many . . . so many questions. Twenty years of questions."

Troy took the corkscrew and opened the second bottle. If there was ever a night to get pissed, this was it.

At the pop of the cork Nell looked up.

"Joe and Judy. They are happy?"

"Yes."

A stretched silence while she took her third glass more slowly than the first two.

"There have been men," she said. "I have not lived the life of a nun. And . . . and there was *a man* in . . . Prague."

She slipped into silence again.

Troy prompted her: "But?"

"Joe Wilderness," she said simply.

She finished the third and held out her glass for a fourth.

Three glasses of *Spätburgunder*, now four, and less than half a chicken sandwich.

She was woozy, gently swaying in her chair.

It was what she wanted.

"You know, I may die a spinster."

She leaned forward, head to forearms once more.

Troy finished a glass or two of the red in blissful silence.

Then Nell started to snore.

He scooped her up in his arms, dumped her down in the first-floor bedroom, slipped off her shoes, drew the counterpane across her and remembered his wife's injunction.

He closed the door quietly.

They could both just sleep it off.

§236

West Berlin: The American Sector
Glienicke Bridge

Monday, September 29
Another Midnight

Hearing nothing at all from the Russians, Frank and Troy agreed they had little option but to go out to the bridge the following night and stand at the midway point.

Troy clutching his briefcase full of cash.

Frank looking at his new watch, a *Lange & Söhne* he'd bought off a kid in the street for ten dollars. Listening for the tick. Shaking it. Cursing it.

"I think I got ripped off again."

Troy said nothing.

"I see you still got Little Nelly in tow. You boffing her?"

Troy ignored this.

"Can you see any lights?" Frank said.

"No."

"Sheeeeeit."

Troy said nothing.

"What do you do besides lording?"

"Lording?"

"Y'know. Being a duke or a prince or whatever."

"Actually I'm just a life peer. A political appointee. It's a title that comes and goes with the job."

"No kiddin'. What kind of job?"

"I used to be a copper. Scotland Yard . . ."

"That gets you lorded?"

"No, it came with my present job."

"Which is?"

"I'm Her Majesty's Ambassador to the Soviet Union."

"Holy shit."

Four headlights lit up the East German end of the bridge.

Frank stuck his right hand in his pocket.

"A gun?" Troy asked.

"Yep. You got one?"

"No," Troy lied.

"So—if shit comes down, I have to handle it?"

"It won't. We have a deal with General Zolotukhina."

"Yeah. Right. That. Twenty-five cents. Cup of coffee. Hold on. I see something."

A man Troy had not seen for almost a year was coming across the bridge. KGB, full uniform, winter overcoat, the hint of blue just visible as he drew closer, the red star on his sable hat blinking in the moonlight.

Frank knew him too. He was older now but still the same skinny kid he'd known back in '48—Kostya Zolotukhin.

Behind him, hunched, maybe cowed, was another kid, a real kid, looked to be about eighteen. Frank had never seen him before. He sure as hell wasn't Joe Wilderness.

Troy knew him.

Jiří Jasný—he had lived in the garden of the Czech embassy when Troy had been ambassador there. Troy's wife had helped him escape over the embassy wall under the noses of Russian soldiers. He'd been arrested at the East German border about a year ago, along with Nell Burkhardt. Nell had been released in the same messy exchange that had got Wilderness kidnapped. Jiří had just vanished. Presumed dead.

Until now.

"Where the fuck is Joe?"

Troy put a hand on Frank's sleeve.

"You shushin' me?"

"I'm a diplomat, Mr. Spoleto, let me dip."

Troy turned to Kostya, noting the promotion in his insignia. A colonel.

"Colonel Zolotukhin? Is there a problem?"

"No. A bonus. We give you the boy for free."

"And Sergeant Holderness? The deal is still good?"

"My mother gave her word."

Frank exploded.

"Her word? This is horseshit! Where the fuck is Joe?"

Frank did not draw his gun. If he had, Troy felt he would have had no choice but to stand between them. But Frank's hand came out of his pocket empty to wave a finger in front of Kostya's face, a reproving schoolmaster.

"Her Word? Word??? You little shit! Since when has your mother's word been worth so much as jar of fuckin' peanut butter? She scammed me in '48 and she's scamming me now."

Troy had no idea what this meant.

"Kid, you produce Joe, or no more moolah. You get it? No more fuckin' moolah. The gravy train stops here!"

Kostya breathed deeply and, almost yelling in Frank's face, spat out a single word.

"Завтра!" Tomorrow.

They'd have stood nose to nose but for Frank's belly.

Frank snorted like a bull and pulled back a few inches.

"What'd he say?"

"Tomorrow."

"Joe will be here tomorrow?"

"Да."

Frank suddenly became aware of Jiří as though he had not noticed him before.

"So what do we do with this one? Is he one of yours or a Polack or a Czech or a what?"

"He's Czech. We take him home. England, not Prague," Troy replied. Then to Jiří.

"I can think of two people who will be very pleased to see you."

Jiří still had not spoken.

It seemed to Troy that the boy was still inside the nightmare.

Frank led off. Back to West Berlin. A snappy "Tomorrow!" barked at Kostya.

"Правда?" said Troy softly, invoking the name of the USSR's best-known newspaper. Truly?

"Правда," Kostya replied.

§237

At the far end of the bridge Frank waited.

"Diplomacy shmiplomacy. Now—how was that for diplomacy, Lord Troy?"

"Please excuse me, Frank. I have to talk to Fräulein Burkhardt."

Nell was out of the car, rushing towards them.

She wrapped Jiří in a hug fit to crack ribs.

"Oh God. Oh my God. I thought you were dead!"

She pulled back, took a look at the boy, hugged him again.

Frank lit up a Lucky Strike.

Nell unwrapped herself from around Jiří.

Glared at Frank.

Frank glared back, blew a smoke ring and stomped off.

"Frank!" she yelled at his back.

Frank turned. Wreathed in smoke. Impatient.

"Thank you," Nell said.

"Think nothing of it," Frank replied, jerking open the door on his BMW.

Then the engine started up and he threw the car into reverse.

Jiří spoke, feeling his way through the English language: "Bass'dor, is your . . . ah . . . wife with you?"

"Only in spirit," Troy replied.

§238

Potsdam, East Germany
The Russian End of the Glienicke Bridge

Tuesday, September 30
Almost Midnight

Even in Kostya's KGB greatcoat, Wilderness was shivering. Kostya handed him a gun, a 9mm Beretta, Frank's gun, the one he'd been carrying the night he was snatched age upon age ago.

Wilderness hefted it. Tucked it into his waistband. The greatcoat had big pockets, but he'd surely want it back.

"A full magazine?"

"Yes, but no firing pin."

"Very wise. I might shoot myself in the foot."

"Worse. You might shoot me."

"No way, Kostya. No way."

"Tell me, Joe, what did you do with your Smith & Wesson?"

Wilderness said nothing.

"Five dead Ivans. Joe, we could have had you shot for that."

"Why didn't you?"

"My mother."

"Your mother?"

"My mother and twenty-five thousand pounds."

"Really?"

"If this goes well, one of those two ghosts in the middle of the bridge is Frederick Troy. He will have the money to buy you back. Judging by the bulk, the fat one is Frank."

Wilderness stared. Mist swirled. Two figures emerged only to vanish in seconds.

"A gathering of the *Schiebers*. Like will o' the wisps. Shall we go? I'd hate the price to go up while we waited."

§239

West & East Berlin: Where the American Sector Meets the Russian Halfway across the Glienicke Bridge, Neither Here Nor There

Tuesday, September 30
When Old Midnight Has Come Around Again

Kostya was right. Frank was fatter than ever. Too many Madison Avenue lunches. Too much of everything.

"What kept you?" Frank said, grinning too much . . . cat, cream, adman—all in a flash of expensive teeth.

"Try asking me how I am."

"That bad, eh?"

Wilderness turned to Troy, ten feet and a world away.

"I hear you have the price of my soul in your briefcase."

"Cheap at half the price," Troy replied.

"I knew nothing about this, you understand."

"Of course. It was the lady at your back."

For a second Wilderness took this for some kind of aphorism, a phrase to trot out when meaning fell flat, but he turned to follow Troy's gaze. A wheelchair was scooting slowly in from the Potsdam end.

Frank said, "I wondered what we were waiting for. I shoulda guessed."

Volga Vasilievna Zolotukhina, grunting her way "westward," cursing as she came.

"Задница. Задница. Задница."

She drew level with her son.

"Arse. Arse. Arse. Was this fucking thing made in a tank factory in Chelyabinsk? My arse feels like some donkey wearing hobnailed boots trampled on it. Next time we get German . . . Mercedes, Audi . . . not this homemade junk."

The chair pivoted. She took in the four men. Her prisoner, her son, Troy, Frank.

"Well, well, well. Frank Spoleto. You old bastard. What's in this for you? Don't answer that, it was rhetorical. You wouldn't be here if there were no profit in it. And the good Lord Troy, I may presume?"

"Can I go now?" Wilderness said.

"Joe, Joe, Joe. This is freedom. Savour the moment."

"Right. I'll do that while you savour your money."

Troy stepped forward, a couple of feet into the DDR. He flipped open the case to let Volga see the money, snapped it shut and set it in her lap.

"Has everyone savoured enough? Because I'm freezing."

"You are no fun, Lordship."

"General, if this were a party you'd have brought vodka and zakuski."

"So happens I did."

"Perhaps when we're both back in Moscow. Not now."

Troy shoved his hands in his pockets and walked away. Wilderness handed Kostya his greatcoat.

"Keep it," Kostya said. "A souvenir."

And much to Wilderness's surprise gripped him in a bear hug.

"До следующего раза." Till next time.

"Nothing personal, Kostya, but I sincerely hope there isn't a next time."

Volga muttered something in Russian, so low Wilderness almost missed it. It didn't translate well.

"Брюзга."

The nearest he could get was "spoilsport."

"Let's go."

$240

Frank and Wilderness crossed the bridge to West Berlin.

Neither looked back.

"What'd the old woman say?"

"Nothing."

"You got the name?"

"You got my cheque?"

"Nah. I got cash. Why change the habit of a lifetime?"

§241

Troy was waiting by the barrier. A few feet behind Nell. An attempt to give her the privacy he was not certain she wanted.

In the minute or so since he had stepped off the bridge all she had said was, "You saw him?"

"I saw him."

And when Frank and Wilderness followed, no hug, no kiss for Wilderness, just a simple question.

"Joe? You are well?"

Wilderness replied, "Shot once, given a bit of a kicking two or three times. Nothing that hasn't happened before. So yes—I'm fine."

Nell turned to Troy. Her back to everyone else

"Then we may go now?"

Troy could read no reaction in Wilderness. Frank looked preoccupied and Eddie looked baffled. As Nell walked towards the Merc, Eddie said "catch" and threw the car keys to Troy.

"They drive on the right here, boss."

§242

Driving north through Wannsee, Nell still hadn't spoken.

Troy said, "Where would you like to go? To your apartment or the British residence?"

"To your residence. I think I deserve one last good drunk."

Troy said nothing.

Nell said, "You are familiar with the American song? 'Gonna wash that man out of my hair'?"

"Of course. *South Pacific*."

"I'm going to wash Joe Wilderness out of my hair, my heart, my gut, off my hands, off my fingertips, off the soles of my feet, off the cheeks of my arse . . . with good German Burgundy. Better *Spätburgunder* than *Neverburgunder*."

Well—at last it seemed as though Nell Burkhardt had a sense of humour. Desperate though it was.

§243

In the morning, Nell curled up next to him, sheets pulled up to the tip of her nose. Troy endeavoured to examine his conscience but was unable to find it.

§244

"Shit," said Frank, watching the Merc vanish with Troy and Nell inside. "Would you fuckin' believe it?"

Then he turned to Joe and Eddie, with what passed for a smile.

"So, here we are again—the *Schiebers*."

Eddie said, sardonic as only he could be, "When shall we three meet again?"

"Say what?"

Wilderness said, "In thunder, lightning or in rain?"

"What?"

"Oh for cryin' out loud," Eddie said. "Do you know nothing? Joe, let's do the hurly-burly and then he can just bugger off back to America."

As they walked to Frank's BMW, he said, "Hurly fuckin' burly curly wurly, what the fuck is that supposed to mean?"

"Hokey Cokey," Wilderness replied.

§245

Frank drove, Wilderness next to him, Eddie in the back seat, hoping for a cloak of invisibility.

"So?" said Frank.

"So what?"

"Aw c'mon. You got the name. You said you got the name."

"No, I didn't. I asked you if *you* had the money."

"I took that as a yes."

"Of course I got the name."

"So who was it?"

"Money first, Frank."

"You must be kidding. I known you what . . . ? Nineteen, twenty years?"

"We've been together now for forty years."

Eddie abandoned his cloak and sang softly, "And it do seem a day too much."

"I heard that, you runty li'l fuck!"

"I think Ed meant you to hear. Don't worry. I'll tell you. All in good time. A bath, a drink. Or maybe a drink, a bath. I haven't had either in the best part of a month. Then I'll tell you."

§246

Wilderness lay in a bath big enough for two.

Frank knocked gently—a newly deployed tact of limited lifespan—and came in.

A bath big enough for two, as long as Frank didn't get in with him. He sat on the loo.

"How much longer you gonna make me wait? I have fifteen grand in cash in a grip next to my bed. I can get it right now if it loosens your tongue."

"Fifteen grand? That's ten percent."

"The rest is invested. Safely. You sure as hell didn't think I'd keep it under the mattress. Joe, trust me."

Had Frank not uttered the last two words, Wilderness might have been tempted to believe him. *Invested safely or lost?*

"Ten percent?"

"Consider it a deposit."

"For ten percent you get . . . one letter."

"What?"

"C."

"Joe, for fuck's sake."

"C. Now send Ed in."

"Jesus H.—"

"If you want a name, just do as I say."

Wilderness ducked his head below the water and blew bubbles till Frank gave up and left.

When Ed came in, Joe said, "I think Frank's fucked up."

"So, what's new?"

"He hasn't got our money."

"Our?"

Wilderness ignored this.

"But . . . I ask myself . . . for all his fiddles, all his bits on the side . . . has Frank ever gypped us out of money?"

"You're asking the wrong person. You have the name. He doesn't have the money. Fukkim."

"No. I don't think I will. Frank has endless resources. He can rustle up the money somewhere else if he has to. Patience will serve us better than anger. Meanwhile . . ."

"I'm listening. God alone knows why."

"I'll give him the name."

"Tell him over breakfast. Let him have a rough night. Just for me."

"Consider it done."

§247

They took breakfast at seven. At Frank's insistence. Sleeplessness gnawing at him like a piranha.

Eddie yawned cavernously.

With his first cup of coffee in hand, Wilderness said simply, "Charlotte Shumacher."

"What the fuck?"

"Or Coky Redmaine, if you prefer."

"She was a Soviet fuckin' agent?"

"Your incredulity could be expensive, Frank. If you don't believe what I'm telling you, you won't get your moneys' worth."

"Charlie named her?"

"No, no, no . . . you get the name. How I got it is my business."

Frank sagged onto the couch, all but buckling at the knees. Had he gone from disbelief to acceptance and missed out on all the intermediate stages?

"Bitch," he softly. "Bitch."

Getting louder with every utterance.

"Fukkin' bitch. Fukkin' bitch. FUKKIN' BITCH!"

Then he was on his feet, sending a table lamp and three cups of coffee crashing to the floor.

"WHATAFUKKINBITCH!"

Ah . . . he hadn't missed out on "rage" after all.

"We have to find her! We have to find her!"

"Your people back in Langley should have no diff—"

"This is going nowhere near Langley."

"Eh?"

"If we track her through the Company, they'll take over—they'll use her in a trade. She'll spend a few months in prison, get treated like goddam royalty and then get swapped on the bridge just like you."

"Frank, I've had several weeks to ponder this. Of course I'd heard of Charlotte Shumacher. In the fifties who hadn't? But lately . . . the last ten years? For all we know she could already be in Russia."

"Nah. If she'd defected, I'd know. You'd know. Things like that do not stay secret."

This was unarguable.

"Then perhaps she's dead."

"Nah . . . she's not dead till I kill her."

From the corner of the room Eddie chipped in.

"She's not dead. Well not officially."

"Eh?"

"She's not officially dead till the London *Daily Telegraph* publishes an obituary. I read the *Telegraph* every day. Have done since 1941. If she'd died, I'd have read her obituary. An' I haven't. They're novels in miniature. Well worth the time. Occasionally I put red rings around them in crayon just to get Burne-Jones to notice. Charlotte Shumacher would have been one of those."

"Obit, shmobit," said Frank. "That's just your English snooty nonsense."

"I couldn't agree more," Eddie replied. "But you're forgetting. Miss Snooty's first husband was a Churchill. Even the *Daily Worker* would give her an obit for that."

Wilderness said, "She's not in Russia. She's not dead. You won't take this to Langley, so how on earth do you expect to find her?"

Frank sank into the sofa, head tilted back, staring at the ceiling. Simmering or steaming. Wilderness could not tell which.

At last Frank drew breath and looked at them both. Head turning from one to the other.

"Joe, as long as I known you, you've been telling me cupcake here is some kind of genius."

Eddie twitched, made to rise but Wilderness waved him gently back down.

"The London archive must be as extensive as ours, and you, my little buddy, have access to it."

"Cupcakes don't do favours for fat fuckers."

"But maybe they do them for nice guys like Joe."

"Don't you dare ask."

"Ed," Wilderness said. "Can you do it?"

"I'd rather not be part of this."

"Can you do it?"

"If that's really what you want."

"How long?"

"Oh flippin' 'eck. Two or three days. Now we've got the new IBM thingy, I could . . . but why the fuck should I? Have you gone deaf in Moscow? He's just said he wants to kill her!"

"If there's any killing to be done, I'll do it. You and I both know our 'ugly American' is all mouth and no tartan trews. No offence, Frank."

"None taken. What's a trew?"

§248

Eddie took to his room. No slamming of doors, just a sad, silent retreat from Frank and Wilderness. Wilderness ordered a second breakfast and a housemaid to clear up the shards.

"Kill her, Frank?"

"She has it coming. If I thought she'd get cooked in Sing Sing like Ethel Rosenberg, I'd let the Company have her. But . . . she's British, so technically not our traitor."

"You're taking this very personally. I thought you wanted a trophy you could take to Langley and put feathers in your cap."

"Yeah. But that was before you gave me her name. Joe, I knew the fuckin' woman. I worked with Avery Shumacher in the run-up to D-Day. He was FDR's eyes and ears in London. I was a witness when Shumacher and Charlotte got married. A couple of times when I was on leave in Washington in the forties I got invited to her soirées. You must have heard of them. Coky Shumacher's political melting pot. Fancy frocks and dinner jackets. Anyone who was anyone was there at one time or another. Later, after Shumacher got killed, I saw her from time to time. Same as I saw Charlie. Fukkit, I even vouched for Charlie to the Company. But it was different. The fifties were different. Redmaine was different. He wasn't Avery Shumacher. He was a hard guy to like, and most people couldn't stand him. The only reason he had friends is they were too scared to be his enemies."

"You feel used?"

"Crapped on, wiped up and dumped in the trash."

§249

Eddie was still in his room, still in need of a Frank-free zone. Wilderness followed.

"Spit it out, Ed."

"I've not often given you advice. Mostly because you ignore it when I do. But as I recall, I've told you a few times that Frank is trouble. OK. I understand you needed him this time, but you've done your bit, so I say again, tell him to bugger off. Whatever stuff is still rattling around between you, let it drop, give it away, throw it away. I don't care what it is. Nothing, absolutely nothing, is worth teaming up with Frank again. You should be back in Hampstead with Judy and the twins, not farting around in Berlin with the king of the dodgy deal. Joe, go back to London. Go back to London and look to your marriage."

"I can't do that, Ed. Not just yet."

"Flippin' 'eck, Joe. How much is it this time? Twenty grand? Fifty grand?"

"A lot more than that. Your cut alone would be twenty-five."

"Well, you can stuff it! I don't bloody want a cut."

"Eddie, if I could stop now, I would, but it's just—"

"Just call Judy! For fuck's sake, Joe. Call Judy!"

"If I call Judy, you'll find Shumacher?"
"Yes."
"It's . . ."
"I know. Seven o'clock in the flippin' morning."

§250

He left the call till eight. Seven o'clock in London. Judy would be having half an hour to herself before the kids woke up. Strong tea and the *Guardian*.

She burst into tears at the sound of his voice.
"Where . . . where are you?"
"West Berlin."
"When will you be home?"
"It'll be a while. Loose ends."
"Loose ends, Joe? Do you mean money?"
Wilderness realised he had hesitated too long for the next lie to carry conviction. Her voice soared, her tone ripped through him.
"Is this about money, Joe?"
"It's about our future, Judy."
"Joe, there isn't enough money in the fucking world to patch up the hole you are blowing in our future right now."
"Tr—"
He had been about to say "trust me," but she had hung up on him.

§251

Wilderness called his father-in-law, not at his SIS office but at his house in Holland Park.

"You should be at home with your wife and children," Burne-Jones said.

"I want to see this through."

Wilderness could almost see the habitual Burne-Jones gesture, glasses whipped off and waved about with his right hand while the left clutched the phone.

"Joe, you have a duty. To your wife. To your children."

Wilderness did not think the sentence would extend to include "your country" and it didn't.

"Alec, I *need* to see this through."

"This . . . this wouldn't be another one of your little fiddles, would it, Joe? Do not tell me all this . . . this diplomatic nightmare has been coffee and peanut butter all over again?"

"No, Alec. It's so much bigger than that."

Burne-Jones was silent for so long Wilderness had begun to wonder if he should just gently put the phone down and sneak away.

At last, "I don't want to know. Really, I do not want to know."

"Eddie," Wilderness said.

"What about Eddie?"

"He's on his way back to London. Later today. If you don't want to know any more, then give him a free hand with what he has to do."

"While you were in Moscow I could and should have retired. I put it off. I put it off every time negotiations with Zolotukhina stalled. I will stall my retirement one more time. Eddie can do what he has to do, and when it's over I shall pick up my gong, retreat to my study, to my pipe, my slippers and my *Observer's Book of British Newts*—and I shall keep my revolver on my desktop fully loaded, and if you ever fuck over my daughter . . ."

"Really, Alec? The f-word?"

§252

Eddie said, "I'd better call the boss."

"I just spoke to him."

"I meant Troy, not Burne-Jones. Just a bad habit of speech."

Troy was still at the residence in Grunewald.

"Boss, I'm nipping back to London for a couple of days. One thirty out of RAF Gatow. We might as well go together. There's nothing to keep you here. And it's not as if you can fly direct from here to Moscow."

"How long will you be gone?"

"About three days."

"Then I'll wait for you."

"'Scuse my cheek, boss, but shouldn't you be in Moscow? Aren't you needed there?"

"Moscow needs me about as much as Welwyn Garden City on early-closing day."

"Come again?"

"Nothing ever happens there. And if it does, Anna can handle it."

"What makes Berlin suddenly so attractive?"

§253

Three Days Later
October 4
About 7:30 p.m.

Frank was enjoying hitting the bottle. Bottles plural, sometimes. Each day earlier than the day before. On their first evening alone he'd knocked back most of a bottle of Haig Dimple—"Pinchbottle," as he called it. On the second he switched to Laphroaig, the favourite tipple of Wilderness's father-in-law, and, feeling patriotic, he was now on Colonel Throckmorton's Old Kentucky Bourbon. It seemed apt to Wilderness, who doubted the good colonel had really been a colonel any more than Frank or the bloke who fried the chicken.

Frank trod drunkenly where Wilderness would tread gently and timely, but no drunk has any sense of timing.

"Your money's safe. Y'know that, don't you?"

"You said. Invested."

"Yeeeeeep."

"So you can get it any time?"

"Kinda. But there's bull markets and there's bear markets. Right now Wall Street is bearish. Bear is not a great time to sell up. Bull? Bull is good."

"You're forgetting duck."

"Uh? Woddafukk's duck?"

"It's a cricketing term. 'Out for a duck' refers to a batsman being bowled out for no runs or, in your case, no money."

"Poor bastards. They get booed?"

"Of course not, this is cricket."

"You ever watch baseball?"

"Are you kidding?"

"'56 World Series. Yankees versus Dodgers . . ."

"Fascinating."

"Fuck yes . . . I was there. In the stadium. Don Larsen took out every Dodger in a row, one after the other, no hits no runs no nuthin', the perfect game—now that's what I call a duck!"

Wilderness silently hoped a paid assassin would creep up behind him and chop off his ears.

Saved. If not by the bell then by the Eddie. He opened the door and sniffed.

"Flippin' 'eck. This place smells like the snug at the Rose and Crown on a Saturday night."

"Li'l buddy!"

"I am *not* your buddy."

Wilderness hauled Frank to his feet.

"Dunk your head under the tap. You need to sober up to listen to Eddie."

"Shpose he don't find out?"

"If he hadn't, he wouldn't be here, would he?"

"I guesh not."

Frank staggered off.

Eddie said, "Why couldn't I have just phoned this in?"

"Because we're in a city where every phone is tapped and Frank wanted it kept secret."

"I find it hard to care what Frank wants."

Eddie shrugged off his coat, flipped open his attaché case.

"I might as well be living on a plane."

"You got the better deal, then. I've been living with him."

"Serves you right. When he gets back I'll say me piece, get some kip, and then I'm on the first available flight back to London. You buggers can just stew."

"I'll follow you as soon as I can."

"Really?"

"Yes, really."

"Joe—if you *really* mean to see this through, you need to know how far you're going first."

Frank emerged from the bathroom rubbing his head with a towel. He seemed to Wilderness to have semi-sobered up with practised skill.

"So, tell us. How far?"

Eddie spread out half a dozen sheets of paper like a casino croupier dealing cards and waited for them to sit down.

§254

Frank's rage was an inferno.

He stood over them like a burning redwood.

"Whatafukkinbitch! Good God almighty, if this damn woman had sailed on the Titanic she'd have floated home on a marshmallow! I mean . . . has she sold her soul to the devil?"

Wilderness sat impassive. He'd seen enough of Frank's dicky fits to just let it ride. Eddie twitched, wishing he were anywhere Frank Spoleto wasn't.

From somewhere Frank had produced a Smith & Wesson—Wilderness's Smith & Wesson—and was waving it around wildly.

"I will kill this fuckin' bitch! I swear I will kill this fuckin' bitch!"

"Bugger," Wilderness said softly. "Time to send for the cavalry."

He got to his feet, knocked Frank to the floor with a single blow and took the gun off him.

"Will you never learn? Leave the guns to me, Frank. If there's shooting to be done, I'll do it. And while we're it at, this is mine. You can have your Beretta back when you calm down."

"Eh? What? Sure. Whatever. Beretta. Sure."

Then he passed out.

§255

Joe and Ed agreed. They had had enough of Frank.

They stood in a drizzle outside the Kempinski. Eddie's hands sunk deep in his mackintosh pockets like a thermometer for his spirits.

"D'y'ever get the feeling life goes round in circles?"

"What's the problem, Ed?"

"Need you ask? Here we are back in Berlin. With Mr. Congeniality. He makes off with the boodle and we're left standing in the soddin' rain. It's 1948 all over again. And me shoes leak."

"Well . . . you leave the boodle to me."

"That's what you just said about guns. I don't mind about the money. I mind about the guns. I mind about what you're getting yourself into."

"You could go home, Ed."

"So could you. I'm back to Blighty on an RAF flight at three o'clock tomorrow. You could just come with me."

"No I couldn't. As you said, I need to see this through."

"But you've packed a bag."

Wilderness glanced at the bag dangling from his left hand as though it had crept up on him unseen.

"I'll stay with Erno until we get a flight. Might just kill Frank if I have to stay here."

"That word again."

"Frank?"

"Kill."

"Forget it, Ed. I'll see you back in London."

§256

Wilderness had called on Erno Schreiber several times in the days since his return. A year ago, on the far side of his time in Moscow—a continent, a constellation away—he had thought the old man was dying. Yet here he was, far from sprightly, but alive and, if not kicking, shuffling. Wilderness had no idea how old Erno was, just that he had survived two world wars, the "stab in the back," a near-miss revolution, the Nazis . . . and the Russians.

"I need your couch."

Erno was hovering by the stove, coaxing the kettle to boil water.

"I had wondered when. Frank wearing you out?"

"Something like. And I have this for you."

He put the bag by the old man's chair.

"What is it? Coffee? Peanut butter? Potatoes?"

"It's not 1948 anymore."

"So . . . money? I remember when a pack of java was worth more than money. It was currency itself. I remember when you stank of coffee whenever you entered the room."

"My *Schieber* days are long gone, Erno."

"Not if you're working with Frank Spoleto, they're not."

Erno eased himself into the armchair, pulled a blanket around his knees.

"I don't deal with cash anymore," he said. "Trudi upstairs will handle it."

"You trust her?"

"And you've met her. I doubt you will meet anyone quite so capable. I'd have died a dozen times without her."

"There's fifteen thousand dollars in there."

Not much startled Erno, but there was a flicker of surprise.

"Your . . . hmm . . . your cut?"

"Shall we say . . . *your* cut. That is a small part of *my* cut."

"*Gott im Himmel*, Joe. What are you planning?"

"Something of nothing—but I'll need a passport."

"I must have half a dozen already made up in your various . . . ah . . . *kriminellen Gestalten*. Who do you want to be? Ludwig, Otto, Johannes? Beethoven, Bismarck or Brahms?"

"German is fine. Preferably not Bismarck. Just someone we've never used before. I'm pretty certain my father-in-law will have people looking out for me."

"And Frank?"

"He's CIA. They probably have a passport shop at Tempelhof that gives Green Shield stamps. He can take care of himself."

"And may I ask where you are going, or is that a secret?"

§257

Eddie, meanwhile, caught a cab to the British residence in Grunewald. His rented Merc was parked outside.

Frau Butterschuhe ushered him in.

Troy was seated in front of an open fire, reading, struggling for the umpteenth time with Goethe's *Elective Affinities*, thinking the English title a damn sight easier on the tongue than *Die Wahlverwandtschaften*.

"When are you going back to Moscow?" Eddie said.

"You didn't come all this way to ask me that. What's up?"

"We need to talk."

Troy closed the book. Eddie could not resist tilting his head to read the spine.

"How rarely you have ever used that phrase, Edwin."

"You're taking the mickey. You always call me Edwin when you take the mickey."

"What's your problem, Ed? Spoleto, Holderness or both of them?"

"Both, but I'll start with you. When I first met you in Berlin I'd just got shut of Joe. He was my best friend and I was so glad to see the back of him. And twenty times gladder to see the back of Frank. They were nowt but trouble. You—I had you down as toff and worked out pretty well on the spot that you might be a bit of a bastard too, but you couldn't possibly be as big a bastard as Joe or Frank. I was wrong. You are. But don't get me wrong. You rescued me from being PC Plod on the soddin' beat in Brum. I'm grateful. I'll always be grateful. Yet you outclassed two of the biggest rogues I've ever met. But . . ."

Eddie's diatribe ground to a halt.

"You need a prompt, Ed?"

"Oh bloody Nora, I can scarcely bring meself to say it. You shot the Ryan twins. OK. They had it coming. Probably not the worst thing you did when you were a copper and if there's more please do *not* tell me. But . . . but this. . . oh fukkit . . . they're going to Italy to kill this woman."

"What woman?"

"The spy. The Washington spy. The one who ran your pal Charlie all those years ago. The one Joe went to Moscow for. That was the deal. Joe would let himself be kidnapped, the CIA would pay him a hundred and fifty grand—'cept Frank's spent it, lost it or just trousered it—then they'd do a swap—'cept the Russians wouldn't when push came to cash—and he'd come back with a name."

"He got Charlie to talk?"

"Oh yes."

"Are you going to tell me or not?"

"She has a bundle of names. Shumacher, Redmaine . . . but I'd bet five bob and a Mars Bar you knew her as Charlotte Churchill."

"Indeed, I did."

"She's now a nob."

"Eh?"

"A toff. Some sort of Italian aristocrat. La contessa di Volpintesta. A title courtesy of her last husband. She's outlived four of 'em now. Left America for good in 1960, when she married Alessandro del Sarto, Count of whatever. He died in '65, left her millions—and I don't mean millions in lire. I mean millions in pounds and even more millions if you do the arithmetic in dollars. Frank did. Drove him nuts. It's one thing to be a Soviet spy, quite another to be a filthy rich Soviet spy.

"She lives in a palazzo south of Naples. And . . . she was bloody hard to find, a pretty good disappearing act. Married in Switzerland, and you know how tight the Swiss are with information . . . a honeymoon cruise around the world that lasted more than a year on his private yacht registered under the name of Horvat in Dubrovnik—Horvat is Croat for Smith or Jones—so by the time they docked in Amalfi in 1961 the paper trail had gone cold. She'd left the USA and more or less vanished.

"Now, boss—why do you not look remotely surprised?"

"Oh I am. I had no idea what deal Joe and Frank had cooked up. The last time we talked about it, you didn't know either."

"But?"

"But what?"

"You knew she was a spy? You knew she ran Charlie Leigh-Hunt?"

"No. Charlie's indiscreet but not that indiscreet."

"So?"

"So I had no idea she was a spy—but I did know she had married again and I have a vague recollection of her moving to Italy. I didn't, however, realise she was widowed."

"Boss, I hate this. I feel like the spare prick at the wedding."

"And you reckon they'll kill her?"

"Frank's threatening blue murder, red murder, every shade on the bloody palette."

"But, Ed, will he actually do it?"

"I don't know. I used to think he was capable of anything, but truth to tell, it's Joe that's got me worried."

A footstep, someone entering the room caused them both to turn their heads.

Nell stood framed in the doorway.

"Worried about what, Eddie?"

Eddie looked at Nell. Looked at Troy. Looked at Nell. Looked at Troy.

"Did I mention the spare prick?" he said.

Fox in the Head

§258

Latana della Volpe, Ravello
Provincia di Salerno, Italia

October 9, 1969

Much to Frank's chagrin it was impossible to get a car within half a mile of the palazzo. An unpaved donkey track led from the village up the hillside. Stunning views of the Tyrrhenian Sea—knocking Clacton, Margate and even Brighton into a cocked hat or two—and a trail of fresh donkey droppings. Not that Frank would know donkey shit from bullshit.

"I swear. I'm gonna kill the bitch twice. Once for treason and once for this goddam hike."

"Frank. You've never killed anyone, and you're not about to start now."

"Watch me, Joe. Just watch me."

A rusty gate creaked loudly enough to attract the attention of two bristling border terriers who came running and yapping only to retreat along a cypress-lined path when Wilderness reached down a hand. It looked to be a long walk still. Frank was sweating. Now he'd kill her thrice.

At the end of the path, emerging from shadow into searing sunlight, a peasant woman, billowing skirt to ankle length, headscarf and apron, stood catching lemons lobbed by a boy up a tree straight into the apron, spread out like a parachute.

It blasted Wilderness back to the 1930s. He'd be the boy up the tree, pitching apples, fat Granny Smiths or fatter Arthur Turners that would not be shaken loose, into his great-aunt's patchwork apron, out beyond the Roding Valley in the not-so-wilds of Essex.

The woman turned to them. Not the face of Great-aunt Elsie. Not the face of an Italian peasant. Not that Frank could see this.

"You speak English?" he asked.

"Better than you do, Frank. I always did."

But . . . Frank rolled with it.

"You've been kinda hard to find. This place is off the beaten track. It's like you're in hiding."

"Not at all. I think that's just Italy. Most of it is off the beaten track. I have a little place in Florence too. Very much on the beaten track. Just a terraced house. 'Earth to roof,' the Italians call them—*terratetto*. So . . . as the old song has it: 'Sometimes I live in the country, sometimes I live in town.'"

"And sometimes you get a great notion?"

"No, Frank. Never. I left such confusion behind long ago. I am happy. *Sono contenta*. But . . . *you* are here—God alone knows why—so some confusion is to be expected."

She shook the lemons from her apron into a huge wicker basket and called out to the boy up the tree.

"*Abbastanza per ora, Gianni. Abbiamo ospiti.*"

Then to Frank and Wilderness—not that she had yet acknowledged Wilderness, not that he had yet spoken—"You will stay for lunch, won't you?"

She pulled off the headscarf. Swirling blonde hair, with just a hint of grey. A face tanned, but hardly lined.

"Now. We are both forgetting our manners, Frank. Introduce me."

"This is Joe Holderness. This is . . . fukkit, who are you these days? You sure as fuck ain't Coky."

"Good morning, Mr. Holderness. I am, since Frank forgets, Charlotte Ophelia Katerina del Sarto, la contessa di Volpintesta."

"And I'm plain Flight Sergeant John Wilfrid Holderness."

"Ah . . . a fellow Londoner. Tell me, Joe, are you MI5 or MI6?"

"The latter, Contessa."

"Hmm . . . not so plain after all. And, Frank, I suppose it was too much to expect you to bring Charlie?"

Frank just glared.

Wilderness said, "I saw Charlie only a few weeks ago."

"Really? In Russia? Is it too risky for me to ask how he is?"

"I think he's happy too. Against the odds, I suppose."

"Oh. Most certainly. We were neither of us destined for happiness."

§259

Charlotte/Coky/Contessa showed them to a downstairs bathroom—fresh towels, olive oil soap, a cool shower. No room in Wilderness's London house was as big.

"Is this her way of saying we stink?" Frank said.

"I thought you wanted a clean kill?"

"Ha fukkin' ha."

All the same he showered.

Not that it did anything for his mood.

Another boy, a taller version of Gianni-up-the-tree, showed them into the sitting room.

"It's like the fukkin' woman has some kind of male harem."

"Or maybe they just work here."

"Yeah, right."

Charlotte/Coky/Contessa was seated at a wide, low, round table—a vast bruised and patched mosaic. She sat with her back to the window, giving them the view of the sea.

The boy poured prosecco for them all.

Frank stared at his glass as though suspecting poison.

"Cook says luncheon will be ready in a few minutes. Have a drink and do try the olives; they're our own."

Still Frank stared.

"Oh for fuck's sake," Wilderness said and picked up his glass in one hand and popped an olive with the other.

At last Frank spoke.

"So. You done well for yourself. House boys, a cook, a palace, if that's what this is."

"Yep," said Coky. "Been in my husband's family since 1633. Bits of it might be newer, bits might be older—and the table is said to have once been part of the floor in Caligula's palace. Or was it Claudius? I can never remember."

"Your late husband."

"All my husbands are late, Frank."

"One in particular."

"Yes, poor Hubert. Only last year. It would have been tactless for me to have attended his funeral, much as I dearly wished to be there."

"I meant Bob Redmaine."

"Surely you're not here for Bob?"

"I'm here to hear you say it."

"Say what?"

"Charlie Leigh-Hunt killed Redmaine. All of Washington bought the suicide line. I never did. Charlie killed him. I know it in my bones."

Coky sipped gently at her prosecco. Regarded Frank with a cool, unrufflable expression.

"Are you sure? Has Charlie ever said he killed Bob? Joe, you mentioned you were in Moscow. Did Charlie tell you he killed Bob?"

"We had better things to talk about."

"Delighted to hear it. Still certain, Frank?"

Frank reached one pudgy paw inside his jacket, laid his Beretta flat on the mosaic, safety off, barrel pointing at Coky.

"Could we just cut the crap?"

Charlotte ignored the gun, fidgeted with the cushion at her back as though physically irritated by Frank.

"Charlie killed a United States senator. I want to know how, and I want to hear you say it!"

"No."

"No what?"

"No. Charlie never killed anyone. He doesn't have it in him. And you don't give a flying fuck about Bob Redmaine. What's bothering you, Frank, is that Charlie and I ran circles round you and yours in Washington for the best part of three years, and you were clueless, completely bloody clueless!"

Frank snatched up the gun.

Coky looked not at Frank but at Wilderness.

Sipped at her prosecco.

Frank looked sideways, followed her gaze.

Wilderness was pointing his Smith & Wesson at Frank's head.

"This could get messy," he said.

"What the—?"

"You want to shoot something, Frank, just try. Shoot a cushion, shoot one of those ceramics hanging on the wall."

"What?"

"Just shoot, Anything, but not her."

Frank took aim at a padded chair by the door and squeezed.

A hollow click. He squeezed the trigger again.

Click.

He looked at the gun as if it had cheated him at cards.

"No firing pin," Wilderness said. "Kostya took it out before he gave it back to me. On the other hand . . ."

Wilderness thumbed back the hammer.

"Stop it. Both of you."

Neither man moved.

"Joe. Please stop. Just empty the bullets out, put your gun on the table, and we're all even. You really don't want to kill Frank, and I'm fairly certain he'd prefer not to kill me."

Wilderness made Frank sweat a few seconds then flicked the cylinder open, dropped the bullets into his hand and laid both gun and bullets on the table.

Coky sighed audibly.

"Now," she said, reaching behind her cushion once more to bring out a Walther P38. "Suckers, the pair of you."

§260

Frank seemed to have lost his appetite. An accomplished trencherman for whom foreign food held no fear, he merely nibbled at the *fagioli e pecorino*, looking as though he'd been served a plate of cat kibble. Sniffed loudly and pulled a face at the *brodo di aragosta*. A dish he'd eaten a hundred times at Harvey's. Perhaps it was the gun, which Coky kept on her side plate, inches from her right hand, throughout the meal.

Wilderness was certain he could grab it off her in two seconds. Equally certain that if Frank tried it he'd end up shot.

But she had stunned Frank into silence.

"You're not here out of any sense of justice. So stop pretending I've offended your patriotism. You're here for vengeance."

Frank pushed his bowl away.

It seemed to Wilderness an age before Frank found the words, but find them he did.

"You're a complete fucking cunt, aren't you? You sell out everyone around you, you ratfink on England, you ratfink on America, then you pick up your reward, a rich widow yet again, a heavyweight professional widow, more bouts than Rocky Marciano—and you think you're invulnerable. You're not. Right now you're just a bitch with a popgun."

"Do get to the point, Frank."

"I did. Forty-five minutes ago. I just want to hear you say it."

"Charlie?"

"Charlie."

"Safely tucked away in the Soviet Union, where you cannot get at him."

"Then you've nothing to lose, have you?"

"Only Charlie."

Frank snorted with derision.

"What were you two? Martin and Lewis? Abbott and Costello? Or Bonnie and Clyde?"

"Do not malign Charlie! I meant what I said. He couldn't kill anyone."

"Yeah right, so who killed Redmaine? Spin me a line, Contessa."

"I did."

§261

"How much will it take for you to bugger off?"

Of course Frank was open to a bribe. That had been a given since the day he and Wilderness had met in Berlin more than twenty years ago. The question now was, did his desire for vengeance impinge on his most vital organ—his wallet?

Wilderness did not give him the chance to dither. He increased the pressure on Frank's foot under the table. If needs be he'd stamp on it. Anything to shut him up.

"One hundred and fifty thousand dollars."

"Ah," she said.

Frank had his mouth open as though ready to speak but lost for words. Wilderness pressed harder.

"Well, Frank. Does Joe speak for you?"

Pulling teeth.

"Yes," he said, not much above a whisper.

Coky rang the bell.

Both the boys came into the dining room. The smaller with a pot of coffee, the taller carrying a grip, which he set down next to Frank.

Frank hefted the bag to his lap, unzipped it.

"Don't offend me by counting it," Coky said. "It's all there."

Wilderness held out his hand.

Silently.

"Sheeeeeit," said Frank, and passed him the bag.

Coky stood up.

"I don't drink coffee in the middle of the day. In fact, I take a siesta, so I'll leave you to it. When you're ready, the boys can call you a cab."

"Sheeeeeeeeeeit," said Frank when she'd gone. "I mean. How the fuck did she know?"

Wilderness zipped up the bag.

Poured himself a coffee.

"Do I care?" he replied.

§262

Four Days Earlier: October 5
A Telephone Call: The British Residence, West Berlin,
to Latana della Volpe, Ravello, Italy

Troy picked up the phone.

"*Herr Troy, ich habe die Leitung nach Italien für dich. Einen Moment, bitte.*"

The crackling was like a breaking storm, and he wondered at the aptness of his own metaphor, then . . .

"*Pronto.*"

"Contessa di Volpintesta?"

"That rather depends, doesn't it?"

All those years in America . . . all those years in Italy and her voice, as plummy as Troy's own, had picked up not a trace of a foreign accent.

"Of course. Frederick Troy."

"Freddie? Fuck me! It's been . . . I mean . . . where are you?"

"It's been about five years. I think we last spoke when you rang me in that sanatorium up the Hudson Valley, when I went down with TB."

"Yep. That was it. And now . . . ?"

"I'm in Berlin. In fact, I saw an old acquaintance of yours just a few days ago . . . I would hesitate to call him a friend . . . Frank Spoleto."

"Oh. How is the fat bugger? . . . No, don't answer, I don't think I care . . . Would you believe he was best man at my wedding? . . . Well, one of my weddings. He was always on the make. What's he after this time?"

"You."

"Me? What could he possibly want with me after . . . after all this time?"

"Are you sitting comfortably, Charlotte?"

"Always."

"Then I'll begin . . ."

Anna

§263

. . ..

The Office of Her Britannic Majesty's Ambassador
to the Union of Soviet Socialist Republics, Moscow

```
Telex/High Commissioner's Residence/West Berlin


               October 11th 1969

               Ref. No. 030849

               Confidential/FYEO



            From: Lady Troy

            To: Lord Troy



         UTTER FUCKING BASTARD!
```

Message ends

. . ..

Stuff

McCarthy: I suppose I've been hearing about McCarthyism most of my life. Socialist parents, after all. My interest was further prompted in 1983. I had given up on England (for the first time, but not the last) and taken a job painting a villa in Spain, in the shadow of the Rock. The villa was empty, so most nights I slept there. At the end of the first week guests of the owners did turn up, an old American couple (old, i.e., the age I am right now), Harold and Florence. They weren't married, they'd just teamed up for travel, and several evenings I stayed on to eat with them.

I asked Florence where she was from.

"Nowhere you'll have heard of. Mineola."

"Out on Long Island?"

"Yes, but how would you know that?"

"Bogart, Cagney, Priscilla Lane. Her character came from Mineola. I forget the name of the film."

"It was *The Roaring Twenties*. Written by Mark Hellinger. I was his script editor."

Florence was the widow of Josef Mischel, a Hungarian-born, blacklisted Hollywood scriptwriter, author of *Mademoiselle Fifi* and *Isle of the Dead*.

I was confused as to what was HUAC and what was McCarthy, and even now, as I read the history of the 1940s and '50s, so many committees seem to have sprung up to investigate loyalty and communism that the confusion scarcely lessens and they begin to blur. To wrap it all up under "McCarthyism" is neat, if crude.

It was not Joseph McCarthy who summoned Josef Mischel—it was HUAC. And Florence was unequivocal:

"HUAC killed my husband."

Josef Mischel died of a heart attack in 1954.

Hence the fleeting character of Joe Tubkis in this book.

Florence lived to be eighty-six . . . but there is more . . . I paraphrase, accurately I hope:

"I did a stint at Warner Bros. Radio in Burbank. In sports. A local LA baseball team was hosting the Chicago Cubs. I thought it would be a good idea to get a local commentator and suggested a man known as 'Dutch,' who had worked at a Des Moines radio station and who'd got a good reputation in ball-by-ball commentary for Cubs games. The studio agreed. I could make the approach to 'Dutch.' For my sins I'm the woman who brought Ronald Reagan to Hollywood."

There is a brief mention of both Josef and Florence in Victor Navasky's *Naming Names* (1980).

H. G. Wells: I have invented very little about H. G.; nonetheless, he is a fiction.

At the time Charlotte first visits H. G. in Essex he was probably building his house in France and spending very little time in England. The mistress he owns up to was Odette Keun, with whom he was building the house, but he spent much of 1927 at Easton Glebe, occasionally visiting France and London.

I also moved his final visit to Russia back to the late 1920s. It took place in 1934.

Balzac: I have no idea whether a signed first edition of *Illusions perdues* exists. Balzac certainly signed books and in at least one instance signed for Laurent-Jan.

Coky and Avery: It's rather obvious that the idea for this couple came from the lives of Pamela and Averell Harriman. But the resemblance is scarcely more than that—a point of departure. Pamela Harriman was married several times—her first husband was Randolph Churchill, son of Winston; hence she was the mother of the Winston Churchill of my generation. There may well be a few similarities between Pamela and Coky, but Coky is not a representation of Pamela Harriman. The contrast between Avery and Harriman (a man said to be a humourless skinflint) could not be starker.

AJ's Weekly: No prizes for guessing that this is a time-shifted, scarcely disguised *I. F. Stone's Weekly*. Shumacher's review of *Birth of a Nation* is a paraphrase of a review written by James Agee for *The Nation* in 1948.

Roundehay: This is a fictionalised Merrywood, much touted as the childhood home of Jackie Kennedy. Before that it was the childhood home of Gore Vidal, from whom I first learnt of it—the owner, Hugh D. Auchincloss, being the second husband of both their mothers. Latana della Volpe was another of Gore's homes, exactly where I say it is, but I changed the name from La Rondinaia. I have never set foot in Merrywood. I visited La Rondinaia several times (lost to Gore at chess). I suspect it is now a hotel rather than the most glorious writer's retreat ever imagined.

Philby: Kim Philby buried his own spy kit, and he describes doing in his *My Silent War*. I had other uses for the story.

Mario Mariotti: The foreign correspondent is pretty loosely based on my old pal Murray Sayle. Perhaps Mario is Italian for Murray? *Chi lo sa?* I worked with Murray a few times in the eighties and nineties. He possessed one of the most enquiring, tenacious minds I have ever come across. Whenever we met, "hello" was like as not instantly followed by a question I could not answer, and I'd spend the next few days listening to Murray answer it himself. He was part of the *Sunday Times* Insight team in the sixties, the first journalist to land an interview with Kim Philby. I think it safe to say the Insight team did eventually blow the lid off successive British governments' insane neglect of Ulster, but that was in 1972, some three years after this novel is set.

I may have made Mario somewhat more Australian in his choice of expression—that I owe to another old friend from Oz, Ugo Mariotti. I do not recall that Murray was quite as fancy-free with the "fucks," whereas Ugo habitually greets me with "What do you want, wanker?"

Peredelkino: This village is exactly where I say it is, but Guy Burgess was never assigned a dacha there. My Peredelkino is fiction.

I have been unable to find out where Burgess's dacha was, and a couple of books ago (*Friends and Traitors*, 2017) decided it might as well be Peredelkino as it was the home of Boris Pasternak and hence much visited and much written about. In short, there are published sources—among others, Pasternak was visited by the English critic Isaiah Berlin and the French-born translator/novelist Olga Andreyeva Carlisle. It would seem to have been exclusively for writers, and I doubt a retired spy or an active cellist would have been allocated a dacha. There was a colony of musicians' dachas near Moscow, at Nikolina Gora. Prokofiev lived there (according to Tass, about five years ago, there was a project to restore his dacha, a stunningly beautiful house, at the instigation of the conductor Valery Gergiev)—but if I'd billeted Méret Voytek there she'd never have met Charlie, so . . .

The real Peredelkino was a "classier joint" than the village I describe—although dachas as tatty as Charlie's were commonplace elsewhere—and it was much more closely monitored by the KGB. Lastly, would anyone have been allowed to keep pigs? Answers on a postcard, please.

Burgess's apartment next to the convent of Novodevichy in Moscow was not left unoccupied for six years—I took a huge plotting liberty here. Burgess left most of his possessions to the Philbys and the Macleans. Eleanor Philby mentions clearing the apartment just a few weeks after Burgess's death in her memoir *Kim Philby: The Spy I Loved*. Rufina Philby's memoir shows a photograph of one of the few things Philby claimed under Burgess's will: a high-backed wing chair in a floral pattern, the sort of thing a sort of Englishman retires into along with slippers and a pipe.

British Embassy Moscow: The British got a brand new, shiny embassy in the mid-1960s. The one I describe is the previous embassy, the same building H. G. Wells stayed in during his Moscow visits. I kept it because there are numerous descriptions of life inside (Humphrey Trevelyan's, Robert Bruce Lockhart's et al.), and I liked the coincidence of Troy and Coky staying in the same house some forty years apart. The line about it looking like a fruit salad I lifted from the memoirs of Sir William Hayter, ambassador to Moscow from 1953 to 1957.

Half dollars and snowflakes: This scene at the Metropol is a geographical sleight of hand. A deliberate if romantic fudge on my part. Round about 1990, after a day at the Actors Studio on West Whatever,

Patty Ewald (whose name I pinch without consent) and I sat in one of the half-moon windows on the mezzanine of the newly reopened Paramount on West Forty-Sixth Street in New York, drinking martinis and watching snowflakes . . . "the size of JFK half dollars," as I put it at the time . . . floating down. There is more than a passing resemblance between the two hotels . . . so . . . fukkit.

Page 196: "I feel sorry for all the gherkins in this world," he said. "Nobody loves them. Always left on the side plate of life." I take no credit for this. It was said to me donkey's years ago in a diner on Second Avenue by that master of the incisive one-liner, Quentin Crisp.

A Legnote (there have been enough footnotes): I came across this quote in a novel by Elizabeth Taylor: "Soyez réglé dans votre vie et ordinaire comme un bourgeois, afin d'être violent et original dans vos oeuvres." —Gustave Flaubert, 1876. Er . . . I could not agree less. If there is shit to kick, put yer boots on.

Acknowledgements

Gordon Chaplin
Zoë Sharp
Sarah Teale
Peter Blackstock
Elizabeth Cook
David Mackie
Clare Drysdale
Emily Burns
Alicia Burns
Cassie McSorley
Sam Brown
Clare Alexander
Cosima Dannoritzer
Allan Little
Alessia Dragoni
Ion Trewin
Giuliana Braconi
Christine Hellemans
Nick Lockett
Pile Wonder
Bruce Kennedy
Patrizia Braconi
Ugo Mariotti
Gianluca Monaci
Erica Nuñez

Tim Hailstone
Kevin O'Reilly
Sarah Burkinshaw
Morgan Entrekin
Amy Hundley
Joaquim Fernandez
Marcia Hadley
Lewis Hancock
Justina Batchelor
Barbara Eite
Lesley Thorne
Deb Seager
Karen Duffy
Frances Renwick
Sue Freathy
Maggie Topkis
Valentina Memmi
Peter Sokole
Oscar Mackie
Zuzanna Budziarek
John Dudley Young
&
Sir Arthur Streeb-Greebling,
Proprietor of the Frog & Peach.